Sight Unseen

Sight Unseen

Suzanne Barr

Five Star • Waterville, Maine

ABERDEENSHIRE LIBRARY AND	
INFORMATION SERVICES	
1764793	
HJ	488354
MYS	£17.99
AD	KINP

First Edition
First Printing: October 2005

Published in 2005 in conjunction with
Tekno Books and Ed Gorman.

Set in 11 pt. Plantin by Carleen Stearns.

Printed in the United States on permanent paper.

Library of Congress Cataloging-in-Publication Data

Barr, Suzanne.
　　Sight unseen / by Suzanne Barr.
　　　p. cm.
　　ISBN 1-59414-300-5 (hc : alk. paper)
　　1. Parental kidnapping—Fiction.　2. Architects—
Fiction.　3. Adoptees—Fiction.　4. Orphans—Fiction.
5. Revenge—Fiction.　I. Title.
PS3602.A77745S56 2005
　813′.6—dc22　　　　　　　　　　　　　2005016253

Sight Unseen

Acknowledgements

For those that make me the happiest. Amy, my daughter and my friend. Jason, my son and my source for "things moms don't know." The sweetest daughter-in-law I could ask for, Lauren and my musically gifted son Michael. My sister Marlene, *kita vata!* David and Mary Barr, family and fellow ski buddies. Quivel and Budbo, normally called Mom and Dad by the rest of the family. My dear friend Mary Kuczkir, who without her guidance, I wouldn't be where I am today. And last but certainly not least, my husband Jay, who has supported me and stood alongside me throughout the years. You are my rock, Rube Dog!

Prologue

Orlando, Florida
December 14, 2002

Susan Johnson stood in the middle of the bathroom staring at her reflection in the bathroom mirror. She refused to acknowledge the glass of water and the bottle filled with Valium. Who was this ugly caricature staring back at her? She glared at the person returning her glassy-eyed stare. Not only did she look ugly, she looked pathetic as well.

Dove-gray eyes shadowed with purple half-moons stared vacantly at the image, as though controlled by a remote. Her shoulder-length hair was a dull coffee brown and hung limply around her face. She looked like an anorexic, ugly, pathetic witch.

Mother of God, how did it come to this?

She fingered the lustrous pearls circling her neck. They looked as dull and washed-out as she did. To still the ever-present tremor in her hand, she balled it into a fist. She winced because her nails were raw and ragged from biting.

She turned around and studied the black, knee-length sleeveless dress she was wearing for the evening's festivities. The off-the-rack Ralph Lauren would do little to disguise her gaunt figure. She could have gotten the same style dress at the Gap for a quarter of the cost and saved some money. Richard considered off-the-rack Lauren and Gap slumming.

God how she hated the son of a bitch.

She deliberately moved away from the vanity and the pill bottle to stare into the massive walk-in closet. Versace, Yohji Yamamoto, Armani, and Escada decorated the long racks and were a healthy tribute to the fashion industry. She'd always been a Levi's and tee shirt kind of gal. Back in the days when Cameron was in her life, but that was all B.A.—Before Ashley.

Today was the day she was taking matters into her own hands. She was too tired, and she couldn't fight anymore. *Couldn't or wouldn't?* What did it matter? It was all a game anyway, a game with no rules. She couldn't win, so why bother to play? She wondered vaguely if this was the way her mother felt when things closed in on her. *God, where did that come from?*

All she had to do was get through the evening. Just one more evening.

Susan reached for a pair of black sling-backs. Slut shoes. Then she remembered that, at five-foot-seven, in heels she would stand taller than Richard, who at five-foot-eight was self-conscious about his height, or lack of it. Her hand reached out for a pair of black flats. She jerked it back and chose the slut shoes. "Fuck you, you son of a bitch!" she mumbled.

"Susan?"

"What is it, Richard?" Susan asked, stepping out of the closet, the slut shoes dangling in her hands.

"What the hell is taking you so long? That goddamn idiot of a caterer your mother hired doesn't understand a word I'm saying, and the fucking bartender hasn't arrived. He should have been here an hour ago." He looked at the Rolex on his wrist.

She'd given it to him as an engagement present. It was

the last gift he'd ever get from her. She felt smug at the thought.

"Move your ass. Christ, can't you do anything right?"

Susan stared at her husband with clinical interest. Richard Johnson was forty-five, fifteen years her senior, and didn't look his age thanks to daily workouts at Elite Fitness, one of Orlando's most exclusive men's clubs. He wore his hair close-cropped, military style, and it had just the right blend of gray at the temples. He thought it made him look distinguished. Deep webbed lines etched the corners of his pale blue eyes. Richard referred to them as laugh lines. She knew better. Full lips, professionally whitened teeth, and skin tanned without any help from Florida's burnishing sun proved he could pass for an often-out-of-work George Hamilton. And to think at one time she'd thought him handsome.

That night Richard wore an Armani suit, pristine white shirt, and a festive red tie, in apparent deference to the holiday. He looked every inch the consummate professional.

Architect extraordinaire.

Susan took a deep breath. *Screw you, you bastard.* "I just need another minute."

Richard scrutinized her. She knew she was coming up short. She felt the urge to laugh in his face. *Just let me get through the night,* she thought.

"Christ Almighty, you look like you just came off Forty-second Street. Fix your goddamn hair. If I didn't need you to help with the bar, I'd lock you in this room."

Lock her in her room. Isn't that what my father did to my mother? He gave her one last disgusted look before he stomped out of the room.

Susan watched her husband's retreating back until she was sure he'd left the room. Her heart pounded with each step. Actually, it roared in her ears. She laughed, a weird sound. It was like putting a seashell to her ear the way she'd done when she was a child. Sweat dampened her palms. Not caring, she wiped them on her dress.

She tottered over to the toilet tank and looked down at a large, white magnolia candle whose scent was overpowering. Next to the candle stood a statue of a naked woman, Richard's sick contribution to the bathroom decor. With one sweep of her arm, the statue shattered, and the candle broke into three jagged pieces. The sound of the breaking statue sounded loud to her. She paused and listened for Richard's footsteps.

Silence.

She was safe.

Lifting the porcelain top from the back of the tank, Susan found her stash, courtesy of Doctor Emily Watts, safe and sound.

The Ziploc bag dripped on her dress. Like she gave a good rat's ass if it dripped. She removed a second brownish gold bottle of Valium and placed it next to the bottle on the vanity. She uncapped the bottle and shook out several of the blue pills.

She looked up then to stare into the mirror. She blinked when she saw, not the haggard woman she'd become but a smaller face with blond curls and clear, blue, puppy-dog eyes. The vision was wearing a little pink tee shirt with matching shorts. The last outfit she had dressed her daughter in.

Susan leaned into the vanity, her knuckles white with the effort. *Dear God, help me. Please, help me.* She managed to open her eyes, but everything was out of focus. Was she having one of those out-of-body experiences she'd read about? Probably not since she didn't see any golden light at the end of the tunnel. Damn, there wasn't even a tunnel. *What is wrong with me?*

Her gaze dropped to the marble vanity and the two bottles of "relief" she'd come to rely on since losing Ashley two months earlier.

She dumped the contents of both bottles onto the vanity. They glowed like a beacon to the lost. She was lost, wasn't she?

Since Ashley's disappearance, her life had been nothing more than a performance for the characters who, like her, merely pretended to care. Their act was so well rehearsed, Susan often believed it herself. Richard. Her father. Her mother. No, she wouldn't think about her daughter. If she did . . . she might not be able to go on.

Her fingers traced the pills on the counter until they formed an A and an R. It took forty pills to make the two initials.

Forty pills should be enough to do the job. She picked them up, one by one, hating to disturb her daughter's initials.

She ran water from the tap to fill the glass in her left hand. From somewhere far back in her mind she could hear a stern voice say, *Oh, no, Sue, that's the coward's way out. No, no, I won't let you do this.*

Susan whirled around. "Cam? Is that you?" She shook her head to clear it. Cameron Collins, her true love. "You dumped me, remember? What do you care what I do?"

She was about to swallow the pills when she heard loud footsteps. Shit! Panic zipped through her as she pulled the stopper to let the pills go down the drain.

"Goddamn it, Susan, hurry up. Your father is asking for you. I want you downstairs now, or I'm going to do something you aren't going to like."

She didn't have to be on the other side of the door to see the controlled rage that contorted her husband's features. Didn't actually have to stand next to him to hear the venom in his words.

God, how she hated him. She looked around for another means of escape. Other than the skylight twelve feet above her, her only other means of exiting the bathroom was to walk out the same way she had walked in.

Susan took a deep breath. The pills she'd taken earlier had finally kicked in. Familiar fogginess descended easing her tension. She smiled at herself in the mirror. She looked crazy, dazed.

She thought about the pills sliding down the drain. Oh, well, she'd just have to go to see Doctor Watts again, and if she balked, she'd simply remind her of what she'd been through. Or, if she was desperate enough, she'd look up that quack González. Just the thought made her stomach roil.

It was time to make her command performance. She splashed water on her face, combed her hair. She didn't look one bit better. She looked just as crazy and dazed as she had before. Stumbling from the room minus her slut shoes, she whizzed downstairs so fast she had to stop at the landing to catch her breath.

Susan viewed the throng of guests as though she was in a fun house, the images distorted. Tall, short, fat, and skinny. Smiling, frowning, talking. She didn't know half of them, and she knew they couldn't have cared less whether or not she made an appearance. This party was all about Richard. Not her. Never her.

Peter Breckenridge, Richard's friend and client, and his wife Marilyn. Tall and gangly, Peter reminded her of the scarecrow in *The Wizard of Oz*. Blond hair in constant need of combing, shirttail out, always in need of a tuck here or there. Peter was the complete opposite of Richard, who never had a hair out of place. Marilyn, on the other hand, was the direct opposite of her husband. Flawless skin, cat-green eyes that couldn't possibly be her real color, and skin so tight, it looked like a mask. Fake. Rumor had it she'd recently undergone a face-lift. Auburn hair cut in the latest short style stuck out from her head like feathers. She'd always reminded Susan of a bird. One of those drinking birds filled with red water she'd seen at Stuckey's as a child. Marilyn's head bobbed up and down, her mouth in a constant state of movement. Chirp. Chirp. Chirp.

She continued to watch the couple chat with Rosa and Reuben Rosenberg, old friends of her father's and once practicing attorneys. Susan had enjoyed many lively debates over the years with the retired couple. Reuben, short and rotund, with a snow-white beard and like hair, could have passed for a jolly Santa. At four-foot-ten, Rosa fit the image of a petite Mrs. Claus. Always animated, Susan watched Rosa's gnarled, jeweled hands wave through the air while she spoke. Take away Rosa's hands and she would become a deaf mute.

She sensed Richard glaring at her from across the room. She held his gaze, and, under her breath, muttered, "Fuck you, Richard. I hate your guts. Do you understand what I'm saying?" She smiled when she realized he understood *exactly* what she was saying. She took a step forward and stumbled. She grabbed for the newel to support herself.

She watched him weave his way through the den, pausing to stop and talk with people who idolized him. *They should only know,* Susan thought grimly.

He was on his way to the bottom step, where she remained a spectator. Scorching anger brightened his eyes. Ashley's eyes.

"Okay, how many did you take this time?" He yanked her by the arm, his fingers digging into the underside of her tender flesh before he half dragged her to the kitchen and slammed her down on one of the kitchen chairs.

Maria, her new housekeeper, looked at her, then quickly averted her eyes. A man dressed in a crisp white shirt and dark, tailored pants, obviously a member of the catering staff, stood at the center island in her stainless-steel kitchen. He was filling a platter with stuffed cherry tomatoes. He looked at Richard, then back at her, his dark brow raised in question. She knew what he was thinking. Was she going to take this abuse or do something about it? She shook her head slightly.

Richard loomed over her like a giant. His voice was little more than a harsh hiss when he said, "What in the hell am I supposed to tell our guests, Susan?" His fingers tightened on her arm.

"I have an idea," she singsonged. "Let's tell them the truth for a change. Let's tell them what a conniving son of a bitch you are. Let's tell them about your temper, how you hit women. Let's tell them *everything*. If you don't want to tell them, I'll do it for you."

She eyeballed him, knowing she'd finally struck a nerve. The last thing Richard Johnson wanted was for his business associates to discover the *real* Richard Johnson.

He released his grip. So predictable.

She was angry now. She wanted to, no, she *needed* to provoke Richard.

"Well?" she prompted.

He leaned over her and met her glassy-eyed stare. He wanted to beat her senseless, but he didn't dare.

She laughed in his face.

"You find this funny? I certainly don't, and I doubt your father will either. We have a house full of guests. This is supposed to be a goddamn Christmas party, not some . . ."

She laughed again. "Some what, Richard?"

Richard looked around before he grabbed her arm again. "You don't belong here, you belong in an institution, Susan. I've warned you that I won't tolerate this behavior. Make no mistake, I will have you committed, and Daddy dearest isn't going to be able to prevent it."

"Tsk, tsk, and just how are you going to do that? Are you going to say *poof* and make me disappear? I don't think so. My father and mother care about me. And you're wrong about one thing; it's you who doesn't belong here. This is all mine. Not yours. Never yours, you son of a bitch."

Susan turned around when she heard the kitchen door open, heard her name called. She stared, unable to believe what she was seeing in her Valium haze. And then her world turned black.

Chapter One

Orlando, Florida
2000

Susan looked up at her father, a speculative look in her eyes. "And I suppose this . . . Richard is another poor, single guy who's going to be absolutely thrilled to spend the holiday with his new employer's daughter?" Her gaze remained speculative as she brought the crystal flute of champagne to her lips.

Ashton Parker Burke III's six-foot-four frame dominated the state-of-the-art kitchen. He was handsome; there was no doubt about it. Even now, at his age, he could still turn female heads. He combed his steel gray hair back from a high forehead, but it was his crooked nose, broken more than once, his eyes, glacier clear and sometimes as chilling, that drew female gazes, and right now those eyes were boring into her.

"Is there a reason he shouldn't be? You're not planning another four year stint abroad, are you?" The cool, glacier eyes clearly said there better not be.

Leave it to her father to pry into her personal life without actually asking her if she were seeing someone. He knew that she and Cameron had decided to call off their engagement, and he also knew how she felt about it. Cameron had opted to stay in Europe. He'd said he needed time. Marriage and family were too important to him to make a knee-jerk agreement. He'd wanted to be sure when he made his

18

final commitment that it was right, and besides, he told her, he wasn't ready to settle down just yet—he had made a commitment to his medical profession.

At twenty-eight, she wasn't getting any younger. She'd always wanted a family. Now, however, she was afraid she'd have to put that dream on hold. They'd promised to write, but secretly Susan didn't think Cameron would follow through. She was still in love with him, and she didn't see that changing anytime soon. Maybe it was best that they didn't write. She wouldn't know what to say if she wrote him anyway. The slick magazines said time heals all wounds. *Right, let's just see how quickly it can heal my broken heart,* she thought.

Her mind wandered to an outdoor café in Paris. Her last meeting with Cameron. He'd brought her a small bunch of violets, violets she still had pressed into her passport. He'd looked so handsome, so . . . so American. Her eyes filled with tears as she recalled his words, remembered how sad his eyes were. Her own just as sad.

Her father cleared his throat a second time. "Susan?"

Susan traced the condensation on the crystal flute. She jerked back to reality. "Of course not. I'm here to stay. I applied for a teaching position at the Art Institute. I rented this condo and bought a car. I don't think I'm going anywhere for a while." Susan surveyed her kitchen, the main reason she'd leased this particular apartment. Copper pots hung from a wooden rack, a new fern hung from the ceiling above the kitchen sink, and her antique wooden table was positioned in the corner, allowing plenty of room for Nipper, her German shepherd, to stretch out in his new bed. Yes, she'd be there for a while.

No doubt about it. Susan and Nipper. A handsome couple. She smiled.

"It's settled then." Her father looked down at his watch. "I'll expect you around noon. Jemma will be thrilled to have someone other than me to cook for. This is my first party in months. She wanted me to tell you she's making your favorite butter pecan ice cream. She also told me I'm not much of a culinary challenge these days."

Susan observed her father. He'd lost weight. Her heart lurched. "You're not ill . . ."

". . . Good Lord, no." Ashton offered up a dry laugh as he walked to the front door. "Though I'd bet my last nickel I know a few who'd give their eyeteeth to see me and the company buried six feet under."

"Bullshit, Dad!"

"It's true, Suzie. Some of my former colleagues would be quite happy to see Burke and Burke languish after that deal with the faulty cement. But thanks to Richard, that's not about to happen. If it wasn't for him landing that government contract with the Pentagon, I'd be standing in the unemployment line right now."

Susan ran to her father and placed her arms around him, pressing her face into the folds of his collar. Cherry-scented tobacco, a smell she remembered from childhood, suggested he hadn't given up the habit after all.

"Burke and Burke has been solid for more than thirty years, Dad. I can't believe you're talking this way. That 'faulty cement' deal wasn't your fault. Your contractors know better than to believe garbage like that. If Stanhope hadn't been trying to save on materials to feather his own bank account, this wouldn't have happened. He's nothing but a corrupt creep, and better you found out now than later. I hope he rots in that damn jail cell. Your people have worked with you far too long to cast you aside now." Her voice rang with loyalty. "He's damned lucky that collapsing balcony didn't injure more than the twelve it did, and he was damn lucky no one died in the accident."

Ashton disentangled himself from her embrace. For one brief second Susan had the feeling he didn't want her touching him. She took a step back, unsure what she was sensing. "Yes, you're right," he said. "But there's still a handful of people who think Stanhope and I were in it together. I won't ever be able to convince them otherwise, and we both know it."

Susan shivered despite the muggy heat that was seeping in and around the windowpanes. He was right, he'd always have to live with that, but she knew her father. He was as decent and honest as they came. If there were those who doubted him, then it was their loss. "You don't have to convince anyone of anything, Dad. The truth came out. Stanhope will never build another structure in the state of Florida. It's time to move on and let it be."

"Easier said than done but yes, you're right. It's just hard after having a decent reputation for so many years. Look, I'd better go; just promise me you'll come to the party?"

She nodded as she followed him out to the steps. She hesitated before saying, "I wouldn't miss it for the world. That was one thing I missed while living in Europe. The fireworks and your steaks. Will Mom be attending the festivities?" He hadn't mentioned her, and Susan was afraid if she didn't, he'd simply avoid the subject.

The silver gray eyes clouded, darted to an unknown object above the steps. "If she's up to it," he said coolly.

"Come on, Dad. Mom is perfectly fine. You know it and I know it. I can't believe the way you keep her away from people."

Her father walked down two steps. She heard him sigh.

Susan knew what was coming next and hated it. If *she* didn't speak up on her mother's behalf, who would? No one, that's who. She could feel her stubborn streak rising to the fore.

"Let's not go there, Suzie." Using her nickname, his tone was one she remembered from childhood. It was meant to soothe and comfort. Sometimes it worked on her and sometimes it didn't. At present it wasn't working.

Anxious to pursue the matter, she grasped her father's arm, preventing him from going any farther.

"Dad, we've got to stop this dance we go through every time I bring up Mom's name. Mom has just as much right as we do to enjoy the party. She always loved parties. You can't continue to keep her hidden away." Susan trembled.

"There are things you don't understand. You were in college for six years, then in Europe for four more. Your mother's changed. I know you love her; I do too. She's just become extremely hard to handle. Last week Jemma caught her trying to climb down from the second-story balcony. Said she needed to get to the garden. Her roses needed her."

Susan smiled. How like her mother to think of the garden she loved. When she was younger, they'd spent many happy afternoons together in her mother's favorite spot, her rose garden.

"Was her door locked?" she asked. Her voice, she realized, was as cold as her father's eyes.

He had the good grace to look away. "I don't have a choice . . ."

"Was the door locked?" Susan repeated, her voice was even colder now, ice dripping from her words.

"Yes."

"That explains why she tried to climb over the balcony.

How can you do that to her? Dad, you can't continue to hide her from the world. I can remember a time when you entertained clients, and Mom acted as your hostess. Now, it's me, or Jemma. Why?"

She'd asked her father this same question dozens of times and always gotten the same answer. *Your mother has not been right for a long time.* It was another subtle way of saying it was *her* fault her mother wasn't normal.

If she was a different kind of person, her father's words might have stabbed at her. No matter what her father said about her mother, he could never deny that she was a warm, loving, wonderful, caring parent. More so than her father had ever been. So what if she had vague little spells from time to time. So what?

She sensed her father's impatience as he again glanced at his watch. "I promise we'll talk after the party." She wasn't sure, but she thought she saw his eyes mist over. Or maybe it was a trick so she wouldn't pursue the matter.

She'd always thought of her father as a good, decent man. He'd been through so much the past two years. He cared about his family, but many times she found herself wondering what had happened in her mother's past that caused her to do the things she did or, as her father put it, didn't do.

There were times when her mother would zone out for days at a time, and then, in the blink of an eye, she would be her normal, cheerful self. She hated those dark moments in her mother's life, moments that cheated all of them of her normal presence. Even so, it was no reason to medicate her so heavily and lock her up until such time as her father said she was all right. Sometimes, like now, Susan thought her father cared more about his firm and reputation than her mother's well-being.

Ready to change the subject, she nodded and squeezed her father's arm. "Sure. Now, about this man named Richard. Tell me, is he tall, dark, and handsome?"

Her father's face brightened at the change in the topic. "Richard Johnson is one of the brightest architects in the business. Graduated from Tulane. Top of his class, though a bit later than most. The man is brilliant. He spent twenty years in the navy. He knows his stuff. As I said, if I hadn't found him when I did, we'd be broke. Richard walked into my life as though fate led him to me."

"Okay, so he's brilliant. What about the rest? What's his Achilles' heel? No one is *that* perfect." That had to be the understatement of the year. She'd thought Cameron was perfect in every way.

Susan observed her father. He appeared to be at war with himself. His eyes darkened as he clenched his hands into tight fists. "Richard's the shot of adrenaline Burke and Burke needs. I'm hoping he'll want to stay on with the company permanently, make a career with us. He says he needs a change, so that makes me hopeful. I think Florida's sun, sand, and surf might be just the change he's after."

"And you want to make sure he's mesmerized with the boss's daughter, so he'll stay on? You're shameless! Just don't get your hopes up too high."

Her father had the decency to look embarrassed. "Am I that obvious?"

Susan gave a comforting pat to his shoulder. "It's fine, Dad. Really. But, promise me one thing?"

"Anything."

Anything meant anything. One hand washes the other, that kind of thing. She knew she could bargain by the desperate look in her father's eyes. Later, or at some point, she was going to have to think about that desperate look. "Bring

Mom to the party. I miss her. We haven't had a good gab in a long time. It'll do us both good."

She knew she was blackmailing her father, but someone had to stand up for her mother.

Ashton Burke stood at the bottom of the steps, staring up at his daughter. "We'll see." Susan watched as he walked out to the parking lot and his car.

"If she doesn't go, I don't go," Susan shouted, knowing her voice would carry across the lot.

Susan marveled at the festive atmosphere. As usual, her father had spared no expense when it came to his annual Fourth of July bash. Tables were scattered on the lawn, each decorated with a bouquet of red and white roses in blue vases in honor of the holiday. Miniature flags centered on each table waved in the humid afternoon breeze.

Damp hair clung to her neck, and she suddenly wished for a cool dip in the pool. Maybe there would be time for a swim after the spectacular display of fireworks her father was famous for. Maybe her father and mother would join her. A family affair. The words brought a smile to her face. *Yeah, and they get ice water in hell,* she thought.

Grills sizzled with filets the size of dinner plates, racks of ribs, and ears of freshly picked corn still in their husks. Two makeshift bars, one by the pool and the other at the south end of the lawn, were stocked with enough liquor to satisfy a small nation of alcoholics.

Susan's heartbeat escalated as she made her way across the pool deck and out onto the lawn. Curious about the man her father wanted her to meet and even more curious to find out if he'd met her demand, she hurried in search of an answer.

Seated at a table with Lily, her youngest sister, her

mother appeared to be animated and enjoying herself. Her father had come through. Susan smiled. This was going to be a great party after all.

"Mom!" she shouted before she reached the table.

Her mother waved, so did Lily. "Dear, come over here! It's so good to see you. Your father just told me you were back. You should have called," she scolded. "You have to tell me about Europe. Did you bring home a handsome Frenchman? Or a dashing blue-eyed, blond-haired Spaniard?" Her mother's smile was infectious. She was having a good day.

Susan embraced her mother. For as long as she could remember, her mother smelled of sweet gardenias. She drank in the scent as a flood of memories washed over her. Her mother sitting at her dressing table, singing softly. She could never understand the words, but remembered they were always calming. Her mother told wonderful tales of her own childhood in Atlanta. Cotillions, white gloves, and fancy dresses. Afternoons were spent on the front porch sipping iced tea and lemonade, and munching on sweet tea cakes and dainty cucumber sandwiches, minus the crust, her mother always added, served by none other than Jemma.

"Oh, Mom, you look absolutely beautiful." Iris Burke was dressed in a tea-length dress of pale pink, the color perfect with her complexion. Her silver hair was piled high on top of her head, and tendrils hung loosely around her ears. Her bright blue eyes glowed with excitement. It was times like this that Susan wondered how her mother could ever have had a sick day in her life, how her father could keep her hidden from a world that Susan knew would only benefit from her mother's kind and generous spirit.

Susan reached for paper-thin hands covered with purple-

and-blue spidery veins and squeezed them tight before she brought them to her lips. Life's road marks. A wave of sadness rivered through her.

"Not nearly as beautiful as you, my dear." Her mother stood up and reached for her daughter's hand. She turned to her sister Lily, and said, "Excuse us for a few minutes."

"Of course," Lily said, her Southern accent as thick as honey. "I wouldn't expect you to share your daughter's company. You never were one for sharing Ashton's wealth. Why, Papa would turn over in his grave if he knew the state of disrepair Prosperity Place fell into."

Prosperity Place had been Iris and Lily's childhood home in Atlanta. Her father had encouraged the sisters to sell the property, but Lily wouldn't hear of it. Susan often thought Lily truly believed Prosperity Place was Tara and she was Scarlett. She'd told this to her mother once, and they'd both had a good laugh.

"Not now, Lily," her mother said firmly.

Susan placated her aunt. "When we get back, I'm going to spend the rest of the afternoon telling you about all the wonderful antiques in Europe. You'll be sick of me by then, won't she, Mom?" Susan looked to her mother for confirmation.

"There's no doubt in my mind. Now, if you'll excuse us, I need to speak to my daughter. *Alone*."

Away from the table and strolling hand in hand across the lawn, Susan asked, "How long is she here for this time?"

"Too long. She's rearranged the dining room furniture three times. Poor Jemma can't find the pots and pans. She threw out all of the daily dinnerware, telling Jemma it was tacky. She redid all the linen closets. Had everything rewashed. Told me it smelled." Her mother laughed and

27

went on, "Said she couldn't understand why I didn't have better help. She reminded me of Maureen. Said they didn't come like her these days."

"Didn't she have a child? A son."

A shadow rested on her mother's face. "Yes, but I never heard anything more about him after she died. That misfit of a husband of hers just lit out and left the boy behind. I guess some relative took him in. I miss her so much at times. My heart actually hurts when I think about her. She was my dearest friend." Her eyes filled with her memories of Maureen.

"I know, Mom. It's always sad to lose someone you love." She thought of Cameron. *No, I'm not going down that road. At least not today. Today is meant for fun, sunshine, food, drink, and a ton of costly fireworks.*

Her mother dabbed at her nose with her ever-present lace hankie. "Very. Now look at me. All gloom and doom. And my mascara is melting."

"When did you start wearing mascara?" Susan asked. Her mother rarely wore any makeup.

"When my eyes started to droop, and I realized how old I really am."

Susan laughed. "Right. I can only hope to look as good as you when I'm your age."

"Said like that, you'd think I was a hundred and three!" her mother quipped.

Susan gave a playful punch to her mother's shoulder. "Stop it! You know I'm teasing."

"I know. But seriously, dear, there is something I want to tell you." Her mother paused. She looked nervous. Always cheerful, her mother's tone suddenly sounded ominous, and it frightened her.

In silence they walked toward the rose garden.

28

Florida's blistering July heat had little effect on her mother's rose garden, it was so carefully tended. Of course the underground sprinkling system might have something to do with the luscious blooms that decorated the yard all summer long.

Roses, deep reds, pinks, and dozens of shades in between, with names like Madam, Classy, and Charlotte, dominated at least half an acre. Different shades of white, their symbol of purity and innocence, a tribute to her mother, Susan often thought, blanketed the ground like soft moonlight. Then there were her mother's favorite Florida hybrids: Old Bush, Summer Snow, and Belinda's Beauty. Lush and full, the garden never ceased to surrender its beauty because the hands that tended to its care demanded nothing less than perfection.

Her mother led her to a stone bench worn with age and cracked from too much sun.

"What is it, Mom? You look worried. Is something wrong?" Susan clasped her mother's small hand between her own.

Praying her mother wasn't about to have one of her spells, Susan waited patiently for her mother to speak.

Iris looked around the garden, as if expecting to see spies, men in dark suits wearing black sunglasses coming to whisk her away. Not an unlikely scenario because it had happened many times before, but those times the men wore white and had pushed a stretcher.

She motioned for her daughter to sit down. She had to be very careful. Just this morning she'd overheard her husband Ashton on the phone with Doctor González. He'd mentioned the word *permanent,* and that scared her. However, if that's what it was going to come to, she wasn't going to fight him. She was powerless anyway. Even though

Ashton never said the loathsome word aloud, she knew he thought her insane, the entire family, including her ditzball sister Lily, thought she was one slice short of a loaf, all except for Susan. Loyal, loving Susan.

Iris searched her mind for the right words, knowing this might be her last and only chance to advise her daughter. As she struggled to find the words, she knew they had to be damn convincing. But Susan was always a quick study. Hopefully, if she didn't choose the right words, her daughter would pick up on it and figure it out on her own. She hoped she wasn't wrong in her assessment of her only daughter.

"You're scaring me, Mom."

"It's *him*. That man your father is going to introduce you to. There's something familiar about him. I'm not sure what it is." Her mother looked from side to side, making sure they weren't being overheard.

"How can that be, Mom? He's just moved here from California. Maybe he reminds you of one of those handsome soap stars you're so fond of," Susan said lightly.

"Oh, Susan, for God's sake, please stop placating me. You sound just like your father. I'm far from the crazy woman he portrays." She stood and paced the spiky grass in front of the bench. "I can't put my finger on it but he . . . he gives me the creeps. I just want you to be on your toes. Watch him. He seems sneaky to me, and way too old to have just finished college. I think he's one of those wannabes."

"He spent twenty years serving his country, Mom. Dad said he's a late bloomer."

"I know all that, but that's not what I'm talking about. I can't think straight now." Her mother sat back down on the bench and leaned against her.

30

Alarmed, Susan asked, "Do you need your medication?"

"Lord no. That's why I can't keep anything straight. I'm sure that old fool, González, is giving me more than I need. I'm going to ditch it all and see what happens. I overheard your father talking to him. He wants to put me away. Permanently."

Susan turned to face her mother. "When did you hear that?"

"Just this morning. I want you to be prepared, that's all. And more than anything, I want you to watch out for that man. Promise me."

This was not the conversation Susan had expected. Needing a few minutes to absorb the information, she walked to the edge of the garden. Yes, her mother had her moments, but certainly she wasn't so bad that her father would have her hospitalized permanently. There had to be a mistake. Her father loved her mother, was always kind and gentle with her. Those trips to the hospital had been in her mother's best interest. Hadn't they?

"Mom—" Susan whirled around when she heard her mother's footsteps behind her "—I'm sure this man is fine. Dad wants to impress him, that's all. After landing that government contract, I think he feels indebted to him."

Her mother's clear blue eyes clouded over with sadness. "It's more than that. I suppose, if you want to believe your father, I'm imagining things. I'm not, but you'll have to make up your own mind in that regard. Last week that man came to dinner. I had the strangest feeling sweep over me when your father introduced us. I had one of those . . . *feelings*. And what's even more strange, I felt as though he felt it, too. He kept staring at me all evening long. My skin actually started to crawl at one point."

31

A feeling of foreboding settled over Susan like a shroud. "Strange as in, how?"

"I don't know. Just strange. I swear I've met him before."

"Mother!"

"I'm sorry. I shouldn't have said anything."

"Of course you should have said something. I'm a firm believer in gut feelings, but most likely he reminds you of someone you've met before."

"You're probably right, dear. Forget I said anything. I think it's time for us to mingle. Ashton likes family to mingle, you know that."

There was nothing for Susan to do but lead her mother back to the table, where she spent the next half hour telling her aunt all about her four years in Europe. She couldn't help feeling apprehensive each time she caught her mother watching her.

She'd been looking forward to the holiday, but their conversation in the garden had cast an air of gloominess. She'd even decided that Cameron could go to hell. He could've come back to the States with her and still saved the world or whatever the hell he'd needed to do, then she wouldn't have been placed on her father's auction block. She hated fix-ups, as she called them. Fix-ups had a way of not working out.

Susan looked up to see her father standing next to her. "I've been looking for you, Susan. I have someone here I'd like you to meet." Her father turned to the man standing beside him. Susan drew in a deep breath. Next to her father stood the most handsome man she'd seen in forever. Not much taller than her five-foot-seven, he appeared much larger. Broad shoulders dipped down to a narrow waist, and legs bulging with so much muscle, his navy slacks looked as though they were about to rip at the seams. This topped with his crisp blue naval jacket made an impressive sight. Dark hair neatly combed to the side, a square, freshly shaved face housed sapphire eyes that stared directly into her own. Her father had an eye for good looks. She'd give him that.

"Susan, this is Richard Johnson. Richard, my daughter, Susan. You met my wife and sister-in-law earlier."

She clasped the hand held out to her. "I'm thrilled, uh, glad to meet you." God, had she really said *thrilled?* How sophomoric. She felt a wave of disloyalty when Cam's face invaded her thoughts. On top of that she could feel her mother's gaze boring into her back.

"I'm honored." He continued to hold on to her hand.

"Susan just returned home from Europe, and I'm hoping she has plans to stay in the States."

Susan shot her father a sour look. "I told you I was staying. Did you say *honored?*" she asked Richard.

"I did."

"Richard. Johnson. His name," her father threw in.

"Yes, Dad. I know. I was paying attention during the introduction." Susan gazed into Richard's eyes, and any regrets she might've had about her breakup with Cameron were put to rest for the moment. His casual touch sent shivers through her. And in July's heat, too. Maybe allowing her father to match-make wasn't such a bad idea after all.

"Truly, this is an honor," Richard repeated, gazing openly into her eyes. "I was actually dreading this meeting." His face reddened at his comment. "I thought you were . . ."

"An aging spinster whose father had to fix her up?"

Richard laughed. "Something like that." Teeth so white

and so perfect must have made some dentist happy on his way to the bank. Cam had a crooked eyetooth she thought of as endearing when he smiled. There was nothing perfect about Cam.

"I can see I'm not needed. Richard, Susan, enjoy the party." He turned to his wife and patted her on the shoulder as though she were a stray dog before he hurried back to his guests, unaware that his departure went un-noticed.

"I'm glad I can put that thought to rest." Susan smiled her first genuine smile all day. She took Richard's out-stretched hand.

"I don't know about you, but I'm starved. Your father passed those tables—" he nodded at the food being served "—a dozen times. Want to bet those steaks are to die for?"

Her stomach rumbled. She hadn't eaten since lunch the previous day. "You're on." She waved airily to her mother and aunt. Her mother turned away, her shoulders sagging. Lily simply gawked.

Hand in hand, they walked to the far side of the lawn, where tables were set up in cozy circles. Waiters dressed in white slacks, red shirts, and star-spangled ties scurried around delivering heaping platters of food. They found an empty table by the pool.

Between picking on the ribs and nibbling on the golden corn, Susan learned that Richard had been adopted when he was twelve. "I can't imagine what that would be like. Were they good to you?"

"They were decent, hardworking people. They couldn't have children of their own. I remember the day they came to the foster home where I'd been staying since my mother's death a few months earlier. I thought for sure they were there to take the baby girl that had just arrived. When

Mrs. Patsy told me they were there for me, I couldn't believe it.

"They adopted me right away. Insisted I use their name. They saw to it that I had all the things a young boy needed. I helped them work in the orange groves in California when they needed me, and they helped me when I needed it."

Susan wanted to ask what kind of help he'd needed, but she didn't think it was any of her business.

"Sounds like you had a stable childhood. I know I did. I never wanted for anything. I had love and discipline and a few extras that I'm sure I could've done without."

"Your parents must be very proud of you," Richard said.

Susan thought it an odd comment but said nothing. "Speaking of parents." The moment she saw her mother heading their way, she struggled to maintain her smile. "Here comes my mother. I just love her to pieces. Isn't she the prettiest woman here?"

Chapter Two

Susan wasn't sure who looked more surprised, Richard or her mother. He stood and held out his hand just the way a gentleman should. "It's nice to see you again, Mrs. Burke. I trust you're feeling well today?"

So, it was true. They'd met before. Not that Susan thought her mother hadn't been telling the truth, but on occasion she had a tendency to "meet" people by watching through a crack in the door. Apparently that wasn't the case this time.

There was no happy smile on her mother's face. She made a point of ignoring Richard's outstretched hand. "I'm fine. I can't imagine why you'd think otherwise," her mother said coolly.

Susan hoped her father hadn't aired their family matters to his new employee. She was a firm believer that family matters should remain family matters.

Richard dropped his hand in his lap and sat back down at the table, apparently unperturbed by her mother's refusal to shake his hand. Instead, he concentrated on his silverware and the food on his plate. She watched as he picked up his knife and fork and expertly sliced into his rare filet. She imagined she was seeing a precision drill.

"Richard, would you excuse us for a minute?" Susan gave her mother a questioning look as she cupped her elbow in her hand to lead her away.

"Certainly." He didn't bother to look up.

Out of hearing distance, Susan said, "Mom, don't you think you were a little rude? I've never seen you act this way before."

"I'm not sorry. I didn't like him the first time I met him, and I don't like him now. Why should I pretend I do? There's just something about that man that gives me the shivers. I really don't care if your father, and even you, Susan, like him. It won't be the first time your father's made a mistake in judgment."

"We're all entitled to our feelings, but it might be a good idea not to wear them so openly. I remember getting the same advice as a child when I told you and Daddy I hated Terry Mullins. You both insisted I play with him even after he'd pulled my hair out by the roots and kicked me in the shins."

Iris smiled. "Yes, I remember that little terror. His father was a client as I recall. I wanted to paddle him myself. Of course, I didn't," she added hastily. "This is different. I'm sorry if you feel I embarrassed you. I'll try to keep my feelings to myself, but Susan, please don't allow yourself to become attracted to this man. You're still smarting from your breakup with Cameron. At best, he's rebound material. He appears to be quite handsome and charming. I could be wrong, but I think it's just a facade. I'd really be crazy if I missed that. I want your promise that you'll be careful. I know what you went through with Cameron. I'd hate to see you get hurt again."

She'd confided to her parents about her breakup with Cam, and was beginning to wish she'd kept her relationship a secret. They'd never met Cam, but Susan had sent dozens of happy letters home filled with details about their relationship, and had even told her mother of their engagement. They were in the planning stages of a visit to Florida when Cameron decided he wasn't ready to settle down.

"I just met the man, Mom. I'm not going to marry him. I *need* handsome and charming, especially now. If it's okay with you, I'm going to finish my lunch and enjoy what's left of the day. I promise I'll be careful." Susan gave her mother a quick squeeze before she went, not to the table and Richard, but to search out her father.

"Just give me another minute, Richard," she called as she raced across the lawn and up to the house.

She found him inside in his study poring over a set of blueprints. How like her father to be working in the midst of a party. "Dad, you're ignoring your guests, or did you forget you're having a party?"

Susan felt the fine hairs on the back of her neck start to prickle at how slickly he covered up the loose papers on his desk. "I was just going over a few minor details on a project. You know how the devil is always in the details. I just want to make sure I don't miss anything."

"Dad, Mom and I were talking a little while ago, and she's worried that you're going to, as she put it, have her put away, *permanently*. That isn't true, is it, Dad?" Her voice was sharp, demanding. She locked her gaze with her father's, daring him to look away.

"Susan, your mother is ill. You don't understand."

"Oh, I understand all right. I think you're the one who doesn't understand. You will only do that over my dead body. Let's make sure we're both clear on that. Other than depression, there's nothing wrong with Mom." Susan banged her clenched fist so hard on the desk that the blueprints slid across the polished surface. "If you even *think* about sending Mom to one of those . . . those places, you'll be in for the fight of your life." She banged the desk a second time for emphasis.

"Susan, listen—"

"No, you listen. For years all I've heard is, Mother is sick, Mother is this, or Mother is that. If you'd taken the time to get her a *real* doctor and not that reject González— who I suspect isn't a real doctor in the first place, and I *will* have him and his degrees checked out—just maybe Mom could've had a more normal life. He should have been treating her for postpartum depression. All he does is pump her full of pills so that she can't function.

"I'm remembering all the times you tried to make me feel guilty for Mom's illness when it was you who should feel guilty. That old dog ain't gonna hunt anymore. You should have taken her to the Mayo Clinic or someplace where she could have had a thorough evaluation. Did you do as I suggested? No, you couldn't take the time. It was easier to let that old fool shoot her up with drugs so you wouldn't have to deal with her." Susan took a deep breath and jammed her hands into her pockets. She was shaking from head to toe. "I'm not going to let this go, so be warned." She stomped out of the den, leaving her father dumbfounded.

To calm her nerves, she stopped at the bar and gulped down two ounces of scotch before she felt calm enough to join Richard at the table.

"Welcome back."

Susan ignored the curiosity she could see in his face. She nodded.

"I take it your mother isn't too fond of me," Richard said. He sounded like he was discussing the possibility of rain.

"My mother has always been a worrier. Put a new face in

front of her and she wants a life history. Usually she wants it yesterday." She had no desire to go into detail about her broken engagement, nor did she want to reveal her mother's warnings.

"It doesn't matter. We're both adults. I make my own decisions, and I'm sure you do, too." He folded his paper napkin into a neat square and reached for another. She always crunched hers into a tight ball for some reason. Military habits. Neat and orderly. Persnickety.

It did matter. She said so. She wanted *both* of her parents to support her choices. "I agree, but I respect my parents' advice; they're the only family I have." Susan regretted the statement the moment the words spilled from her lips. She didn't want to come across as being a female *wuss* or a Pollyanna.

"Of course. I wouldn't imply otherwise." Richard continued to eat.

Susan watched him out of the corner of her eye as she finished her own meal. Each bite of his steak was cut in exact lengths. His baked potato was sliced, not mashed and gooey with tons of butter and sour cream the way she liked hers. He ate his salad plain, and hadn't lathered an ounce of butter on his ear of corn. He hadn't added any salt and pepper either. She wondered what her mother would think of that. Maybe he was one of those health nuts. Then again, maybe it was a military thing.

"I didn't mean it the way it sounded," she said defensively. "I don't ask for my parents' advice, but when they offer it, I owe it to them to listen. I'm an adult, and they respect me as an adult. Now that we've established I'm of age, what would you say to having a glass of wine?" Susan hoped he picked up on her teasing tone. The sun was setting, and the humidity wasn't as bad. A slight breeze scented the evening air with her mother's roses. In another hour her father would begin his fantastic display of fireworks. She wanted nothing more than to enjoy them, her mind devoid of anything unpleasant.

"I'll come with you." To Susan's relief, nothing more was said about their respective families. Richard walked with her to the bar and ordered a ginger ale while she reached for a glass of white wine. A health-conscious teetotaler. Wrong, teetotalers usually sipped at a single drink the entire night. She wondered if he had an alcohol skeleton in his closet.

Uncomfortable with the silence between them as they wandered through the gardens, Susan groped for something to say. "So, what do you think of Florida compared to California?"

"They're like day and night." He threw his head back and laughed.

He looked incredibly sexy when he laughed like that. She found herself smiling. "How's that?" she questioned.

"For starters, I believe the average age of a Californian is nineteen, and Florida's average-aged citizen must be at least eighty-five."

He smiled again, and Susan felt her heart flutter. Cam had an endearing smile, too—a smile that often invaded her dreams. She shook her head to clear her thoughts.

Richard continued with his assessment of the two states. "The weather is much nicer out West. We don't have the humidity Florida has. They have snow, beaches, and mountains. I guess you could say California has it all."

"Do you miss it?"

"Not really. Perhaps a little when I first left, but you get over it. I've spent most of the past six years in New Orleans. Now, if you want to talk about humidity, that's a good

41

place to stay away from. It's almost worse that Mississippi."

"I didn't know. Dad said you were in the navy, I assumed . . . I don't know what I assumed," she said lamely. "So tell me about life in the Big Easy."

"It wasn't so easy. I studied at Tulane's School of Architecture, got my graduate degree in preservation studies, and went back to California right after graduating. I hated the crime in particular. The weather was something I couldn't get used to. The food is quite decent, and I do miss that, but as for the rest of it, you can keep it. I wouldn't ever want to go back."

Susan knew he'd done a twenty-year stint in the navy, but wasn't going to question him on his sudden desire to go to college and study after the service. She'd wait for him to tell her.

"I'm glad my father hired you," she blurted suddenly, and was, again, instantly sorry she'd said the words aloud.

They stopped simultaneously. Richard tucked a strand of hair behind her ear. "You don't know how happy I am to hear you say that. It makes it all the more worthwhile."

Her stomach fluttered. "Thank you. I think."

"Your thinking is right on the money. A job with a firm like Burke and Burke is a lifelong wish of mine. With you as a bonus, it's a dream come true."

Susan smarted at his words. "I'm not sure I like that comment. I'm not a part of the career package, Mr. Johnson, so if you've got any preconceived notions where I'm concerned, you'd best clear them out." She removed his arm from her shoulder and headed back to the festivities.

"Susan, wait!"

She almost stopped but kept on going. Let him follow her.

He found her ten minutes later at the bar, this time with a scotch on the rocks, straight up, in her hands. She looked at him. He'd really ticked her off just when she was beginning to think he might be the one to help her get over Cam.

"Why, he's back! No, it's not the hunky bowler; nor is it the beach-going dreamboat; I'm sure it's not the dapper young dancer—I always thought he was gay anyway. It can't be . . . but it is! It's every girl's Mystery Date nightmare, the Dud! If you're going to apologize, forget it. I'm not accepting, so save your breath." She drained the last of her drink and asked for another.

"Fine." Richard turned away from her and continued speaking. "It's one of my known faults. Putting my foot in my mouth. You know, words that missed the brain's filtration process. Not one of my better habits. But the Dud? For years I thought of myself as the beach-going dreamboat. I'll no longer suffer from that delusion." He paused and saw her grin.

"Okay, so you're not the Dud, but you're sure not Prince Charming either."

"Charming? I've never been called that."

"I'm sure."

"Susan, I do apologize. That came out the wrong way. God forbid, the last thing I want to do is offend you. You're like a breath of fresh air in my life. The excitement in meeting you overwhelmed me. I'm sorry. I would be honored if you'd have dinner with me tomorrow night."

He *was* sexy as hell, she'd give him that. Well-mannered, sort of. He hadn't spilled his food or drink. Healthy. Employed. So what if he put his foot in his mouth? She'd been known to do it on more than one occasion. She'd give him a second chance. "What time?"

"Seven thirty? I'll pick you up, if that's agreeable with

you." He sounded like a schoolboy who'd recently been punished.

"It's agreeable."

Lights suddenly exploded in the sky. Green, gold, and red sparks shot upward, then arced down like an umbrella. "You've got to see this. Dad puts on the best fireworks display in Orlando. He gives Disney a run for their money."

"Let's go." Together, holding hands, they raced across the lawn to join the other guests.

For the next half hour Susan and Richard watched the sky light up with bright, fiery lights. Some sounded like shrill bombing whistles as they were released, and others simply exploded, eliciting "oohs and aahs" from the guests. Once again, her father's Fourth of July bash was a success.

Susan set out a fresh water bowl, another bowl of dry dog food, and two rawhide chews for Nipper to indulge in while she was gone. She felt guilty leaving him alone.

He was dogging her footsteps, knowing she was leaving. "I won't be long, I promise. He'll probably turn out to be a dud after all, though he sure can be charming when he wants to be. I think it's a selective charm. He pulls it out, then puts it away. It's not natural is what I'm trying to say." She looked down at the bowl of dry dog food before she picked it up and poured it back into the doggy barrel that guaranteed the food would stay fresh. "You're getting my leftovers. Steak, medium rare, no garlic." She warmed the meat in the microwave and questioned her sanity. She wondered if Richard liked animals. It said something about people when they loved animals. Her mother always told her you could judge a person's character by observing how they behaved around animals. She'd always had a pet growing up, except in Europe. She'd missed their affection and company. As soon as she returned, she'd found Nipper at the shelter and immediately bonded with him. A German shepherd, he'd been left behind when a family relocated. Susan was sure the people hadn't meant to leave him, but was glad they did because he was the perfect dog, especially when she gave him extra doggy treats and wrestled with him. He was still a pup with lots of energy. She'd lost several pillows already, and her sofa was showing signs that Nipper had mistaken the legs for a chewie. In the scheme of things, it hardly seemed important. Cam would have loved this dog, and Nip would have loved him. She closed her eyes and imagined she could see the two of them rolling and tussling on the floor, with Nip winning and Cam growling. She smiled, almost laughing aloud. It always came back to Cam.

The door buzzed to life. "Be right there," she called. She wiped her hands on a kitchen towel, stopped and gave herself the once-over in the foyer mirror. Basic little black dress, high-heeled sandals, hair pulled into a chignon, just enough makeup for a night out. She rubbed her lips together. She'd have to pass inspection. The buzzer sounded again, not allowing another second to primp. The earmarks of an impatient man. A timetable man. A controlling man.

"I'm coming. I'm coming," she called.

She paused at the door. It was now or never. She opened the door. She was surprised to see that Richard had left his navy uniform behind, substituting it with an all-black suit. It looked like Armani, but she couldn't be sure. Cam wore Armani but beat-up, wrinkled Armani, and on him it looked good. He wore a pearl gray shirt with a matching tie. Cam never wore a tie unless he was going to a funeral. His dark hair was neatly combed. A tinge of spicy aftershave scented the space around him. She took a deep breath. He was

45

handsome; there was no doubt about it. But she didn't feel anything. When she looked at Cam, even after four years of being together, she would get weak in the knees.

"Is there a password?" Richard asked.

"No. Come in."

Before she had time to close the door, Nipper made a beeline for the front room, stopping dead in his tracks when he saw Richard. He let loose with a fierce growl, the hair on the nape of his neck standing on end.

"Nipper! Shhh, boy, it's okay." She dropped her hand to tickle him behind the ears. He continued to growl as his lips peeled back to show a magnificent set of teeth.

"Let me." Richard took a step toward the dog, and, before Susan could stop him, Nipper lunged, locking on to Richard's leg.

"Nipper! Down!" At her iron command, the dog released his hold on Richard's leg. He backed up a step, then another, as his tail dropped between his legs and his ears went flat against his head. The hair on his neck still stood on end. All signs of the playful pup she knew him to be were gone.

"I don't know what's wrong with him. He's never attacked anyone before," Susan said, a frown building between her brows.

Richard smiled. Susan thought it a forced smile. There was no smile in his eyes, though. "He was just protecting his woman. Right, boy?" He stooped to pet the dog, who would have lunged again if Susan didn't grab for his collar. Her mother's words about dogs and people rang in her ears.

"Give me a minute so I can crate him." She turned to Richard. "There's wine chilling in the fridge. Glasses are in the cupboard to the right of the sink. I'll be right back."

Susan scooped the dog into her arms and took him to

her bedroom. "I don't know what's come over you, Nip. Is it that you don't like men, or is it this one in particular?" She recalled her father's visit a few days ago. Nipper had greeted him, barked, held out his paw, then trotted over to his bed. He hadn't made another peep during her father's visit. She hated to put him in his crate. He didn't like it either.

"It's just for a little while, Nip. I'll give you a bacon chewie before I leave." She reached between the bars and scratched the dog's head. "I'm sorry, Nip. Tomorrow we'll work on your social skills." Nipper continued to whine as he lay down, his big head nestled between his paws.

"Everything settled?" Richard asked as he handed her a glass of zinfandel.

Susan took a long sip of wine. "Hmm. For a bit. He's still a pup. I got him when I returned from Europe. He's not used to strangers. I guess you're the first stranger I've invited over since we moved in."

"Well, let's hope I won't remain a stranger for long. I'd like to get to know you better. Your father seems to think you need a change. He said you'd had a rough time of it lately."

Susan was speechless with his confession. How dare her father discuss her like she was something on the auction block. How dare he . . .

"I've made a reservation at Charlie's Steak House. Your father recommended it. He told me they had the best steaks in town. He said the company even had its own special table. That's the mark of a successful company." He glanced at this watch. "Our reservations are in an hour."

It figures, Susan thought. A man's place. All macho leather, dark wood, and cigar smoke. Pictures of celebrities hung on the walls showing those who could afford to dine there just how famous they were. They'd never advertised, as far as she knew. They offered superb service and their food was top-notch, but it was *her father's* favorite restaurant, not hers. That nice little Japanese place around the corner would have suited her just fine. Her father must still be trying to impress Richard even though they'd landed the contract with the Pentagon. Burke and Burke was back on top again, thanks to Richard's sharp mind and military connections. Or was it? Was there more she didn't know? Her father had always been reluctant to discuss business with her. Maybe it was time to start prying into that business.

She thought Richard assumed too much too soon, and almost said so, but decided to give him the benefit of the doubt. She'd see how their date went. "Charlie's it is." She swallowed the last of her wine and declined his offer to pour her another. "If we want to make our reservation, we'd better leave now. Orlando traffic is murder."

Susan gasped in surprise when Richard led her to her father's Jaguar, parked beside her red Saturn.

"Mine is being repaired," Richard offered as he opened her door.

Her father *never* let anyone drive his pride and joy. Just how close was Richard to her father? She knew he'd been working for him the past three months, but certainly not long enough to get father-son car-sharing privileges. Something was awry.

"So, tell me about you. Dad says you're the best architect he's had working for him in years."

Richard slid into the driver's seat, adjusted his seatbelt, and gave her a questioning look.

She clipped the shoulder strap in place.

"They make these things for a reason, you know."

"What things?"

"The seatbelts."

"Oh, yes, they do." That military arrogance again. He wasn't her father. She felt totally and unequivocally chastised. "I don't usually wear one when I'm in Dad's car. He doesn't either." *Let's just see how he likes that,* she thought smugly.

"He should. It's for his own safety. I'll mention it to him. Now, you were asking about me. What would you like to know?"

This guy had balls. Nothing. Everything. Anything you want to tell me. "You *seem* to know everything. And what you don't know, you have an opinion on. Why don't you just tell me what you think I *need* to know," she said, daring him to chastise her a second time.

She observed whitened knuckles gripping the steering wheel, jaw clenched, all typical male symptoms of some kind of rage. Then nothing. She'd never seen a person's expression change so rapidly. Cam never got angry. Cam was always big on talking things through, and if something bothered him, he'd go off in a corner and work it out. She'd never once seen Cam with white knuckles.

"I guess I deserved that. I could blame it on the military, but that wouldn't be fair." He reached for her hand.

She let him hold it, but she didn't relax. She had to shake Cam out of her thoughts. "Yes, you did. We need to get some things straight before we go any further. Pull over." She pointed to a McDonald's parking lot. He did as instructed.

The moment he slid the gear into PARK, Susan let loose. "First, I'm a grown woman. If I don't wear my seatbelt, it's my business. I know it's for my own good, and I'm working on it. Second, I don't want to go to Charlie's. And third, I haven't had a rough time of it lately, and I resent my father confiding my business to you. I also want to know how in the hell you talked my father into borrowing his car."

Richard shut off the engine and turned to face her. "Your father offered me his car when he learned mine was in the shop. I want you to be safe when you're with me. Your father wanted the same thing. Jaguars are very safe cars. I think that's the main reason your father *insisted* I take it. Ashton told me about your engagement being called off. I'm not sure why he felt he had to share that with me because I certainly didn't ask." He held up his hand. "Now it's my turn. I know I can be an obnoxious ass at times. I'm trying not to do that." He offered up a rueful smile. Her heart fluttered. "I've been alone too long, and I've become set in my ways. Twenty years in the navy can do that to a person. I know, I know, that's not a good reason to act so . . ."

"Controlling?" Susan interrupted, thinking he reminded her of her father.

Richard nodded and went on. "I need to get out more often, I suppose. I've been alone for so long, I think I've forgotten how to act like an ordinary citizen. If you want me to take you home, I'll understand."

"No, you're right. Granted your social skills are lacking, but we're here." She nodded toward the golden arches. "We might as well have dinner."

Richard laughed. "You're serious? Here?"

"Why not?"

"I can't think of one good reason."

"I'm game. And since you're so out of touch socially, let's go to Church Street Station. That ought to liven things up a bit." Susan wasn't going to waste the night out. She wore makeup and had one of her best black dresses on. If it were to be worn at McDonald's and clubbing for the night, then so be it.

"I've heard of it, but first let me call Charlie's and cancel our reservation. I wouldn't want them waiting for us."

"I doubt they would, but there's a public phone right there if you don't have a cell phone. Go ahead."

While Richard used his cell phone to cancel their reservation, Susan went inside and ordered for the both of them. Big Macs, fries, and vanilla shakes. See how Mr. Richard liked this. She hadn't quite figured him out. She was attracted to him but didn't like him all that much. He wasn't Cameron, that's for sure. Cam was fun, outgoing, and, most of all, kind and considerate. So far, Richard was arrogant and at the same time, boring. Until he smiled. Then his face totally changed. *He was meant to smile,* Susan thought.

She needed a diversion in her life after Cam. Richard was older than she by fifteen years, yet in the short time she'd known him, she felt she was the more sophisticated of the two. Never mind that Richard had been in the navy. He'd been isolated from the real world. Join the navy and see the world. It didn't compute.

He found her at a back booth munching on fries.

"We'll do Charlie's another night. If you're up to it." Richard was about to sit down when he leaned over to reach for a napkin. He swiped the crumbs from his seat. "Kids."

"Let's see how tonight goes. And what's wrong with kids? Don't you want them?" Susan asked.

"I've never really thought about having children, though the thought doesn't repulse me if that's what you're asking. As far as tonight, I know I screwed up big time. I put my foot in my mouth. I don't know why you'd want to go out with me ever again, but if you do, I'm optimistic." He gingerly took a bite of his Big Mac, careful not to drip any special sauce on his suit.

"I'll make you a deal. Let's just forget about stepping on one another's toes and have a good time. We'll go to Rosie O'Grady's. If you don't have a good time there, I won't go out with you again. Deal?" She held her hand out for him to shake.

Apparently amused, Richard shook her hand. "That's easy enough, though I have to admit I haven't a clue what we're in for at this Rosie O'Grady's."

"You'll like it, I promise."

"Whatever you say. I like the company; that I do know."

They finished their burgers, then headed south on I-4 to downtown Orlando, then on to Church Street Station. Concrete block, high-tech glass, and highways wound through the downtown area like a maze. Susan was comfortable in the area, having spent most of her childhood in Orlando. She'd observed the growth, the tourists who came in droves, and the fast money made by the many entrepreneurs who flocked to the state in hopes of catching whatever it was that had inspired Walt Disney to draw that little mouse on that long ago train ride in 1928 when he traveled from New York to Los Angeles. The results, an empire with no equal. That little drawing was now recognized around the world. In Orlando those big ears meant big business. Everything from ice-cream bars to telephone power lines were shaped like mouse ears. Susan never tired of it and the excitement she'd see in the faces of those who were visiting the vacation city for the first time. A land of fairy tales, where dreams came true. *Another crock to the public.*

Cruising along at a decent speed considering the traffic, Susan told Richard about her job at the Art Institute. "It's just what I need right now. I'll be working with local artists setting up showings, and, two nights a week, I'm instructing a live art class." She grinned. "That promises to be different."

"Nude?" Richard asked.

"The old cliché 'a form of art' it is. It's nothing, really. Most of the models are young college students trying to earn extra money. I took a few live art classes myself in college, though I never posed."

"Why not?"

"I wasn't asked," she shot back.

"So you're saying you would have posed nude had you been asked?" She heard the annoyance, or was it anger, in his voice?

"I might've. I don't know. Why?"

"You don't seem the type." He pushed down on the accelerator.

"What 'type' do you think I am?"

"I don't know, but I hope to find out." Richard took his eye away from the road for a split second, and, before she knew what was happening, they were eating the metal bumper of the car in front of them. Steam billowed out from beneath the Jaguar's hood, and angry voices shouted from the vehicle behind them.

It took Susan a few seconds to get her bearings. She quickly felt for anything that was broken or bloody and came up with nothing. Richard groaned in the seat next to her, but appeared alive. He could kiss that state goodbye when her father learned of their accident. His precious Jag, which had probably been totaled. So much for the safety of the famous Jaguar. She dreaded making the call because she knew the dark stuff was about to hit the fan. She could hardly wait to see what her father's reaction was going to be. A part of her knew she was going to be disappointed. A deep sigh escaped her lips.

Chapter Three

October 2000

Susan and Richard finally made it to Charlie's Steak House on their sixth date. Susan wasn't sure if it was a wise choice or not, since Friday nights were always crowded with a long line waiting to get into the popular restaurant, not to mention another long line at the packed bar. More often than not, you literally had to shout to your dinner companion to be heard over the babble of voices. The maitre d' led them to Burke and Burke's reserved table.

Richard held her chair, then handed her a napkin before he seated himself. "This is quite a place," he said, craning his neck to look around. Susan watched as his gaze took in the richly paneled walls covered with celebrity photographs of men, and a few women, in business suits, quite possibly discussing Disney's latest architectural venture, other diners, and possibly the waiters. She didn't know why, but she rather thought her dinner companion was doing a cost analysis.

She wasn't wrong.

A waiter appeared, menus in hand. "It's nice to see you again, Miss Burke."

Susan nodded as she waved away the menus. "It's nice to see you, too, Lionel. I'll have my usual, the special, medium rare, a loaded baked potato, and ranch dressing on the side for my salad."

The waiter looked at Richard, his pencil posed. "I'll have the filet, rare, plain baked potato, salad, and no dressing."

Richard waited until the waiter was out of earshot before he spoke. "It would have been nice, Susan, if you had introduced me as an employee of Burke and Burke." Susan frowned at the edge in his voice. "I imagine I'll be coming here with clients. It helps when the staff know you."

"I can't believe you expected me to introduce you to the waiter, Richard." Susan rolled her eyes to show him what she thought of *that* comment. He certainly *was* a finicky eater, she thought. One would have thought he'd be conditioned to eat anything after spending twenty years in the navy. The government wasn't exactly known for its gourmet food.

The waiter reappeared with a bottle of wine. Richard waved the cork under his nose as though he was a wine connoisseur before he took a sip of the purple liquid. He inclined his head slightly to show he approved. She'd just as soon have a Coke but didn't say anything.

"So, tell me. How was your first week at the Art Institute?" He reached for her hand.

Susan paused, taking a minute to clear her head. She was always unnerved when Richard touched her, and wasn't sure why. Just last week, she'd invited him over for pizza and videos. They'd eaten the pizza, but had never got around to the movies. It was the first time they'd been together since that night. Her face grew hot with the memory. He was a skilled lover, even a satisfying one, but he wasn't Cam.

"Susan? Is something wrong?" His voice was deep and sensual-sounding, like he'd rehearsed what he'd just said in front of a mirror, right down to the facial expressions.

"No, nothing's wrong. I just got lost there for a second."

It happened to her every time Cam invaded her thoughts. "You asked me about work. It's going great. I have a new assistant, Tristan. She's about my age, married with two kids. She just went back to work after her son William started school. If it weren't for her, I'd be lost. She's a great help."

"That doesn't bother you?"

"What? That she's a good employee? No, should it?" Susan sipped at her wine, eyeing her dinner partner over the rim of the wineglass.

"Are you sure she's not after your job?"

"Richard!" Susan looked around the restaurant to make sure they weren't being overheard. "Of course I don't think she's after my job. Why would I? Tristan doesn't want to work as many hours as I do. She's happy working part-time. I can't believe you'd even think something like that. This isn't Burke and Burke, where things like that are a daily occurrence. I'm a teacher, for God's sake, and so is Tristan!"

Richard folded and unfolded his linen napkin. If Susan didn't know better, she would have thought him nervous, but he was way too confident for nervousness. Suddenly she felt uneasy and didn't know why.

"Do you discuss your business with your father, or does he run things by you?" Richard asked, his gaze intent.

She gave a wry laugh. "Hardly. My father doesn't make a habit of discussing business with me; nor do I discuss my business with him."

"And you don't find that odd? I thought close families like yours discussed things like that."

"Hardly. Richard, let's get something clear. My father *is* Burke and Burke. My grandfather was Burke and Burke. It's a part of my family's heritage. I don't want or need to know its daily functions. I teach, my father runs his archi-

56

tectural firm. On occasion we'll discuss a project he or I might be on, but that's the extent of it. So, to answer your question, no, I don't find it odd in the least. Do you have a problem with all of this? Why are you asking me all these questions? I almost think you're writing our . . . our life story or something."

"I just wondered. Not having grown up in a close-knit family like you have, I guess I thought you'd know more about your father's business."

The waiter brought their salads then and refilled their wineglasses. The tinkling of glassware along with the drone of voices wasn't the most romantic setting. The acoustics were terrible, Susan thought. Apparently Richard liked this macho atmosphere, as did her father, and she had to admit, aside from the ambiance or lack thereof, the food was excellent. After their last date, she'd imagined a more intimate setting, but Richard was determined to come here to eat at the private, reserved Burke and Burke table.

"You know what they say about assuming . . ." She let her comment trail off as she forked a leaf of romaine.

He laughed. "Okay, you got me. Next time I want to know something, I'll just come right out and ask."

She nodded. "I like the direct approach myself. Cut out the middleman and get straight to the heart of the matter and cut the bullshit." That had always been Cam's MO. Obviously, she'd adopted it herself.

Richard chopped his lettuce into bite-size pieces, pushed the croutons to the side, and carefully set the onions on the side of his plate. Susan supposed he was being considerate. She hadn't bothered since she liked onions. They'd already been to bed, so she wasn't going to worry about her breath. Besides, she had a package of Listerine breath fresheners stashed in her purse.

Their entrees arrived, and they gave the meal their full attention.

Two hours later, on her front stoop, Susan handed her keys to Richard. He was gallant and old-fashioned, Susan thought. Opening the car door, pulling out her chair, unlocking her door, not eating onions. She decided then and there that she liked his gallant attitude. Cam would have said something like, "Did you break your wrist or something?" Then he'd swoop her up and carry her over the threshold.

Nipper growled from the bedroom. "Settle down, boy," she called out. "Richard, would you mind waiting a few minutes?" She'd promised him coffee and dessert. "Nipper's going to want a walk."

"Of course not. I'll come with you."

Susan hurried into the bedroom, changed out of her silk slacks into jeans and a tee shirt before she let Nipper out of his kennel. He ran around the room like a cyclone. "Easy, boy, easy." Susan hooked his leash on to his collar. Richard waited in the front room.

Nipper practically dragged her to the front door. "He's more than ready. I shouldn't have left him so long. He's all energy right now, and he has to release it."

"You weren't gone *that* long. Besides, he's *just* a dog. He's not your timekeeper."

Richard's tone of voice was so annoyed, Susan stopped in her tracks, bristling. "Yes, he is *just a dog*, but he's also my best friend, and it's my responsibility to care for him—a responsibility I take very seriously. I take it you didn't have pets growing up." His insensitivity to animals bothered her. Cam had loved animals and would have taken in every stray he came across if the landlord had permitted it.

"I'm sorry. I don't know why it is, but I can't seem to

strike a happy medium with you. I've upset you, and I apologize. You're right, I never had a pet growing up."

Nipper stopped in front of a cluster of shrubs to do what he had to do. "Yes, you did upset me, Richard. I love this dog. I understand that everyone is not an animal lover, but I refuse to accept callousness and snide remarks where my dog is concerned."

"Okay, okay!" He held his hands up, palms outward as he bent over to pet Nipper. The dog's ears went flat against his head as he bared his teeth. "See? He doesn't like me either."

"Dogs know when they're not liked. They react."

"Are we having our first argument?" Richard asked lightly. A wry smile tugged at the corners of his mouth but didn't extend to his eyes.

Susan frowned. "Actually I think it's our third argument, but who's counting? C'mon, Nipper, time to go back in."

Back in her apartment, over coffee and fresh strawberries, Susan shared her experiences in Europe at his insistent urging.

"So you came back to the States on the rebound?"

Maybe it was the bluntness of his statement, or maybe it was the truth of it, whatever it was, it didn't sit well with her. One minute she liked him and the next she wanted to smack the hell out of him. "If I didn't know you better, I'd give you what for. You might have spent the last twenty-six years in the navy and college, but that doesn't give you an excuse to sum up my life in such a blasé manner. My life is none of your business, past or present. You don't see me asking you questions about your past, do you? That's because I'm not interested in what you did before you met me. Why don't we just drop the subject." Her voice was cold, verging on frosty.

"I'm sorry. I can't seem to stop apologizing, Susan. I guess I'd better leave while I'm ahead."

She walked him to the front door. "Who said you were ahead?" she all but shouted before she slammed the door.

He'd called three times last night and twice tonight. Maybe she should give him another chance. He *had* been out of circulation for a while. Susan wondered how she would act if she'd spent the majority of her life in the navy with barely a connection to civilian society. She'd tried to compare her time in Europe to Richard's time in the military. She couldn't. The time with Cam was the most special time in her life. One small part of her liked Richard, yet another part of her wasn't sure what it was that she liked about him. He was courtly, almost too much so, but at the tick of a clock he could become crude and callous. However, it was hard to forget their one romp in bed. She almost felt ashamed for her wanton behavior that night, but then she was an adult, entitled to some pleasures in her life. Sex with Richard was satisfying. Nothing could or would ever compare to the sex she'd shared with Cam. Did that mean she was settling? She summed it up in her mind as nothing more than a physical attraction.

The phone rang.

"Hello."

"So, you're not avoiding me any longer."

Richard.

"I didn't know that I was. Avoiding you, that is."

"You were. Your father told me you've been home in the evenings. He said he'd talked to you on the phone."

"My father needs to . . . never mind. Actually, I *was* avoiding you. I don't think we have much in common, Richard. You irritate me, you don't like my dog, and I seem to irritate you. Therefore, I see no reason to pursue this relationship." *Shit!* There was no relationship to pursue.

"I agree. I just called because I wanted to hear your voice. I've been thinking about that night . . ."

So had she.

Maybe she was being a bit too hasty.

"All right, one more date, but that's it. If you so much as say one thing out of order or if you pry into my life—past, present, and that also includes the future—we're done. Oh, one last thing. You will refrain from making comments about my dog. Is it a deal?"

"Yes. You're quite good at stating your case. You tell me where and when you'd like to see me again. I'll abide by the rules."

She hesitated, a frown building between her brows. She'd expected a little more give-and-take. Somewhere safe, neutral, sexless. "How about McDonald's?"

She heard his intake of breath and crossed her fingers.

"What time?" he asked.

"Let's make it around seven. Tomorrow night. I'll meet you in the play area." *How childish was that?* She hung up the phone and burst out laughing. What had happened to that sophisticated woman who cruised around Europe quite comfortably, dined in the finest restaurants, slept in the best hotels? She'd been so enamored with Cam back then. They'd enjoyed Paris's fine cuisine and nightlife. Their relationship had been anything but neutral, safe, or predictable. They were so in love neither one of them could see straight much less think straight. Would she ever find that kind of relationship again?

With the rest of the evening at her disposal, Susan decided it was the time to start her search into Doctor González's background. She'd been away at college when her mother became his patient and had no clue as to what his redeeming qualities were, if any. None that she could see on the surface, given the state of her mother's health. She was almost convinced her mother suffered from a serious mental condition, something more than the clinical depression for which she was being treated.

For the next hour she wrote letters to the American Medical Association, the Immigration and Naturalization Service, and the State Medical Licensing Board. Surely between the three organizations, something was bound to surface that would shed some light on the doctor.

She placed a call to her friend Tristan, who picked up on the first ring. "Hello."

"Hey, Tristan, it's me. Got a minute?"

"Absolutely. What's up?"

"Remember when we were talking the other day about my mother? You told me the name of a female psychiatrist? I can't seem to recall the name."

"Oh, you mean Doctor Watts? She's listed in the phone book. Want me to find the number for you?"

"No, I can look it up. I want my mother to see her as soon as possible. I think that quack González is over-medicating her. It wouldn't surprise me in the least to find out he doesn't have the slightest clue as to what's really wrong with her."

"I feel bad for your mom. Why would she allow herself to be treated by a doctor who wasn't qualified?" Tristan asked.

"The short answer is, she wouldn't. My father hired González. If Dad told Mom he was the best, she'd take him at his word. If he told her the moon was green cheese, she'd believe that, too. She's incredibly trusting."

"I don't understand why your father wouldn't want the

best available care for your mother." Tristan sounded confused.

"I don't think he knew what he was getting himself and Mother into. The sad truth is, my dad was too busy with the company and didn't want to be bothered, so he got a doctor who took care of things. A bottle of pills here, two bottles there, and Mom was out of his hair. My father's first and only love has always been Burke and Burke. It's entirely possible I'm wrong, and Doctor González is perfectly legitimate. There's just something about him that doesn't ring true to me. When Mom told me she overheard the good doctor talking about committing her, I knew there had to be more to the story than meets the eye. I intend to find out just what the real story is. Before it's too late. No one," she said adamantly, "is going to lock up my mother."

"If there's anything I can do to help, all you have to do is ask. Speaking of asking, did Mr. Navy-College-Man-Richard call again?"

"Actually, he called earlier this evening. I've decided to give him another chance. No one else is knocking on my door."

"Are you out of your mind? I thought you said he was a real toad," Tristan said, referring to the girl talk confidences they shared.

"I did say that. I'm never going to get over Cam if I don't date and circulate. Walking my dog for entertainment just doesn't cut it. He's not bad in bed. Very self-assured, very skilled. The guy's been around the block a few times. Did I say *skilled?*"

"You never told me you . . ."

"You're right, I didn't. He called, said he was sorry. I didn't want to overreact. I decided to give him another chance." Susan waited for Tristan's response.

"I guess if he's that good, I'd give him another chance, too."

Susan was glad Tristan couldn't see her face. Heat crept up her neck and into her cheeks. "What can I say? We're going to McDonald's."

"Besides being *skilled,* you didn't tell me he was a cheap-skate! That takes balls if you want my opinion. Susan, you deserve better. If a man asks a woman out, that man should at least be able to afford to pay for a decent dinner. Jeez!"

"I picked the place, Tris. I wanted somewhere boring. Nonsexual."

"Ohhhh, I get it. You don't trust yourself with him?"

"Exactly!"

"We'll talk more about this in the morning," Tristan said.

Susan knew her friend was smiling. "Thanks, see you bright and early."

Susan hung up and immediately picked the phone back up from its cradle to call her father. "Jemma, I need to speak with my father," she said when the housekeeper answered the phone.

"Let me go fetch him. I think he's in the study." There were no phones in the study because when her father retired to his inner sanctum, he didn't want to be disturbed with phone calls. She thought it rather ridiculous, considering how many hallways he had to traverse to get to the nearest phone. She waited.

A few minutes later her father's voice came over the phone. "What is it, Suzie? Is something wrong? You don't usually call so late."

She glanced at her watch. It was after ten. "No, you're right, and I'm sorry if I woke you."

"No, no, I was reading. Is something wrong?"

"I want to know how you met Doctor González."

"That was a long time ago. Why on earth do you want to know that?"

She immediately picked up on the change in her father's tone. Susan drew in a deep breath. She didn't want to lie to her father, but at that point she wasn't willing to tell him what she was doing. He already knew she was suspicious of his friend Maximus González. She didn't want to tip him off for fear of what might happen to her mother. As it was, this was probably a definite heads-up. Whatever.

"Because I want to know. We're talking about my mother's treatment here. I also know about your notorious memory. How'd you meet up with him?"

"He came to my office. Said he'd recently relocated from California. He wanted me to design his office building. One thing led to another, and I asked him to check your mother over when her little spells seemed to accelerate. It's nothing sinister, I assure you."

You don't know that. "I think he gives her too much medicine. Where is Mother now?"

"She's sleeping. She spent most of the day weeding her rose garden, not that it needed it, but you know your mother. She had supper sent up to her room and went to bed shortly thereafter."

Susan wondered how much medication it took to get her to go to sleep right after dinner. "Tell her I called. I'll stop by one evening this week." She was about to hang up when she heard her father speak.

"Susan . . ."

"Yes?"

"Are you going to see Richard again?"

Damn him! "Actually, Dad, we have a date tomorrow night."

The silence on the other end of the phone bothered her. "I see. Well, good night, honey."

Puzzled, Susan dropped the phone back in the cradle. Was it her imagination or was that fear she'd just heard in her father's voice?

Susan spent most of the morning with Tristan arranging a display called Seascapes and Beaches for a local artist. Personally, Susan didn't see that this particular artist's work was anything different from the hundreds of other "Florida theme" paintings she'd viewed, but this was part of the job, and she was determined to give each and every artist a fair chance.

"There. I think that about does it." She brushed dust from her slacks and stood back to view her handiwork.

"You really do have a knack for this," Tristan said. "Sometimes you absolutely amaze me."

Susan laughed. "Thanks. This is what my parents sent me to college for all those years ago. I enjoy doing it. Want to have lunch with me? I'm starving."

"You're on."

Directly across the street from the Art Institute was Rosie's, the best delicatessen in Orlando. It was owned and operated by an older couple who'd moved from New York to the Disney community twenty years earlier. Susan had discovered the place years earlier. She often indulged herself with their corned beef on rye, with a good smear of spicy brown mustard.

Today was no different.

"Miss Suzie, Miss Tristan. What will it be today?"

This was a private joke between her and Hector, the owner. Susan never ordered anything *except* the corned beef.

"I don't know. What's good?" Susan grinned, playing the game the way she always did.

"Everything," Hector replied, grinning from ear to ear.

"Then I'll have one of each." She reached for a Styrofoam cup from the red counter, filling it with Coke. Tristan did the same. They found their usual red plaid Formica table by the window and waited for the sandwiches Rosie would serve minutes after they were seated.

"All excited about tonight's date?"

Susan grimaced. "Yes and no."

"What's that supposed to mean?" Tristan inquired.

"Am I excited about going to McDonald's on a Friday night? No. Am I excited about seeing the man who is to be my date? More or less. Probably more than less."

Rosie plopped red plastic plates filled with huge sandwiches and oversized portions of potato salad in front of them. Red plastic flatware was wrapped in red-checkered napkins.

"If I keep eating like this, my dates with Richard are numbered. He's obsessed with physical fitness and healthy eating habits. Did I tell you he *runs* on the beach with a telephone pole on his shoulders? I think it's *half* a telephone pole. Navy SEALs do that," Susan said as she chomped down on her sandwich.

"A man shouldn't care about a woman's size. It's what's inside that counts. I can barely get my feet out of the sand to *walk* on the beach. He must be one magnificent specimen."

"Exactly. What's inside makes what's outside look . . . overstuffed!"

"Then tonight you'll want to go light on the fries and milk shakes."

"You can count on that," Susan said.

Two hours later, Tristan cleared her desk, leaving Susan to finish the mound of paperwork on hers. She glanced at the clock. Four o'clock already. She'd have to leave early herself to take Nipper out for a run. With that in mind, she put the file folders in a neat pile on her desk, made sure the lights were out, and quietly closed the door behind her. She took one last peek inside the studio just to make sure everything for tomorrow's showing was in order. She didn't want the artist to find a crooked painting or anything out of place. She sighed; everything appeared to be in order.

Nipper's run was short but exhausting. She ran a hot bath that was relaxing and delicious. She soaked for twenty minutes before she hopped out to dry and spread her favorite Lancôme lotion, Miracle, over freshly shaved legs. She'd shampooed her hair twice, applying a deep conditioning treatment and was now waiting for the face mask to dry on her face. *A lot for a trip to McDonald's,* she thought. But just in case . . . she wanted to be prepared. Her mind wandered to the little white Victoria's Secret panties and flimsy bra she'd bought a week ago, knowing they would go perfectly underneath her Levi's and tee shirt.

At six thirty on the dot, Susan headed south on I-4 to McDonald's.

She spied the golden arches and made a sharp left turn into the parking lot. She recognized Richard's new sleek black Porsche, parked between an SUV and a Dodge pickup truck. Susan swerved the Saturn into the next empty space. Porsches were incredibly expensive.

Surrounded by overhead slides, colored nets, and hundreds of multicolored plastic balls, children whooped with excitement. Susan watched from her vantage point as Richard seated himself at a small child's table, knees scrunched up, his flat stomach practically scraping the edge of the table. She lifted her hand to wave. He saw her and stood to greet her.

"You look absolutely ravishing." Richard pulled a child-sized chair out for her.

Susan thought he looked enticing. Her heart kicked up a beat. Dressed casually in khaki slacks and a light blue pullover, his hair windblown, he made one hell of a tempting sight.

"I haven't ordered. Figured I'd wait. I didn't know if you'd want another Big Mac or something else."

Something else, she thought, but that remained to be seen. "I promised Tristan I'd go easy. How about a salad and a Diet Coke?"

"Works for me."

Richard went to the counter and placed their order. Susan liked observing him from behind. Nice buns. Narrow waist, broad shoulders. He would have been perfect if he was just a few inches taller. She sighed. No one gets it all. Besides there was no such thing as a perfect man. Except maybe Cam.

Richard returned with plastic bowls of salad and paper cups of soda. "I guess I deserve this after our last date. I talk too much sometimes."

"Before you put your foot in your mouth, *again,* let's eat and play it by ear afterward."

"Anything you say, Susan. *Anything.*" He emphasized the last word. Susan knew exactly what he was referring to.

They spent the remainder of the evening doing *every-thing.*

Susan ripped open the envelope from the American Medical Association. It'd been four weeks since she'd mailed out her letters inquiring into Doctor González's past. She'd been ready to place phone calls to find out if somehow her query letters had gone awry when the response arrived in that day's mail.

Dear Ms. Burke,
  Please find the following information you requested enclosed. If we can be of further assistance, please do not hesitate to contact us.

She scanned the letter looking for anything unusual. Apparently the good doctor had a few malpractice suits against him, nothing especially peculiar about that. Most doctors at one time or another have had a disgruntled patient willing to sock it to both the doctor and the insurance company. She flipped through the pages. Damn. This one went back over thirty years. God, how old was this quack? Susan knew he was long past retirement age, but that hadn't really concerned her. A lot of medical professionals worked well past the usual age of retirement. She firmly believed as long as one was able to function in their chosen profession, age was simply a number.

Everything seemed to be in order as far as the Immigration Department was concerned. Maximus Eduardo González became a citizen of the United States in 1960 when he was thirty years old. He then studied medicine at UCLA, graduating at the top of his class. Nothing wrong there. For several years he worked with a group of physicians, then dropped out of sight. Then in the late seventies, he resurfaced. Susan was curious. Where had he been all those years? Maybe he went back to his birthplace, San Pedro de las Colonias, Mexico, to practice medicine. No matter. She'd read enough.

She found the number for Doctor Watts. "I'd like to make an appointment for my mother. Yes, Monday is fine.

Iris Burke. Ten o'clock."

The voice at the other end of the line said she was looking forward to meeting her and her mother.

"I feel foolish and disloyal sneaking behind your father's back like this, Susan." Iris sat in the front seat of her Saturn, looking better than Susan remembered her looking in a long time.

"Mom, you stopped taking all those pills González prescribed, right?"

"I did exactly what you said, Susan. This is all so cloak-and-dagger," Iris fretted.

Susan watched the road ahead, glancing up every so often to peer in the rearview mirror to see if anyone was following them. She wasn't sure if she was being paranoid or not. Better to be safe than sorry. One of Cam's mottoes. She'd told her father they were going shopping and from there, out to lunch. She'd taken the day off from the studio, knowing Tristan could handle things in her absence.

"I know, Mom. But it has to be this way. I don't want Dad locking you up somewhere for all the wrong reasons. And I sure as hell don't want you taking any more medication. You did bring some of your pills for Doctor Watts to look at, didn't you?"

Iris patted her purse. "I have them right here, inside a tissue. I just held them under my tongue till Maximus or your father left the room. Nothing to it. I can't believe how alert I am these days! Things aren't fuzzy or wavy anymore. I haven't wanted to rest for days now; well, other than getting a good night's sleep."

"Mother, when we talk to Doctor Watts, I don't think I'd go into our concerns about González's past, just his treatment plan, okay?"

"Of course. I don't really care about his past. I just want a doctor to tell me what's *wrong* with me. Why do I have those terrible dark days, then suddenly feel as if I'm bathing in a pool of sunlight? It started before you were born, no matter what your father says. He wants me to think it was *after*. He knows exactly when it all started."

Her mother's voice was hard with an edge to it and more determined than Susan could remember. "Then if he knows, Mom, why hasn't he taken you to another doctor, one that could help you?"

"Oh, he thinks there's no need. He and Maximus are close, personal friends, and he trusts him. They golf together, and they socialize at times. Your father designed his office building years ago and some other buildings, if I'm not mistaken."

"I know all of that, Mom. I just think there's something strange about the man. I can't put my finger on anything other than his over-medicating you, but something about him doesn't ring right with me. I'm also trying to figure out Dad's role in all this."

"You've just described the way I feel about Richard. Your father tells me you have been seeing a lot of one another."

Susan wondered if there was anything about her personal life her father *didn't* know. She debated saying something to her mother, then changed her mind. In her own way, she'd let her father know she didn't appreciate him prying into her affairs.

"I wouldn't say I'm seeing him a lot, Mom. We've been out a few times. I kind of like the guy. He's sort of old-fashioned, and that appeals to me. He opens doors for me, orders for me, and makes me feel as though there is nothing more important in the world than his spending time with

me." She and Richard had reached an understanding the
night they'd eaten at McDonald's. They agreed not to question or comment on one another's past. It was one foot forward, one step at a time, and it seemed to be working. They
were getting along very well these days. In and out of bed.
She wasn't obsessing about Cam, but he still wasn't totally
out of her thoughts. She wished she knew if that was good
or bad.

"Don't say I didn't warn you, Susan. I know that somewhere along the way I've met that man. I just don't know
where or when. Eventually, though, I'll remember. He is
not the man for you. I wish you'd listen to me."

"Mom, I think you've really mistaken him for a movie
star. I know how you watch *Inside Edition* and *Entertainment
Tonight* and all those talk shows with celebrities. You aren't
exactly a gadabout, so I don't know how or where you
could have seen the man, much less met him. I think he
looks like George Hamilton, with blue eyes, of course."

"I would never mistake Richard for a movie star. For one
thing, he's much too short. Short men have all manner of
complexes. Just look at Napoleon. Nothing comes back
from his eyes, they're dead. Eyes are a mirror of one's soul.
I don't think that man has a soul. If you don't have a soul,
that means the devil took it; therefore, he's evil. What was
Cameron like, Susan? How does Richard compare to
Cameron?" Iris said, all in one breath.

It was the last thing she thought her mother would ever
ask. A chill chased itself up her arms at her mother's ominous words.

Susan drew in a deep breath, wishing she could close her
eyes to call up their last evening together in Paris but
couldn't because she was driving.

"Cam was everything, Mom. That once-in-a-lifetime

kind of guy. He was so clever and witty. We used to laugh over everything and nothing. He was real easy on the eyes, too. He was six-foot-two, a hundred ninety pounds. A real hunk of muscle and good looks. He has this crooked grin that made me melt. He loved children and animals. I think if we had married, we would have started a family right away. He was . . ." She stopped, tears clouding her vision. She couldn't go back there. Ever. There was no point.

"Was what?" her mother insisted gently.

Susan sniffed, and murmured, "He was perfect, Mom. Absolutely perfect."

A minute later, Susan pulled in the parking lot to the doctor's office. She jumped out and opened the door for her mother, thankful for their arrival. She couldn't take another trip down Memory Lane. "This looks like a nice place," she said.

What might have been an old house years ago was painted a bright cheerful yellow, with white shutters. White wicker chairs along with clay pots full of colorful blooms were scattered along the front porch and down the steps. Susan watched her mother. Already she was seeing a marked change in her. She watched as she stopped to pick a dead leaf from a plant. She smiled. "Mom, I'm sure Doctor Watts has someone who tends to her plants. I know, I know, you and plants go together, and it's hard to resist a dry old leaf.

"Are you ready, Mom?" Susan asked as she held the door for her mother.

"Yes, dear, I'm ready. Let's do it!"

Chapter Four

Doctor Emily Watts was a small, plain woman with warm, brown eyes and a perpetual smile. Within minutes she managed to put both Susan and her mother at ease. Iris had relaxed immediately when the doctor took both her hands in her own and squeezed them gently.

They watched as she poked at the pills from the balled-up tissue. "This is Stelazine, an antipsychotic medication that's used to treat schizophrenic behavior."

"My Lord! I'm not . . . are you saying I'm . . . ?" Iris placed her hand on her chest. Her eyes implored Susan, who was busy shaking her head.

"Don't worry, Mrs. Burke, you're not schizophrenic."

"But how can you tell? Are you sure?"

"I reviewed your medical records sent here from Doctor González, who is a . . . passable physician, but not the brightest star in the sky. That remark stays here in this office. I've examined you myself. Doctor González has been treating you for a disorder you don't have. The treatment is far worse than what I suspect we may be dealing with here."

Susan spoke up. "And what is it that my mother has?"

"A simple case of depression. Usually you'll have your first depressive episode after a stressful event. A death in the family, loss of job, sometimes the death of a beloved pet, a divorce, that kind of thing. What one person might call stressful, another may accept as normal. However, no matter what triggers the episode, the organic cause is a chemical imbalance in the brain that involves neuro-trans-mitters called dopamine, norepinephrine, and serotonin. Low levels of these brain chemicals prevent the nerve cells in the brain from transmitting normal signals. This creates chaos in the centers of the brain. Appetite, concentration, sleep, mood, and even your libido are out of whack. Given these facts, then add the Stelazine, which itself can cause a number of side effects such as drowsiness, weakness, blurred vision, constant fatigue, agitation, and sometimes insomnia, and you have a problem. It's no wonder you don't know which end is up, Mrs. Burke."

"What can I do?" Iris asked.

Doctor Watts's ready smile lit up the room and reassured Susan she'd made the right choice for her mother.

"For starters we'll need to wean you off the Stelazine."

"But I haven't taken it for three days now," Iris said as she tried to come to terms with everything the doctor had just said.

"That's fine, but if we simply allow you to stop the medication all at once, you could experience withdrawal symptoms. I don't want that to happen. Instead, I'll gradually ease you off the medication, and I'd like to try some Paroxetine. It's also called Paxil. We'll see how you do on that. If it doesn't work for you, there are a host of other medications we can try."

"I feel like I've lived in a gray fog the past several years," Iris said. "I want to move into the sunshine. I'll do whatever you say."

"That's what's so wonderful about these new meds. You won't be sleepy or tired. Most patients experience few side effects. Those who do experience side effects say they are so minimal they can live with them."

Doctor Watts scribbled a prescription and handed it to Susan. "Have this filled for your mother and, Mrs. Burke, please follow the directions carefully."

"Of course. And the other medication?" Susan wanted to know what her mother's treatment plan would be. She'd see that her mother followed the doctor's order to the letter.

"I'm going to recommend a dose of Stelazine every other day for two weeks, then twice a week for two weeks. We'll wait a week before she starts on the Paxil. She only needs to take it once a day. If you have any questions or problems, call me. Day or night. My service can always reach me."

Susan stood and helped her mother out of her chair. "Doctor Watts, I can't thank you enough. You don't know what this means to my mother and me. I wish I knew why Doctor González was treating Mom for schizophrenia. It's bizarre."

"Doctors are human, Susan. We all make mistakes. Though off the record, I don't think Maximus González took the time required to diagnose your mother properly. Your mother told me there have been many doctors throughout her life. She said she's been in and out of the hospital so many times she can't recall the exact number. I'm confident my plan of treatment is a new beginning for her."

"I'm sure it will be. Once my father sees the change in her behavior, I don't think he'll be so quick to call Doctor González or the men in white jackets. Now that I think back, it seemed like he always did that right before a big event of some sort. It was almost like he was afraid Mom's illness or her behavior would embarrass him."

"Sadly, that's not unusual either, Susan. Mental illness is greatly misunderstood. Most people recognize alcoholism as a disease, but when it comes to mental illness, it scares them, makes them think the patient is crazy. But there is hope. I'm trying to spread the word little by little, day by day. Now, I'd like to see your mother in a month. We'll talk more then."

Doctor Watts led them down the long hall to the front door. "Good luck, Iris. Susan. Call me if you have any questions."

Susan waved with one hand and held her mother's elbow with the other. The moment she was belted in the car, she looked to her mother, who was smiling from ear to ear. "I liked her, Mom. Did you? I think she's on the money, too."

"I can't wait to tell your father. I'm so angry at that man right now I could . . . sever his . . . his . . . oh, never mind."

Susan bit her lip to keep from laughing. She *liked* this new side of her mother already.

Iris looked at her daughter, and they both burst out laughing at the same time. This was they way it was supposed to be. Mother and daughter sharing a day together and loving every minute of it. Susan made an immediate promise to herself. She would never allow her father to take control of her mother's medical treatment ever again. And if it meant fighting him in a court of law, she was prepared for one hell of a lengthy battle. She prayed it wouldn't become that drastic once her father saw the change in her mother. For now all they could do was wait and see.

Knowing her mother's love of celebrities, Susan had planned a surprise luncheon at Emeril's, a new restaurant at Universal Studios. Advance promos said the man himself would be there today. Susan hoped they got a chance to see him.

First things first. She made a quick stop at Walgreen's to fill her mother's prescription, then another at the ATM.

Fifteen minutes later Susan whipped her bright red car into the closest space possible.

"Oh, Susan, not the City Walk!"

"Yes, Mother, the City Walk. What's the big deal?"

They both stepped out of the car at the same time. Iris waved her arms about. "This is all your father talked about when he designed these buildings. He was obsessed with the project. I promised myself I would never come here."

"Well, you're about to break that promise because I have a big surprise for you."

Susan took her mother by the arm to lead her through the throngs of tourists. The City Walk was one of her favorite places to visit in Orlando. It had everything and more.

Through a concrete maze, Susan found the Food Network's top chef's current place of employment. Emeril's.

Susan stopped outside the glass doors. "Well?" she asked her awestruck mother.

"Oh, my dear, this is delightful! You always know just the right places to go. I love that man. I watch him on TV all the time. Why, just last week I was telling Jemma she ought to try some of his recipes. I ordered his new Cajun cookbook, too."

"Richard told me about this place. He said they just opened a few months ago. I guess he learned to love Cajun-style food while he lived in New Orleans."

The sudden, ugly look on her mother's face stopped Susan in her tracks. "What? You look like a bomb just went off. What is it, Mom?"

"I just wish you wouldn't talk about than man around me. I can't stand him. I think he's trying to control your father in some insidious way. I know he thinks I'm a mental case. I can see it in his eyes. That's probably due in part to your father. Can't you find someone else to date? There are millions of eligible men in Florida."

This wasn't what she wanted to hear. "Mom, please! Let's not spoil our day. We're supposed to be having fun. I won't talk about Richard if you'll stop telling me how much you hate him. Deal?" Susan looped her arm through her mother's and led her inside the restaurant.

Iris clenched her teeth. She nodded. "Since you've gone to all this trouble, I guess I can hold my words. For now. And we *do* have something to celebrate, don't we? I can't wait to tell Maximus to kiss my tush. I don't think your father will be happy about that. I'm on the road to becoming a new woman and I like the feeling!"

Susan smiled at her mother. "Let's not be too hasty. Why don't we wait and see if Doctor Watts's treatment plan works, then you can tell Max to bite your ass, chew it up, spit it out, or choke on it! Your choice."

"I do love that scenario." Iris twinkled. "It gives me something to look forward to. Did I tell you your Aunt Lily is seeing someone? She says he's a *stud*. He's ten years younger than she is."

The hostess seated them and discreetly placed menus in front of them so as not to interrupt their conversation.

Was this her *mother* talking?

"That's wonderful. Tell her I'm giving her the high five. Where did she meet this *stud?*"

"At church. Do you believe that! Still waters, hidden fires, whatever that saying is. He's a deacon. A widower, too. Lily told me they were going on a cruise together. You know what that means?"

"That they like each other's company?"

"Yes. Apparently in and out of bed." Iris smirked at her revelation.

"Mother! I can't believe what I'm hearing! You've never been . . . so . . . so outspoken."

"I was very outspoken when I was younger, young lady. Where do you think you get that thumb-your-nose-tell-it-like-it-is attitude from? Your father always said he liked that trait in me. Somewhere along the way, he switched up on me and ordered me to be quiet. Back then I didn't care what I said or to whom I said it, as long as it was the truth. Though I never hurt anybody's feelings. At least not intentionally. I'm going back to my old ways," her mother said smartly, her eyes sparking with humor.

"I'm glad. Now tell me more about Aunt Lily and her new lover." Susan wanted to keep the atmosphere upbeat.

"There's nothing else to tell. All I know is what I told you. Maybe it will shorten Lily's surprise visits and keep her out of Jemma's cabinets."

Susan grinned. Lily's visits were legendary. Everyone dreaded them. "After Uncle Gavin's death, I thought she'd never look at another man. Fifty-six is young by today's standards, so maybe she might marry this . . . stud."

"Yes, fifty-six is still young. However, I'm not sure if Lily is ready for marriage. I think she just wants to have some fun. Gavin was such a . . . horse's patoot. We'll have to wait and see."

The waiter materialized, putting an end to their discussion.

Susan ordered first while her mother continued to peruse the menu. "I'll start with the Creole-marinated calamari, the wilted spinach salad, and for an entrée I'll try the pecan-crusted redfish."

"I guess I'll have the same." Iris closed her menu and handed it to the waiter.

"We won't eat for a week," Susan teased her mother.

"Jemma would croak if she couldn't cook for us. She spoils your father. I think she needs to slow down. She's got to be nearing eighty by now. She was just a teenager when my daddy hired her."

"I really missed her cooking when I was in college. I even tried making her butter pecan ice cream once. It was a disaster."

"I'll leave the cooking in her capable hands. Though I've often wanted to try my hand in the kitchen. Maybe I should take lessons," Iris said thoughtfully. "I think I'm going to be trying a lot of new things in the coming weeks."

"I think that's a great idea. Perhaps you could take them from the man himself." Susan focused her gaze on the tall, dark-haired man emerging from the kitchen.

Her mother turned to see who she was looking at. "It's *Emeril!*"

The tall, dark-haired man approached their table. "Good afternoon, ladies. I trust everything is to your liking?"

"Well, we haven't gotten our food yet, so . . ."

This must be a page out of her mother's old book. Say what you want when you want as long as it's the truth and you don't hurt anyone. "Yes, very much so. The atmosphere is very pleasing, the selections on the menu sound wonderful. I'm sure the food will be as delicious as it sounds," Susan said.

"Enjoy your lunch, ladies." Iris almost swooned when Emeril offered up a low, courtly bow before he made his way to the table next to them.

"I thought *he* was the chef. Isn't he supposed to be back there cooking our lunch?" Iris nodded in the direction of the kitchen.

"Shhh. I'm sure he has assistants to do that since he became so famous. He just makes up the stuff. And look—"

she turned to see the waiter bringing their appetizers "—this looks scrumptious."

They turned their attention to their food, making small talk between bites. Two hours later, they were in the Saturn headed for home.

"This is the best day I've had in ages," Iris said to Jemma when she entered the house through the kitchen. "My daughter certainly knows how to treat her mother to a wonderful afternoon." Iris smiled at Susan, then winked.

Susan was stunned at the sudden change in her mother in a matter of a few hours. This was the mother she knew and loved. It was almost a miracle. And she did believe in miracles. She prayed Doctor Watts's treatment plan would work. It was time her mother had a chance at a normal life. Her heart fluttered in her chest when she realized her father wouldn't be too thrilled about giving Maximus the medical boot. She wondered if they would still golf together. Would there be ramifications? She didn't know.

"It's been a ball, Mom, but I've got a date tonight. I think a nice hot bath is in order." She gave her mother a quick kiss and Jemma a hug.

"Oh, I wish you hadn't said that," Iris said.

"Mom . . ."

"Oh, all right. Have fun. No, on second thought, don't have fun," Iris snapped.

Susan rolled her eyes for Jemma's benefit. "Bye, Mom." Susan let her words trail off as she closed the door.

Susan wrapped her hair in a towel and pulled a pink nightshirt over her head. Her favorite outfit. She plopped down on the sofa next to Nipper.

"According to Richard, you're really not supposed to be

up here, boy. Do we care what Richard thinks? No, we do not."

"Woof."

"I really don't care if you sit on the furniture or not, Nip. You live here, too. Besides, you've earned it. I've left you alone too much the past few weeks."

The dog stared at her as though he understood every word she said.

"It's that man, I'll admit it. He just makes me so . . . excited and so . . . angry all at the same time."

Nipper growled. Maybe he really *did* understand what she was talking about. The shepherd did not like Richard at all. Some people simply weren't animal lovers. Richard was one of those people. It didn't make him a bad person. But admit it, a niggling voice whispered, it does bring him down a notch or two. He makes up for it in other areas. Speaking of which, she did have a date to dress for. Or undress for, as she hoped was the case. She'd invited Richard over again. Movies and dessert. She didn't tell him that *she* was the dessert. If he was half as smart as she thought him to be, he'd know.

Susan rolled over on her side and squinted at the oversize, red numerals on the alarm clock. Three in the morning! God, where had the evening gone?

She tugged at the sheet and jumped when she felt a hairy leg rub up against hers. *That's* where her evening went.

"You sleeping?" Richard murmured.

"Hmm. You?"

"Nope. You hungry?" Richard asked.

"Hmm."

"I take it that's a yes."

He reached for her and pulled her next to him. Their

bodies were damp from lovemaking. She instantly responded to his touch. With his fingertips, he traced her neck, lips, tucking a stray hair behind her ear. He kissed her softly, his tongue teasing, probing. She felt that familiar fire stir in her belly and opened herself up for him for the third time that night.

Minutes, or it could have been hours later, Susan descended from the euphoria of sexual bliss. She was sure she'd died and gone to heaven.

"Susan?"

She licked her swollen lips before answering. He'd kissed her with his entire being. God, it was almost sinful the way he made her feel. Her whole body ached, but it was a good kind of ache. "Yes?"

"Let's get married."

For a minute she thought she was hearing things. Surely Richard hadn't just said what she thought he said. She remained quiet, wondering if she had imagined the words. She didn't want to spoil the moment.

"Susan?"

It hadn't been her imagination.

"I heard you." Marriage? To Richard? He hadn't even said he loved her . . . or had he, and she'd just chalked it up to words said in the heat of the moment?

"So?"

So? That was all he could come up with. She needed a few minutes to get her thoughts together. Lying naked next to the man who'd just fulfilled her every sexual fantasy wasn't going to cut it. Lust was one thing, love was something else entirely.

She grabbed the sheet and wrapped it around her. "I'll be right back." She practically ran for the bathroom, closing the door and locking it behind her.

Marriage to Richard?

She dropped the sheet and turned on the shower. She stepped inside and let the warm spray wash away the traces of their long evening. She shampooed her hair with kiwi shampoo for the second time that night, then shaved her legs again. She didn't know why.

Marriage to Richard?

She got out of the shower. The mirror was foggy, and she had to have a clear place to see herself. She swiped at the damp glass with her hand. Underneath the glare of bright light, she scrutinized herself. Crow's feet had developed around her eyes; too many years in Florida and not enough sunscreen. Small wrinkles that would turn into larger wrinkles were starting to show around her mouth. Too many cigarettes in her youth. The skin beneath her chin wasn't as supple, and her ass was starting to droop like a hothouse daisy. Her breasts weren't in too bad a shape. Her legs were still lean and well toned, but she needed some work. When had this happened? When had she let herself go? *Why* had she let herself go? She'd always been athletic and fit. She never had to diet or work out extensively, as many of her friends did.

Marriage to Richard? Was it possible?

She turned away from the hateful mirror. She grabbed her robe from a hook on the back of the door and went back to the bedroom. Richard sat up in the bed with pillows propped up behind him reading her latest copy of *The New Yorker*. He looked satisfied and sexy at the same time. Satisfied and sexy did not a marriage make.

He tossed the magazine aside. "Is it that bad?"

She had the grace to turn away. "It's not that."

Richard tossed the covers aside and made his way to her side of the room. He held her. "I shouldn't have asked you now. It's too soon. I've fallen in love with you, Susan. I thought you felt the same way. We're good together." He held on to her as if he was a drowning man and she was his life raft.

"It's not what . . . what you said. It's me. I just need some time to think, that's all. I really never thought . . . marriage is . . . a serious step."

"Then it isn't a no?" Richard said, relief ringing in his voice.

Was it? She wasn't sure herself.

"I need time. We've only known each other a few months. This is so sudden." She moved away from him to walk back toward the bed, where she sat down and contemplated her bare toes with their cherry-red nail polish.

"Of course you need time. I don't expect an answer right away. Well I did, but—" he raked a hand through his dark hair "—I understand. I love you, Susan."

Where was the passion that was supposed to be in the words? Cam had almost turned himself inside out when he proclaimed his love. She'd known in her gut, in her heart, and in her mind that Cam meant it when he said he loved her.

She allowed herself to be wrapped in his arms. Could you build a marriage on sex? Was that enough? She cared about him. He was old-fashioned. Sometimes she felt protective of him. Her heart warmed. It was all too new to her. It hadn't been that long since she and Cam . . .

"Susan, what is it? You look like you're ready to cry." Richard ran his hands down the sides of her back, then stopped at her waist. He found the belt to her robe and gave a gentle tug. Her breasts exposed, he skimmed the pebbled peaks with the pad of his hand.

Before she knew what was happening, they were tangled

beneath a mass of sheets, with yet another erotic round to their credit.

Somewhere far off in her mind she made a mental note to explore it all later. It was all about sex.

It was still dark when Susan woke. "Time to rise and shine, Richard!" Suddenly feeling energized and playful, she snatched the blankets away from Richard's naked body, grinning from ear to ear.

He jumped off the bed with both pillows in his hands swinging them back and forth.

"I'll get you!" Richard whopped the pillow against her rear end.

"I-don't-think-so!" She snatched the pillow from him and jumped up on the bed. Swinging the pillow left to right, Susan fell to the bed in a fit of laughter as feathers gushed from her favorite down pillow.

"Look what you did! I hope you don't expect me to clean this up." Richard sat down beside her.

"It's only a pillow. I'll buy a new one. Now, before we get into another . . . uh, situation, let's race to the kitchen. I'm famished."

"I'll let you win this time. I'm going to take a quick shower. Get the coffee started."

Susan stared at Richard's retreating back.

Get the coffee started!

Craving a cup herself, she relented to his command. Scooping a large heap of coffee from the canister, she poured water in the coffeemaker. Watching the brown aromatic fluid as it filled the pot, she contemplated Richard's marriage proposal.

They both enjoyed one another's company. In and out of bed. They had a lot in common. He liked her family, or at least he liked her father; she wasn't quite sure what he felt about her mother. They both liked art. She tried to think of something more, but for the life of her she couldn't come up with another thing. Then there was Nipper. Maybe they didn't have as much in common as she'd originally thought. Maybe this wasn't the time to start a like/dislike list.

They'd been dating for more than four months. She thought she knew him as well as she would ever know him. Was that enough? In some respects, Richard was a simple man. He'd told her quite clearly what he wanted from life— a good job, a family of his own, to be needed. There was nothing really special, nothing that stood out as out of the ordinary. But that was just it. There should be something *special* about Richard. Not like with Cam. Just thinking about him had been special.

Before she could give Richard an honest answer, there was something she had to do first. She had to try one last time to reach Cam. If she didn't get an answer, then that would be *her* answer.

Richard emerged from the shower smelling of Dial soap and her kiwi shampoo, a towel wrapped around his middle.

"I'll have some coffee now that I'm fully awake." Richard grabbed a mug from the stand and held his cup out to her.

She made no move to pour the coffee. Instead, she pointed to the pot.

There was no time like the present to set some ground rules. She was not going to wait on him hand and foot. This wasn't the navy.

"Okay, okay. I just thought after last night you'd be feeling a little . . . grateful."

"Grateful? For what?" He was of course referring to their sexual romps. "Maybe it's you who should be grateful."

"You're right, I am grateful. But not for last night. I'm captivated by you. I'm grateful you gave me a second chance. About my proposal, take all the time you need. I'm real good at waiting for what I want."

Susan shivered at his words. For some reason they almost sounded like a threat. Taken aback, she just nodded and poured more coffee into her cup.

"I have to get going. I told your father I'd be in early to look over those Disney plans one last time. This is going to top the Pentagon deal. I need to go home to change my clothes. I don't want anyone seeing me in the same outfit I was wearing yesterday."

She watched him. He had a faraway look in his eyes, almost dreamy. She shivered again. At least he enjoyed his work.

He swallowed the last of his coffee and put his cup in the sink. "I'll call you later." He gave her a quick kiss before he headed back to the bathroom for his clothes. She didn't see him leave because she was walking Nipper.

Susan didn't have to be at the Art Institute until ten. She had a few hours to kill. Before she lost her nerve, she went to her desk and took out her monogrammed paper and a pen.

Dear Cam,

I hope this letter finds you well. I know we agreed to write that day in Paris, but I felt it would be for the best if we left things as they were. I guess you more or less felt the same way since I haven't heard from you. I found a great condo as soon as I arrived home. You'd love the kitchen. It has every gadget known to man. Even a built-in espresso maker. I went to the animal shelter and got a dog, too. His name is Nipper. He's a shepherd and so full of energy. He keeps me running, but I love it. I'm teaching at the Art Institute, remember the place I told you about? I have a great assistant, Tristan. She's married and has two children. We've become great friends.

There is no other way to say this except to come right out and say it. I understood how you felt when we broke up, wanting to be sure that you could keep your promise to all those people in third world countries. I know what being a doctor means to you. I know it's soon, but I find myself currently in that same situation. I met a man recently, and he's asked me to marry him. I can't give him my answer until I'm certain in my own heart that there isn't anything left for me in Paris.

If I don't hear from you, I'll understand there is nothing to wait for.

Always,
Susan

Chapter Five

Richard cradled his head in his hands, propped his feet on the corner of his desk, and let his thoughts go where they wanted to go. He felt so pleased with himself he wished there was a way to celebrate. Things were going even better than he'd hoped. Why the gods were looking down on him so benevolently at the moment he didn't know, but he certainly wasn't about to question his good fortune. After all, it was his turn. So what if he'd manipulated events? People did it all the time. It was what you had to do in business to stay at the top. In his case, he'd simply started his planning early, very early, at the tender age of twelve.

All the loneliness, all the years of neglect, all the unending criticism, were about to culminate in one masterful payoff. And there was no one he had to share the credit with but himself. *He* was the mastermind of his destiny.

All he had to do was continue living his life. He saw the way *she* looked at him. The only flaw in an otherwise perfect plan.

Flaws could always be corrected.

His feet hit the floor with a loud thump as he prepared to go about his usual morning routine. He skimmed through *USA Today*, the *Wall Street Journal*, and the *New York Times*. He allowed himself one hour for this rather small indulgence. Time was a precious commodity, and if there was one thing he was known for, it was that he didn't waste it, but today, his thoughts were on *her*. He cringed when he thought of what she'd done to him. The bitch. She'd had no right to take his life away the way she had. She'd made a sacred promise, then broken that sacred promise. His only advantage, even now, after all those years, was that she didn't know he knew about the promise.

He hadn't forgotten. You never forgot the things that turned your life upside down. He'd spent untold sleepless nights entertaining thoughts about what he would do to *her*. While plotting her destruction, he hadn't dared dream it would be so easy. He laughed, a cruel sound.

Richard folded the newspapers and stacked them in a recycling box by the back door. He hated sloppiness because he viewed it as a form of laziness. His apartment was immaculate. There was no way he wanted some cleaning service touching his belongings. To that end, he cleaned the apartment himself. Strangers tended to pry, to snoop, and, oftentimes, to steal. If they put two and two together, not that they would, he'd be fucked. That wasn't going to happen, he reminded himself, because he wasn't about to hire a maid, and he sure as hell wasn't going to start entertaining in this pissant apartment.

At the current stage of the game, he couldn't risk even one question cropping up in regard to the reputation he'd worked so hard to achieve.

Most people thought him well-to-do, or at least comfortably off. Though far from poor, he wasn't a wealthy man. Yet. Poor as a child, he vowed he would never live that life as an adult. He wanted more, what rightfully belonged to him, and he'd get it if it harelipped the governor, and he didn't see that happening anytime soon.

Now the waiting game was about to begin. He knew his

next move, as well as the outcome. He laughed again, delighted with the way things were going. There wasn't a damn thing *she* could do about it. She was going to be as powerless against him as he'd been against her years ago. What she cherished most in the world was almost his.

Mentally crossing her fingers, Susan inserted her key in the mailbox. She could feel her heart slamming back and forth inside her rib cage. *Please, please let there be a letter today. Please.* Unaware that she was holding her breath, she felt tears sting her eyes as she scanned her mail.

Utility bill. Phone bill, car insurance bill, an ad from Burdines department store. Nothing else. Damn. She'd waited almost eight weeks. International mail didn't take more than a couple of weeks, at the most, to reach the United States. She might as well face the fact that Cam wasn't going to respond to her letter. Every day for the past month, she'd hurried home, her heart racing, palms sweating, as she ran to the mailbox in hopes there would be a response.

There was nothing today, just as there had been nothing during the previous days. Did she dare hope that her letter had somehow been lost in the mail and that was why Cam hadn't written? She wanted to cry but knuckled her eyes instead. All she was doing was prolonging the inevitable. What was it Aunt Lily always said? Fish or cut bait. Translation . . . accept Richard's proposal and get on with your life.

Nipper nudged her leg. Time to go for a walk.

"Okay, big guy, let's go for a walk. I think both of us could use some fresh air." She hooked the leash onto Nipper's collar and grabbed her keys. Her thoughts ran every which way as she walked alongside her dog. Richard had been more than patient with her these past few months. They'd shared a lot during the past few weeks. Susan felt she knew Richard as well as she would ever get to know him. She knew, sensed, that there was another side that he would never allow her to see, the side that he hugged to his chest. She wasn't getting any younger. All her friends were married with children or children on the way. Twenty-eight, almost twenty-nine wasn't that old, she told herself. She wanted a family while she was still young. Her mother had been older when she was born, not that it mattered, but she'd secretly wished sometimes that her mother was younger like her friends' mothers. Her mother was wonderful, and she hadn't really missed out on anything, but there had been times when she wished her mother would've spent the night with her watching old movies, talking about guys, but she'd been sick then. It was now that mattered. The past was prologue, as Aunt Lily would say. Her mother was as spry as they come these days, alert and vibrant with a mind of her own and a vocabulary that left nothing to the imagination. Doctor Watts's treatment was nothing short of a miracle.

Two hours later she decided to accept Richard's proposal. Why, she wondered, didn't she feel happy at the decision? Before she could change her mind, she ushered Nipper into the Saturn. Their destination, her parents' house.

She made her announcement quietly, unsure how her parents would react. Nipper sat on Susan's feet, his ears straight up, sensing the tension she was under.

Iris's face turned bone white. "Susan, are you sure? You just met the man eight months ago. Ashton, say something, for God's sake. Susan, you're making a mistake. Can't you wait a little longer? You're settling for this man because of

Cameron. Please, don't rush into this. Ashton, if you don't say something, I am going to throw this teapot at you."

"Mom, we've been over this a dozen times, maybe two dozen times. You don't have to know someone ten years before you get married. Richard and I get along very well together. We enjoy our respective careers, and neither of us is getting any younger. You do want grandchildren, don't you? The only way you're going to get those grandchildren is for me to get married."

Susan risked a glance at her father. His face was red, the veins in his neck popping. The news didn't appear to elate him any more than it had her mother. She wondered if she should worry about his lack of a reaction.

"You know better than to say a thing like that, Susan. Your father and I would love to have grandchildren. I don't like Richard Johnson. I will never like Richard Johnson." She turned to her husband and said, "This is all your fault, Ashton. You introduced her to that . . . that . . . man. You mark my words, you are both going to rue the day he came into our lives."

"Mother!" Susan wailed. "Why are you spoiling this for me?" She looked to her father, hoping he'd step in and side with her. Instead, he looked away. He was still distant over her interference with her mother's medical care. "Richard cares about me. He cares about our family. He's going to take over Burke and Burke so Dad can retire soon. Isn't that what you both want? This is supposed to be the happiest time in a woman's life. All you're giving me is grief. Maybe we should elope. Forget all the hoopla. I'm going home now and I'm taking my dog with me. After I leave, you can talk it to death, do whatever you want. Call me when you're ready to plan my wedding. Stay where you are, I can see myself out. I mean it, you two, either be happy for me, or I'm eloping." She kissed each of them on the forehead before she led Nipper out of the house and into the car.

Her thoughts were like a runaway train as she drove home. *What is that saying, where there's smoke, there's fire? What* is *Mother's fear? Is my father having second thoughts?*

Richard certainly wasn't the man she'd thought him to be six months earlier. He'd mellowed during their relationship, allowed himself to be human. Susan suspected he'd grown up in a cold environment, never receiving what she termed "real motherly love." Sure, he'd had his adoptive parents, and they'd taken care of him, but she wondered if they'd really *loved* him. They were still alive, but, as far as she knew, he never wrote or called them. Some instinct, and she didn't know where it came from, warned her not to pry into that aspect of Richard's life. Now, she wished she had. Surely, he would invite them to the wedding. She would insist on it.

Her chaotic thoughts turned to her parents. With her mother's health improving in the past months, her father had become withdrawn. The more vitalized her mother became, the more the light dimmed in her father. While he still controlled Burke and Burke, she suspected he was more of a figurehead than anything. Richard was top man now.

"Oh, Cam, why didn't you answer my letter?" Tears gathered in the corners of her eyes, then rolled down her cheeks.

The die was cast now. Cam belonged to her past.

"Then it's settled. The seating arrangements are final," Iris said, making a note in the planning book at her side. "I can't understand why Richard doesn't want his foster parents seated at the parents' table. It seems rather strange, don't you think?"

"I don't think they're very close, but it's the only request Richard has made. I'm sure he has his reasons. Let it be, Mom."

"This is so irregular. Everything about that man is irregular. All right, Susan, I won't say another word. Obviously, your father isn't going to say anything either. Suddenly, he seems to have hit a silent spell."

Her tone was so accusing, Susan blinked. *I don't want to travel that road today,* she thought.

"You worry too much, Mom. I've got a thousand things to do with the wedding just three weeks away. I've got to meet with the realtor, and I'm already late. Richard hasn't a clue that I'm surprising him with the new condo. I have a few details that I need to work out. I'll call you guys tonight."

Iris's features tightened. She forgot that she wasn't going to say another word. "Why don't you just turn your trust fund over to him and be done with it? The man appears out of nowhere like some sphinx and within weeks is going to head up the family business and marry the boss's daughter. We're buying and paying for him to marry you. It's making me sick. What's wrong with this picture?"

Susan stared at both her parents, her shoulders slumping, before she turned and left the room without replying. *She's right and you know it.*

Susan spent the remainder of the day with the realtor and the decorators. She wanted everything to be perfect when she gave Richard his wedding gift. When you were buying your way into something, you might as well go for the best. What a bitter thought.

The condo in the posh neighborhood filled with elaborate furnishings, the Italian leather in his study, the desk imported from Spain, she knew would please. It was more than she needed, but Richard had grown up poor, and the trimmings of wealth and success seemed important to him at the current stage of his life. Too important. And yet, here she was, bending over backward to give him those things. She knew in her heart he wouldn't have done the same thing for her. Cam would have. Richard wasn't Cam. Cam would never accept anything so lavish from her. Richard would have no trouble accepting it and holding out his hand for more.

She tried to squelch the sick feeling in the pit of her stomach when she forced herself to think about her other surprise.

A surprise for him that she hadn't even told her parents about, a surprise that at some point, was probably going to come back to bite her on her rear end. She'd purchased twenty acres of land in Western North Carolina near Asheville two weeks earlier on a quick turnaround trip. Richard had often told her about his dream of having a cabin in the mountains where he could go to get away from it all. Well, she didn't have the cabin, but the land was a start. Richard could design the cabin to his specifications. They could spend their vacations there. She was already looking forward to it.

Iris blotted a tear with a delicate lace handkerchief while Karen Carpenter's "We've Only Just Begun," an all-time favorite at weddings, or so they were told by the wedding coordinator, played softly in the background.

Midmorning March sun glistened through the stained-glass windows, casting the church in an iridescent glow. Iris glanced around the packed church and scrutinized the guests.

Seated on walnut pews covered with rose-colored fabric, Iris spotted family members she hadn't seen in years. Distant cousins and their offspring. She surveyed the rest of the crowd packed inside Orlando's First Methodist Church. Many of the guests were strangers to her. Most of them were business associates of Ashton and Richard.

The organist began to play the "Wedding March." Iris stood with the rest of the guests and turned to see the bride, her beautiful daughter, and Ashton strolling up the aisle.

She had personally, with Jemma's help, decorated the church with an assortment of prize roses from her own gardens. She'd fashioned cream-colored velvet bows at the end of each pew and placed candles throughout the church, creating a soft, romantic glow. Considering that she'd only had seven weeks to pull everything together, Iris couldn't have asked for a more elegant ceremony for her only daughter.

Father and daughter made a beautiful couple. Ashton, with his steel-gray hair and black tuxedo, still presented a dashing figure. Susan, with her delicate features, looked perfect. Wearing the same dress she'd worn when she'd married Ashton, Iris thought her daughter exquisite in the simple ivory lace gown.

Ashton stopped when they reached the end of the aisle. He took a step backward and waited. Iris wished she could see her husband's face. Her heart fluttered in her chest as she realized, right this moment, this very second, a turning point was taking place in all their lives. Was she the only one who recognized it? Her stomach roiled at the thought.

Ashton would relinquish partial control of Burke and Burke to Richard, hoping to slide into semi-retirement, then they could travel as she'd dreamed of. In the early years of their marriage, when she was a young bride just out of her father's house, she couldn't have imagined wanting to do anything other than raise a family. Well, she had raised one child, who had grown into a beautiful, independent woman. Her life hadn't been perfect, but now that Susan had found the new doctor, and her medicine no longer left her in a deep fog of depression, she had a new attitude as well as a new lease on life. She was looking forward to Ashton's retirement and the future.

She let her gaze travel to the man who was going to be her new son-in-law. No, she was wrong, she wasn't the only one who knew this was a turning point. Richard Johnson's smug features told her he was prepared for the turning point. He turned slightly and met her gaze, his expression triumphant. She felt fear for the first time in her life. She was the one who looked away first.

Was it Ashton's hand that was trembling, or was it hers? Had he reached for her hand, or had she reached for his?

The next words she heard were the minister's as he pronounced Susan and Richard man and wife.

Iris looked around at the reception room with the eye of a connoisseur. The Grand Cypress Racquet Club had done a magnificent job with the decorations. Susan's favorite color was yellow, and the wedding planners had kept it in mind. The tablecloths were pale yellow with yellow lace overskirts. Ceramic bowls, a shade darker, held yellow roses nestled in between delicate fern and baby's breath. The candles, in frosty little porcelain jars, were yellow, too, and smelled faintly of vanilla. The room was beautiful, and she had no complaints. The two hundred and fifty guests milling about were laughing and talking and enjoying the hors d'oeuvres. The band was playing but not too loudly. You could actually carry on a conversation and not have to shout.

Iris let her gaze circle the room as she looked for Vilma and Buddy Johnson, Richard's adoptive parents. Last night, the Johnsons hadn't attended the rehearsal dinner. Why, she didn't know. Richard said later that they were tired. How could a seventy-mile trip from Lakeland be tiring?

She saw them at the far end of the room and made her way through the crowd. She should have been introduced to them long before now. *They must think I have terrible manners,* she thought.

Iris turned when she felt a hand on her shoulder. "Everything is beautiful, Mom," Susan said, her eyes sparkling with happiness. "You did a really good job on such short notice. Where are you headed?"

"To introduce myself to your new in-laws. They are your in-laws, aren't they?" she asked fretfully.

"Yes, Mom, they are. Richard said they got in late last night and were tired. I only met them myself this morning. Right before we left for the church. They aren't very talkative. They don't appear to be very sophisticated either. I think they're just nice, simple people. Come on, I'll introduce you."

"Did they bring a present?" Iris snapped irritably. She was instantly ashamed of the question. Anything and anybody having to do with Richard Johnson brought out the worst in her.

"Richard said they gave him a card with five twenty-dollar bills in it. They manage an orange grove, and I don't think there's a lot of money to spare."

"That's not the point," Iris snapped.

"What is the point, Mom? You asked if they gave us a present. I told you, then I gave you an explanation. You've already made up your mind not to like them because you don't like Richard. Look at them, Mom. They aren't used to such . . . for want of a better word, opulence. Behave yourself now when I introduce you."

"Mom, I'd like to introduce you to Richard's adoptive parents." She wished she didn't feel compelled to put the word *adoptive* in front of the word *parents*. Richard always did, so maybe it had rubbed off on her. "This is Vilma and Buddy Johnson. This is my mother, Iris."

Vilma Johnson, dressed in a flowery dress that shrieked Wal-Mart, stood up and held out her hand. Iris smiled. "I'm so pleased to meet you, Vilma, and you, too, Buddy. Is there anything I can get you, some champagne, some shrimp or lobster?"

"No. We're fine. It was a lovely wedding. You have a beautiful daughter," Vilma said quietly. "This is all so very grand. I've never seen anything so pretty."

Iris warmed to the shy woman immediately. "Yes, she is beautiful, and she's just as nice on the inside as she is on the outside." She'd be damned if she'd compliment their adopted son. "Are you staying at the club?"

"No," Buddy Johnson said gruffly. "We drove here in our camper."

Iris cleared her throat. *Camper.* "How nice," was all she could think of to say. She wasn't a snob; she wasn't. "I was wondering if you would like to come out to the house tomorrow morning for breakfast. I feel terrible that we're meeting for the first time at the wedding. I was hoping to spend some time with you last night at the rehearsal dinner. My husband and I would really enjoy having breakfast with you and getting to know you," she said graciously.

Vilma looked at her husband, her thick glasses fogging up.

"That's mighty nice of you, Mrs. Burke, but we have to

leave at first light. I was wondering something. Are we sitting at the wrong table? We don't want to do nothing that will embarrass you and your family. My wife said we were supposed to sit up there," he said, pointing to the bridal table.

Iris could feel her daughter start to tremble. "Actually, Buddy, you and Vilma *were* supposed to sit there. I don't know how it happened, and I do apologize, but the person in charge of the seating arrangements made a mistake. I can't tell you how upset my husband and I were when we found out. I hope it won't spoil the reception for you," she lied smoothly.

"I told you, Vilma, he doesn't want us sitting up there with him," Buddy said out of the corner of his mouth.

"No, no, no, Mr. Johnson, it wasn't Richard, it was the person in charge of the seating," Iris lied a second time.

Vilma's back stiffened as she threw her shoulders back. "Is it the same person who forgot to ask us to be in the wedding pictures?"

"No, Vilma, that was Richard's idea. He said you were his adoptive parents, not his *real* parents. He said only real parents should be in the picture." Iris wondered if her voice sounded as desperate as she felt. She looked at her daughter, who had tears in her eyes.

"I can remedy that right now," Iris said. "Come with me, both of you."

"Mom . . ."

"Hush, Susan. Find your friend Tristan. I saw her a few moments ago, and she was carrying a fancy-looking camera. I want her to take some pictures of all of us by the wedding table. Be sure to bring your new husband," Iris trilled.

Vilma was protesting, as Iris literally dragged her across the room. Buddy, in his polyester suit, locked his jaw, his face grim as he trailed behind.

"Ashton, come with me. Susan's friend Tristan is going to take some pictures of all of us." She pulled her husband away from a group of former associates.

"Now, that sounds like a plan to me, Iris," Ashton boomed.

Susan returned, Tristan in hand, her new husband bringing up the rear.

Iris waited. She knew what was coming the moment Susan joined her, her husband on the left. The line was drawn. *Us versus You.* There was nothing for Richard to do but stand next to his adoptive parents. *He's full of rage,* Iris thought. *No, that's wrong, he's full of* blind *rage.* She smiled, for Richard's benefit, as she moved forward to cup Vilma's palm in her own. Vilma turned to stare up at her. She was stunned to see *fear* in the woman's eyes. She looked across at Buddy Johnson and saw only defiance.

Dear God in heaven, what has my daughter gotten herself into?

Richard smiled through the obligatory pictures and left immediately afterward, giving his parents no more than a cursory wave.

Susan stood rooted to the floor. She turned to her in-laws and smiled. "I hope you're enjoying yourselves. I'll have the pictures blown up and send you a whole set. I hate to admit this, but I don't have your address. Before you leave, will you give it to my mother?" Vilma's head bobbed up and down. "Ooops, my maid of honor is calling me. I'll see you all in a bit." She rushed off, dreading the confrontation she knew was coming with Richard at some point during the evening.

Iris led the Johnsons back to their table at the far end of the room. She strained to hear what Buddy was saying to his wife. She thought he said, "He's angry that we drove to church, and here to this fancy resort, in the camper. He said we were like white trash, and he was embarrassed."

The rest of the day was a complete blur. Up until the moment the sick feeling hit Iris in the pit of her stomach. The sick feeling happened when she watched through her tears as Richard led his new wife, her only daughter, to the waiting limo. Would their lives ever be the same again after today?

The long and short answer was, no.

Iris said a prayer because she didn't know what else to do.

Chapter Six

October 2001

The Johnsons had settled into their new life with relative ease. The weeks and months followed one another in a near-identical pattern. They both worked, they came home, they showered, and they went out to dinner almost every night with prospective clients. It became a routine within a matter of weeks, one that Susan wasn't overly fond of but she endured because she knew it made Richard happy. He didn't seem to worry too much about making her happy. She sucked that up, too, because she had very little choice.

Saturdays Susan spent with her parents while Richard golfed. Sundays were a hit-and-miss day. If a client was in town on a Sunday, Richard played golf or tennis with him, then they went to the country club. Lately, to get out of the business on Sundays, she lied and said she had to go to Tristan's house to catch up on work. Then she would either go back to her parents' or to the park, where she sat on a bench under a tree and read.

She was lonelier than she'd ever been in her life. Or, as Iris put it, the bloom was off the rose. And they had only been married for seven months.

Susan patted her stomach. Her dream come true. She was six months pregnant. The baby was due shortly after New Year's. Her parents had almost orbited at the news. Richard had said he was delighted, adding, "Make sure it's a boy now." Secretly, she hoped for a girl. She'd had a sonogram but, as many mothers did, refused all information about the sex of the baby. She had not told Richard about it.

She was exceptionally tired today, and the morning sickness she'd had during the first three months had returned with a vengeance. She'd called Tristan after Richard left for work and asked her to cover for her, saying that if she felt better she'd go in around noon. It was six thirty, she was still in her nightgown, and she didn't feel one bit better.

She flinched when she heard the front door slam. Richard, for some reason, felt the need to slam doors.

Susan padded into the kitchen, hoping some ginger ale might settle her stomach. She gulped at it, then crunched on the ice. She wondered if she would dehydrate with all the throwing up she'd been doing. Maybe she needed to call the doctor. Her hand was on the phone to do just that when Richard appeared in the kitchen.

She knew the ginger ale and the crackers she'd eaten earlier were going to come back up. She waited.

Her husband looked at her with disgust. "You look like a goddamn Ethiopian, with a basketball stuffed under that nightgown. Can't you find something to wear that doesn't make you look like a blimp? I can't believe you're still in a nightgown. Have you looked in the mirror today? Christ, don't tell me you're sick again. This whole place smells like puke."

Susan bit down on her lower lip as she struggled not to cry. She wouldn't give him the satisfaction. "The house does not smell like puke. Yes, I'm sick again. I was about to call the doctor when you came in. Before you ask, no, I will not be going to dinner with you tonight. I've been out to dinner with you three nights this week. I'm tired of it. My father never dined clients every night of the week." This was all said in a flat, even monotone.

"Wining and dining is how you get ahead in business. I don't do business the way your father did business. You don't have to eat, you can just sit there and pretend you aren't dead. You are not an asset, Susan; at this point in time, you're a goddamn liability. Christ, I can't wait till you pop that kid. I hate seeing you looking like a beached whale. On top of that, you're starting to bore me. I'm sick of talking about baby names and baby furniture and baby this and baby that. You are not the only person in the world ever to have a baby."

"I'm six months pregnant, Richard. I am only going to put on more weight during the next three months. Right now, I am the only one having this baby, so that does make me the only person in the world to have *our* baby. Do you want to hear something else? You started to bore me *months* ago. This type of life is not what I signed on for. I did not agree to marry Burke and Burke. I'm already a Burke. You are Richard Johnson. You will never be a Burke. The only reason you want me at those stupid dinners is so you can say and this is Ashton Burke's daughter, my wife. Get it!"

She was used to his rages, but she still stepped backward. "Don't even think about it, Richard. One false move and your ass is on the highway. Now, what part of I am not going to dinner with you didn't you understand?"

"You're getting pretty mouthy, Susan. You're starting to remind me of some trashy people I've come across in my lifetime. Now, get dressed. This is an important client. I won't take no for an answer."

"You better take no for an answer because I'm not going. Now, if you want to bring all this to a test, why don't we call my father to settle things."

Richard reached for her wrist and swung her around so fast, she turned dizzy. "Don't ever make the mistake of threatening me again, Susan."

She tried to hold it back, she really did, but her stomach had other ideas. The contents of her stomach came out with projectile force to splatter over her husband's pant legs and Brooks Brothers shoes. Richard jerked backward, releasing her arm at the same time. Her back hit the edge of the kitchen counter with a painful thud.

"Christ Almighty, now look at me!"

Susan wiped her hand across her mouth. "I warned you if you ever touched me again what would happen. Pack your things and leave now! *Now* means now!"

Richard's eyes were like shards of glass when he spoke. "What are you going to do, Susan, run to Daddy and tell him your big bad husband touched you?"

"That's exactly what I'm going to do. I should have listened to my mother. She said you were *evil*. She's right, you are! Now get out of here!"

"Fine. I'm leaving. Call me when you grow up and come to your senses. I'll be at the Embassy Suites."

"The Embassy Suites! Are you going to charge it to Burke and Burke? Of course you are. Richard Johnson would be lucky to sign in on Senior Day at the Best Western. Don't hold your breath waiting for me to call, Richard," she snarled, as her stomach heaved a second time.

Susan didn't cry until she heard the front door slam thirty minutes later. She watched as he climbed into the Porsche that was leased through Burke and Burke.

Two days later, Richard returned with a bouquet of yellow roses and a box of Godiva chocolates. He looked humble, his voice contrite when he made his apologies.

Susan eyed him warily, telling herself a child needed two parents. Two, not one. She nodded but moved into the guest bedroom. Her excuse—she wasn't sleeping well and didn't want to keep him awake. He readily agreed.

Appearances were important to Richard.

Life settled into a routine orchestrated by Susan. She did her own thing and Richard did his thing, which was to work eighteen hours a day and entertain.

The day Ashley Rose made her appearance in the world, Susan had to call her father to take her to the hospital because Richard couldn't be located. He showed up at the hospital shortly before midnight with more yellow roses and a stuffed teddy bear bigger than she was. Susan pretended to be asleep.

She now knew she hated her husband. As soon as she was on her feet physically, she was going to head for a lawyer. It couldn't happen soon enough for her.

Cam had always said when you make a mistake, own up to it, don't lie, correct it, and move on. Life is too precious and uncertain to wallow in misery.

"Son of a bitch! Can't you keep her quiet? I have to get up in two hours," Richard snarled. "That kid has been squalling like this every goddamn night for two weeks. Give her a pacifier or a goddamn bottle. If it isn't her, it's you getting up every ten minutes to check on her. I need more than two hours of sleep a night, Susan."

Susan clenched her teeth as she swung her legs over the side of the bed. She unclenched her teeth long enough to say, "She's only three weeks old, Richard. She doesn't have a routine yet." She knotted her robe as she headed for the nursery, Richard right behind her.

The birth of her daughter had turned her life into sunshine and roses those first few days. And then, before she knew it, the sunshine turned into black storm clouds, and the roses became dry and wilted.

There were no words in her vocabulary to convey how much she loved the pink bundle in her arms. She knew in her heart, if need be, she would give up her life for her daughter. She rather thought all new mothers probably felt the same way.

The day after Ashley Rose's birth, Richard had looked at her, a strange expression on his face, and said, "She's the icing on the cake, Susan." She remembered how she'd smiled at his comment. She wasn't smiling now, though.

Susan sat down, Ashley Rose in her arms, in the antique rocker that had been a gift from her Aunt Lily. She opened her gown, aware that Richard was watching her. She hated it when he watched her nursing. Nursing was a private, mother-child-bonding experience. Since her return from the hospital, she hated everything about her husband.

"That's another thing, Susan. I hate seeing that kid hanging on your tit. It's been three weeks now, give her a damn bottle already. She probably isn't getting enough milk from you. That's why she's always screaming her head off. She needs a supplement. And she goddamn well needs a nanny. Do you have any idea how disgusting you look with your clothes soaked with milk? This whole thing is getting real old, real quick. Are you listening to me, Susan?"

Susan refused to look at her husband or even acknowledge him. She knew if she was jittery and tense, Ashley Rose would become colicky no matter what the doctors said.

The moment the baby finished nursing, Susan burped her and laid her back in the cradle. She checked to make sure the baby monitor was on and left the room, leaving the door slightly ajar.

Richard followed her to the kitchen. Why wasn't he back in bed for the precious sleep he claimed he was losing?

The coffeepot in her hand, she turned, finally, to face her husband. "Richard, I think it might be a good idea if you went to see Doctor Watts. You seem to be having a hard time coping with our new life. I told you when I was pregnant that our lives were going to change. You said you could handle the change. You are not handling it, Richard. I know what a hard time you're having, and I think it would do you some good. All you have to do is look at my mother to see what a wonderful job Doctor Watts did with her care."

"Are you out of your fucking mind? You think *I* need to see a shrink? I think you're the one who needs to visit the good doctor. I'm not *obsessed* with Ashley. I'm not the one who won't make a sound when she's sleeping. I'm not the one who hasn't left the house since she was born. I'm not the one who hears her crying when she isn't crying. I'm not the one who sits by her bed watching to make sure she's breathing. It's you. Nutcases are always the last to know they're nutcases. Didn't *that* mother of yours have the same problem at one time? While we're on the subject, I have another applicant coming by this afternoon to apply for the nanny position. I want her hired. You *will* do it, Susan."

"I don't want a nanny. Don't bring this to a test. I'm perfectly capable of taking care of my own child, which is what I want and what I intend to do. If you make another remark like that about my mother, you'll find yourself on the other side of the door. If that happens, you won't get back in, so remember that. I don't want to fight with you, Richard, but if you're looking for one, I'll give you a battle you'll never forget. We have a child together, a beautiful baby daughter. Can't you understand the importance of loving and raising a child? Newborn babies need to feel the closeness of a parent. But then I guess you wouldn't know about such things since you were raised by people who didn't love you." She turned to reach for the coffeepot.

Susan didn't see him raise his hand, didn't see the slap coming. The thin china cup dropped from her hand, shattering on the floor.

"Susan, I'm sorry. Jesus Christ, I'm sorry. I didn't mean to do that."

Susan stood rooted to the floor, her body stiff with shock. A cold wave of anger washed over her as her hand went to her cheek. "Oh, yes, you did mean to do that, you son of a bitch! Pack your bags and get out of my sight! Now!"

"Susan, I'm sorry. I don't know what came over me. I'll never do it again! I swear to God, I'll never do that again."

"You're damn right, you'll never do that again. *Sorry* is just a word. I told you to get out of my sight. My mother was right about you! She warned me, but I didn't listen," Susan declared, her voice ringing with unbridled anger.

My mother was right about you. She warned me but I didn't listen.

"Susan, you need to listen to me. You have got to get a hold of yourself. We haven't had a normal life in months. Look, I'm willing to take half the blame here. Hell, I'll take all the blame if that's what you want. I'm putting off all kinds of invitations because of you. I don't know how much longer I'll be able to do that."

"Do you think I care about your social invitations? I don't care about them, Richard. I care about my home, my child, and I did care about you. Do you really think I give a good rat's ass about an invitation to some dry dinner talking about blueprints? I just had a baby. Can't you see that I'm not up to socializing yet?" She reached for the broom and swept up the broken shards of the cup. She had to remember not to tell her mother she had broken one of the beautiful cups that had been her grandmother's.

"You know how I hate it when you use profanity. It sounds trashy. Susan, please, I really am sorry," he pleaded.

"I really don't care what you think right now, Richard. What I do think is, it would be best if you went to work now. Burke and Burke might fall apart if you're not there. Please, just go. I'm getting sick just looking at you. I'll have your bags packed by the time you get home this evening. And I'm changing the locks and the code to the alarm system."

She walked out of the kitchen and upstairs to her room. She locked the door. She was tired. Since Ashley's birth she hadn't had much sleep, with two-hour feedings around the clock. Slipping into a fresh gown, she almost missed the red trickle of blood on her neck. She leaned into the vanity and plucked a tiny shard of glass from the cup she'd dropped. She soaked a tissue and held it to the nick in her neck.

She didn't want to remember why she'd dropped the cup. She couldn't comprehend Richard's behavior. Yes, he was jealous of the time she spent with Ashley. Jealousy she could understand, but not his scorching anger. She would not tolerate his abuse. There was too much focus on domestic violence these days. More often than not, when a man hit once, he'd hit again. It scared her. Physical violence had occurred twice now. The third time, and there would be a third time, she might not be so lucky. *God in heaven, why didn't I listen to my mother?*

Only in these dark moments, when she was alone, could she admit that she'd made a mistake marrying Richard. She was sick and tired of trying to make the marriage work. It was so one-sided, it was pitiful.

Aside from her devotion to her daughter, she hadn't neglected her husband. She made his meals, washed his clothes, got up when he did, kissed him goodbye. The only thing she hadn't done was go to his silly dinners and luncheons so he could feel important. She knew in her gut that all he wanted to do was show off his trophy wife, Ashton Burke's daughter. Somehow he thought that reinforced his position in the company. It was all about Richard and his ego.

Suddenly, she thought of Cam; she always thought about him when things were sticky or dicey. Cam would never lay one finger on her. Just thinking about him hurt. She'd tried too hard and too fast to forget him. Her present circumstances were the result.

She fell asleep thinking about that last day with Cam in Paris. If only she'd listened to her mother . . .

Ashley's soft cries woke her.

She looked at the clock and saw that it was ten o'clock. Ashley had slept longer than usual. Maybe she was finally going to put herself on a schedule. She raced to the nursery. Her angel was sucking on her fist. Nipper sat by the crib, his eyes alert.

She made fast work of bathing Ashley, feeding Nipper, and getting herself dressed. For now she had to shelve what had happened earlier until she was ready to deal with it. For Ashley's sake she had to work harder at her marriage. At least for a little while longer. She hated the way she was vacillating. Earlier she'd thrown her husband out. She'd offered to pack his bags, and now she was thinking about continuing with the marriage for Ashley's sake. *What kind of sick thinking* is *that,* she wondered.

They hadn't even celebrated their first wedding anniversary yet. She wondered if there would ever be a second anniversary. Growing up with two parents was important to a child. Though Richard had grown up with adoptive parents, Susan knew he hadn't been loved as a child should be loved. On more than one occasion she'd asked him about his real mother, but he'd brushed off the question by saying he didn't remember her. She knew it wasn't true because he'd been eleven going on twelve when he was sent to the orphanage where he'd been adopted by the Johnsons. Richard flat out refused to discuss his background, other than the time he spent in the navy.

Now, with a new daughter in her life, there was more at risk. She needed to find out about Richard's background. If he or any of his biological family members suffered from any strange mental disorder or chronic disease, she wanted to know.

What she was about to do went against every grain of her being. As she looked at her daughter sleeping peacefully in her cradle, she knew she'd do everything in her power to protect her.

She picked up the bright red phone book and let her fingers do the walking. A dozen calls and two hours later, she started her search. It was amazing what one could do with a credit card, a phone, and the Internet. She didn't even have to leave the house.

With an empty afternoon looming before her, she decided Richard was right about one thing. It was time she got out, back into the world, but with Ashley and Nipper at her side.

Before she called her mother, she threw Richard's clothes into trash bags and lugged them to the hall foyer. Let him get a taste of living alone for a while. If she backed down now, it would just give Richard a license to repeat his actions. She then called a locksmith, who promised to be there in fifteen minutes. While the locks were being replaced, she called her mother. "Are you up for a visit with your granddaughter?" She didn't have to see her mother's face to know that she was smiling.

"Always. And your father is home, too."

An hour and a half later, she steered the car into her parents' circular drive. This was her first outing with the baby. She'd packed more for the short visit than she normally would pack for a week-long trip.

The front door opened before she could get out of the car. "Need some help?" her father called.

"Yep. I need a Mack truck to haul this kid and her diapers. Here." Susan gave him Ashley's diaper bag, the Portacrib, and the rocker seat.

"Is that all?" her father asked as he struggled to distribute the weight evenly.

"No, there's more."

"There can't be more. A man could go to war with less gear."

"I've got the biggest and best load right here." She took Ashley from her car seat and hefted her onto her shoulder. Even though they lived in Florida, it still got chilly in the winter months. She'd wrapped Ashley in an extra blanket, plus her cap and a pair of tiny pink mittens.

The baby settled, the gear stowed, Iris leaned over the crib, drinking in the sight of her new granddaughter. Ashton smiled when he, too, stood over the crib. "She looks just like you looked when you were born," he said quietly.

"So how does it feel to be a new mother?" Iris asked. "I can't tell you how many times I wanted to stop by, but I know how hectic the first month is. Your father felt the same way. Now, you're here. We'll be more than happy to baby-sit Ashley, honey, if you have to get back in the social swing with Richard."

Susan smiled, her eyes lighting up. "It's the best feeling in the world, Mom. But of course you already know that. You can baby-sit anytime you want, but it won't be for social engagements with Richard. It'll be because I want to have lunch with Tristan or to go shopping. Burke and Burke is not my life." She pointed to Ashley, Nipper, her father, and her mother. "You guys are my life."

"What about us men?" her father asked.

Susan smiled and nodded. Now wasn't the time to go into detail about Richard's lack of fatherly skills or jealousy, whatever he was experiencing, or the fact that she'd kicked him out for the second time. Later she would discuss Richard's current actions with her mother when her father was out of earshot.

Jemma entered the room carrying a tray loaded with baked goods, a steaming pot of tea, and other mysterious drinks she was known for concocting. "Now, I know you're watching your weight, not that you need to, but you've got to eat now. You're feeding that blessed child, and a few sweets aren't going to hurt one bit."

Susan hugged her dear friend. "You're absolutely right. I'm famished and wouldn't think of passing up your goodies. What do we have here?" She peered at the tray laden with food.

"There's your favorite peanut butter kisses. Then, of course, your father's oatmeal raisin cookies. I have red velvet cupcakes, S'mores, and those old Rice Krispies treats dipped in chocolate that you're so fond of. Hot tea, cocoa, and fresh milk. I want to see you swig down a couple of glasses of that milk while you're here, too. You look bushed."

"Thanks, Jemma. You're too kind." She took the glass of milk Jemma poured and a Rice Krispies treat. "Yum, these are so delicious. I haven't had one of these in years. I think the last time you made them for me was right before I left for Europe."

Jemma, Susan's mother, and her father rehashed old times, played with Ashley when she woke from her nap. "She's all yours, guys. Nipper and I are going for a run."

Susan found her old Frisbee in the laundry room and off they went. The exercise felt good. Maybe Richard was right. She should start going out more. But not without the baby. That's what she would tell him. Maybe that would keep him off her back for a while. Then she remembered she had booted him out. She could now do whatever she wanted, when she wanted. She no longer had to worry about Richard's state of mind. At least until she received the information from the private detective she'd hired earlier. When the reports came in, then it would be time enough to decide if Richard was going to be a part of her and Ashley's future.

Nipper growled and tugged at her shirtsleeve, his signal that he had enough. She looked down at her watch; time to go inside, pack up, and head back to the condo. She'd wanted a few minutes alone with her mother before she left, but if her father didn't disappear into his study for a while, it wasn't going to happen.

Inside, she packed up Ashley's gear. She turned to her mother and said, "Mom, let Dad hold the baby. I have something I need to ask you. A woman thing," she called over her shoulder to her father.

"Of course, dear. Here, Ashton," she said, handing the baby to her grandfather. "Careful of her head, you know, that soft spot and all. Hold her right."

"Yes, dear. Like I've never done this before." Ashton smiled.

In the kitchen, Iris looked at her daughter, a murderous look on her face. "Before you say anything, Susan, I want to know why that son of a bitch hit you? Don't even think about denying it. I see the cut on your neck, and you're still wearing the red mark on your cheek. It's going to turn black-and-blue. Now, tell me why that bastard hit you."

Hot tears pricked Susan's eyelids. "I kicked him out this morning, Mom. I threw all his stuff in garbage bags and left them by the front door. I even changed the locks. I'm not saying this is forever, but unless he changes big-time, I'm going to file for a divorce. I never thought I would say this, Mom. I wish I had listened to you. God, you don't know how much I wish that."

Chapter Seven

The manila envelope bearing the return address of Apex Investigations glared up at Susan like a square, malevolent, yellow eye. Her hand reached out three times before she was finally able to pick it up. It took another three tries before she could undo the clasp and rip at the tape that held Richard Johnson's secrets. She knew they were secrets because Richard was a secretive person.

Apex Investigations was one of the best investigative firms in the state of Florida. It was run by a grizzly old man named Charlie La Toya. Charlie was a Tex-Mex and proud of it. He was also proud of saying, "Been there, done that," and "I've seen it all." What that meant was no one could get past his eagle eye, evade him, or try to put something over on him. He had a staff of twelve and every high-tech gizmo known to man.

Charlie hated being called a private dick, and if someone had the balls to refer to him in such a manner, he turned down the case. He didn't take offense at being referred to as a gumshoe extraordinaire.

She'd met Charlie for the first time in a seedy bar where no one looked at anyone once, much less twice. He was fat but light and fast on his feet. A beard that was snow-white matched his mop of unruly hair. He barely fit into the grimy booth. Out of the corner of his mouth, he said, "Don't eat anything in here or you'll get sick. I just pay to sit here. They know me." He was smoking a cigar that smelled like a cross between burned rubber, scorched coffee, and vanilla. It was a test. If a client complained, he simply got up and walked out.

Charlie La Toya loved money. Actually, he worshiped it. She remembered how he'd smiled when she wrote out the check for five thousand dollars. She hadn't asked what she would get for her five thousand dollars. She knew better.

What she liked about the detective was that he listened. When she was done, he'd looked at her and said, "Sounds to me, little lady, like you got yourself a bad apple. I'll be in touch."

The palms of Susan's hands started to sweat when she pulled the stapled report out of the envelope.

Outside, rain fell in torrents against the skylight. The sky was dark and ominous looking. Susan reached up to turn on the light. She needed mega-wattage to read about her husband. She wiped her palms on her jeans. Taking a deep breath, she started to read through the report. Disappointment clouded her features. Richard excelled during his twenty-year stint in the navy. He'd done well in college. He was personable. She read through his shopping habits, viewed his driving records. He'd been adopted at the age of twelve by Vilma and Buddy Johnson. The adoption records were sealed. A footnote at the bottom of the page said for megabucks, maybe Charlie could get those records unsealed, but there was no guarantee. He'd spent nine months as a very troubled child at the Oakhurst Orphanage *in Florida.*

In Florida.

Susan sat up straighter in her chair.

She continued to read. Vilma and Buddy Johnson had

lived their entire adult lives in a trailer park in the town of Lakeland, Florida. Seventy miles from Orlando. The Johnsons managed two orange groves. Richard Johnson had worked in those orange groves, not *California* orange groves, until he left at the age of seventeen to join the navy.

Richard had lied to her father and he'd lied to her. He said he was from California and he'd never been in the state of Florida. Susan shook her head to clear her thoughts as she finished reading the report that turned current. Richard was staying at the Embassy Suites. He dined out seven nights a week. He made excellent use of Burke and Burke's credit cards. He was a healthy tipper. Drove a Porsche that was leased to Burke and Burke. He obeyed the speed laws, wore his seatbelt at all times. He played golf but was terrible at the game. He played a lousy game of tennis, but he could still leap over the net to congratulate his opponent.

He got his hair trimmed once a week and the Porsche washed every morning on his way to work.

Susan bit down on her lower lip and tasted her own blood. She reached for a napkin just as a wicked bolt of lightning ripped across the sky. The thunder was so loud the window rattled. She looked down at the report. Just how bad was the lie? Maybe he was ashamed of living in a trailer park, ashamed of picking oranges, ashamed of his adoptive parents. She could almost understand that. But it was more than that, and she knew it.

Well, there was no time like the present to confront her husband. She folded up the report and stuck it in her carryall. But in order to do that, she had to call her mother and ask her to come over to baby-sit.

"Oh, honey, your father and I would love to sit with Ashley. We were sitting here having coffee. We'll be right over. It's terrible out there on the roads, so give us a little time. You aren't in a hurry, are you?"

Yes, she was in a hurry. She wanted to get this over with as soon as possible. "Take your time, Mom, and drive carefully. It's just a lunch with Tristan that I postponed one too many times. I don't want to disappoint her again. I might also have a touch of cabin fever." She knew her mother would love hearing that.

"I'll be there within the hour."

She glanced at the clock. Eleven fifteen. Richard was so obsessed with Burke and Burke she knew she would find him in the office, and if he wasn't there, he would be at Charlie's Steak House. It didn't matter. She'd find him no matter where he was.

Susan checked on Ashley, smiling when she bent over to kiss her on her downy head. Nipper whimpered softly at her feet. She dropped down to her haunches and hugged him. "Keep your eye on her while I'm out, boy," she whispered.

She was a whirlwind then as she stripped off her sweats. She chose a skintight black skirt with a slit up the side that revealed a generous expanse of thigh. She pulled on a pale yellow cashmere shell with a matching long-sleeve sweater. Understated but elegant was always best. She looked down at the shoe rack. Normally, when she was going to be in Richard's company, she wore flat-heeled shoes so she wouldn't be taller than her husband. Today, she chose a pair of two-inch sling-backs. Who cared if she got her feet wet? As Richard said, appearances are everything.

Rummaging in her underwear drawer, she withdrew a small white velvet box. Nestled in the white velvet bed were the two-carat diamond earrings her father had given her last month for her thirtieth birthday. She wasn't a diamond kind of gal and knew she'd only wear them for a special occasion where her father was in attendance so she wouldn't seem ungrateful. She preferred small plain gold hoops. The diamonds in her ears looked like the headlights on her Saturn. In spite of herself, she giggled. She dabbed some perfume she'd bought in Paris behind her ears and sniffed appreciatively. The French certainly knew how to make perfume.

She was ready.

For what she didn't know.

Fifteen minutes later, her parents arrived. From the grim set of her mother's jaw she knew they'd been arguing. Well, she couldn't worry about that now.

"All you have to do is warm the bottle. Ashley should sleep for at least another hour. She's pretty much on a four-to-six-hour schedule these days. The diapers are on the dressing table. She likes that gizmo on the living room floor. It has all kinds of bells and whistles. Nipper loves it. All you do is crank the handle. I'm not sure what time I'll be back. You aren't in a hurry, are you?"

"Not at all, dear. Where are you having lunch?"

Where indeed. "Charlie's Steak House. It's my treat since it's Tristan's birthday. Well, actually, her birthday was last week and I had to cancel." Lord, how easy the lies were coming.

"That might be a problem, honey. I was speaking to Richard this morning, and he's having lunch there with some developer who drove up from Miami late last night. He wants us to design a mini mall on Emerald Island. Richard said he was taking him to Charlie's," her father volunteered.

Susan and Iris both stared at Ashton.

"Take care of it, Ashton. Now," Iris said coolly. "Family comes first. You have a lot of kissing up to do, so let's get a head start here." Iris winked at her daughter, who could only gape at her forceful mother.

My God, I've created a monster. A monster she loved and adored. She winked back.

Both women listened when Ashton called the restaurant. "That's too bad, Marco. My daughter wants the table. I hope you aren't going to give me a hard time over this because if you are, we can take our business to McDougal's. What time is Mr. Johnson's reservation? One o'clock. Sorry, that conflicts with my daughter's luncheon plans. Oh, you don't have a reservation for my daughter. The object of reserving the table, Marco, is that we don't have to make a reservation. The only other table you can give Mr. Johnson is one by the kitchen!" He looked up to see his wife's and his daughter's fists shoot in the air. "That will be fine, Marco."

"Thank you, Daddy," Susan said sweetly.

"And what is this going to cost the family, Ashton?" Iris asked coolly.

Susan didn't want to be around to hear what it was going to cost the family, nor did she want to be a witness to her mother's newfound independence. "I'll see you when I see you. Don't spoil my kid, okay?"

In the Saturn, Susan clicked on her cell phone to call Tristan. "Listen, girl, don't ask questions. Close the gallery and hotfoot it over to Charlie's Steak House. Tell Marco you're meeting me for lunch if you get there before me. We absolutely have to be there by twelve forty-five, not a minute later. I'll explain it all to you when I get there."

It was a game plan.

Susan turned the Saturn around and stopped for a moment to stare up at the condo. She wondered what was going on inside.

"Would you like some coffee, Ashton?"

"Actually, I would. Listen, Iris, are we going to rehash all that garbage again?"

"Yes, Ashton, we are going to hash and rehash it until I get it all out of my system. And you're going to listen even if it takes forever. Now that I'm clicking on all cylinders again, you are going to do some major sucking up. Because if you don't, I will call in my notes. You remember, all the money I put up time and again for Burke and Burke. Remember how when you took it over, it was in the crapper. I bailed you out. Then, of course, I will leave you a broken shell of a man, and move in with Lily, who, by the way, has three gentlemen friends. That's two more than she can take care of at the moment. I can handle the overflow."

Ashton's shoulders slumped. "You aren't going to do any such thing and you know it, Iris. Why do you keep tormenting me with these threats?"

"Because, damn you, you stole years out of my life in the name of Burke and Burke. How many of your clients ever knew I was the second Burke? None, that's how many. My money was good enough for you but I wasn't good enough to be known.

"That's for starters. Actually, it's number two on the list. Number one was me giving you the money to jump-start the firm when your father ran it into the ground. Three is that business with Maureen. *That,* I will never forgive you for. Never, Ashton. You zapped the life right out of me over that. That's why I went into such a tailspin. I'm over it now, but you still have to pay for it. Then there is that reject doctor you sicked on me. You both had me convinced I was suicidal. You have to pay for that, too. Then there is Richard Johnson. That's the biggie, Ashton. That's the one you have to lose sleep over."

"Iris, I don't want to talk about this anymore. We go

through this every day, sometimes twice. You're making me crazy."

"Get over it, Ashton. How does it feel thinking you're going crazy? Tomorrow I might lock you in your room. You know, with one of those special locks you're so fond of."

The implied threat was there, and Ashton heard it, recognized it. *Who the hell* is *this woman?* His shoulders slumped even further. "Aside from tormenting me and making my life miserable, what the hell do you want from me?"

"Do you know what I really want, Ashton? Really and truly want? I want to burn Burke and Burke to the ground. I never want to hear the name ever again. First, though, I want you to fire that . . . that . . . man. That damn company ruined my life and it almost ruined yours. You were obsessed. I think you're still obsessed. These are our golden years. We're supposed to be enjoying them. We should be traveling, playing with our new granddaughter, loving our daughter. You said you were retiring. The damn phone is growing out of your ear. Half the time you still don't know I'm around. Lily's friends are starting to look real good to me. And that exciting lifestyle she's leading. She shops at Victoria's Secret these days. I'm going to give it a whirl myself."

"Iris, shut up!" Ashton said wearily. "I can't fire Richard. I gave him an ironclad contract. It's good for two years."

Iris poured coffee into a cup and handed it to her husband. "Buy him out," she said bitterly. "Before something terrible happens. I keep telling you, I have this *feeling.*"

"Don't start with that spook stuff, Iris. I can't buy him out. Where's the cream and sugar?"

"Drink it black. You don't need the calories. Then you'll

leave me no other recourse, Ashton. I'll have to call in my notes. I hope you haven't forgotten who my attorneys were at the time. All I have to do is give you thirty days, and you have to liquidate or the company goes to me. Is there any part of this that you don't understand?"

"Why are you doing this, Iris?"

Her husband looked so miserable Iris almost took pity on him. Almost. She leaned across the table, her eyes wet. "Because I'm afraid of that man, Ashton. I'm as afraid as you are, but you won't admit it. I'm going to tell you something I shouldn't tell you. Susan told me in confidence, and I feel terrible breaking that confidence, but if it's the only way to get through to you, then so be it. He hit Susan. Not once, but twice. Susan kicked him out. What if he does something to Ashley the next time? He's not even living here, but he does come to see the baby. If you don't believe me, check the closets. He's staying at the Embassy Suites and charging the room to Burke and Burke.

"He's not who he says he is. This would be a really good time for you to say something, Ashton. Make it good because my patience is running so thin right now, it's transparent."

"I think I know who he is, Iris," Ashton whispered.

Iris had to strain to hear the words. "Who?" she whispered in return.

Susan looked down at her watch: twelve fifty. She'd made it on time. She got out of the car and stood under the umbrella the valet held out for her. She sighed with relief when she saw Tristan waiting for her. "Hurry," she said. "We have to get to the table before Richard gets here."

"Oooh, I do love a good mystery. Are we eating or drinking our lunch?"

"Both. We are just two lovely, fashionable women out for the day. Make sure you laugh and giggle and pretend you're really having a good time even if you aren't. Richard is bringing someone here for lunch, and they're giving him the table by the kitchen. I want to see *that*. Here's how I look at it: you and I are more important."

"Speaking of fashionable, you look . . . sylphlike. I always wanted to use that term. You look smashing, Susan. God, I should be so skinny. This is the first time I've ever seen you wear high heels. Like I said, sylphlike. And, we won't need a candle on the table with those earrings you're wearing."

"They were a birthday gift. I'm not a jewelry person. I just wore them to please my father and to make Richard's eyes pop. Sometimes I am so bad, I can't stand myself. Thank you, Marco," Susan said, when the man held her chair for her. "Is something wrong? You look worried. It looks to me like business is wonderful even with this horrible weather. We'd both like a whiskey sour, Marco."

"This is a table for six, Susan. Maybe he's grouchy because he's going to lose four meals with just you and me."

"He'll get over it. My father pays for this table by the year even if no one eats here. One minute to go. If nothing else, Richard is always punctual."

Their drinks arrived just as Richard walked into the restaurant. She watched the byplay, saw Richard glance her way and then away. Marco's elaborate shrugs told her, he was smart enough to back the right horse. She knew he was saying, "There is a table by the kitchen, Mr. Johnson It's a take-it-or-leave-it offer. There are people waiting behind you." Or words to that effect. The table by the kitchen was the worst table in the restaurant, with the swinging door and the clattering that could be heard in the kitchen. She

131

watched as her husband followed Marco to the table. For some reason she'd expected a scene. Even from a distance she could read his rage. She waited until he was seated before she got up to go to the restroom. She knew his eyes were following her as she weaved her way through the crowded room.

When she returned to take her seat, Tristan murmured, "He couldn't take his eyes off you. Half the men in this room almost fell off their chairs. I think you made a statement that was loud and clear. Now, fill me in before I explode."

Two hours later she was in the elevator on her way to her father's, *now Richard's,* tenth floor office. Instead of seeing her father's beautiful, antique furniture, there was chrome, glass, and strange-looking wire things that she supposed were some sort of modern sculptured plant. They looked like a bunch of screws and bolts to her. She didn't see Sally, her father's receptionist of more than twenty years, at the front desk, either. Instead she saw a young girl who couldn't have been a day over twenty, if that, leafing through *People* magazine. Disarmed by the unfamiliarity, she stepped away from the elevator and glared around at the reception room. She hated it.

The young girl looked up long enough to ask if she could be of help.

"I'm here to see my husband. Don't trouble yourself. I can find my way."

"Do you have an appointment? Are those earrings real?" she asked in awe.

"Diamonique. I don't need an appointment. My father owns this firm. I'm Susan Burke."

"Oh. I guess it's all right then."

Susan tripped down the long hallway, mentally preparing herself for the change she was about to experience. Not bothering to knock, she pushed open the mahogany door. Apparently Richard's decorator hadn't made it this far.

Her husband's back was to her as he talked on the phone. He swiveled around, sensing a presence. "I'll get back to you by the end of the day." He glared at her, his lips pressed tightly together. "If you ever pull another stunt like that again, you'll wish you hadn't. We don't just barge in here anymore. We make appointments. This is a working office."

She hated the look she was seeing in his eyes. The truth was, she hated everything about the man sitting in her father's chair. Susan reached inside her purse and took out the investigative report. "I'd like you to explain this." She tossed the papers on his desk.

He didn't bother to look at them, but his expression turned wary. "Explain what?"

"The papers, Richard." Susan seated herself in one of the matching leather chairs usually reserved for business associates. She wiggled her foot so he could see her high heels. It was a small, silly thing to do, but it made her feel better. Since she wasn't going anywhere until she learned the truth, it could turn out to be a long afternoon.

Richard picked up the papers and skimmed through them. Was that a tremor she saw in his hand? She watched him closely. Today he was wearing his favorite navy Brooks Brothers suit—the one she had puked on—a navy and yellow tie, and starched pale yellow shirt. There was nothing casual about him. His shirt collar and tie were in place; he hadn't removed his jacket. Even here in the office, he was the impeccably dressed man that he loved to be.

There wasn't a hair out of place or a wrinkle to be seen on his bronzed face.

What *had* she ever seen in him? How could she have been so blind? Flashes of Cam assailed her. She couldn't go there now. Thoughts of her former fiancé were too precious to waste when she couldn't give them her total attention.

Richard flung the papers to the side. "What's the big deal, Susan? Are you bored, with nothing better to do? Maybe you need to go back to work part-time, occupy your mind." The tone was different, blustery. His expression was still wary.

That couldn't be fear she was seeing in his eyes, could it? Suddenly she felt all-powerful. "Dammit, you lied to me! When Dad hired you, you told him you'd never been to Florida. How do you explain that report? Come on, Richard, spin me a fairy tale."

Susan crossed her fingers, hoping Richard wasn't going to pitch one of his insane fits. She reached for the papers and shoved them back inside her purse. "I'm taking this information to my father. I made copies," she lied.

He wanted to hit her. She saw it in his face, in the way he clenched his fists.

"You know if I wanted to, I could do this to you, too, but what's the point? I can't imagine why you would hire a private detective to check into my background *after* we've been married for almost a year. If it will make you feel better, show your papers to your father. I promise you, he won't be as surprised as you think he will." He stood and walked to the door, opening it. "Now, if you don't mind, I have work to do. Don't ever come here unannounced again."

"That's it? You're not going to explain to me why you lied about never being in the state of Florida when you lived here for almost eighteen years? Do whatever you want, Richard. You always do. You lie, you cheat, and you probably steal, too. Just remember this, money can buy almost anything in this world. Think about those sealed adoption records. Think real hard. I'll just bet you for the right price, someone somewhere will open them up. Now I'm leaving. Do you know why I'm leaving? I'm leaving because I'm ready to leave. You really are short, aren't you?" she said, standing next to him for the barest second when she reached the door.

God! She couldn't believe the mess she'd made of her life. When she'd returned from Europe, it had gone totally downhill. Except for Ashley and, of course, Nipper. They were the only sunshine in her life at present.

She stepped into the empty elevator, grateful to be alone for a few minutes. She pressed the button for the first floor. She knew he was inside his office with the door closed as he tried to battle his rage. In the year they'd been married, she'd never come there. Not even once. She'd wanted to keep Burke and Burke out of her personal life. This was what she'd gotten for her efforts.

When she tossed him and his bags of clothes out the door, it hadn't fazed her, hadn't changed her or Ashley's life in any way. She didn't have to work, but the work at the Art Institute was important to her. And besides, her parents would love to watch Ashley. *So why do I feel such a tremendous sense of guilt right now?*

The elevator doors opened and she rushed out. She didn't have time for guilty thoughts. She was going to have a heart-to-heart talk with her father and mother. She hoped it wasn't too late.

In the car, Susan called Tristan to recount the past

hour's events. "Did you get the name of that divorce lawyer?"

"Yep, and you have an appointment with Gerald L. Reinhold one week from today."

"You work fast," Susan said.

"There's no reason to let the grass grow under *our* feet. As they say, 'There's no time like the present.' "

Susan loved how she'd said, *our*. Tristan was in this with her for the long haul. "Okay, what do I do next?"

"You go to your parents, and I feel strongly that you include your mother in the conversation, and tell them everything you know, everything you suspect, and what you're worried about. Tell your father to step back into harness and not to let Richard make any hard business decisions. If things fall into place, you can begin divorce proceedings next week."

"You make it sound so simple."

"It is simple. You made a mistake. Now you're simply going to rectify that mistake."

"I hope so." Defeat rang in her words, and she hadn't even started the battle.

"I know so," Tristan concluded.

"Then why don't I feel like fighting? The thought of dealing with Richard legally scares the hell out of me. I don't know what he's capable of."

"No, we don't know what he's capable of doing. You have to tell the lawyer everything. That's why you ask for a restraining order and do this legally. Richard might be smart, but he can't fight the system. If he tries, he's gonna lose," Tristan said with an air of confidence that Susan couldn't feel.

"I don't know what I'd do without you. You've been such a good friend. I'm sorry to burden you with all my problems. It seems that's all I do."

"Oh, now don't go getting all hangdog and mushy on me. What are friends for if you can't lean on them in a crisis?"

"You don't know how much your friendship means to me. You're a true friend. Promise me something, will you?"

"Anything. Just name it."

"If something were to happen to me, make sure Ashley Rose is cared for. Do whatever you have to do to keep her out of Richard's custody. Promise me?"

"Susan! Stop being so morbid! Nothing is going to happen to you, and if it did, which it won't, I'm Ashley's godmother. Of course I'll take care of her. Now don't say another word."

"Sorry. I just can't imagine him taking care of Ashley on his own, that's all."

"Well, you're not going to have that problem, so forget about it. Your parents would fight for Ashley, too, Susan. Don't underestimate your mother. Since she's been on her new medication, the woman is a powerhouse. God help Richard if he causes her any trouble."

Susan laughed. Tristan was right; her mother was a powerhouse.

If only she'd listened to her mother on that fateful Fourth of July. Sadly, now that it was after the fact and the damage done, Susan was only all too ready to listen to her mother.

For Ashley's sake, she prayed it wasn't too late.

Chapter Eight

February 2002

Richard scanned the papers in his hand a second time, then a third. There was nothing in the papers he was holding that held even a vague hint about his biological parents, and that's the way he intended to keep it. It was enough that Susan had hired a private detective to explore his past. It was quite another thing for him to hire a private detective to investigate the detective Susan hired. He felt reasonably sure he was on safe ground. As far as he could tell, there was nothing new, or at least nothing that could possibly expose his background in the papers he was holding.

He remembered how stunned he'd been when Susan sent him the entire investigative file through the mail. It was Susan's way of telling him not to underestimate her.

Richard got up and walked around his desk—the papers still in his hands—to stretch his muscles. He really liked this new apartment. In fact, he liked it a lot. Living at the Embassy Suites the past few weeks had had a temporary feel. If there was one thing he didn't want in this new life of his, it was the feeling of anything temporary. The word *permanent* was at the top of his vocabulary these days.

Sandy, his new receptionist, had found him this posh, elegant apartment. Who cared if the rent was four thousand a month? It certainly didn't faze him. Burke and Burke could handle the loss. Besides, they owed it to him.

She owed it to him. Big-time.

Located in Orlando's newest and most expensive complex, Splendor House was perfect for his needs. Four bedrooms completely furnished. Top of the line. Each room a total contrast to the others.

First there was the master suite. Decorated in dark greens and navy, the room was the perfect complement to his own darkness. A dark cherry four-poster bed dominated the center of the room. Directly opposite the bed, a large, marble, gas fireplace covered an entire wall. A built-in television, DVD player, and compact disc were discreetly located behind cherry cabinets on the left wall. To his right was a hallway leading to the master bath. Done in the same subdued, manly colors, the room housed a Jacuzzi tub, a shower with six rotating showerheads, heated towel racks, and a vanity any woman would die for. Italian marble floors swirled with blues, greens, and just the right amount of cobalt streaks. To the right of the bathroom was a complete mini-gymnasium. He could kiss the smelly, sweaty gym he went to every day goodbye. He had his own now. He'd taken the apartment for that room alone.

The remaining bedrooms were decorated in different color schemes and styles. The room next to his was done in pale pink, the one across the hall a soft yellow, which reminded him of Susan; and then there was the room that he was sure was meant for a child. Red, blue, yellow, and green. The room had bunk beds, red and yellow wainscoting, with walls painted bright blue. A rug with a hopscotch pattern covered the middle of the floor. It would be Ashley's room when she came to visit him. The other two bedrooms would be perfect for guests should he ever have them. He thought of Vilma and Buddy, and cringed. There was no way in hell he would ever allow them to step inside his new home. They belonged in that run-down, dirty trailer park where he'd spent so many years dreaming and planning. No, this was his apartment, and he'd make damn sure they never came near it.

He placed the reports in the wall safe. The wall safe was the second reason he'd signed the lease on the apartment.

His agile mind raced. He wouldn't gain any favors with Ashton if he were to learn he'd hired a private investigator with company funds. Ashton had been in the palm of his hand until that fucking wife of his had found a new doctor. He had Susan to thank for that little favor. And now, Susan was trying to ruin him. His beautiful wife didn't know what she was up against. He smiled. If he chose to look in the large mirror above his dresser, he knew he would see an evil glint in his eye and wickedness in his smile. He'd practiced that look so many times it was second nature.

Everything he'd schemed, conned, and lied for was finally his. Twenty years in the navy, six years in that Southern armpit known as Louisiana. Of course he would never forget his first six miserable years working as slave labor for the Johnsons. He'd endured and suffered enough. Now it was their turn to go through what he'd had to go through. He wondered if they'd buckle or endure the way he had.

Four months later

"I'm glad that you two are finally coming around to seeing things the way I do," Susan said. She swiped a tissue over her daughter's mouth. Ashley cooed while she sucked on a graham cracker. She was just a little over four months old, and already she looked like she might be getting ready to cut her first tooth.

"If you recall, dear, I said from the beginning that I

didn't like Richard Johnson. The first time I set eyes on him, I knew he was a sneak and a liar. Your father is to blame for all of this. Yes, Ashton, you are the one at fault here. You couldn't wait to introduce our daughter to that . . . that . . . wannabe. Your greed and your ego are why we're sitting here discussing that evil person. If Burke and Burke flounders, it's your fault, and you damn well better be man enough to stand up and take the blame. If it isn't too late already," Iris said ominously.

"You made your point, Iris. All you've done is harp on this twenty-four/seven. I know now that I made a terrible mistake. I didn't know it then. I also know I need to cancel Richard's contract, but I have to do it legally. He's got me over a barrel. I simply do not have the stomach to go through another lawsuit. I talked with Sol Bloomberg again last night. He said lying on a contract about living in Florida isn't enough to warrant dismissal. He also said one lie leads to another lie, but so far that seems to be the only one we can nail him with. There could be a dozen reasons why he lied. Emotional reasons, bad memories, trauma. Even something like a bad auto accident that would trigger bad memories would enter into play. According to Bloomberg, a judge would toss it out in a second. We're working on it, that's all I can say. Yes, Iris, for the moment, we are at Richard's mercy. Please, cut me a little slack here.

"What about the divorce, Susan? Do you have a hearing scheduled yet?" Ashton asked as he tried to switch the focus away from himself.

Susan wiped what was left of the cracker from Ashley's chubby fingers. Ashley howled her outrage. "Yes, four weeks from next Monday, on June 16, at nine o'clock in the morning. I'm not looking forward to it, either. Richard has something up his sleeve. I can feel it. He's only been to see

Ashley twice since that day I saw him at Charlie's three months ago. He stayed five minutes with her and another thirty minutes threatening me. I know he was served with the divorce papers at work. I don't know why, but I expected him to go crazy and come after me with a gun. He didn't do that. He's playing it real cool, and it's starting to spook me. It's like holding your breath for the other shoe to drop."

Seated in Susan's stainless-steel kitchen, Iris shivered. She'd never liked the room much, thinking it cold and sterile. Like Richard. She knew Susan had decorated the kitchen and the rest of the house with her husband's taste in mind. She wondered if she regretted the sterile look. Her voice was calm, almost conversational, as though she were discussing the heat and humidity. "The day that happens is the day I put a bullet right between his eyes."

"Mother! You're getting meaner by the day." Despite the underlying meaning, Susan laughed.

"I'm serious, Susan. You need to wake up to the fact that this is no laughing matter. That man has the power to turn all our lives upside down. He's proved that already. We have to stop him before it's too late. What does your attorney say about Richard's missed visits?"

"I couldn't be more serious, Mother. I am not burying my head in the sand. Mr. Reinhold thinks Richard is going to hang himself. Those are his words, not mine. He hopes once we appear before the judge, his visitation record, or lack of, will stand on its own. Richard Johnson is not a changing diapers, warming formula kind of guy. God, he'd die if Ashley so much as drooled on him. I can't imagine what a full day of her spills would do to him. I just hope the judge is female and has children."

"Don't count on it, Susan. And, if that turns out to be

the case, Florida courts are well-known for awarding custody to the father. It would surprise me if Richard doesn't ask for full guardianship," her father said.

"Ashton, for heaven's sake, watch what you say. You're upsetting Susan."

Susan was shocked at her father's comment. "Dad, tell me you're joking? Do you really believe a court would grant Richard full parental custody? The man doesn't even know how to change a diaper."

Susan adjusted Ashley on her hip and leaned against the countertop. "I'll never let him have her! I don't give a damn what the court says. The man is crazy. And I'll do whatever I have to do to keep my daughter safe!" She held up her free hand to prevent any interruption. "I don't care if it's legal or not." Her face was full of panic as she held her daughter fiercely.

All Ashton and Iris could do was nod in sympathy.

"That miserable cretin doesn't know who he's up against. Ashton, doesn't Judge Barclay owe you a favor? Didn't I just see him on the news last week? Something about family court. You need to call him. *Now,*" Iris said adamantly. She pointed to the phone. *Now* meant now.

"It's an idea. I don't know how receptive he'll be. Favors on the outside are different from favors involving the law. Lord, before this is over, we may all go to jail!" There was a new spring in his step and a spark in his eye when he got up from the table. "I won't let that son of a bitch destroy my family any more than he has already." He shot Iris a you-know-what-I-mean look. He picked up the phone.

Iris and Susan remained silent as they listened to Ashton go through the amenities, the weather, the family, each other's golf scores, the crowded court calendar, and the judge's new car that got twenty-two miles to the gallon. Iris rolled her eyes. She mouthed the words, "It's part of the game."

"This afternoon. Four thirty? We'll be there." Ashton hung up the phone, a satisfied look on his face.

Susan tilted her head to the side as she watched her father. In a matter of moments, he was his former self. He even appeared taller.

Her gaze switched to her mother. Something was going on between them, something they weren't willing to share with her. They both appeared powerful and determined, not to mention strong. Her father was acting like the head of the family again.

Her father had finally stepped up to the plate and was taking charge once more. She felt like clapping.

"We're meeting Judge Barclay this afternoon. Jemma can look after the baby," Ashton said.

"Thanks, Dad. I appreciate your support. Doubly so because I know this isn't easy for you." Susan shifted Ashley to her other hip. "Now, you take your granddaughter, while I change my clothes."

Her father smiled as he reached for the baby. "Take your time, dear. The judge is a family man."

The moment Susan was out of earshot, Ashton spoke. "Iris, I realize I'm at the bottom of your ugly list right now, and I understand, but let's try to keep our personal matters private for the moment. Susan is going to need our support now more than ever, and there's no point in muddying the waters. That bastard is out to ruin everything this family stands for. It's my own fault. I now have an inkling of what you went through all those years. I swear to God, Iris, I will make it up to you. I swear on this child in my arms."

"I like this side of you, Ash. I only wish you'd been this aggressive when Doctor González was doping me up for all those years. Maybe then it might have meant something. For Susan's and Ashley's sakes, I'm willing to call a truce until we get this settled. Afterward, we'll talk. You owe me, Ashton, big-time, and don't ever forget it either because my memory is long and unkind!"

Ashton nodded, his eyes miserable. "A truce it is." Ashton held out his hand.

Iris grasped it. "This isn't the last of it, Ashton. We have to help Susan escape from that devil she's married to. I could kill the man with my bare hands if I got the chance. He's not going to end this until we stop him, you realize that, don't you?"

Ashton heaved a mighty sigh. "More than you know, Iris. More than you know."

Susan entered the room, their signal to put their conversation on hold. "So, how do I look?" She twirled around. She wore a simple white blouse tucked neatly in the waistband of tailored black slacks. Three-inch-high black boots covered her feet.

"You look like a woman ready to do battle, doesn't she, Ashton?"

"Yes, she does. Now if we're going to take Ashley to Jemma and make that four-thirty appointment, we'd better get a move on. Judges go by the clock and they do not like to be kept waiting."

Ten minutes later they were out the door.

Located in one of Orlando's oldest neighborhoods, Judge Martin Barclay's office was quiet so late in the afternoon. Four Queen Anne chairs covered in a faded gold brocade fabric were placed in a circle around an antiquated coffee table in the waiting room. The table was covered with equally old magazines. Live plants with dusty leaves, graced the corners of the room. Sunlight and airy dust motes filtered in between the slats of an old-fashioned blind, making the small waiting area appear more drab and dusty than it actually was.

"How old is Judge Barclay?" Susan whispered to her father.

"This was his father's office, too," Ashton said as if that explained the judge's age.

"Shh. Here he comes," Iris whispered.

"Ashton. How are you?" Judge Barclay held out a long, scrawny hand.

Tall and thin, the judge stood well over six feet, and Susan guessed he weighed somewhere around a hundred and fifty pounds. His egg-shaped head was covered with sparse brown hair. His eyes were the color of faded denim and were almost hidden behind horn-rimmed glasses. He looked more like a librarian than a judge.

"I appreciate your seeing us on such short notice, Martin. My wife, Iris, and my daughter, Susan," he said, introducing his family.

"Pleased to meet you, sir." Susan shook his proffered hand. Iris nodded.

"We'll be much more comfortable in my office." The judge motioned for them to follow him down a dark hall. Up two small flights of stairs and they were in the judge's private office. Unlike the waiting room, it was bright and cheerful. Different shades of pale blues adorned the walls. Sky-blue drapes were parted to admit the May sun's golden rays. Cream-colored file folders were scattered across his oak desk. Instead of the usual chairs, a sofa with pale blue flowers sat in front of the judge's desk. Susan sat in the middle with her parents on either side of her.

The judge took charge immediately. "I understand

there's a problem with the son-in-law?" The judge looked at Iris, but he addressed his comment to Ashton.

"Yes. He's working for Burke and Burke. I made a serious mistake when I hired the man. In some respects I may have made a *deadly* mistake. I'm now trying to rectify that mistake and break his contract. Sol Bloomberg is handling that end of things for me," Ashton said.

"You can't do better than Sol Bloomberg when it comes to contracts. You chose the right man, Ashton."

"Yes, Sol is a good man. But that isn't why we're here today."

Ashton looked at Susan.

"Go ahead, Dad, you can tell him. Everything. Every last bit."

"I think it's best if you tell Judge Barclay in your own words. Tell him about the abuse."

Susan drew in a deep breath, uncertain where she should start. The beginning seemed like a good place. She took another deep breath. "When Richard and I first met, he was perfect. Well, almost. He wined and dined me. Eight months later we married, and a month afterward I became pregnant. Things went downhill from there. We argued constantly. Richard refused to understand that I couldn't handle going out every night of the week to entertain clients. I gained too much weight. I spent most of my days, and sometimes my nights, throwing up. He had no patience for my condition. At that point, he started showing his true colors. He slapped me once. I put it down to stress. I tried convincing myself I deserved it. That's a defense most battered wives use. When he hit me a second time, I asked him to leave. He did leave and then he came back. He goes into these rages. When he did it a third time, well, that was enough for me. I have a child I have to think about now. I don't want to raise her in a home where her father batters her mother.

"Richard has never hurt our daughter, Ashley, and I don't think he would, but he frightens me because I've seen his rage. I know what he's capable of doing. Since I served him with divorce papers, he hasn't acted normal. What I mean is, normal for Richard."

"Could you explain that to me?" Judge Barclay asked.

Susan had a captive audience in the judge. "Richard has a violent temper. He likes things to go his way. When they don't go his way, he reacts. Oh, it's not always violent, but he does *react*. Since the papers were served to him, he hasn't done a thing. He's missed almost all his allowed visits with Ashley, and he hasn't tried to contact me. Normally, he would have shown up and broken down the door. What I'm saying is, to me this feels like the calm before the hurricane. It simply is not like him. He has something up his sleeve, and I'm afraid." Susan's hands started to shake.

"Have you given any thought to the possibility that his lawyer told him not to bother you? That's standard procedure. Visiting his daughter might make him angry, and he would take it out on you. Better to stay away. Do you have a restraining order?"

"Yes, but it has stipulations. He is allowed to visit the baby at our home. I have to leave the room. He came twice the first week as ordered by the judge. He played with Ashley for a few minutes, then he started threatening me. I got upset and threatened to call my lawyer. He just laughed and said it was my word against his. But he did leave at that point."

"What kind of threats did he make? He could be charged with a felony in the state of Florida if your life was threatened in any way."

"He never came right out and said he'd kill me or anything like that, if that's what you're asking, but he did imply that I could get hurt or maybe have an accident if I pushed him too far. Of course, he would deny ever saying that."

"I see." The judge steepled his hands in front of him, weighing the information he'd just heard.

Why did her parents think they could pit this old man, a judge no less, against someone like Richard?

"Can you help us, Martin?" her father asked.

"I'm not exactly clear as to what you're asking me to do. From what you've told me, it appears as though you've covered all your bases."

"Legally, we have done everything we can do. There are two things Richard wants. He wants total control of Burke and Burke. I can handle that. What I cannot handle is his abuse of my daughter and getting away with it. What's he going to do to Ashley Rose? That scares the living hell out of us all, Martin. I want something done about it and I want it done quickly." Ashton banged his fist down on the judge's desk to make his point.

Iris fixed her gaze on the judge. "Richard wants all of us out of the way so he can control the company. Only God knows why. For some strange reason, he thinks he deserves it. I don't know how he persuaded Ashton to hire him in the first place." She gave her husband a cut-eye look.

Ashton wilted, his voice weary. "The company was in serious financial trouble. We were a hair away from closing our doors. Richard arrived with a big Pentagon contract in his hip pocket. He's a superb architect. I can't take that away from him. He just recently signed another *multimillion*-dollar deal with the Disney empire. He's got two more deals, just as big, just as impressive as the Disney deal.

That's why I hired him, Iris. The man is a goddamn genius. I wish you'd stop implying that it's something else." Ashton could feel the veins popping out on his neck as blood pulsated in his ears.

"Isn't it?" Iris charged.

"Mom, Dad, let's not fight. We're here to solve a problem, not start another one." Susan was uncomfortable acting as referee to her parents' public argument.

Iris waved her hand through the air. "I'm sorry. Just talking about the man makes me crazy. Judge Barclay, please accept my apology."

"I understand. I have children and grandchildren of my own. If they were threatened in any way, I'm sure I would be reacting the same way you are. No apologies are needed."

"So, tell me, Martin, is there something you can do to help us? Legally, of course," Ashton inquired. He didn't need to remind the judge of the favor owed to him. Men his age understood one another.

"Let me take a look at the docket to see who the presiding judge is. Maybe I'll have a talk with him or her, explain a few things." The judge stood up, towering over the Burkes, who remained seated on the sofa. It was a clear signal that the meeting was over.

At the door, the judge said, "Ashton, can I speak with you in private for a moment?"

Ashton looked at the women who were his life. He'd do anything to protect his trio of ladies. He nodded. "Wait for me in the car. I won't be long."

Susan reached for her mother's hand and literally dragged her out of the office.

"I don't understand your father," Iris grumbled as she settled herself in the backseat of the car. "One minute he's spitting fire and the next minute he's sneaking behind my back. What could he possibly say to the judge that we can't hear?"

"He isn't sneaking behind your back, Mom. He's talking with the judge. Private stuff the judge didn't want us *ladies* to hear. The judge is the gentlemanly type, couldn't you tell? I'm sure there's something he can do and he doesn't want us to know what it is. In other words, Mom, guy talk, but *serious* guy talk."

Iris peered out the window. "Let's hope that's all there is. I find it very hard to trust your father these days. I'm trying, but it isn't easy."

"I just think Dad was duped by your doctor the same way Richard duped us. I'm not discounting his obsession with the company, Mom. But if you think of it in those terms, maybe it won't be so hard to swallow. Speaking of doctors, how are you and Doctor Watts getting along?"

Her mother's face brightened. "Susan, Emily Watts is the best thing that's ever happened to me. She told me to call her Emily, and she calls me Iris. Isn't that nice? She listens to me, she doesn't judge me. And she certainly doesn't think the answer to my every need lies in a prescription bottle. She thinks in a few months I can go off the Paxil completely. I agree. I lost so many years. That's what is so hard to forgive." Iris looked off into the distance, a wave of sadness washing over her face.

"You're not that woman anymore. Don't dwell on the past, Mom. Here comes Dad," Susan said, relief ringing in her voice.

Ashton slid behind the steering wheel. "Sorry about that. Some unfinished business from way back when. Martin didn't want to discuss it in front of you girls."

"What sort of business? Are you sure it isn't something I

should know? There will be no more secrets in this family," Iris said coldly.

"Sometimes, Iris, you are like a dog with a bone. The year before last, I bet Martin a thousand dollars on a round of golf. He lost. He was really embarrassed when it was time to pay up. He didn't have the money. I told him to forget about it."

"You mean *that's* the favor he owed you? I'm scared out of my wits to face Richard in court and we're wasting time on a man who can't pay his golfing bet! Dad, for crying out loud, you can't be serious about asking him to help me." Susan didn't know whether to laugh or cry.

She was due to face Richard in court June 16. She needed anything and everything to go in her favor. The last thing she needed was for Richard to find out she'd consulted with her father's golfing buddy in hopes he could bribe the presiding judge. All in the name of a good game of golf, of course.

"Susan—" Ashton viewed his daughter in the rearview mirror "—it's not what you think. Martin *will* help you. Trust me."

"I'm sorry, Dad. I do trust you, and the judge . . . it's just that this isn't a game of golf. This is my life. It's Ashley's future. I don't want anything to spoil my day in court. Mr. Reinhold thinks the judge is going to grant me full custody. I can't do anything that doesn't pass the sniff test."

"Iris, is this the same woman that only hours ago said she'd do anything to protect her daughter?"

"I think it is, Ashton. Trust us, baby."

"C'mon, you two, I'm serious. I appreciate your trying to see some humor in the situation. Richard *is* something to laugh at. Ashley's future isn't a laughing matter. My God, can you imagine what would happen to her if Richard got custody? It doesn't bear thinking about."

"It's not going to happen, I promise," Ashton said.

Susan's father had never made promises to her that he couldn't keep. Even when she was a child he'd gone to great lengths in order to keep his promises. Like the time she'd wanted a dog for her birthday. When her father found out the dog she'd wanted had been adopted, he'd found the family and practically begged them to take another dog. They did. And he'd kept his promise. On her tenth birthday her father gave her a full grown eight-year-old basset hound named Pepper.

"You're right. I'm just being paranoid. I'm scared, that's all."

"Why don't you invite Tristan and her family over tonight? We can cook outdoors, and the children can play with Nipper. We'll rent that new Ashley Judd movie. The one with Morgan Freeman. He's such a good actor, and I think he's so handsome, don't you? Then you girls can have some time for girl talk. Your father and I will take care of the children. It will be good experience for when Ashley is older, and we have to chase her around. Besides, you need to do something to get your mind off that devil you married."

They were flying along I-4 at record speed. Susan looked up to see the odometer. They were going fifteen miles above the speed limit.

"Okay, whatever you say as long as Dad promises to slow down. I want to live to see my daughter start elementary school."

Her father looked in the mirror for the second time. Susan felt the car slowing down. "Sorry. I get carried away. It's a miracle I haven't gotten another ticket since this whole thing started."

"You're damned straight it is. Now slow down and get us home in one piece. We've got to make dinner and baby-sit tonight," Iris said.

Ashton reached across the seat and took Iris's hand in his. He did love his wife. He'd been wrong about so many things. Now, he had more going for him than he ever had in his life. He had a loving daughter, a wife who was mentally sound, and a granddaughter who was perfect in every way.

Life was as it should be. He and Iris would travel the world once the mess with Richard and Susan was finally over. Maybe they'd go to Paris. Iris had always wanted to go to France. They'd take Susan and the baby with them. Maybe by some stroke of luck, she'd meet up with that Cam fellow. Maybe they'd fall in love all over again and get married.

Maybe his ass.

Maybe you'll mind your own goddamned business this time. Next time Susan marries, if there is a next time, you'll make sure the man she marries doesn't come fully equipped with a past.

He'd make sure of it or else.

Chapter Nine

August 2002

Susan checked her camera kit for extra film one last time.

"If you keep diddling around, the party will be over by the time we get there," Tristan grumbled, as they loaded the kids in the backseat of her Explorer. The birthday party she was referring to was being held at the Chuck E. Cheese restaurant.

"This is the first time Ashley's gone to a birthday party. Speaking for myself, I have never been to a kid's party. I just want to make sure I have everything. Thanks for inviting us, Tris. I really needed a diversion today. I can't wait to see Ashley's face when she sees all of those musical characters come to life. She's already hooked on the Big Blue Bear videos." Susan placed the camera on the dashboard before she strapped Ashley into her car seat. Satisfied that the harness was secure, she walked around to the back to load the stroller and diaper bag into the cargo hold. *I probably forgot half the stuff I was supposed to bring,* she thought ruefully.

"Okay, let's get this show on the road. I don't think Billy Bob and Jasper are gonna put the party on hold for us," Tristan said as she climbed into the driver's seat.

"Billy Bob and Jasper?" Susan repeated.

"They're characters. They sing with Chuck E. Cheese. The big mouse." Tristan laughed at the bemused look on

155

Susan's face. "Welcome to motherhood. It gets better as they get older. Barbie dolls, Easy Bake ovens. Stuff we identify with from our own childhood. At least I do."

"Hey, I had my share of Barbie dolls, too. My mother kept most of them. Actually, she kept just about everything. When Ashley's older, I'll give it all to her. I'm going to start my own traditions. You know, the holiday ornament, Christmas Barbie, Christmas whatever."

Amy and William started to act up, hating the car seats that held them prisoners. As they punched and gouged at one another, Ashley watched, her chubby fists trying to reach out to the children who were causing her to gurgle with laughter. "Now that you've made such an important decision, reach in that cooler at your feet and grab two juice boxes. They need something to do. Eating and drinking always helps. It's a short ride."

Susan gave each of the older kids a juice box and lifted a finger to her lips, indicating they should quiet down a bit. She winked at them so they'd know this was just an act for their mother. Ashley was all drool and giggles sitting next to Tristan's two kids.

At seven months, Ashley was sitting up on her own. Susan was glad she'd let Tristan talk her into coming to the party for her neighbor's youngest son's fourth birthday.

Tristan tooled the Explorer down International Drive, known as I-Drive to the locals. I-Drive was Orlando's most exciting street, excluding the Disney empire. Anything and everything could be found on I-Drive, both day and night.

FAO Schwarz stood out among the many stores. Giant Raggedy Anne and Andy dolls framed the entrance. Jack-in-the-boxes stood like armed sentries. Susan couldn't wait to take Ashley into the famous store. She remembered her first trip to the famous toy store as a child while on a visit to

New York City. It fascinated her then, and she was sure Orlando's famous store would do the same for her daughter once she was old enough to appreciate it.

"I can't wait for Ashley's first party. I'm going to hire clowns and have ponies, I'll rent a merry-go-round. And a magician, too. And a dollhouse. She has to have a dollhouse. Life-size of course. We'll do it in pink, just like all little girls should have."

"Whoa! Isn't this a bit premature? Ashley might like a Game Boy or computers. I can't keep Amy off the Internet and she's only five. I think dollhouses and ponies are leftovers from our generation. Kids are smarter these days. They want to be challenged."

Susan smiled. "Whatever you say. It's nice to imagine her life so simple, that's all. I want that for her more than anything. Being shifted from one parent to the other isn't going to be good for her. I know half the kids in the country have two sets of parents. It confuses kids. What's going to happen once she starts school?"

"Worry about that when it happens, Susan. If it happens at all."

"There is no *if*. It will happen. Richard will never give me total custody of Ashley. Never."

"She's not a thing, Susan, she's a person. Promise me something?"

Susan nodded. "Sure."

"Let's not let that scummy husband of yours ruin our day with the kids. All we talk about when we're together is Richard. Let's shift into neutral, so we can have fun today. I want to see you enjoy Ashley instead of worrying about her. That's a damn order, Susan."

"That's easier—"

"Said than done. I know. You can do it if you put your

mind to it. I want to see you stuffing your mouth with pizza piled high with too much cheese and mushrooms. Have regular soda instead of diet, and I want a full bowl of chocolate ice cream under your belt before we leave here. Understood?"

Susan laughed. "You got it, but when I start to look like a blimp, I'm going to say it's all your fault. You sound just like my mother, Tristan. She's always harping on me about eating."

"Fine, I'll take the blame. You really need to put on some weight. You're starting to look anorexic. That is not a good thing."

"You've been talking to mother or Jemma. Which one?"

Tristan swerved into the crowded parking lot. Her kids whooped with pleasure as Ashley bounced in her seat. "Neither, I have eyes of my own. Now, let's get these kids inside and enjoy ourselves."

With Tristan's help, Susan managed to unload the stroller, fasten Ashley securely, and stuff the diaper bag and her purse beneath the seat. "You're a pro at this I see," she grumbled good-naturedly.

"Hey, I've done this a whole bunch of times already. If there was a way to simplify things, I found it. You'll learn in time that one free hand is better than none."

Susan pushed the stroller with one hand and held Amy's with the other. William raced ahead, anxious to see his friends who were attending the party. Tristan removed the invitation from her purse and stuffed it inside her pocket. "Just in case," she said as they walked into Chuck E. Cheese, a restaurant created exclusively for younger kids. She was relieved that there were no loud, rowdy teenagers in sight.

A giant mechanical mouse was center stage in the restaurant. Next to him stood two cartoon characters just as tall. One wore a badge saying his name was Billy Bob; the other, dressed in bright colored clothing with a goofy face, wore a hat saying his name was Jasper. "Rockin' Robin" blared from the Chuck E. Cheese figure. Ashley bobbed up and down in her stroller, her eyes big as saucers. "She loves it," Susan yelled to Tristan. The noise was deafening. The background was filled with high-pitched squeals from excited children. Bells, whistles, and zinging sounds emanated from every corner of the restaurant. It was a musical jungle, and the kids were lapping it up like soda pop.

Tristan searched out her birthday group as Susan tagged behind to sit with the other moms. "This is Susan, my friend from the Art Institute. She's a new mom."

"Nice to meet you."

"Good luck."

"Sleeping through the night yet?" someone else asked.

Susan nodded, then laughed as she slid onto an empty chair. "So, you've all been there, done that, huh?" she said, her eyes twinkling.

A petite blonde spoke for them all. "Yes, we have. We're experts on everything from bug bites to freezing popsicles faster than the freezer. Ask us anything you can't find in a book and one of us will have the answer. I say this with no shame."

The woman held out a hand for Susan. "I'm Laura Thompson. I have the twin boys with the red hair." She pointed to two laughing boys who looked to be around seven or eight.

"Twins! How in the world do you manage? You don't look tired at all."

"They keep me hopping, but I love every minute of it. You learn to roll with stuff. You also learn real quick what's important and what isn't. I'm not supermom, and I don't want to be supermom. If things get done, they get done. If they don't, oh, well!"

"That's a great attitude. I'll have to try it," Susan said, laughing.

"That's more like it, Susan. Never sweat the small stuff. I never liked changing dirty diapers and cleaning up vomit at three in the morning. Motherhood definitely has its up and downs. You just roll with it," Tristan said.

Suddenly, the talkative bunch of moms turned silent. Susan looked to Tristan, who shrugged her shoulders, indicating she had no idea why her friends clammed up so suddenly.

"It's *them*," the mother of the twins whispered to the woman on her right.

Susan followed Laura's gaze to the couple that had just entered the restaurant. The woman carried two large packages. The man with her had a giant box up on his shoulder. It was obvious they were there for the party. She was about to ask why the little group turned silent when her heart started to pound so hard she thought it was going to explode right out of her chest. She squinted, certain in the dim light that she was seeing things. She closed her eyes, opened them, and looked again. No, she was not seeing things.

It was Dylan Stockard in the flesh. Cam's best friend.

"What?" Tristan poked her in the side.

"It's Dylan."

"You know Dylan and Renée?"

Susan struggled to take a deep breath, aware that Tristan was looking at her in alarm. "I know Dylan," she finally managed to gasp. "I've never met his fiancée, but I've heard about her."

"Then you're behind on your news. Renée and Dylan got married a year ago." Tristan leaned over and continued talking, this time in a much lower voice. "They've been trying to get pregnant since day one, only to find out Renée can't have children. I heard Dylan was devastated."

Susan nodded, her eyes on the handsome couple. "How do *you* know Dylan and Renée?"

"I met them in a parenting class last year. Most of us in our little group went to that class, but that was before they knew they weren't able to have children. We stayed in contact because they're both so likable. It's easy to see how much they love kids. We're all hoping they make the decision to adopt, but that has to be their decision. We see each other a few times a year. Birthday parties, picnics. Come on, I'll introduce you to Renée."

Susan scooped Ashley out from her stroller and followed Tristan to the front of the restaurant.

"Tristan, hi!" Renée gave her friend a hug.

"Susan? Is that you? With a . . . baby? My God, I had no idea! Come here." Dylan grabbed her and Ashley and gave them a big squeeze. "Cam never told me! That son of . . ."

"Dylan, watch it, there are kids everywhere!" Renée jabbed her husband in the side with an index finger.

"Uh, sure. Sorry. Damn, Susan, Cam never told me."

Susan didn't know what to say. It had been almost three years since she'd seen Dylan. He'd been with a medical group of volunteers headed for Borneo. He'd spent a week with her and Cam in Paris. He wasn't sure how long he was going to be in Borneo, and he'd wanted to see Cam and Paris before he committed himself to an indefinite stay in a third world country.

Dylan was the complete opposite of Cam. Close to six feet, built like a boxer, with bright red-gold hair and clear blue eyes, his Irish heritage shone through like a beacon. Cam was taller, leaner and darker. Black hair and green eyes. Eyes that lit up when she entered the room. Eyes that revealed his thoughts. Eyes that she'd wanted to spend the rest of her life looking into, but, sadly, it hadn't worked out.

"Susan!" He pushed her away so he could look down into her eyes. "God, I'm so glad to see you!"

"Dylan. Of all the people in the whole world, you're the last person I expected to see here. In this place—" she motioned around her "—in *Florida*. How did you wind up in the Sunshine State of all places?"

"First, meet Renée."

Susan clasped a tiny hand and looked into deep brown eyes. They smiled at one another but Renée's eyes immediately went to Ashley. She held out her arms and Ashley went willingly into them.

"Dylan told me all about you and Cam." She looked down at Ashley with such longing, Susan felt a lump start to grow in her throat. "But he forgot to mention this little bundle."

"She's heavy." She watched in horror when, with a stubby fist, Ashley bopped Renée on the nose, then grabbed a fistful of hair. "Ashley, no!" Susan laughed and picked Renée's hair out of Ashley's grasp. "She reaches for everything. I don't wear earrings or necklaces anymore. She's just a busy little girl. Everything is new and exciting to her. On top of that, she seems to love everyone."

"It's okay, right, little lady? You can pull my hair all you want." Renée nuzzled her cheek. "She's beautiful, Susan. You're so lucky."

"Yes, I am. She's going to drool all over that lovely jacket," Susan said, reaching for her daughter. "I'm going to put her in her stroller. I'll be right back. Don't go away.

We have so much to talk about."

Instead of waiting, they followed her. They watched as she settled Ashley and handed her a pacifier. "That should keep her occupied for two minutes at least. Please, join us, we have enough soda and pizza to feed an army."

"Dylan, do you want to stay? We were just dropping off the presents," Renée said.

"Why not? Looks like we've got some catching up to do. Besides, I haven't had my turn at getting my hair pulled." He reached over and patted Ashley's downy head.

The moms made small talk with Dylan and Renée for a few minutes before they trailed off to participate in a game with their kids. Tristan remained seated at the table with Susan.

"Okay, I want to hear everything that's happened to you since I saw you last."

"No, you don't, trust me. Will you settle for the high-lights?"

Dylan laughed, a robust, hearty sound. "I guess I'll have to. Cam can fill me in on the details later."

"That won't happen, Dylan. For starters, Cam and I broke it off not long after you left. There were things he said he needed to do, and things I thought I needed to do in the States. I met my husband, Richard, right after I moved back to Florida, got married, and had a baby. That pretty much covers it."

"I'm having a hard time believing all this. Jesus, Susan, what the hell happened? You and Cam were so perfect for each other. Just you wait till I get hold of my old buddy."

"No . . ."

"Yes, you were and you know it. Something happened, and it's obvious you don't want to talk about it, but I know someone who will."

"What is that supposed to mean?" Susan suddenly felt an attack of the jitters.

"Cam. I'll ask him. Man-to-man."

"But, he's . . . I hope you have better luck than I did. I sent him a letter, I called, e-mailed, faxed. Hell, I did everything I could to try and locate him in Paris. It was as if he dropped off the face of the earth. And you as well. I'm not discounting the fact that he might have been avoiding me." Susan felt drained. Empty. Like she'd walked through the Mojave Desert for miles and miles with no water. Her throat was dry. She took a drink of Coke. She watched Ashley leaning over her stroller, looking at something on the floor.

Dylan and Renée exchanged glances as Dylan bent down to pick up Ashley's pacifier. He handed it to Susan, who slipped it into her pocket.

"What? Did something happen to Cam?" Her heart pulsed.

"No." Dylan somehow managed to drag out the word. "I think I'm missing something here. Cam is in the United States. He's been here for over a year now. His group left for Somalia not long after I left. A few months later, they joined me in Borneo. He said you left to return to the States. I thought everything was fine between the two of you. We returned to the States together last year." Dylan shook his head. "I can't believe he didn't try to contact you. He was devastated when you left."

"Bullshit, Dylan. He was no more devastated than the man in the moon!" Susan raised her voice, then, remembering where she was, she lowered it. "He didn't seem to be the least bit unhappy when I left. He was committed to the work he was sent to do. He told me I would be miserable where he was going. He said it wasn't the kind of life I deserved. I came home. I tried to call him."

She stopped. It didn't matter anymore. She was married to Richard, soon to be divorced from Richard. She had Ashley Rose. Cam could never be a part of her life. She had to accept that.

Then why did she feel as if her entire world was suddenly turned upside down?

"I don't care what the contract says, Richard," Ashton's voice boomed over the phone. "I want you and your piss-poor excuse for a secretary out of the office by the end of the week, and that's final. If I have to have the police remove you from the premises, that's just exactly what I'll do! The courts will iron it out." He inhaled, his nostrils flared wildly. "Is that understood?"

"Ashton, calm down. I'd hate for you to have a heart attack. Actually, that *would* settle my problems right now, but it wouldn't be very fair, would it?" Richard said calmly.

His calm voice only incensed Ashton further. "You let me worry about my heart, you piece of shit. I know who you are. I know what you're doing. Let me rephrase that. I know what you're *trying* to do. I'm just sorry I didn't catch on sooner. Rest assured, you son of a bitch, if I had, you would never have stepped inside my home, let alone married my daughter."

"Now, now, Ashton, let's not be too hasty. Of course I would have married your daughter. You practically insisted on it. Damn, you threw us at each other. She was ripe and ready. Hell, if memory serves me correctly, it was your daughter who fucked my brains out. On our second date. Fine job you did, *Dad.*"

"Don't you ever talk about Susan that way again. I swear I'll kill you if you do. And don't *ever* call me Dad. I'm not your father. Fortunately, the poor man who had that job is probably six feet under by now."

"Yes, he is. Sad, isn't it?"

"Richard, I'm going to give you one more chance. I called you, man-to-man, to step aside. I don't think either one of us wants a protracted, bitter court battle. I've offered you a hefty settlement. You can keep the Porsche. What more do you want?"

Ashton had expected Richard to take his offer and run with it. He was more than willing to lose a few million for the sake of his family. Hell, he was willing to close the doors to Burke and Burke if he had to. He was prepared to do whatever he had to do to get the conniving son of a bitch on the other end of the phone out of their lives. He'd been so confident when he told Iris and Susan the man could be bought off. Any man could be bought if the price was right. The big question now was, what did Richard want?

"You know what I really want, Ashton? What I wanted all those years ago. The basic things that every boy needs. Promises kept. A home. Parents. Food. Shelter. Just the basic things. You do understand me, don't you, Ashton?"

"Yes, all too well. I understood then and I understand now. You didn't convince me then, Richard. You might've had your mother wrapped around your little finger, but I saw through you. I saw what you did." And he'd never told. He'd made a promise to himself and he hadn't broken it. Things were different now. Circumstances changed. Old promises could be broken.

"What are you talking about? If you're trying to scare me, you are not succeeding. Do whatever you feel you have to do, and I'll do what I have to do. Know this, though, *Dad*. If I go, and I said, if, the Pentagon, Disney and the other three go with me, too. You didn't even read the damn contracts did you? They're my clients. If I go, they go with me. Shame on you, *Dad*. What were you talking about again?"

"Let's just say I saw something I wasn't supposed to see. Something that involved a pillow. Something that could put your ass away for the rest of your fucking life." Ashton glanced behind him, making sure Iris hadn't come in the den unnoticed. "As for your precious Pentagon and the others, take them. Just leave. Like I said, the courts will handle it. If you're stupid enough to think the Pentagon or Disney want to see their names plastered all over the front page of the *Wall Street Journal*, then go for it. I-don't-think-so."

"Stop with the stupid games already, Ashton. I'm in no mood for pillow talk, whatever that's supposed to mean. I swear, *Dad*, you're starting to lose it. If there's nothing else, I'm going to hang up. Someone in this company has to work. I'm doing my very best to earn the salary you're paying me so you and yours can live in the lap of luxury."

"I'm not finished with you. You either take the deal, or you leave it. I don't care either way. I want you out of our lives. You have one week, Richard! At the end of the week, the police will escort you off the premises." He broke the connection before his son-in-law had a chance to say anything. Score one for Team Burke.

Damn the bastard to hell! He had thought for sure he could buy him off with money and the threat of exposure. Obviously, he'd underestimated his son-in-law.

Ashton's mind wandered back to when Richard Johnson had first entered his life. At first he thought his mind was playing tricks on him. Richard's sly references to his past when they were alone. The knowing looks, the secret smiles. How could he have been so gullible? How? What

167

was it Iris said? Oh, yes, you only see what you want to see. Well, she was right about that.

He'd been right to do what he did all those years ago. Now he was even more certain that he'd done the right thing. The years, and time, the healer of all things, faded, and finally he was eventually able to put the horrible memory out of his mind. When had he become so soft and weak?

Oh, he'd been happy for a while, lured into a false sense of family. He convinced Iris they were doing the right thing. Then Iris became ill. Now he knew she was sick with guilt, but he didn't know that back then, or if he did, he closed his eyes to it. With his hands full at Burke and Burke, he hadn't questioned the doctors who cared for his wife. There was no reason to question them. He simply accepted that Iris's mind couldn't handle what had happened. Finally, after a few years, Susan was born; but Iris, to his mind, was never the same after their daughter was born. Guilt again. But it was more than that. If he were half the man he claimed to be, he would admit that not only had he failed as a husband, he'd failed as a father. By God, he wasn't going to fail as a grandfather.

What kind of man was he if he couldn't protect his family? He slumped in his chair, the fight temporarily gone. He opened a drawer and found his pipe. He stuffed cherry tobacco inside and struck a match. He puffed a few times, enjoying the fragrance. A habit he'd had most of his life. He'd given it up more than once. Why was it when a man was down he resorted to his old habits, most of them bad? He often wondered about things like that. No matter. He liked his pipe and was going to continue smoking it until they threw dirt on his face.

"Ashton, I've called you a dozen times. Jemma has

dinner ready. I think you're losing your hearing. Ashton!" Iris called from the doorway.

"Yes, yes, Iris. I hear you. I'm relaxing. Tell Jemma I'll have something to eat later."

Iris entered the den to perch on the edge of his desk. "What is it, Ashton? I know you only smoke that nasty thing when you're upset. Did something happen? Something I should know about? Remember what I told you about secrets in this family."

She knew him too well. "I'm not upset, just tired. Why don't you have dinner with Jemma? I'm not really hungry right now."

"I'm not leaving this room, Ashton Parker Burke, until you tell me what's going on. Why is it women are always the last to know? Are you ill? Is that it? Or are you having an affair? That's it, isn't it? Need I remind you of my sister Lily and all her eligible friends."

"Iris, shut up!"

"Don't tell me to shut up you, you old buzzard. Say that again and I'll . . . I'll cut your gonads off!"

Ashton burst out laughing, hard belly laughs. He rolled to the side and dropped his pipe in the ashtray. Tears streamed down his face. He coughed, then fell into another fit of laughter. He couldn't stop.

"I think you need to be committed! I'm calling Doctor Watts." Iris was about to leave the room when Ashton was finally able to control his laughter.

"C'mere, woman."

Something in his tone of voice must have struck her, too, because in the next instant she was on his lap doubled over with laughter.

"What's . . . what's, oh hell, Ashton, we're some old pair, aren't we?" She gave him a wet kiss on the cheek and placed her head against his.

"That we are, my dear. But not so old that I've forgotten how to—" he reached beneath her blouse and cupped her breast "—do this."

"Mmm, you need to get angry more often. Or laugh. Whichever." For the first time in more years than they both could remember, they forgot the troubles between them and did what came as natural as breathing.

Ashton dimmed the lights and locked the door. He took the phone off the hook—the same phone Iris had installed while he was playing golf one day because she said she was sick and tired of chasing him down to take his calls. He loosened his tie. For the next hour he made love to his wife on the sofa in his den. It was as good as he'd remembered. Hell, it was better.

When it was over, Iris lay with her head on his chest, her legs tossed over his. She played with the soft hair on his chest and nibbled his neck. "Ashton?"

"Hmm?"

"We haven't been together like this in . . . forever. Tell me something."

"What's that?" His words were almost a whisper. He hadn't been so relaxed in years.

"Has there ever been someone else? You know, all those years with me in and out of the hospital. I've often wondered. I wouldn't blame you if there was. I just want you to know that."

He'd had plenty of opportunity, but that wasn't what he was about as a man and a husband. He and Iris had their ups and downs, more downs than ups, but he had remained faithful to his marriage vows. At least he had that to hold on to.

"Well, you can stop wondering. You know me better than anyone, Iris. What do *you* think?"

Chapter Ten

Susan was on the phone with Tristan. "Okay, back to the matters at hand. Are you sure that you want us to be a part of your trip? I don't want to be a third wheel. I don't want to intrude on a family outing."

"Of course I'm sure. It's not really a family outing. It's another one of those group things I told you about. To keep us all sane a few days longer." Tristan laughed. "It was Laura's idea. She asked me to invite you and Ashley. Even if she hadn't asked, I would have invited you. It'll be a blast, and besides, you mentioned that Ashley's never been to the Magic Kingdom. She's old enough now to enjoy the bright colors and all the activities. Not to mention the thousands of kids running around. Babies like little people."

"Then we accept. But first I'll have to call Richard. He called last night and said he wanted to see Ashley on Saturday. I'll have to tell him we have plans and see if he can make it on Sunday or Monday. There shouldn't be a problem. It's not like he's been the most attentive father in the world. I will have to get back to you, though."

"You better. I'm counting on you. It will be good for all of us," Tristan said.

"You know me, Tris. A promise is a promise. I'll get back to you as soon as I can."

Susan hung up the phone, her thoughts jumbled. She

dreaded making the call to Richard, but he *was* Ashley's father, and he *had* called asking to visit her during the weekend. Sometimes plans had to be changed. If she had to, she would remind him of all the visits he'd missed. She didn't think it would come to that, but Richard was unpredictable. Just last Wednesday, he'd called her twenty-three times and hung up each time without speaking. His way of harassing her, trying to beat her into the ground. She did find it unnerving since she'd had caller ID installed on her phone and Richard knew it. He took great joy in trying to torment her. She hadn't told her attorney or her father. It was probably a mistake on her part, but she would have to live with it just the way she lived with all her other mistakes.

She dialed Burke and Burke. Despite the threat of a lawsuit, Richard had remained at the firm, refusing the golden parachute Ashton Burke had offered him. "I need to speak with Mr. Johnson," she said coolly. *Mr. Johnson, my ass.*

The receptionist put her on hold. She was about to hang up when Richard's voice came over the wire.

"What do you want?" he asked coldly.

"And hello to you, too, Richard. There's been a change in plans. Do you have any objection to visiting Ashley on Sunday instead of Saturday? We're going to the Magic Kingdom Saturday, and it's too late to cancel on my part. I'd forgotten about it when you called last week." A polite question. She was civil.

"It's nice of you to ask." Sarcasm reverberated over the telephone line.

"Richard, I haven't asked you for anything. I put up with your no-shows on visiting day. Not to mention your harassing phone calls. Let's not turn this into a legal hassle. This is a big outing for Ashley. Will you please just give me a break here? I'm not asking for anything outrageous and I'm trying to be fair."

He paused for what seemed like forever. "I suppose I could do Sunday instead of Saturday. You damn well better be home. I don't intend to drive across town to find out you found something else better to do."

"I'll be home. Ten o'clock?"

"Whatever."

She stared down at the pinging phone. She had a mental picture of Richard slamming down the phone, his face contorted in rage.

Being civil to her child's father was rapidly becoming a white knuckle experience. She didn't know how much longer she could keep it up. Thanks to her attorney, she now had temporary custody of Ashley, but their divorce was going to take longer than she'd originally thought. On top of all that, there was her father's attempt to oust Richard from Burke and Burke. She sighed. When would the legal mess end? Not in the near future, that much she did know.

It was a perfect Florida day or, as those in Orlando liked to say, a perfect Disney day. There wasn't a cloud in the sky. It wasn't too hot and it wasn't too cold. Best of all, there was no humidity.

He couldn't have chosen a better place or a better time to put his plan into action. His time was running out where Ashton's threat was concerned. He'd been rattled, even frazzled, until Susan called him. Then, with a little ingenuity on his part, it all fell into place.

It was the debut of Disney's latest creation, the Mammoth, a roller coaster soaring up to eighty miles per hour. Fifteen hundred feet high, it promised to be the biggest and the best ever. He should know, he had the inside track with the Disney people. Crowds had gathered from all over the world to share in the magnificent unveiling. The excitement was catching. *I might even take a ride myself, but definitely not today.* Then again, maybe he wouldn't ever take the ride.

His brilliant scheme had hit him like a ton of bricks on Thursday afternoon. He wondered why he hadn't thought of it sooner. Probably because of Ashton's threats and having to deal with his ultimatum. When you were between a rock and a hard place, you used whatever crumbs came your way and hoped for the best. What had come his way wasn't crumbs, though, it was the whole loaf.

It seemed like half of his childhood and his entire adult life were geared to that moment in time. When he *really* thought about it, he likened it to being in a holding pattern, waiting for just the right moment. He was finally *in* the moment. He couldn't cave in.

. It was all *her* fault. *His,* too. He hadn't known that until last week, though. He couldn't wait to see how they reacted when they heard the news.

Then he saw them. There looked to be about twenty people in the group straggling along. All of them were laughing and talking, the children poking and punching one another. He guessed that's what you did at Disney to make it an enjoyable experience. He looked around to confirm his thought. Yep, everyone was laughing, talking, and jostling one another.

The group he was interested in consisted of twelve adults, six or eight children of various ages. They all wore bright-red tee shirts with some family name emblazoned on the backs in big white letters. Red was a color easily identified, easy to spot in a crowd. He wondered how his wife managed to get herself invited to what looked like some sort of reunion. He laughed. What did he care? He'd lucked out. Big-time. Who was he to question the whos and whys of it?

Once again, fate had intervened on his behalf.

Richard saw Susan pushing Ashley in her stroller. She was laughing. Ashley was sleeping. A red-haired man bent down to whisper something in Susan's ear. She looked up at him and smiled, her face alive with joy. He watched as the red-haired man took his wife's hand in his, gave it a squeeze, just as a small, dark-haired woman appeared at his side. She said something to Susan that caused her to erupt in laughter. Ashley started crying. The red-haired man leaned over the stroller and gave Ashley her pacifier. She spit it out. He heard his daughter let out another cry. He continued to watch as Susan removed a yellow plastic bottle from her diaper bag and handed it to Ashley, who reached for it greedily. He continued to watch his wife and child from his position behind a huge sign telling Disney's visitors they were about to enter the home of the Lion King.

He stayed where he was because he didn't dare get any closer to the group. He waited patiently while his daughter sucked down her bottle. The others read maps, bought sodas and balloons. Irritation clouded his features. None of them were in a hurry. There was no way for them to know he had a schedule to stick to. If he strayed at all, his plan would fail. He looked at his watch: 11 a.m.

He'd given himself exactly two hours inside the park. Though he had no idea where the *actual event* would take place, he knew his escape route. He'd done nothing for the past forty-eight hours except study the Magic Kingdom's blueprints. He'd memorized every exit, above ground and below. He would find a way out. That had been the only part of his plan that left him with doubts. If the authorities were to learn of his plan before he'd left the park, then he'd be done for. The key to the success of his plan was to make his move when their guard was down.

He was so relieved when the group split into two, he felt light-headed. It was easier to track ten people rather than twenty, even if they were all wearing red shirts. Half of the group splintered off, going in the opposite direction, waving and shouting, saying they'd meet back at the front gate at three o'clock.

Susan and her little group moved forward. Pushing the stroller, she followed the man with the red hair and his companion. All of them were laughing as they took turns peeking at Ashley under the sun cover on the stroller.

Gradually, the group made its way inside the cool, dim studio where they would see a magician make an audience member disappear. He couldn't help but laugh at the irony of the situation. Disney, with no help from him, had just made his day.

He was hot and sweaty. At first he'd planned on a disguise. A wig with a beard that really wasn't a disguise at all. He'd had second thoughts, and he was glad he'd rejected his earlier idea. Dark glasses and a baseball cap would be enough. Just about every man in the Magic Kingdom, old to the very young, wore dark glasses and a cap. If, *if* something were to go awry, they'd stop every single man in the park. That would take hours. By then, he would be long gone.

He allowed several groups to move ahead of him in line. He didn't dare get too close to the group in the red shirts. He could barely see Susan, but he could see the stroller, and that was all that mattered.

Inch by inch, the long line made its way inside the crowded auditorium. It was surprisingly cool, yet filled with the stench of sweaty bodies. He put his hand over his nose. He hated these fucking places. People packed together like sardines were something he had no desire to be a part of.

He tried breathing through his mouth.

It was his turn to saunter down the aisle. The seats were arranged like those in a movie theater, but he was sure they were closer together in the auditorium. He sat down in an aisle seat next to an incredibly overweight woman in a flowered dress and huge straw hat. He watched as she struggled to fit her girth into the seat. A water bottle hung from her neck, rolling back and forth over her ample bosom. She smelled.

He strained in the darkness to see where the group he'd followed were sitting. Their heads together, they appeared to be whispering to one another. They stopped when the announcer made his way down the aisle and up onto the stage. He had a clear view of Ashley's stroller at the end of the row. He crossed his fingers that his daughter was sleeping.

It would take only seconds for him to do what he had to do. He'd be gone before any outcry could erupt.

A man dressed in a black cape, wearing a purple wizard hat, popped on stage in a cloud of smoke. The audience sucked in their breath when he pulled a dozen bright-colored kerchiefs from thin air.

The red-haired man in his red shirt got up, distracting him for a second. He watched him walk up the aisle, presumably to leave the building. Probably a trip to the men's room. *That's good,* he thought. *One less person to worry about.*

As the magician began to twirl hoops of fire, his assistant, a Red Riding Hood look-alike, did a handspring through the fiery hoops. Another huge sigh from the audience, followed by loud applause.

He glanced at the illuminated dial on his watch. According to the sign posted outside the auditorium, the show lasted thirty minutes. He'd used ten precious minutes already.

He looked at the overweight woman on his right, but she was mesmerized by the performers and paid no attention to him or anyone else. To his way of thinking, she posed no problem.

Before another precious second could pass, he stood up, then hunkered down and crab-walked down the aisle until he reached the stroller four rows ahead, where he banged his knee on it. Susan and the dark-haired woman sitting next to her watched the magician, who was clearly captivating his audience. He really should thank Disney again. He risked a glance at his wife. She was totally oblivious to everything but what was happening onstage.

He squatted behind the stroller, momentarily thankful for the large, cumbersome contraption. It was big enough to hide behind if he remained in his current position. He peered above the stroller one last time. His little group, like everyone else in the auditorium, was engrossed in what was happening on the stage. *Good.* A quick glance at his watch told him they were sixteen minutes into the show.

Leaning to his left, he saw his daughter lying on her back, sucking on her fist. With one deft, swift movement, he caught her up in his arms and whizzed out the side entrance on his left.

Outside in the sunshine, with thousands of tourists milling about, he allowed himself to relax. He placed the still-sleeping baby over his shoulder as he sauntered along like he didn't have a care in the world. Two women pushing a park-rented stroller that looked like a jeep smiled at him as they passed by. He nodded. He was a father walking through the park with his sleeping child. Nothing unusual about that.

Suddenly, he became aware of a change in the crowds milling about. They were stopping, bumping into one another as they tried to focus on something beyond his range of vision. He tried to see past the thick crowds. It looked like they were staring at the auditorium he'd just vacated. He, too, looked, shielding his eyes the way other people were doing. Shaking his head, he maneuvered his way through the thick crowd of curious adults and squalling children.

His heart started to race. He adjusted his cap by pulling it down farther. Maybe he should just get rid of it. He stopped at a garbage can bearing the Disney logo. His gaze swept through the park as he nonchalantly removed the baseball cap and dark glasses, tossing them inside the trash can.

He slipped inside a Disney Store that was packed from floor to ceiling with every character created by Disney in the last six decades. He spied a rack of souvenir shirts. He reached for a bright yellow shirt with the Goofy character stamped on the front. He needed to get rid of Ashley's pink outfit. He moved forward to grab a green sleeveless Little Mermaid dress. He had no idea if it was the right size or not.

The cashier, a young girl of sixteen or so, stopped talking to a pimply-faced youth long enough to say, "Is that it, sir?"

Richard nodded as he handed her twenty-five dollars. He moved in double time as he pocketed his change. He needed to find a restroom. Now they had those family rooms. Another thing in his favor.

Up ahead, next to the "It's a Small World" attraction, he saw the sign: FAMILY RESTROOMS.

Ashley took that moment to wake up.

"Shhh, it's okay." She peered up at him with her big blue eyes, lavishing him with a grin. He smiled down at her.

After a two minute wait in line, he entered the restroom and waited for a stall to become available, where he removed Ashley's pink outfit. He tore the tags off the Little Mermaid dress and flushed them. Pulling on disposable gloves in order to avoid leaving fingerprints, he stuffed the clothes into a white plastic bag before placing it in a metal disposal meant for diapers.

Ashley wiggled and he almost dropped her. "Look at this." He held the dress up so she could see the cartoon picture of the Little Mermaid. Another grin. In seconds he had her dressed. He marveled that by pure dumb luck, he'd somehow managed to get the correct size.

Tucking her under his right arm, he managed to strip off his tee shirt and pull on the Goofy shirt. He tied it around his waist—another neat trick—while he jiggled his daughter from arm to arm. The extra large shirt covered the bulge. He looked at his watch. He'd had Ashley for exactly eight minutes.

He was right on schedule.

Not wanting to draw any undue attention to himself, he strolled through the park at a normal pace. The baby gurgled and dribbled on his shoulder, but she didn't cry or fuss. Apparently there was enough action with all the Disney characters, bright colors, and kids whooping and hollering to keep her occupied.

He nodded and smiled at an elderly couple who whizzed passed him in electric wheelchairs. They returned his smile. Dad and baby. They were probably thinking, isn't that sweet.

He was almost to the exit. *God, it's really going to work.* Now, if *they* were as willing to help him as they said they would on the phone last night, he'd actually pull it off. No one would get hurt and he would come out smelling like the proverbial rose.

Then he remembered he hated roses.

Two long strides took him through the exit gates. A young girl with a rubber stamp in her hand stopped him. His heart fell to his feet and back. "Sir, would you like a stamp to reenter the park?"

He pretended to debate the question. "No, I think she's had enough Disney for one day. Right, *Jenny?* Her mother's waiting over there," he said, pointing to a bunch of young women with toddlers at their sides. He made his way through the contraption that counted the comings and goings of the thousands of people who exited the park daily.

"Come see us again," the girl with the rubber stamp called.

He waved to her. "We'll be back, won't we, Jenny?" he said loudly enough for the young girl's benefit.

He'd parked a car in the preferred parking lot. He didn't want to ride the tram to Daffy Duck six or whatever the hell they named the lots. This was not the time. He grinned. It was all so fucking easy. He could probably make a career out of snatching kids if he wanted to.

He found the white Toyota Corolla he'd stolen at three o'clock in the morning. At three fifteen, he had switched license plates with a Honda Civic parked in the long-term parking lot at the airport. Grabbing the key that the considerate motorist had left in his glove compartment from his pocket, he unlocked the back door and put the baby inside the car seat he'd purchased the night before at Babies "Я" Us. The trunk was loaded with enough supplies to last at least six months. He'd bought twenty-four bags of diapers and another dozen bags in a larger size, just in case. He'd gone from store to store, not wanting to arouse suspicion. Undershirts, pajamas, booties and socks. Three pairs of tennis shoes all in different sizes because he didn't know her exact size, plus he had to assume she would grow in the coming months. Babies grew fast, or so Susan said. It might be cool in her new home, so he'd purchased three little jackets, all equipped with hats and matching gloves. Long pants and tights in a half dozen sizes, too. He bought twelve cases of formula, ten cases of various kinds of baby food, and Playtex bottles with disposable bags. Three aqua blue curved spoons with matching bowls. Twelve large boxes of Wet Wipes. Blankets and a handful of toys, and he was set. If he needed more, he'd see that *they* had the cash to purchase whatever they needed. Not bad, if he said so himself.

He secured the infant in her seat, double-checked the device, then stole another glance at his watch. Thirty-three minutes in all. Not bad. He was certain the authorities would be closing the park within minutes. He swerved through the parking lot, wound his way through a group of teenagers, all wearing pants three sizes too big, the crotches hanging down between their knees. He looked at them in disgust. They should be working. They probably had parents who thought fifty dollars a week was the minimum required allowance.

Up ahead he saw a string of police cars, their sirens screeching, the blue lights flashing brightly, swerve through the entrance. They didn't bother to stop for a parking receipt. He laughed again. *God, this is too easy.* He made a right turn, then another to his left. He was out of the park.

He'd done it.

Let the games begin.

Susan clapped along with the rest of the crowd. The magician was good, actually, he was exceptional. She leaned over to Laura. "Do you think that kid was a plant?"

"Of course. You really don't believe this stuff, do you?"

Susan laughed and whispered, "Sure I do. But then I believe in the Easter Bunny and Santa Claus, too." She grinned at Tristan, who rolled her eyes, then focused her attention back on the performance.

Susan was pleased that Ashley was being so good and not disrupting the magician's performance. Overall, she was a good baby, fussing mostly when she was either hungry or needed to be changed. As her mother said, she'd lucked out where Ashley was concerned.

She'd had nightmares the last few nights, worrying about having to walk out of every show to quiet her child. Most babies would be wailing by then, wanting to be held and played with. Somehow, Ashley managed to sleep through the noise, the applause, and the laughter.

Susan leaned over to peer inside the stroller. A receiving blanket covered her child. She pulled the blanket aside. "Ashley. Let Mommy—"

She looked again. And again. Then she screamed her daughter's name. "Ashley!"

Tristan and Laura jerked around. "Susan, what's wrong?"

Paralyzed with fear, it took a second for Susan to find her voice. "She's gone! Look for yourself! Ashley is gone! She isn't in her stroller. Somebody call the police!" she screamed at the top of her lungs. "Someone do something!" she continued to scream.

The magician, clearly flustered, stopped what he was doing on the stage as the lights were raised. People stared at her unaware of what had happened.

"Dylan probably took her, Susan. Calm down. He went

to the men's room," Renée said in a calm voice.

"Why would your husband take my daughter to the men's room with him? Give me one damn good reason why he'd do a thing like that and not tell me," Susan continued to scream. "Someone, please call the police. My baby is missing!" Susan screamed over and over until she was hoarse.

Tristan turned to face Susan. "I want you to calm down. Renée's probably right, and Dylan simply took Ashley with him while we were engrossed in the show. Take a deep breath. You need to keep your wits about you. Do what I say, Susan."

Susan clenched her teeth, her whole body shaking.

One of the ushers leaped onto the stage, microphone in hand. "Ladies and gentlemen, if I could have your attention, please. Will you all please return to your seats? We're going to close and lock all the doors until we can—"

"You can't close the doors," Susan shouted, interrupting him. "We need them open. He's coming back. He just went to the men's room!" She heard the doors slamming shut just as she finished speaking.

The usher, via the microphone, directed his words to Susan. "I have to follow procedure, miss. All entrances and exits must be closed until we determine exactly what happened. Please return to your seat."

"No! You can't do that! He's coming back with her. Please! Let him back inside!" Susan started to sob hysterically.

Tristan placed an arm around Susan's shoulders. "Shhh, this is only going to take a few minutes." She looked at the boy center stage. "Right?"

The young usher, clearly out of his depth, strained to hear her above the din of voices that had now become louder. He watched as parents checked their own strollers. They pulled their older children closer or placed them on their laps.

"May I have your attention, please. I want you all to remain calm until we can figure out what happened." The boy looked anything but calm; he looked terrified.

Just the way Susan looked and felt. "Don't tell me to sit down! My daughter is missing! Someone took my daughter! Open those damn doors and let me out of here! I have to call the police. Does anyone in here have a cell phone? Please, if you do, dial 911!"

"Ma'am!" the boy shouted. "Please. We have to follow procedure. My supervisors have contacted Disney security. They're on their way. Please just calm down." The boy sounded as if he were about to cry.

"Someone just stole my daughter and you want me to sit down? No! I will not sit down! Let me out of here before I break your neck! Now!" she screamed at the top of her lungs, a pure primal scream of fear.

"Susan, please." Tristan wrapped her arms around her. "Screaming isn't going to change things. Take a deep breath. We'll have this under control as soon as security checks the men's room."

"Are you out of your mind? If this was one of your kids, you would be doing the same thing I'm doing. My daughter is gone! She's gone, Tristan. That means someone kidnapped her." She pushed her friend aside and ran to the front of the auditorium and up to the stage.

She yanked the microphone from the usher's hand. "Don't say a word!"

She took a deep breath and tried to still the trembling in her hands. Her heart was pumping as though she'd run a marathon while sucking in big gulps of nicotine. She was getting light-headed and the room was starting to spin. Her world was about to close in on her. She took another deep breath.

Ashley. Missing. She had to remain in control. She had to find her daughter. She closed her eyes and inhaled, then exhaled. One more time. She opened her eyes.

Yes, this is real. Yes, this is happening. Jesus Christ! Why are all these people staring at me? She looked at the microphone in her hand. Calm. Yes, she needed to remain calm. Hysterics wouldn't help Ashley Rose. Later, after she was found, she could collapse in hysteria.

"Please." A loud squeal blasted from the microphone. She tried to steady her hands. They were shaking uncontrollably. She saw confusion at the end of the stage.

Had they found Ashley? She dropped the microphone and ran to the end of the stage. "Miss." A man grabbed her. "Please, this way."

Tristan appeared at her side. "It's okay, Susan. These people are park security. They've got people looking for Dylan in all the restrooms. I'm sure that's where we'll find Ashley. Dylan probably got bored with the show and decided to take Ashley with him. You know how he loves kids."

She nodded. But he would have *told* her if he had taken Ashley, wouldn't he?

Then she remembered Renée.

She looked for the small woman. There she was. Something snapped in Susan. "You!" She tore at her shirt, grabbed a fistful of hair.

"Susan, what the hell do you think you're doing?" Tristan struggled to pull her away from Renée.

"It's her! They had this all planned! Don't you see?"

"Ma'am, if you'll follow us," the uniformed security man said.

186

"No! Please, it's her! Them. They took her. They must have planned this. That's why they all invited me to come here. Dammit, do something!"

"My God, Susan, what are you saying?" Tristan was so agitated, she started to cry.

The group in the red shirts were staring at her, mouths agape, eyes the size of half-dollars. What were they doing? Why were they staring at her like she'd suddenly sprouted a second head? "Isn't someone going to arrest her? She knows! She planned this. Please, Tris, you know what I'm talking about, don't you? Please, someone do something!" Susan fell to the floor, her body racked with sobs.

She was back up and on her feet a second later, screaming, a bloodcurdling scream. "Please. Someone call the *real* police. I'm telling you, they've kidnapped my daughter! I know what I'm talking about. Why won't you stupid people do something? Someone, anyone, do something! Tristan, please, please help me!"

Susan pleaded with her friend through streaming tears of fear and disbelief. "Remember? You told me? At the party? No baby! Remember?" Susan shrieked.

Tristan looked at Renée, who appeared to be in shock. Renée shook her head. "No, Tristan, I would never do anything like that! My God, I couldn't do that to anyone! How could you even think such a thing? Please, you've got to believe me!"

Tristan nodded, then sat down on the floor next to Susan, where she'd collapsed a second time. She *wanted* to believe Renée, but maybe Susan was right and this had been planned. She was suddenly unable to meet Renée's tortured gaze.

A large shaft of sunlight appeared when the doors to the main entrance slammed open.

She saw him through her tears. Dylan. Yes, thank God!

"Susan, it's Dylan. They found him."

"Ashley!" She found her footing and ran to the entryway, toward the sunlight and Dylan.

But her daughter wasn't there. Only Dylan, outlined in the bright sunlight.

The bright sunlight shone down on the handcuffs he wore on his wrists.

Susan's world turned black as she slid to the floor.

Chapter Eleven

Ashton Burke idly swung his indoor putter. He could hear music playing from somewhere. Iris and Jemma both liked music when they were puttering around. Didn't they hear the damn phone? Where were they? He slapped at his forehead. Where would Iris be at this time of day but her rose garden? He just knew there would be American Beauty roses on the dining room table tonight. Probably yellow ones. Iris did love her roses. The phone continued to ring.

He'd spent most of the morning with his putter and green in the dining room practicing for tomorrow's golf tournament. Following Sunday brunch, the country club was hosting a golf tournament for the senior members. If nothing else, it promised to be entertaining. Maximus González would be there. It was time to say a few choice words to old Max. He wouldn't mince them either.

Thinking about Maximus was better than thinking about his son-in-law. Thinking about *anything* or *anyone,* and that included Maximus, was better than thinking about the biggest mistake of his life. Meaning Richard Johnson. After Richard had refused his buyout offer, he'd waited until his attorney had come up with what he thought was a way to oust him, then given Richard a week to get out of their lives. That was three days ago. The countdown was on, with four days to go. It would be just like the bastard to wait till the last day before he stole off into the dead of night.

The phone continued to ring. "All right, all right, I'm coming," he muttered irritably. He dropped the putter on the dining room carpet and walked into the kitchen.

He could see Iris and Jemma in the garden through the kitchen window. His greeting was a harsh bark. "Ashton Burke."

"Are you the father of Susan Burke Johnson?" a strange voice inquired.

"Yes, this is Ashton Burke. I'm Susan's father. Who is this?" Thinking it was a telemarketer, he was about to hang up when the caller acknowledged he was still on the phone.

"This is Detective Simmons. Orlando Police Department, Special Investigations."

"Yes?" Ashton's heart rate quadrupled. Outside the kitchen window, Iris waved a rose under Jemma's nose, then sniffed it herself before she added it to the dozen or more flowers in her basket.

"Your daughter would like to speak with you, Mr. Burke."

All Ashton could hear was mumbling and sobbing. "Susan? What's wrong?"

"Dad, she's gone. Dylan took her. They don't believe me. Please, can you come here? Please?"

Ashton hadn't heard his daughter cry like this in . . . ever.

"I'll be right there, Susan. Put Detective Simmons back on the phone. Calm down, honey."

Ashton tapped his foot to more muffled noises, phones shrilling in the background. He could still hear his daughter sobbing. She sounded hysterical to him.

"You'd better have a good reason for holding my

daughter. I've got the best lawyers in the state. If I hear that's she's been . . ." Reality set in. She'd said something about some guy named Dylan taking someone. Who? Her friend Tristan?

"Sir, please. Your daughter hasn't been charged with anything. It's your granddaughter."

"Ashley Rose? What's happened? Put my daughter back on the phone. Now!" He raised his voice. Susan came back on the line.

"Dad, Ashley's been kidnapped. At Disney. Please, just come downtown to the police station on South Hughey. Hurry. I have to hang up now, Dad."

Ashley Rose. Kidnapped?

This had to be some kind of ugly mistake. No one in their right mind would take Ashley. Susan never took her eyes off that child. Never. *Why* would anyone take his granddaughter? Iris, he had to find Iris.

He tossed the phone on the counter, raced through the dining room, found his Docksiders beneath the coffee table. He slipped his shoes on and hurried out the French doors to Iris's garden.

"Iris, Jemma!"

Iris appeared from behind a rosebush that was in full bloom. She wore a straw hat, bib overalls, gardening gloves and was carrying a basket of fresh-cut flowers. "Ashton, what in the world is wrong with you? You're as white as my Snow Bush! Ashton, are you sick?" Iris placed her basket on a nearby bench before she walked toward him, her hand open so that she could feel his forehead.

"God, no. Iris, I'm not sick. Susan just called from the police station. The baby is gone." He could hardly believe his own words. "Susan said she was kidnapped. This can't be happening. It has to be some kind of mistake."

Iris stopped, her hands flying to her face in shock. "You're right, this has to be some kind of horrible mistake. Who in the world would kidnap that precious child?"

"Susan wants us down there right away, Iris. We can talk on the way. She was hysterical. Hysterical means it is not a mistake. Our granddaughter is gone."

"Don't make dinner, Jemma. We'll call you when we know something." A year earlier, she would have fainted at hearing such news. Her daughter needed her. She followed Ashton but stripped off her gardening gloves on the way. There was no time to even think about changing her attire. Her daughter wouldn't care what she was wearing.

Together, they climbed into the Lincoln Navigator and headed for South Hughey Avenue.

"Ashton, what happened? Do you know more than you told me? I . . . this is insane! This can't be happening to us."

Ashton nodded as he tromped on the accelerator, passing the small car in front of them. "I know. We aren't going to know anything till we get there." He swerved back into the right lane, cutting off the car he'd just passed. The driver blasted his horn.

"Ashton, slow down. I want to get there alive," Iris pleaded.

"I'm sorry. Look, I'm just as nervous as you are." He eased up on the gas pedal. "Susan said something about a man named Dylan. Do you know anyone by that name? She said he took Ashley Rose. It was the first time I ever heard her mention his name. I don't even know what his last name is. He's probably some sleazy-ass friend of that slimeball Richard. Jesus Christ!"

"Ashton, you're scaring me!"

"Richard. I bet that bastard is behind this. He's just

brazen enough to try and pull a stunt like this. Oh God, Iris, why would Richard kidnap his own daughter? He's crazy, but he's not stupid. What would he possibly have to gain? Dammit, Iris, just think about it for a minute. He's only got four more days to clear out. There's a lot at stake for him. In a way, it's his whole life. So, to answer your question, he has a lot at stake. Money. Burke and Burke. The divorce. God knows what else. His reputation, his high-powered friends and clients."

"Susan said she switched his visitation day from today till tomorrow and said he was okay with the switch. Don't you think if he planned on kidnapping his daughter, he'd do it tomorrow, when he would have Ashley all legal and aboveboard?" Iris could see her husband was thinking about what she said.

"You could be right. Right now, I have a hate on for the man and it's clouding my thinking. This family is unraveling, and it's all because of him. Unfortunately, it's all I can think about."

"And you, Ashton. You played a role in all this. You're going to have to step up to the plate and take responsibility," Iris said quietly, so quietly that Ashton had to strain to hear the words.

When he heard them, his shoulders slumped. "Let's not go there now, Iris. We have to think about Susan and Ashley. They're the only ones who matter right now."

"I'm quite aware of that, among other things. We have to talk about it, deal with it. There's never going to be a right time, if that's what you're thinking."

"Please, Iris, be quiet! I can't deal with you . . . this . . . this, whatever it is, right now."

Iris reached across the seat and placed her hand on her husband's thigh, her signal that she understood. "We *will* talk about it later, Ashton. I realize you're upset. I'm just as upset, possibly more so. Ashton, we need to pray that our baby girl is alive!" Iris almost broke down then. Her grandchild could be in harm's way, and here they were wasting their precious time talking about . . . *him*.

Iris was right. He needed to pray. "This has to be some kind of horrible mistake. I promise you, if it's the last thing I do, I will get to the bottom of it."

Located in downtown Orlando, at 100 South Hughey Avenue, the Orlando P.D. had three main investigative units. Violent Crime handled assault and battery cases, homicide, and robbery cases. The Special Investigations division dealt with sex crimes, economic crimes, and crimes against children. Detective Simmons was in charge of the Crimes Against Children Unit. Comprising only seven personnel—five detectives, one detective's assistant, and one sergeant—the Crimes Against Children Unit, known as CCU, was responsible for investigating missing juveniles, though much of its focus recently was on child custody cases.

At forty-eight, Detective Joshua Simmons had been with Orlando P.D. for twenty-six years. He'd been a patrol officer when little Adam Walsh had been abducted from Sears in the early eighties. He'd met the child's father, John Walsh, years later when he came to fame hosting *America's Most Wanted*. He'd both admired and pitied the man. It was a terrible way to gain fame.

Simmons had been through two marriages, the loss of his parents, and had one grown son who was a rookie cop. He liked his lifestyle. He was single with no one to account for other than himself and the department. It was another way of saying he was married to his job. He intended to keep it that way for at least another ten years. Maybe then he would think about retiring. Maybe.

He knew he looked ten years younger by the grace of good genes, and if he followed in his father's footsteps, he'd live to the ripe old age of ninety. He still boasted a full head of blond hair, though middle age had begun to creep up in the last year, taking up residence in his gut. The extra day at the gym was starting to pay off.

It'd been three weeks since they'd had a new case, and that was the good news. New cases in the CCU meant a child had suffered in some way. All of the officers had children of their own or nieces and nephews. Each missing child, whether it was a runaway, a parental abduction, or foul play, held a special spot in the hearts of CCU personnel. Their goal was always the same: return the child to his or her rightful home, unharmed.

That day, when he'd gotten the call telling him there had been an abduction at Disney's Magic Kingdom, his gut churned. It was a favorite hangout for pedophiles and sex offenders, so he'd learned to dread a call to the famous theme park.

He finished filling out the required forms for a missing child, then readied himself to begin the *real* work. He shifted in his chair, waiting for the young mother. He looked at his notes. Susan Burke Johnson and her friend, Tristan, returned from the ladies' room. Mrs. Johnson had been hysterical, just as any mother would be if her child was abducted, when he'd arrived at the park. If he'd had a Valium, he would have slipped it to her.

Lucky for her, they'd apprehended a suspect almost immediately. Doctor Dylan Stockard, a friend of Mrs. Johnson's ex-fiancé, Cameron Collins.

Doctor Stockard was still being questioned by Detectives

Nicholls and Davis. The doctor's wife, Renée, had asked to use his telephone to call a lawyer. She appeared to be just as upset as Mrs. Johnson. He almost felt sorry for her, but then it was her husband who was being questioned in the disappearance of Ashley Rose Johnson. It could all be an act. He'd seen it before. It was entirely possible she was also in on the abduction. Time would tell. It always did.

Simmons was shaken from his thoughts when Susan Johnson and her friend entered the office. He immediately pushed a box of tissues to the edge of his desk.

"Thanks." Her nose was red from crying, her eyes almost swollen shut, her skin blotchy. The woman was no fake. She was shattered to the core of her very being.

"Are you all right?" he asked. She looked at him, her eyes glassy and blank. Of course she wasn't all right. Her daughter was missing. "I'm sorry. I do have a way with words." He offered up a wan smile. Tristan just stared at him.

"Detective, I want to know exactly what you're doing to find my daughter. Has that woman told you anything? Have you at least questioned her?" She pointed to Renée, who was standing outside in the hall waiting for her attorney to arrive.

Simmons cleared his throat. This was the part he hated. Everyone wanted instant gratification. Instant everything. "Mrs. Johnson, we are following procedure. We know how to do our job. It's just been a matter of a few hours, so keep that in mind. Disney executives have closed the park. Their security team, along with more than two dozen police officers, are searching for your daughter, Mrs. Johnson. No one will be allowed to leave the park without passing through security. We're searching every place humanly possible. We'll find her, Mrs. Johnson. I promise." What he didn't say was when they did find her, and they would, she might be dead. No, he would never say that aloud to a grieving parent.

"Where is your husband? Has he been contacted?" Simmons asked.

Susan looked at Tristan, her eyes widening. "My God, I didn't even think to call Richard! Tris, will you call him for me? Are you sure your kids are okay with Laura?"

"Be glad to. Don't worry about my kids, they're fine."

The fine hairs on the back of Detective Simmons's neck prickled at Susan's declaration. Not calling your husband when your child was abducted sent alarm bells ringing all over the place. Maybe this was more than a kidnapping. He sat up straighter in his chair, his eyes on Susan. "Mrs. Johnson, do you want to tell me why you haven't called your husband? Is he the child's father?"

"Of course Richard is my child's father. We're in the process of getting a divorce. Richard has never really been much of a father to Ashley. I simply didn't think about him. I was centered on Ashley." She blew her nose and reached across his desk for another tissue.

"And why is that, Mrs. Johnson?" Detective Simmons asked.

More tears flowed. As upset as she was, she knew she had to choose her words carefully. "Richard is not a nice person. Unfortunately, I didn't find that out until after we were married and I had become pregnant. He likes to hit women, and he has a rage in him that is frightening. I met him when he came to work for my father two and a half years ago. My father can tell you more if you need to know about his business background."

The fine hairs on the back of Detective Simmons's neck were still prickling. "You're his wife. I would think you would know more about your husband's background than your father."

"You would think so, wouldn't you? Richard isn't an easy man to get to know. He's very secretive." Her eyes filled with tears again. "Look, Detective, all I want is to find my daughter. I don't care if Richard falls off the face of the earth. Right now, I hate the man and I won't make a secret of it either. It might be best if he did fall off the face of the earth. It would be the biggest favor he could do for me. Do everyone a favor."

Simmons was starting to feel intrigued. There was always more to the story than met the eye. Especially in the beginning. His area of specialization. Reading between the lines. Getting down and dirty, straight to the nitty-gritty or the heart of the matter. Whatever you called it, this part of his first interview with the parents was always the most crucial. This was when they were raw and honest, before the lawyers appeared; after that, everyone had selective memory lapses out the kazoo.

"I take it the divorce isn't amicable?"

Susan shook her head. "Are they ever? I don't know, Detective. It's my first. Why do you care? What does this have to do with finding my daughter? You're wasting time! Shouldn't you be out there trying to locate her?"

"Ma'am, we're doing all we can do for the moment." Of course she couldn't or wouldn't understand that. All she could see was him sitting in front of her, asking questions she'd rather not deal with. "I need you to trust me." That was the key. Trust. Gaining the parents' trust only made his job easier. "Tell me about—" he looked down at the yellow legal pad he'd been scribbling notes on "—Richard."

Tristan came back in the office. "There's no answer. I tried Richard's apartment and the office."

She nodded, her eyes miserable. "I didn't think he'd be home today since we switched visitation days. He's probably playing golf or tennis with a client. Richard doesn't like to sit around. He's one of those people who has to be moving about."

Simmons jerked to attention. "Tell me about these visitation changes, Mrs. Johnson."

"Don't tell them anything, Susan!"

Susan turned around in her chair at the sound of the man's voice. "Dad! Thank God you're here. Mom, someone took Ashley," she wailed, as her mother wrapped her arms around her. "God, I'm so glad you came, too."

"Sir, I'm Detective Simmons. We spoke on the phone."

"Ashton Burke, my wife, Iris."

Simmons shook their hands. "Please, sit down." He motioned to two chairs placed next to where Susan and Tristan had been sitting.

While they situated themselves, Simmons took a moment to observe them. Both parents appeared to be in their mid- to late-sixties. They looked well cared for despite the woman's gardening attire. Even he, stupid man that he was when it came to women's fashions, knew she must have been working in the garden when the call came through. Her hands were manicured, showing no signs that she'd been in the dirt. Gloves, he thought. The father wore khakis, Docksiders without socks, and a denim shirt that was not tucked in. They had left their home in a hurry, not bothering with appearances. So far, so good. This was just the way he liked it. No one was trying to fool anyone.

"Detective, what are you doing to find my granddaughter?" Iris asked, her voice forceful and determined. "And why aren't *you* out there looking? Is this our tax dollars at work? You sitting here on your duff while some . . .

some madman absconded with Ashley!"

Absconded. He hadn't heard that one in a while. Still, they were running true to form. All those who came before her and had sat in the same chairs, said just what Mrs. Burke said.

"Iris, please." Ashton took her hand. "She's right, though, Detective. Tell me what happened. From the start. Then I want to know what's being done to locate Ashley Rose. If you don't have enough manpower, I'll bring more in. Tell me anything you need and it's yours."

"Thanks for the offer, Mr. Burke, but we're up to speed here. We really do know what we're doing. As I told your daughter, we have two dozen officers at the park and Disney's security team, which is massive. Remember that we're dealing with Disney. They don't want this kind of publicity. They'll help us in every way they can to locate your granddaughter, Mr. Burke. They're all at the park, scouring the grounds as we speak.

"As I understand it, your daughter, along with a group of friends, was inside a magic show at the Magic Kingdom. Let's see, there was your daughter, Susan Johnson, her friend Tristan, and three other couples who were seated a few rows ahead of them in the auditorium." He referred to his notes again. "Doctor Dylan Stockard and his wife were clearly engrossed in the program until Doctor Stockard left to use the men's room. About fifteen minutes later, your daughter checked on the baby, who was presumably sleeping in her stroller parked at the end of the row, and found that she was gone.

"The park is closed, no one is allowed in or out right now. This may take a few hours, Mr. Burke, but we will locate your granddaughter. You have my word on it."

"Then what can we do to assist you? There has to be

something we can do, other than sitting here. Please just tell me," Ashton pleaded. "We need to do something. Surely, you can't expect us to just sit around and . . . wait."

Simmons looked at his watch. It'd been a little more than three hours since the child was reported missing. Davis and Nicholls were still questioning Doctor Stockard. A feeling came to him out of nowhere. He knew instinctively, somehow, that they were not going to find Ashley Rose Johnson that day in the Magic Kingdom. He hoped he was wrong. The first four hours were extremely crucial. He'd just received some new stats on that the other day. Four lousy, stinking hours.

"Do any of you have a current picture of Ashley Rose with you?"

Ashton Burke reached in his hip pocket for his wallet. "My wife took this a few weeks ago when we were baby-sitting."

Susan bolted out of her chair at the sight of her daughter's picture. "Why do you need a picture? That man has her. All you have to do is find out where he took her. He was gone long enough to . . . to hand her to someone else. That person had time to leave the park, that's what I can't seem to make you all understand. Dylan was gone for almost twenty minutes before security found him returning to the auditorium! If you won't ask him, then ask his damn wife. She's the one who can't have a baby!" Susan shrilled before she collapsed against her mother.

"Who is Doctor Stockard, Susan? I've never heard you mention him," her father asked.

"He was a friend of Cam's. I met him in Europe. He was engaged to Renée then, but I never met her until the birthday party at Chuck E. Cheese a while ago. They were in Tristan's parenting class last year."

Tristan remained quiet, still in her chair, seeming to absorb all that was going on around her. She confirmed Susan's statement. "Yes, we were all in class together. I never thought . . . dear Lord, but I just can't imagine them doing something like this. They wanted to become parents more than anyone. They tried so hard, but then Renée learned that she would never be able to carry a baby to full term. I cannot believe they would resort to something this horrifying! People like the Stockards do not go around stealing children. They're decent people. I'm sorry, Susan, that's how I feel. I think you are all making a mistake if you just concentrate on them. The real person could be miles away by now. I do not think Dylan took Ashley Rose," she said adamantly.

"Back up, Tristan, and tell me about the class. Who was the instructor? Where was the class held? How many were in your group? And, more than anything, I want you to tell me about the Stockards' inability to conceive. If you know, that is."

Tristan jumped out of her chair. "I'm not a doctor, I don't know anything about their infertility troubles. What I do know is this, Officer, Detective . . . whatever. Sitting here on our asses trying to assess why Renée Stockard can't get knocked up should be the least of our worries. We have a nine-month-old baby out there, God only knows where, and you want to discuss their fertility problem." Tristan sat back down and hugged Susan. "I'm sorry. I think they had the wheels set in motion to adopt."

"It's okay, Tris. Detective Simmons, would it be possible for me to talk with Dylan?"

"I think I can arrange that." Then he noticed Seamus Clay Franklin sauntering down the hall and knew any chance Susan Johnson might have had to speak to the suspect had just gone right down the drain.

"You'll have to ask his attorney," Simmons amended, motioning to the hall.

Seamus Clay Franklin, Frankie to his friends, See-My-Ass to his enemies, who was sorely lacking in the former, notorious for the latter, gazed out the window of his battered Thunderbird and raked a hand through his nubby black hair.

He scrutinized Orlando's seedier side as he made his way downtown to the jail. Grass burgeoning from the cracks in the sidewalk. Homeless, both male and female, black and white, loitered on the streets. Buildings unfit for rats, let alone the families they sheltered, were spray painted hot pink along with profanity and obscene suggestions. Seamus shook his head. The tourists never got to see this side of Orlando. The only mice on this side of town were the rats gnawing their way into the homes of the unfortunate and the destitute.

This was a far cry from his family home in Mississippi. A far cry from the lucrative law firm he'd envisioned when he'd been fresh out of Ole Miss determined make a difference. He'd made a difference all right. Yesterday, another sick bastard had been freed simply because it was his job to provide his clients with the best defense possible.

Cal Burns had been charged with lewd and lascivious behavior. Seamus knew the truth. Cal had whipped his dick out and jerked off in front of a group of high school girls. Of the four girls, only one had been willing to testify. Tammy Lynn Monroe had been so scared and unsure of herself when he'd cross-examined her, Seamus knew the verdict even before the jurors were led out of the courtroom.

Not guilty.

What a crock of shit.

Now this. Another pervert had found his way into Disney's land of make-believe and abducted a child. The call from the doctor's wife had come through a little over an hour ago. He thought she said her name was Renée. She said he'd been recommended by one of the officers on duty. That meant he must be some needy son of a bitch. Lately, that's all his clients were. Needy and greedy.

His years at Ole Miss hadn't prepared him for the career he'd landed. He was going to make a difference. *Yeah, right, asshole.*

He recalled five years back when he'd brazenly offered his services, pro bono of course, to the first man in the state of Florida convicted of murder without the evidence of a body. Seamus had been only too happy to provide Bobby Leroy Talbot with a defense. Not only was he sure this would bring more clients his way, he was positive his client would be found innocent.

He'd had a rude awakening. Not only was Bobby Leroy Talbot found guilty, he'd been tried and sentenced, all within a matter of months. That was almost unheard of. Word had spread that he wasn't worth the powder to blow him to hell and back, or the chair and back, as was the joke. No, this isn't what he'd imagined his life would be when he'd been fresh out of law school.

A white man, a doctor no less, was being held downtown on charges of child abduction. Ashley Rose Johnson, granddaughter of one of Orlando's top dogs, Ashton Parker Burke III. The missing child, Ashley Rose, was the daughter of Richard and Susan Elizabeth Burke Johnson, labeled one of Orlando's most fashionable couples. Their union had been much publicized in the local papers. They'd even been featured in *Town and Country*.

Jesus. This could get interesting. He swerved the old T-Bird into his usual shitty parking space, three blocks away from the jail, honked at Henry, the parking attendant, and proceeded to go about his business of defending human rights.

Inside the police station, he waved at two officers, who were constantly sending clients his way. Then he stopped at the front desk. The buck stopped here, he always liked to think.

"Hey, Seamus, what brings you downtown on this fine Saturday afternoon?" a uniformed female officer asked.

"Now jus' what do you think, Miss Lisa? Could it be yore pretty face? Nah. Could it be some sick bastard wantin' to harm some little kid?" Seamus teased, nodding in the direction of the jail. "The doc's wife called. The one you all brought in a couple hours ago."

"That one," Lisa said. "He sure doesn't look like the type, but you know what they say."

"What's that, Missy Lisa?" Seamus asked, talking in his infamous Southern slang. He thought it fit the image some of his clients had of him.

"They're usually the ones who are guilty. Friendly, the neighborly type. I always like it when the reporters talk with a neighbor of one of these sickies. 'I couldn't believe Mr. So and So would do such a thing!' " she mimicked an imaginary person. "I always figured they weren't gonna go around advertising their peculiarities, if you know what I mean."

"That I do, Lisa, I certainly do. Now, if you'll let me know where they're holding this new client of mine, I'll be on my way," Seamus said, his tone suddenly serious and professional.

"He's still being questioned. Holding-cell two, I believe.

Davis and Nicholls are in there. They haven't had a break. Most likely they're ready to take one."

"Thanks, Lisa." Seamus saluted and walked down the hall. Seamus followed the familiar path to room two. He tapped on the door.

"Frankie! What brings you here?"

"A little of this, a little of that. Or, how about my new client in room two."

"We're about to take a break, here. You caught this one, huh?"

"Maybe. I don't know yet. I haven't even talked to him yet. Now you two boys go on and get yourselves some soda pop and a doughnut. I need to speak with Doctor Stockard."

"Seamus, you're so full of it, your eyes are brown. Give us a minute, okay?" Nicholls said when he poked his head out the door.

"One minute." He winked at Nicholls. They all played basketball together every Sunday at the rec center. They liked to tease him. He took it good-naturedly, but they knew when enough was enough. This was serious business for all. Seamus knew they were simply trying to make light of another revolting case. Child abduction was never nice.

Sixty seconds later, Detective Nicholls and Sergeant Davis departed, headed for Simmons's office. Davis stopped a minute. "I don't know about this one, Frankie. He's either one hell of a good liar, or he's just what he says he is. My personal opinion is the latter. Another poor guy at the wrong place at the wrong time. I'll let you draw your own conclusions." Sergeant Davis gave him a friendly slap on the back as he followed his partner down the hall.

Seamus paused in the doorway to observe the man seated at the plain, wooden table. Cigarettes, matches, and an ashtray lay next to a can of Diet Pepsi on the table. The cigarettes were untouched, the ashtray surprisingly clean, but the soda had been opened. Doctor Stockard must not be a smoker. He remembered he was a doctor. Probably health-conscious. Lisa was right. He didn't look like a pervert, but as she said, they never did. Something in the pit of his gut told him this case was not going to be one for the books.

"Doctor Stockard." Seamus stepped fully into the room. "Seamus Franklin. Your wife called me." He shook his hand.

"Thanks for coming. Maybe you can straighten this mess out. I can't believe anyone in their right mind would even suggest I have Ashley or had anything to do with her disappearance! My God, do you know that Renée and I would give anything in the world to have a child of our own?"

"I'm afraid so, Doctor Stockard, and that's what makes you such an interesting suspect, according to the police. Add in the fact that you disappeared from the auditorium for twenty minutes, then the child turns up missing during your . . . absence, and I'd say they have a good reason to question you. You want to tell me your side of the story?"

"I'll tell you the same thing I told the two detectives. I left the theater, went to the restroom, then went to the refreshment stand to get something to drink. There was a long line. Disney always has long lines at the refreshment stands. Hell, you can ask anyone who's ever been there, they'll tell you."

Dylan Stockard was upset and frightened. Seamus could see that. Now, the big question: Was he upset and frightened because he was afraid he'd been caught, or was he upset and frightened because he was being accused of something he had nothing to do with?

"That's what your wife told me when she called." Seamus took a legal pad and pen from his briefcase. He jotted down the date, the pen in his hand poised.

Most of his clients were guilty of the crimes they were accused of. Lewd and lascivious behavior. Drunk and disorderly. Exposing oneself to minors. Once in a blue moon he had a legitimate client. For the sake of Doctor Stockard's wife, who'd sounded so desperate when she'd called, he hoped like hell this man was one of the innocents.

"I usually have a standard list of questions I ask my clients, Doctor Stockard. However, I'm not sure they're suitable given your circumstances. So, I'm going to ask you one question to get started, and this will be the only time I ask you." He paused, more for effect than anything. This sometimes scared his clients, giving him the answers he needed in order to defend them properly.

"Ask anything, Mr. Franklin. I have nothing to hide. I'm innocent. I wish they'd let me out of this hellhole so I could help search for Susan's daughter." He palmed his forehead, and Seamus could feel the fear emanating from him. This guy was scared out of his wits. With good cause.

"Do you know where Ashley Rose Johnson is, and did you have anything to do with her disappearance?" Seamus demanded, his deep voice sounding unusually loud in the empty room.

Dylan shook his head from side to side. "No! For the hundredth time. I did not do anything . . . take, abduct, steal, that beautiful child. You've got to believe me. Why hasn't someone asked me to take a lie detector test? That would prove I'm telling the truth!"

Seamus wondered the same thing himself but didn't say

anything to his client. In due time.

"I'll see that it's arranged. Now, Doctor Stockard, tell me about you and your wife." Another pause. "Tell me just exactly what you *would* do to have a child?"

Chapter Twelve

Sweat rolled down Dylan Stockard's face. It was unbearably hot in the airless room. His eyes were wild and glazed over. "I sure as hell would never do what I'm being accused of! Listen, I want a child as much as any family man, but I'm not willing to kidnap someone else's kid in order to say I have a child. My wife and I are planning on adopting. We've already spoken with an agency. Several times as a matter of fact."

Seamus brightened at Dylan's words. "Can I confirm that with the agency?"

"Of course you can confirm it. The agency is in downtown Tampa. Renée has all the information, telephone number, address, the caseworker. The gentleman we're working with is David Houston. He'll confirm everything I've said." Dylan got up and paced the room, mopping at his sweaty face with the sleeve of his shirt.

"When can I see Renée?" Dylan asked. "She must be in a state of shock! Are you sure you want to represent me? I guess I should ask *if* you're willing to represent me. Are they going to arrest me?"

Seamus would of course represent him. He could always use the extra cash, and the case was beginning to intrigue him. It had been a long time since a case had appealed to his keen legal mind. "Yes, Doctor Stockard, I'll represent you when they arrest you. Make no mistake, they are going to arrest you."

Dylan sat down with a thump. "I have a feeling we're going to get to know each other quite well, so you can stop with the Doctor Stockard bit and call me Dylan."

"Of course. And I'm Seamus." The lawyer shuffled through his briefcase, looking for a consent form giving him permission to delve into Doctor Dylan Stockard's—Dylan's—past. He'd already discussed his fees with Mrs. Stockard. It hadn't been an issue. He briefly outlined the contents of the form and handed Dylan a pen.

He signed his name and shoved the paper to the side. "I still can't believe I'm here under these ugly circumstances. Tell me, Seamus, what can you do to get me out of here? Where do we start?"

"Once they formally arrest and charge you, I'll make a formal motion for bail. If everything works out, you could be out as early as next week."

"Next week! I'm a doctor, for God's sake! I've only been practicing in Orlando for a year! I have patients, rounds at the hospital! What am I supposed to tell them?" Dismayed at the news, Dylan shook his head and sat back down in the metal chair. Sweat continued to roll down his face. He mopped at it again.

"I would suggest finding a colleague to cover for you. Don't you doctors do that all the time? My doctor is always doing that. He takes more vacations than any man I know."

Seamus's voice was so affable, so cheerful-sounding, Dylan winced. "Yes, but that's for normal things. Like you said, mini-vacations, conventions. Those three-to-four-day things. Personally, I haven't heard of anyone having their practice covered because they're in jail. I can only imagine what the hospital administrator is going to say about this.

He isn't fond of me as it is."

"Aren't you a general practitioner? I would think you'd be able to get just about any doctor to cover for you."

For the first time since he'd been in jail Dylan's tone held a tinge of humor. "You'd better think again. With lawsuits the way they are today, believe me, no one wants to take over another doctor's turf. We don't want to make you lawyers any richer than you already are. And I'm a pediatrician."

"That's not the case here. That means I am not rich. Trust me. And besides, I'm not a personal injury lawyer. They're the ones who laugh all the way to the bank. Now, tell me, why does the administrator have it in for you?"

"After I completed my residency, I spent a couple years with some of my peers, and my best friend, doing volunteer work in Borneo, India, and Iran. It's tragic the way some of those people live. And die. I wanted to help, to make a difference, that's all. We all did. That's why we volunteered. We wanted to give back a little. For some reason, the hospital administrator resented that time in my life. I think he thought I was just another wealthy college brat spending daddy's inheritance while I played doctor to the natives or something like that. That's my personal opinion."

"Were you?" Seamus questioned.

"Hell no! We worked our butts off. I lived in a damn tent. No water; sanitary conditions were what you could find. The food . . . let's not even talk about that. We were there as medical professionals and nothing more. I felt it was my duty. Like I said, I wanted to give back. Seamus, my family may have a little more than most, but rest assured, my grandfather worked for every penny he ever earned. Real estate and construction. And my father, too. Both of them were hands-on and wore hard hats."

Seamus nodded as he scribbled something on his legal pad. "Okay. So you're not a spoiled rich kid. Tell me more about yourself, your past."

Dylan rolled his eyes. "What does my past have to do with this missing child? You just said there is only circumstantial evidence. I'm not a legal eagle by any means, but I know enough to know they've got to have something more if I'm to be arrested. What about security cameras, that sort of thing?"

Seamus pretended to think for a minute. In today's world with all the high-tech forensic science, not to mention the advances with DNA, it didn't take much to convict a man. One tiny fiber and boom. The rest was history.

"They're being viewed as we speak. I haven't read the reports yet. Now, I know you've gone over this with Nicholls and Davis, but I want you to write down everything you did once you entered the park. No matter how small or insignificant you might think it is. Write it all down. Some insignificant detail might tie in with something someone else says. I'm going to talk to Simmons, see what they have. If they're going to arrest you, it's best they do it while I'm present."

"Why?" Dylan asked.

Seamus laughed. "Trust me on this one, okay?" Seamus reached for the signed consent form. He slipped it back into his briefcase. "I'll be back. Meanwhile, don't say anything more than what you've said already. That means do not open your mouth even if you have to yawn."

"Sure. Seamus, what about my wife? Can I see her? I'll need to make some arrangements. You know, the hospital and all."

"I'll see what I can do." Seamus waved to his new client and left room number two. He strolled down the hall to Detective Simmons's office. They had a lot to discuss. He

213

tapped on the detective's door.

"I take it you're going to represent the doctor." Simmons motioned for him to come in.

"Yes. Only I'm not so sure if my client is the man or woman you're looking for."

"What's changed?" Simmons asked.

"I've talked with Doctor Stockard's wife."

Simmons jerked to attention. "You mean the family actually hired you?"

"Now, why is it I don't find that particularly funny?" Seamus asked, but wore a grin. "Yes, the doctor's wife called me. Tell me, Sims, do you have any hard evidence on him, other than him being in the wrong place at the wrong time?"

The detective sighed. "We still have officers searching the park. That could take all night. Disney is bending over backwards helping us. They don't want this leaked to the media. It could cost them millions. At the moment, I'm waiting for Davis and Nicholls to draw up a warrant. I think we have enough to arrest Doctor Stockard. Let a jury determine his guilt."

"You're serious about this, aren't you? Is it pressure, Sims, 'cause if it is, I gotta tell you, you're barking up the wrong tree. I'll call the media myself. I've talked with Doctor Stockard. He swears this is all a mistake. Coincidence, that's all it is. He and the wife are trying to adopt a child. He told me so. Gave me the name of the adoption agency, too. They're pillars of the community. You might want to tread a little lightly there."

"Frankie, that doesn't mean squat and you know it. What we have is a man, a doctor no less, telling you his side of the story. You should talk with the mother. Mothers know things, you know, intuition and all. Susan Johnson is sure this man knows what happened to her daughter."

"I'm sure she *thinks* she knows. She just lost her kid. I'd be grasping at anything I could if I were in her shoes, too. By the way, where are they?" Seamus wondered if they'd been questioned as thoroughly as his client.

"They're talking with Nicholls and Davis in the front office. The park just called. They think they've found something. I'm waiting to hear more myself. I hate it when you call me Sims, Frankie."

Seamus ignored him. "Good. Maybe then you'll know whether you're going to arrest my client. You know, Sims, you can't keep him much longer. Either you make an arrest right about now, or let him go. No one calls me Frankie but you and your buddies, *Sims*."

Simmons's telephone rang. "Yes. I see. He's still here. Of course, we'll do it right away." He put the phone down and looked at Seamus. "I'm afraid your client's luck just ran out. They found the clothes the Johnson baby was wearing stuffed inside a disposal unit in one of the bathrooms at the park. Apparently it's from the same restroom that Stockard used."

Seamus shook his head. "That isn't enough and you know it. Anyone could have stashed the baby's clothes there. Tell me there's something more, because if not, I'm going to insist that you release my client."

"There is. We searched his vehicle. There's a pacifier. A pink one, with a cord and clip attached to it. We're waiting for an officer to bring it in. If the mother can identify this, your client's in a heap of doo-doo, Frankie."

Resigned to spending the rest of Saturday at the jail, Seamus replied, "I'll want him to take a lie detector test."

"As soon as it can be arranged."

Commotion from the hall made both men turn to look

at what was going on.

"That belongs to Ashley! I wondered what happened to it! Where did this come from?" Susan cried, excitement ringing in her voice. "Did you find her? Well, did you?"

Simmons and Seamus walked out into the hall. "What's going on? Are you all right, Mrs. Johnson?" Simmons asked.

Susan Johnson stood in the middle of the bleak hallway, shaking from head to toe. Her parents were at her side. Sobs ripped from her throat before she fell into her father's arms.

Simmons hated this part of the job.

"I'm ready to go home, Dad. I want to get out of here."

Ashton Burke nodded as he whispered something to his wife. The two women walked down the hall. Ashton Burke stayed behind. "Detective, can we talk for a minute?"

"Sure, Mr. Burke. In my office." He opened the door. "Seamus, I'll catch you later?"

Seamus simply nodded and headed toward the front offices. It would be a long night for Seamus and his client. A very long night.

Ashton didn't bother with pleasantries this time. "Has anyone thought about a ransom? Aren't you supposed to call the FBI when something like this happens?"

Here we go, Simmons thought. *J. Q. Public telling me how to do my job. It never fails. Hell, I could write a book.* "Yes, we've got that covered, Mr. Burke. Davis and Nicholls alerted them earlier. They're aware of the situation. When and if it comes to that, and I don't think it will, they'll be contacted and told to stand by."

"That's it? What am I supposed to tell my daughter? She's not going to hold up much longer. She's stressed to the max. So is my wife. I'm not doing so well myself in case you're interested."

"I can only imagine, Mr. Burke, but we are very serious about the suspect we have in custody now. Your daughter's identification of the child's pacifier will only cement the charges. We'll run this to the lab for DNA analysis. That's going to take a while even if we put a rush on it."

"Then do it. Do whatever it takes to get my granddaughter back!" Ashton shouted. "I'm sorry, I didn't mean to raise my voice. I know you know what you're doing. I just feel so damn helpless. This isn't supposed to happen, is it?"

Simmons perched on the edge of his desk. "No, Mr. Burke, it's not supposed to happen, but it does. Sadly, there are some sick bastards out there. It's our job to find them and put them away. That's what we're trying to do. It may appear that we're all just a bunch of coffee-drinking, middle-aged doughnut eaters, but we're not. We all have children, or nieces and nephews. Each case is personal. We want to find your granddaughter as much as you want her found. Has anyone located the father yet?"

"As far as I know, Susan hasn't reached him. She told me her friend Tristan tried several times and wasn't able to reach him. It's Saturday afternoon. Men like Richard are either playing golf or tennis, or out spending money. You might be able to find him at Coral Point Country Club. He's been a member since he married Susan. He used to spend his Saturday afternoons there."

Men like Richard. What have we here? he wondered. Simmons noted the name of the country club. It was Orlando's most exclusive club. In a million years he wouldn't be able to earn enough money to join. The Burkes were well-off, he knew. Maybe more so than he'd originally thought. He called Lisa at the front desk and asked her to put him through to one of the detectives out in the field. "Lowell, I need you to check out the Coral Point Country Club. Richard Johnson, the child's father, is a member. See if he's there. If he is, bring him in." He hung up. "They are going to send someone over there now. I take it your son-in-law isn't the most popular member of your little family?"

Ashton dropped onto a chair. "You don't know the half of it."

"That's true. Why don't you tell me why there is such discord where he's concerned."

Ashton knew he'd have to talk about Richard sooner or later, he just wished it was later. He sighed. Whatever it took to bring Ashley Rose home, he'd do, no matter what the consequences. "It didn't start out that way. He's a genius. I hired him about thirty months ago. Burke and Burke was in serious financial trouble. I'd made a hefty mistake with one of my subcontractors, who used some faulty cement. It almost cost me my business, and it would have if I hadn't had Richard working for me. He's brought more business to the company in the past year than I did on my own in the last three. I don't like the man because of what he's done to my family, but he is one hell of an architect, I'll give him that.

"My daughter's marriage started going downhill when she got pregnant. Susan is closer to her mother than she is to me. My wife told me Susan said Richard hit her. More than once. I suppose she'd had enough, and the marriage broke up. Richard has a new apartment, a leased Porsche, and a pocketful of money. I'm in the process of terminating his employment. Legally. When I hired him, I didn't think it would ever get to the point it's at now, so I gave him an ironclad contract that's going to be hell for me to get out of. I'm waiting for a hearing on that as we speak."

"So, not only did this guy take your business right out from under your feet, he took your daughter, too. Tell me something, Mr. Burke."

"Anything."

"Would this man attempt to kidnap his daughter?"

Ashton shook his head. "Hell no! He doesn't even want to take care of the child. I think Susan told me once he'd never changed a diaper. No, he wouldn't have any reason to do something like that. Personally, I don't think he likes being a father. Not good for his image, if you get my drift. He's a bit of a ladies' man. I didn't know that either until just recently."

"All right. I just wanted your opinion, Mr. Burke. Your daughter said pretty much the same thing. We'll have to talk with him as soon as we locate him."

"He'll talk with you. He's slick, so be prepared. It's my personal opinion that Richard Johnson is a dangerous man."

"Burke, why is it I'm getting the feeling there's more to this son-in-law story than you're telling me?"

"I haven't a clue, Detective Simmons. Your guess is as good as mine."

Susan curled herself into the fetal position. In a matter of hours, her world had shattered into a million pieces. How was she going to go on without her daughter?

She wanted to die.

A knock sounded at the door.

"Susan?" Her mother's voice was hushed.

"Come in, Mom." Her throat was dry. It hurt to talk and swallow, and her head felt like it was going to explode right off her neck. "Is there any news? Has Dad called yet?" She sat up in bed.

"I'm sorry, dear, but there's no news yet. I called the station, but your father had already left. Here, I want you to drink this. It's just hot tea with a little brandy. Drink it. It will help you to relax."

Susan took the cup and sipped at the hot liquid. The day was a living nightmare. How could there be no news? Hours had gone by. If something didn't happen soon, she was going to lose it; she was barely holding it together as it was.

Ashley was gone. Ashley was hurt. Ashley . . . no! She couldn't think that way. She had to think positive thoughts. A positive attitude would see her through the crisis. Her baby was alive. Someone had her, that's all. Maybe Dylan took her to a family that loved children. Maybe Renée knew her whereabouts and would confess under pressure. Maybe . . . no! God, she had to get a hold of herself. She took a deep breath and then another. She continued to sip the tea. She'd talk to her mother. That's it. Then when her father came home everything would be like it used to be when she was a little girl. Jemma could make ice cream. It'd be like old times. Everything was going to work out. They'd find Ashley any minute now. Then they would really have something to celebrate. Pineapple ice cream with two cherries on top. Jemma would serve it in one of the little crystal dishes that had a stem on it.

"Nooo!" When the scream came, it came from the depths of her soul. Savage. Primal. "Please, God, let them find my baby." She rocked back and forth on her mother's bed, seeing the fear in her mother's eyes, knowing she was afraid for her, yet not caring about anything except the missing child that had become her life.

"Susan, I'm going to call Doctor Watts. I'll ask her to make a house call. Would you like that, dear?" Iris sat on the bed next to her daughter.

Rage, unlike anything she ever experienced, rivered through Iris. She closed her eyes and knew her rage was directed, not at the circumstances but at the man her daughter had married. *Hate* was too weak a word to describe what she felt for Richard Johnson. She knew in that moment, she could and would kill the man if the opportunity presented itself.

"No, Mom. I don't want a doctor. I have to be awake so I can deal with this. I just want them to find her!" Susan started to shiver. Her teeth chattered, and the cup and saucer in her hand clattered. "I'm so cold."

"Here, let me help you." Iris took the cup from her daughter's hand and pulled the down comforter back. "Get under the covers, Susan. Jemma!" Iris called at the top of her lungs.

"I'm on my way!" Jemma hurried as fast as her old bones would let her to the master suite upstairs.

"Try and keep her warm. I'm calling the doctor. I think she's going into shock." She found Doctor Watts's number on one of her business cards in her purse. Her hands trembled as she dialed the emergency number.

"Hello, Doctor Emily Watts here."

"Emily, it's Iris Burke. I've got . . . it's Susan. She needs your help. I think she's going into shock. I'm not exactly sure what shock is, but she can't get warm, she's screaming, and her eyes are glazing over. Someone abducted her daughter this afternoon while they were visiting the Magic Kingdom. Can you please come to my house? Susan is staying with us." Turnabout was only fair. Her daughter had taken care of her in her time of need, and now it was her turn to do the same.

"Give me your address, Iris."

Iris gave her the address.

"I'm fifteen minutes away."

Iris hung up the phone. She struggled to take a deep breath and then another. When she felt calmer, she headed for the stairs that would take her to her daughter.

To her mother's eyes, Susan suddenly looked like a child herself. Snuggled beneath the covers, she looked frail and weak. Iris felt her heart lurch. God, this was her daughter. She'd die for her if she had to. She could only imagine what she was feeling about Ashley Rose.

As she sat staring at her daughter, she felt her mind drift. She hadn't been the best mother in the world. She wanted to be, but things in her life had gone awry. She had so many regrets about that period in her life. Her shoulders straightened imperceptibly. That was then, this was now. She wasn't that drugged-up woman any longer. Today, thanks to her daughter, she had her wits about her and a wonderful, healthy life.

"She's dozed off for a minute. She keeps mumbling something." Jemma tucked the blankets under Susan's chin. "I can't believe someone took this child's baby. Lordy, Lord, what is this world coming to? I don't know, Iris. I just don't know." Jemma sat on the edge of the bed. It was then that Iris realized her dear friend and housekeeper was old. Too old to keep working. Why hadn't she noticed it before? Because Maximus had kept her drugged, that's why. By God, she was going to find a way to make him pay for what he did to her. It was time for Jemma to have a life of leisure. Ashton would agree. It was their turn to wait on her hand and foot. She'd do it cheerfully, happily. She knew her husband would, too.

The downstairs doorbell rang.

"I'll get it," Jemma said.

"No, stay right there, Jemma. Your stair-climbing days

are over. I'm going to install an elevator for you."

Iris went out into the hall and leaned over the balcony. "Emily, come in. We're up here," she shouted.

The front door opened. "Iris, what happened?" Doctor Watts raced up the winding staircase.

"Susan and a group of friends were at the Magic Kingdom today. They were in one of the magic shows, and someone took Ashley Rose right out of her stroller. That was hours ago, and she hasn't been found. The police are searching for her, the park's security team is looking for her. Ashton is . . . I don't know where he is, but Susan is losing it. She's been trying to hold herself together all day. She just can't take any more. If you could give her something, maybe to sleep. Then when she wakes up, Ashley will have been found. I don't know if that's wishful thinking on my part or not. By tomorrow, the press will be here. It will turn into a circus."

Doctor Watts placed an arm around Iris's shoulders. "Let me take a look at her. Wait in the hall. I'll call you when it's time to come in."

"She's not very coherent right now. She needs some sleep. Please, you will help her, won't you?"

The doctor nodded.

Ten minutes later, Jemma and Iris, their steps quiet, entered the room. Iris gave the doctor a questioning look.

"This is Ativan. It will help her sleep and keep her calm when she wakes up."

The two women watched as the doctor rubbed an alcohol pad across Susan's upper arm. She tapped the end of the needle before plunging it into Susan's arm.

"What . . . stings," Susan muttered.

"Shhh, it's nothing, Susan, just a little something to relax you," Emily Watts said in a soothing voice.

Doctor Watts turned to the two women. "She'll sleep for most of the night. I have a suggestion. What do you think about having Susan transferred to The Willows? She'll get twenty-four-hour care. If you're right, and it is going to be a media circus by morning, all the more reason to get her out of here. I'm sure you know The Willows is very private, very exclusive, very costly. You might want to weigh all that before you make your decision, Iris. I recommend it. The decision, of course, is up to you."

"I don't know. I'd hate to lock my daughter up because she's upset. She'd never forgive me. I remember only too well what that feeling was like."

"The Willows is not a lockdown facility, Iris. Privacy is what you need for Susan right now, and The Willows will give you that privacy. It's just till she gets a grip on the situation. A day or two of complete rest can only help her. No harm will come to her at The Willows."

"I'll talk to my husband about it as soon as he gets home."

Susan bolted upright in the bed and let out a bloodcurdling scream. "Nooo!"

Iris shivered as she clutched at Jemma's arm. "On second thought, I'm her mother and I can make that decision. Yes, yes, let's get her to where she can be cared for. I'm sure, if my husband was here right now, he would agree with me." Her shoulders squared. Her first momentous decision in far too many years. In her heart, she knew it was the right one.

"You've made a wise decision, Iris. Susan does not need to wake up to the media dogging her tomorrow morning. Sometimes those reporters are like ghouls. They want every gory detail, and Susan is too fragile at the moment to force her to deal with something like that. Two days, three at the most, maybe just overnight. Who knows? When she wakes she might be ready to bear the media. If you're sure, I'll make the arrangements right now."

Iris nodded. Susan wasn't going to like being carted off to a private hospital. But if she was as fragile as Doctor Watts thought she was, it was what she needed. In the meantime, she and Ashton could do whatever Susan herself would do. She knew it wouldn't take much convincing to get Ashton to hire the best team of detectives in the state if he hadn't already done it.

"I called the hospital. They're sending an ambulance over. I'll follow them."

Iris felt the tears build, then flood her eyes. "I think this is the worst day of my life. I know for certain it's Susan's worst day."

"Look how far you've come, Iris. When this is all over, I'm going to remind you of this day and how you took charge. I am so proud of you. Now, let's get a bag packed for Susan. No one wants to wake up in one of those old scratchy hospital gowns."

"Jemma, will you help me find something? Do you know where those old pajamas of Ashton's are, the ones with the frayed edges? Susan used to sleep in them when she came home from college. She dearly loves those pajamas."

"I know just where to find them," Jemma responded. On a top shelf in Ashton's closet were the pajamas she was looking for. "I think Susan still has some underclothes here, too. She left shorts and tee shirts a while back. You know how Ashley was always dribbling and throwing up over her. She just showed up one afternoon with a whole duffel bag of clothes for herself and Ashley."

"I hear the ambulance, Emily. They just turned into the driveway. Jemma and I will follow you to the hospital. I just need to leave a note for my husband." She looked over at Jemma. "We need to take the cell phone with us." The old housekeeper trotted off to fetch it.

Iris scribbled off a terse note, telling her husband to call her on the cell phone. The day was only getting worse with each hour, Iris thought as she took the keys to her old Volvo from the hook on the back of the kitchen door. She hadn't been behind the wheel of a car in *years*. One look at Jemma's frightened face told her the housekeeper knew it too.

Sunlight filtered in through a single window, casting the room in a golden blanket of warmth. Footsteps muffled by rubber soles made their way around the bed as if leery of what lay beneath the starched sheets.

The figure moved. A sound, almost like a kitten's mew, came from the bed.

The footsteps paused but only for a second.

More curious than careful, gentle hands tugged at the sheet and moved it aside.

The nurse looked down at the still form in the bed. She was used to the rich patients who came here to hide or to lick their wounds. Often times, to dry out in the privacy of The Willows.

Her movements were brisk, professional as she wrapped a blood pressure cuff around the woman's thin arm and proceeded to pump the attached bulb.

Faded blue eyes glanced down at a white, plastic wristwatch. She tugged the cuff free and rolled it back up. Without a second glance at her patient, Mona Embry jotted numbers onto a chart before she hung the metal clipboard at the foot of the bed.

Sometimes she didn't like the patients she was saddled

with. But she never let her dislike interfere with her job. The well-to-do patient that visited the clinic with a hangnail or when a hair was out of place, or as must be the case with her present patient, the good life just seemed to be more than they could handle. They took a handful of pills, hoping their so-called agony would come to an end. Usually it didn't end.

She looked at the woman and felt a momentary pang of guilt for her thoughts. When Doctor Watts admitted her last night she'd explained about her missing daughter. Mona was glad she'd never had children. As hard and jaded as she was, she couldn't imagine what it would be like to lose a child.

In a rare moment of kindness, she reached up and touched the woman's pale forehead, pushing back a limp strand of hair. She *was* different from the others. Her skin didn't have the usual, I've-just-had-a-facial glow, nor were her nails manicured to perfection. Instead, Mona saw pale skin, dark circles beneath her eyes and nails that had been chewed down to the quick.

The soft whir of the door opening made her turn around. Doctor D'Angelo entered the room. "How is she, Mona? Doctor Watts asked me to cover for her this morning."

Mona cleared her throat and thrust her shoulders back. "Her vitals are normal. She's still groggy from the Ativan."

Doctor D'Angelo's name fit him perfectly. Tall, ebony hair a shade too long and eyes as clear as the morning sky winked at her. He looked angelic, almost dreamlike. He took the metal clipboard and perused the chart. Closing it, he looked up at the nurse and winked a second time. She blushed. The doctor was a noted flirt, but otherwise an excellent physician.

"As always Mona, I value your opinion. So what gives?"

He nodded at the patient in the bed.

Mona met the doctor's questioning stare. For a moment, she felt uncomfortable with his familiarity. She busied herself tucking the sheet more snugly around her patient. "She's been very restless. A few times I thought she was trying to tell me something. Mostly it was just mumbling. If she was trying to tell me something, I didn't understand what it was she wanted to say."

"That's a good sign. I'm glad she's coming around because she has a visitor."

"I didn't say she was ready to run a marathon. Doctor Watts said no visitors except her parents."

The doctor smiled at her attempt at humor. "Right now, her husband wants to see her. I can't think of a legitimate reason to keep him waiting any longer, can you? Are you sure Doctor Watts said parents only?"

Mona bristled. "There's nothing wrong with my hearing, Doctor." It was a guy thing. Husband, guy. One guy making things happen for the other guy. She could turn that around right now to a girl thing. "Oh, yes, I'm sure."

A soft moan came from the figure in the bed. Mona moved to Susan's side. "I told you she was trying to tell me something. Maybe you can make out the words, Doctor. It's obvious Mrs. Johnson is upset about something. Now why would she be upset? She's just now coming fully awake. Unless, of course, she heard us talking."

Doctor D'Angelo stood on the opposite side of the bed. Taking his penlight out of his shirt pocket, he gently lifted an eyelid and shined the light in his patient's eye. After he examined both eyes, he placed the penlight back in his pocket, apparently satisfied with the results.

"Her pupils are no longer dilated. She's coming right along. She needs plenty of bed rest; and we'll have her out of here later today, if she wants to leave. Doctor Watts has prescribed some Valium for her to take while she is going through this ordeal."

Another groan came from the woman in the bed. Mona leaned over her patient. "What is it, honey?"

Sticklike fingers clawed at the nurse's wrist. "Please. My daughter. Help me, please." It was all Mona needed to hear. Someone needed her help. That's why she had gone to nursing school and continued to work at her profession. She couldn't remember the last time she'd heard such despair in a human voice.

Susan's first thought when she opened her eyes was she'd finally encountered that warm, bright, welcoming light she'd heard about so often. She blinked, then blinked again. The warm welcoming light she saw was sunlight streaming in through a window.

Unfamiliar with her surroundings, the panic she'd become accustomed to in the past twenty-four hours drenched her like a monsoon. She could feel her heart rate increase. Her mouth, already dry, became even drier. Her palms dampened with sweat.

A sudden movement captured her attention. Through slitted eyes, Susan viewed a heavyset woman writing on a chart. She licked at her dry lips. Water. She needed something to drink. Her mouth was as dry as an empty well.

"Drink." Sure the woman hadn't heard her, Susan closed her eyes. She tried to open them again and couldn't. She felt like weights were forcing them shut. She lost the struggle to stay awake and gave in to the battle.

Seconds, minutes, or it might have been hours later, Susan felt cool liquid drizzle across her lips and down her throat. She tried to smile.

229

"Shhh. Just relax. Let me help you."

A hand reached behind her and plumped her pillow. A mechanical sound let her know her bed had been raised to an upright position. She opened her eyes. The room was a blur. She blinked and tried to focus on something that didn't move.

In the upper left corner of the room she spotted a square black box. She concentrated on that. It must be a television. She remembered then. Her heart fluttered in her chest as she gasped for air. Her fingertips went numb. "No! Stop, please!"

"Slow and easy, little lady, you're going to be just fine. I'm here. Shhh, it's all right."

She was in a hospital. It smelled like a hospital. Something rustled and squeaked. A nurse's starched uniform, rubber soles and heels always squeaked.

Susan tried to raise her arm to point at the television set.

"I see. You want to watch some TV. Wouldn't mind catching up on the news myself. Seems all I do is work, eat, and sleep. I'm so tired at night, watching the tube is the last thing on my mind."

Susan observed the nurse as she searched for the remote control. Shaking her head from side to side, she again clutched the nurse's arm. "No!"

"Well, I haven't got it turned on yet! Give me a minute."

A loud knock, followed by an angry male voice interrupted her. "Is she ready? How much longer is this going to take? It's not like I have all damn day. Could we move on this already?"

Richard! Her heart started to race as her forehead broke out in perspiration.

The nurse stopped in her tracks. Susan jerked her head toward the door. Weak and frightened, it was all she could do to whisper the words, "Please, don't let him in."

The nurse nodded as she moved toward the door. Susan heard hushed whispers, then saw the door close.

She almost fainted with relief. "Thank you."

The nurse wore a name tag that said her name was Mona. She pulled a chair up beside her bed and reached for Susan's hand. "Do you want to tell me what this is all about? I have all the time in the world and I'm a good listener."

"It's Richard, my husband. Someone took our daughter. He . . ." Tears rolled down Susan's cheeks.

Mona Embry's heart started to ache for the young mother.

Susan chewed on her dry, chapped, lower lip, as she eyed the door a second time and motioned for the nurse to pull her chair closer to her bed.

"What is it, Susan? Don't be afraid, he's gone."

"Can you make sure? He . . . he doesn't give up. Don't trust him."

Mona peered out the door, her head turned left, then right.

"He's nowhere to be seen," Mona said, sitting back down at the side of the bed.

Susan nodded as she struggled to sit up in bed. "Promise me you won't go to him?"

Mona gave a puzzled laugh. "Why would I do that? You're going to be released this afternoon. The way I look at it is this, if your husband wants to see you, let him visit you at home. The Willows is off-limits to visitors where you're concerned."

Her instincts to trust Mona had been right. "Thank you. If he comes back, tell him I can't have visitors. Don't explain. When you explain anything at all to Richard, he takes that to mean you're willing to debate." Susan fumbled with the blanket, twisting the end into a tight knot. She wondered if she was losing her mind.

My daughter has been ripped away from me. The man who is my husband is standing on the other side of the door, a man I despise. Is this going to be my life from here on in? If this is all I'm going to get, I might as well close my eyes and never open them again.

Chapter Thirteen

Sunday, 11:14 a.m.

Doctor Tony D'Angelo looked at the blustering man standing in front of him. This was one dude he'd never want to meet in a dark alley or anyplace else for that matter. He felt sorry for the patient in the room behind him. No wonder she didn't want to see this man. He hoped he wasn't going to have to call Security.

"Listen, *Doctor,* I want you to tell my wife I need to know what the hell is going on. Last night when I got home the police were at my apartment! I want to know what she did with my daughter, and I damn well want to know *now.* What part of that don't you understand?"

"The part where I should care what you think. First of all, Mr. Johnson, your wife is not my patient. She's Doctor Watts's patient. I'm merely making rounds. Doctor Watts left orders that your wife was not to have visitors. If you have a complaint, I suggest you take it up with your wife's doctor. Now, if you'll excuse me."

"You're excused. I'm not going anywhere, so you might as well tell her that, too. I'll camp out here if I have to."

The young doctor slipped inside the room, careful not to let Mr. Johnson see inside. His patient was sitting up in the bed sipping a glass of ice water. "Mrs. Johnson? Your husband insists on speaking to you. He's outside waiting. He said he would camp out there if necessary."

Susan looked to Mona. "I guess I might as well get this over with. Send him in, but I'd like you to stay in the room with me if you don't mind."

"Are you sure, Mrs. Burke? You don't have to see anyone you don't want to see. Would you like to freshen up?"

Susan shook her head. "No, just give me a minute. I need to think. My head still feels fuzzy." Her voice was hoarse; her throat felt like she'd swallowed a bucket of rocks. Maybe Richard had news of Ashley! She knew that wasn't the case, but until she heard him say no, he didn't know where she was, she could still hope. "Send him in now."

Mona opened the door. "Mr. Johnson, your wife will see you." She stepped aside to allow Richard to enter the room. She planted her feet firmly on the tile floor, her arms crossed over her bosom. She looked like a ferocious bulldog.

Their daughter's disappearance certainly hadn't affected her soon-to-be-ex-husband's grooming. He was his usual immaculate self, dressed to the nines. "I guess the police notified you. Do you have any . . . ?"

Richard strolled over to the side of her bed. "Yes, I heard Susan." He laughed as he stuffed his hands in his pockets before he assumed a stance of nonchalance. "Surely you don't expect me to believe this cockamamie story? I know what your father is capable of. This is just another one of his ploys. I thought the old man was smarter than that. I knew you were stupid, Susan. Do you really think you can pull this off? A judge isn't going to view this too kindly. All you're doing is trying to keep me from seeing my daughter? If that's your game, I don't think it's the least bit humorous. Actually, it's sick. You're a loony tune like your mother. The police spent an hour questioning me on my whereabouts last night. I wasn't pleased. I'm not pleased now either. Just so you know."

Susan's head whirled sickeningly. "You really believe this is all about *you?* My God, I'm in the hospital and you think this is a joke! You need to spend a night in here!" She tossed the covers aside, saw that someone had dressed her in her father's old pajamas and her feet were covered with beige hospital-issued booties. This was a dream. No, it was a nightmare. She actually pinched herself. She felt the pain. No, this was real.

"What's wrong with you?" Richard insisted. He reached for her hand and practically yanked her from the bed. "Get up, dammit!"

Before Susan's heart could beat twice, Mona Embry had a chokehold on Richard's neck as she bellowed at the top of her lungs. *"SECURITY!"*

"All right, all right!" Richard said. Mona loosened her hold and Richard stepped away from the bed. "I'm Ashley's father. All I want is for you to tell me right now what is going on! This . . . this place, isn't this just a cover-up? Isn't it? Damn you, Susan, answer me."

Nothing around her moved. Even the air she was breathing seemed to stop flowing. "Get out! How dare you suggest such a thing. You sick son of a bitch, do you really believe I would stage such a thing? You're crazier than I thought you were! Get out, Richard, before I—"

"Before you what? Call Daddy? Daddy can't help you this time." He turned to leave just as two burly security guards rushed into the room. "Easy does it, gentlemen, I was just leaving."

"Richard, Ashley is missing. She was taken from her stroller yesterday at the Magic Kingdom. If I find out you had anything to do with it, I will kill you. You do understand that, don't you? I will personally blow your fucking brains out! Me, no one else. Look, I even said it in front of a witness!"

Richard stopped at the door and turned around. "Susan, calm down. Who in their right mind would take Ashley? My God, she isn't even a regular kid yet!"

Susan's mouth fell open. "You bastard! Get out now before I call the police. Don't come near me again, Richard. One phone call, one anything, and I'll call the police and have you locked up. You do remember that restraining order, don't you?"

"Whatever. Let me know when you decide to bring Ashley home. You're in violation of a court order yourself. Another visit gone. I'm keeping a record."

She was a robot as she slipped out of bed and tottered over to the closet for her clothes. She reached for them with arms that were like limp spaghetti. It took her twenty minutes to pull on her underwear, shorts, and tee shirt.

"The man really is insane. I have to get out of here and find Ashley Rose before he does. I can't trust him." She was talking to herself. She had to get out of that place, fast.

Was it only twenty-four hours since she'd dressed herself and Ashley for their big day at Disney? Ashley in her little pink Guess shorts and tiny tee shirt had looked adorable. Hot tears pricked at her eyelids. Susan knuckled her eyes. Somehow, some way, she was going to find her.

Susan almost jumped out of her skin when she walked out of the bathroom. He was back.

"Susan, I'm only going to ask you this one more time. What are you and your father up to? You're really starting to piss me off, and you know what I can do when I'm pissed off."

Susan bolted out of the bathroom. "Yes, you coward. I know what you do. You hit women." She screamed then, the sound coming from the depths of her soul. Suddenly her room was full of people and Richard was dragged out and down the hall.

"You'll be hearing from my attorney," Richard blustered as he was literally lifted off his feet by no fewer than four security guards.

Mona walked over to her. "Are you all right, Mrs. Johnson?"

"No, but thanks for asking. I just need to get downtown to the police station; and I need to call my family to let them know where I'm going. Is there a phone I can use?"

"Right this way." Mona opened the heavy door and waited for Susan to get her bearings. "You okay?" she asked again. "I'm not sure you should be leaving here, but I certainly understand you wanting to go home. Doctor Watts said you could leave anytime you felt up to it."

Susan nodded. She felt light-headed. She knew the feeling would pass when the drugs in her system started to lose their efficacy. She'd be wise to take advantage of her semi-calm state before the drugs totally wore off.

Susan followed Mona to the nurses' station. "Use this phone in here so you can have some privacy." Mona motioned to a small office just behind the nurses' station. Inside were a desk, two chairs, and a telephone.

"I'll just be a minute." The nurse left her alone. She dialed her parents' house. Her mother answered on the first ring. "Mom, any news?" She held her breath as she offered up a silent prayer.

"Susan! No, dear, there's no news. Are you all right? I

thought it best to get you away from here, even if it was for just a little while. Do you feel at all rested?"

"I'm rested. I'm headed to the police station. If Dad's there, I'd like to talk to him."

"Hold on! Let me see where he is."

Susan heard her mother calling her father. He came on the line a minute later.

"You okay, Susan? I was just going to stop by and see you. I was about ready to go back to the police station."

"No, Dad, I am not okay and I won't be okay until I find my daughter. Come and get me. Don't even think about trying to talk me into staying here. I'll be waiting out front."

Susan checked herself out of the hospital. Forty minutes later her father drove up. "Any news yet?" she asked her father as he pulled away from the circular drive.

"Nothing. I called Detective Simmons. He knows we're on our way. Apparently they questioned Richard last night. Richard thought it was all a setup. I guess he got a little abusive and the officers had to threaten him. Simmons thinks he's crazy. As far as an alibi goes, he said he was working out at home, then went to the club."

"He's right, he is crazy. He came to the hospital this morning. He accused me and you of orchestrating this entire thing so he wouldn't be able to visit Ashley. The man is insane. Why did I get mixed up with him? Why?" Susan struggled to fight the tears that were threatening to overflow. It was almost twenty-four hours since her daughter had been reported missing. So many things could happen in twenty-four hours. Especially to little baby girls.

"Damn! I want to kill them! Whoever is responsible for this, I will kill them. I—"

"Susan, I know. I feel the same way, but we both have to

stop thinking like that. We'll find the person responsible for this. I promise. You will get Ashley back. I want you to believe that."

Susan nodded. What good were promises? Promises were nothing but words. She'd had her fill of promises. All she wanted was to see her daughter's chubby little face and those bright blue eyes.

Ashton parked the Navigator. He held his daughter's arm as he led her into the station. It looked exactly the same way it had looked yesterday. "Detective Simmons is expecting us." The desk clerk nodded and motioned for them to enter the detective's office.

Detective Simmons still wore the same clothes he'd had on the previous day. Susan was thankful he was so dedicated to finding her daughter.

"You all have a seat. I'll be just a minute. There's coffee and doughnuts if you want." He pointed to a counter behind him where a full coffeepot and a box of fresh doughnuts sat.

"Here, have some. It'll perk you up. You look pale."

Susan took a cup of hot coffee from her father and sipped. It tasted fresh. "Mmm, this is good. That medication they gave me was terrible. Whatever it was, I don't want it again. I felt like a zombie all night long. I can't believe I actually slept while my baby is out there . . ."

"They'll find her. Here comes Detective Simmons now."

Susan blotted her eyes with a tissue from the detective's desk and sat down. Nausea overwhelmed her. She looked for a restroom; not seeing one, she reached for the brown metal trash can, where she threw up. "Damn!"

"The ladies' room is down the hall, second door on your right." After Susan left, Detective Simmons took the trash can and placed it out in the hall. "Happens more than it should. I'm surprised she's held it together this long."

"She hasn't. Last night she lost it. Her mother sent her to The Willows for the night. They gave her something to calm her. I guess I shouldn't have given her coffee with all the Ativan she has in her system."

"Not to worry. That's a common occurrence around here as much as we hate to admit it. Are you aware we formally arrested Dylan Stockard last night? He's hired an attorney named Seamus Franklin. He's good. He may want to talk with you and your family. I don't know yet. Hell, I'm not sure I'd talk to him if he's defending the man accused of kidnapping your granddaughter."

"Yes, I called and spoke with Davis. He told me you'd made the arrest. I don't want to come off as a know-it-all, but Detective, something isn't right; this whole investigation seems ass-backwards to me. I've watched enough television to know we need to get the media in on this. I don't give a damn what Disney says." Ashton poured two cups of coffee and handed one to the detective.

"Thanks. I was going to talk to you about that. There isn't anything to prevent your family from talking to whomever you like. Disney wants it under wraps for at least forty-eight hours. But I don't think I'd advise you to do that. Between us—" Detective Simmons closed the door to his office "—I think we're wasting time. If you know anyone in the media, it might be a good idea to contact them. If not, I can put you in touch with Channel Eleven's anchor, John Stone. He lives next door to me. I have to warn you, it will turn into a circus. News lately is slow, so they'll run with this. Privacy as you know it will be gone."

Susan came back in the room. "You gonna make it, hon?" Ashton asked.

"I don't know, Dad. Is there any news at all?" Susan

asked desperately. "Any little thing?"

"Nothing. Other than the clothes we found at the park and, of course, the pacifier in Stockard's car, we haven't any more information. We questioned everyone who attended the magic show yesterday. Nobody saw anything. Almost every single person we talked to commented about how it was pitch-black at several points during the show."

"Yes, it was. I remember once peeking over and checking on Ashley. She doesn't like the dark. She sleeps with her Humpty Dumpty night-light on." Susan drew a cleansing breath and raked her hands through her stringy hair. "What about the employees who stand at the door? Were they there? Surely they saw something?"

"Nothing. Or if so, they're not remembering. That's not uncommon. Something may jar their memory. They know to contact us. I told your father, I think it's time to go to the news media. We need to get the baby's picture out there."

"What will the Disney people think?" Susan asked, suddenly pumped with this new suggestion.

"I don't care right now. In my opinion, your daughter is more important than their image. They can either cooperate or not. I'm sure they will. They don't need any bad publicity now. After September 11, they had to make some major cutbacks. It would behoove them to cooperate."

"Then what are we waiting for? Detective, call your friend. We'll meet him and do whatever he says," Ashton said.

"Yes. I'll do anything to get my daughter back."

"She was last seen in the Magic Kingdom with her mother, Susan Burke Johnson, and family friend, Tristan Morrows. A second couple attending the magic show with Mrs. Burke, Doctor Dylan Stockard and his wife, Renée,

have been questioned in the disappearance of Ashley Rose Johnson. Doctor Stockard was arrested late yesterday evening in connection with the missing child. No more arrests have been made. If anyone has seen or has any information, please call . . ."

"You fucking bitch!" Richard seethed as he clicked the remote off, then tossed it on the floor. Any minute he expected the phone to start ringing. Why couldn't she have kept this quiet? This was family business, not national fucking news! Damn. Going public like this could kill any future deals he might have with Disney. He had to make this right with them. He'd arrange for Thompson to meet him later. First, though, he had a role to play.

He showered and changed into dark gray pants and a navy cashmere pullover. He didn't want to look unkempt in case he was to be on the news. He had an image to uphold. And besides, his daughter would be fine. He knew it.

According to the news report, Orlando P.D. had set up a hot line. Anyone with information could call night or day. The report went on to say that Mrs. Johnson and her family would be waiting by the phone. Nothing was mentioned about a ransom. He needed to be there to show his support. He could fake it. Hell, he often thought he'd missed his calling in life. He should have been an actor. He was quite good at it after so many years of practice.

Ten minutes later Richard sped down I-4, heading for Hughey Avenue. When he turned the corner and saw a half dozen news vans, reporters, and cameramen camped outside the police station, he almost turned around, then changed his mind. Appearances. It was all about appearances. And disappearances.

He left the Porsche with the parking attendant across the

street from the police station. The grieving father. A new role. He'd master it.

He walked over cables and wires and bumped into a woman fixing her lipstick. "Damn, can't you watch where you're going!" she said.

Now was his chance. He dug in his pocket for a tissue. "Here, ma'am, let me. I'm sorry. I need to go inside. My daughter is—"

"You're the father of the missing baby?" the woman asked.

"Uh, yes. Here, take this." He held out the tissue. Mr. Considerate even at a time like this. "I have to see my wife."

"Wait—"

"Mr. Johnson—"

"Is it true they've arrested your wife's ex-fiancé's best friend?"

The words paralyzed him. He turned to find the voice. "Where did you hear that?" Shit, he'd actually blurted out the question.

"Mr. Johnson." A perfectly made-up blonde shoved a microphone in his face. "One, two, three . . . we're here at Orlando Police Department. With me is the father of missing nine-month-old Ashley Rose Johnson. Mr. Johnson, what are the police doing to locate your daughter?"

Wife's ex-fiancé's best friend. What the fuck does *that mean?* For once he was speechless. He didn't have an answer. "Please, I'll talk to you later. Right now I have to get to my wife." He pushed through the crowd and made his way up the stairs to the police department. Two officers stood watch at the main entrance. They must have seen the spectacle because they opened the doors for him. He nodded briefly, then went inside to find Susan.

"Where can I find the Burkes?" Richard asked the desk clerk.

"They're with Detective Simmons. Right down the hall, then to your left," Lisa, the desk clerk, directed him.

"Thanks."

Richard found the office. Filled with cops and his nutty-ass bunch of in-laws. He stepped inside the room. His gaze raked the occupants in the room. He saw her then with her father and a tall blond man he didn't recognize.

"Susan, why didn't you tell me this morning? My God, I thought this was some joke. Ashton, I'm sorry, will you excuse us? I need to talk to my wife. Alone."

"Detective Simmons, this is Richard Johnson, my soon-to-be-ex-son-in-law," Ashton said coldly.

"Sir." Richard held out his hand. Simmons didn't extend his. He let his arm hang loosely at his side.

"I want to talk with you, Mr. Johnson. As soon as you're finished speaking to your wife, come and see me. We need to talk."

"Look, Detective, my child is missing. Don't order me around. Get some of these cops out there on the street; they need to be searching for my daughter. Whatever you have to say to me will have to wait." Richard turned, expecting Susan to follow him. *Wife's ex-fiancé's best friend.*

She didn't.

"I have nothing to say to you, Richard. Here or in private. I told you this morning Ashley was missing. You laughed and accused me *and* my father of trying to stage some . . . some charade. Get out of my sight! We managed so far to get along very well without you. Go back to your golf, your luncheons, or your meetings. Or go to hell for all I care."

"Whoa!" Detective Simmons said. "Calm down!"

"I have nothing to say to him, Detective. I can only speak for myself. He's a bastard. He has no interest in our daughter. He only wants to be in the limelight. It's all about him. If I were you, I'd ask him to leave. I have a restraining order against him. Unless you want to arrest him for violating it."

Detective Simmons smiled at her. "It's your call."

"Tell him to get lost and not come back as long as I'm here. Tell him he'll have to call in advance next time he wants to come down and to be sure to ask if I'm here first. Let him think he's gotten away with something for now. Richard likes that. It makes him feel like a man. I'm sorry to say, I can't stand the sight of him."

She watched the detective walk over to where Richard was standing, trying to look patient. Until you looked into his eyes and saw all that built-up rage. Whatever the detective said worked because Richard left the room without another word.

Susan went out in the hall where the noise was mindboggling. Phones were ringing, reporters lurked everywhere. Maybe this wasn't such a good idea after all. But then she reminded herself, this is what it would take to get Ashley back. So far, they'd had a dozen calls. Detective Simmons said they had to check them out. It would be a long and tedious job, but she was thankful for the officers and their devotion.

Her father came outside and stood next to her. "Why don't you go home and rest? Your mother could use the company, and that dog of yours needs some attention. You didn't forget about him, did you?"

"Oh, Dad, give me a break. Mother is fine and Nipper can practically take care of himself. Mom and Jemma can look after him. I can't leave. I have to be here when they find Ashley. She'll need her mother." Susan broke down again and sobbed.

Her father wrapped his arms around her. "It's all right, Susan, I understand. But you know, it might do you good to get out of here for a bit. Go home and have a hot shower. Have Jemma fix you some soup. Take Nipper for a run. He misses you. Clear your head. You're going to need all the energy you can muster, kiddo." He patted her head the way he had when she was little.

"Dad, you're good to me. Thanks. Maybe I will go home and clean up. I'll bring you something back to eat." She was about to leave when her father called out to her.

"Susan, here." He tossed her the keys to the Navigator. "Are you sure you're okay to drive?"

"I'm okay to drive, Dad. I'll be back in a little while. Be sure to call me the minute there's news."

"I promise. Now go on, get away from here for a while."

Seamus pitied his client. Something he didn't do too often. But this poor guy was sick with worry. "Renée can't handle this, Seamus. She's too fragile. I want you to make sure the media can't get to her. She'll have a breakdown."

"Renée is going to be just fine. She's tougher than you think." She was tougher than her husband and he didn't even realize it. It always amazed him just how tough and resilient women were. His own mother had been like that. "I am not deciding what she should or shouldn't do. I am telling *you* what to do, though. Let me take care of this. Monday you'll go for what we call a first appearance. I'll ask the judge for a hearing so we can post bail. Right now, we can post bail on a kidnapping charge. If something else comes of this, well, we will not be able to post bail on a capital offense."

"Look, I just want out of here. I'm worried about my wife. Dammit, Seamus, I did not steal that child."

"Man, this isn't about me! You don't get it, do you? If they don't find that little girl real soon, you are going to be charged with murder. Don't worry about me. You got enough of that to do for yourself." Seamus paced the small cell. His client was idealistic. *If my client thinks this is going to be a simple case, maybe I'm not doing my job well enough.*

"You mean they'll charge me with murder if they don't find the baby? No matter what?"

"Now you're gettin' it. That's exactly what I'm saying." Seamus stood in front of his client. "And they don't need a body either, if that's your next question. Special circumstances. I know three people who've been convicted of murder without a corpse right here in the good ol' Sunshine State. It happens. So, tell me, we're not going to have that problem, are we?"

"Jesus! I told you before I didn't have anything to do with the child's kidnapping or whatever the hell you want to call it; and before you ask, no, I did not have her kidnapped, abducted, I didn't sell her to the black market and I don't have her hidden away somewhere." Dylan sighed wearily.

It was hot in the airless room and he felt sticky. He wanted out of there. He needed to be with Renée, and he needed to make another call to get someone to cover his patients at his office. When he was first detained he'd been too shocked to think clearly. Today his thoughts were clear. He knew Cam Collins would cover for him in a heartbeat.

Seamus held up his hands. "I got it. Now, I'm going to get out of here. I want to see what the cops out there have learned. I'll be back this evening."

"Seamus, can I ask one more favor?"

"Sure, what is it?"

"I have a friend, he's a doctor. I know he'll cover for me if you call him. He's in Memphis now. He's been there since the earthquake last week. If you could call him, tell him what's happened. He'll come."

"I can do that. How do I find him?"

"I don't know. The Red Cross, maybe? He's a pediatrician but he has emergency room experience. Find him, Seamus."

"I'll do my best, ol' boy. Hang in there. I'll be back later."

"Cameron Collins, you have an emergency phone call. Please pick up mobile line six."

He'd set three broken arms, one fractured ankle, treated two women with cracked ribs and stitched another woman with a six-inch gash on her forehead. They would all survive, thank God. He'd seen enough dead bodies in the last week to last him a lifetime. It was horrendous. His year abroad working in third world countries was a breeze compared to what he was doing in Memphis. But, this was what he wanted. A medical career with no strings. He wanted to go where he was needed, when he was needed. When he'd heard about the earthquake, he drove from Florida directly to Memphis. He was needed there.

He walked down the makeshift hallway in the tent where he was working. They had cellular phones everywhere. Number six. "Doctor Collins." He toyed with a string caught on his stethoscope.

"Yes, is this Cameron Collins?"

"The one and only."

"I'm calling for a friend of yours, Doctor Dylan Stockard."

Cam laughed, "What's that *schmuck* got himself into now?"

"Well, Mr. Collins, that *schmuck* has gone and got himself arrested for kidnapping a little baby girl."

Cam froze. This had to be some kind of sick joke. "Who is this?"

"Seamus Clay Franklin, attorney-at-law. Your friend Dylan asked me to call you. He's in jail. He hasn't been released on bail yet. There is every possibility bail will be denied. He seemed to think you'd be willing to cover his practice for him until he's, well, you get the picture."

"This isn't a joke, is it?" Cam said.

"No, Doctor Collins, it is not a joke. Dylan asked me to call you and that's what I'm doing. He was arrested Saturday at the Magic Kingdom here in Orlando, Florida. He went with a group of friends he met at some parenting class. They were in a magic show. A woman in their group brought her little baby along. While they were watching some young thing show his magic prowess, someone was performing a little magical disappearing act of their own. Whoever it was, they took the child right out of her stroller with the mother sitting right next to her."

"Damn. This is serious. Tell Dylan I'll be there as soon as I can. I have to arrange a few things first."

"That's what he said you'd say. I'm going back to the jail this evening. Here's my number. Call me when you arrive." Seamus gave Cam his private and cell phone numbers. "If you need a lift from the airport, let me know."

"Thanks, man, I appreciate it. Tell Dylan the cavalry is on the way and to hang in there."

"He's doing that for sure."

The cell phone crackled, then the line went dead. Cam placed it back in the charger. Dazed by the news, he knew he wouldn't be any good for the rest of the day. He reported to the chief of emergency operations.

"I have a family emergency. I hate to go, but I have to cover a friend's practice. When he's back on his feet, I can come back if you still need me," Cam said.

"Do what you have to do. Thanks for all your help, Doctor Collins. You saved a few lives during your stay."

"Anytime. Later."

Cam arrived at the airport two hours early, and that had been plenty of time. Security was still tight over a year after the World Trade Center attack. They'd checked his luggage, his carry-on, and even asked him to remove his shoes. A couple in line in front of him had pitched a fit when they were asked to remove their shoes. Cam didn't mind. It was for his own safety.

"Flight 1345 for Orlando is now boarding at gate twelve."

Cam stood in another lengthy line, gave his boarding pass to a cute little redhead and finally crashed in first class. He hadn't really relaxed since coming to Memphis. He hadn't wanted to. His services were needed more than ever. The devastation from the earthquake was unreal. People were comparing it to the San Francisco earthquake that had essentially destroyed the entire city. He tried to put it out of his mind for now.

Think happy thoughts.

With his best friend in jail for kidnapping, he'd have to schedule his happy thoughts for later. At the moment, he wanted a cool drink and some quiet time. He didn't want to think at all. If he did, he'd think about *her*.

She was in Orlando. He'd sent her running home that day in Paris, telling her he wasn't ready to settle down. His career had been much too important to him then. Since viewing the loss of innocent life from the Memphis earthquake, he'd had a change of heart. Hell, who was he kidding? He'd been lost without Susan. He hadn't trusted himself with her love. It was so new back then. He hadn't been out of school that long when he and Dylan decided to save the world. With their pockets full of money and hearts full of hope, they'd traveled abroad with the Corps to a different world.

He'd met her in Paris. She was studying art. For him, it had been love at first sight. For her, well he wasn't sure, but he knew she'd loved him. And he'd screwed it all up with his big-headed ideas about saving the world.

The flight attendant began her safety speech and he actually listened. He looked around the Boeing 747. All the passengers were giving the attendants their undivided attention. *You never knew when it would be your last minute,* Cam thought.

More and more he thought about his life. He worked. He ate. He slept. He came back to a hotel, a tent, a cabin, whatever and he was always alone. Then he would think of Susan and all that he'd lost. He could kick his own ass for telling her goodbye. He was heartbroken, but too much male pride prevented him from calling her.

Not this time. He loved the way she laughed. She had a wicked sense of humor. Her love of all animals. And children. Right then he made a promise to himself. If he was lucky enough to get a second chance with the love of his life, he sure as hell was going to take it.

Chapter Fourteen

Sunday afternoon

Iris stared at her daughter, appalled at what she was seeing. She wondered how it was possible for a person to change so much in a matter of a few hours.

"Thanks for the tea, Jemma. It was just what I needed. I'm going to shower, then go back down to the police station. I know it's going to be a circus, but I want to be there in case . . . in case. Right now I'm so relieved the press hasn't gotten around to hounding us. We'd be prisoners. I know that's going to change, and I'm not sure it will be a bad thing. I can put up with anything if it helps find Ashley Rose. It's not about what I can tolerate, it's about my baby."

"Run along, dear. I went over to your house earlier to fetch some clothes for you. I wanted to pick up some of Nipper's toys and his dog food. He misses the baby, too. He's been carrying around one of her rubber ducks."

"Dogs know when something is wrong. I'll make it all up to him later. Promise me if you hear anything, anything at all, that you'll come and get me out of the shower?" Susan pleaded.

"Susan, you know better than to say something like that. Of course I'll come and get you. Now scoot. You look terrible. Put some makeup on."

Susan took a deep breath. At present she didn't care how

she looked. She only cared about finding Ashley Rose. "All right, Mom."

"That's what mothers are for." Iris struggled to smile and knew she was failing miserably. When the door closed behind her daughter, she sat down. She looked at Jemma. "I think I might like a cigarette, Jemma. Along with a cup of black coffee. No, no, I don't want you to get it. Your days of waiting on me are over. I want you to sit down and talk to me. I'll get your coffee. Do you want a cigarette, too?"

"Absolutely," Jemma said smartly. She'd never smoked a cigarette in her life. "Don't you be thinking you're putting me out to pasture, Missy Iris. I wouldn't know what to do with myself. I'd like to keep muddling along if it's all right with you. You know I love to cook."

"And that's all you're going to do from now on. I already called the agency to send someone over to do all the other stuff. In addition, Jemma, I am not helpless. I never said anything about putting you out to pasture. I just want to make things easier for you. The truth is, Ashton and I wouldn't know what to do without you. I was so devastated when my old friend Maureen died. Lately, I've been thinking about her a lot. I think that was one of the worst times in my life. C'mon, Jemma. I know how you hate to waste things. We might as well smoke these since they were in the drawer. We won't smoke any more after we finish these. Is that all right with you, Jemma?"

"Yes, that's all right. How many did you get from the drawer?"

"Mercy, about twelve. That's six each. I don't think I can smoke six cigarettes. Do you? Maybe we should just throw them away."

Jemma was relieved that she was not actually going to have to smoke. "Yes, throw them away. You can always buy some if you feel like it."

Iris reached across the table to pat Jemma's hand. "Whatever would I do without you?"

"You'd manage," the housekeeper said gruffly.

"No. No, I wouldn't, Jemma. You're as much a part of this family as Susan, Ashley, and Nipper are. The way Maureen was part of the family. I know what you're thinking, Jemma. Don't say it. It's apples and oranges."

Iris stared off into space, her eyes filled with sadness.

In the bathroom adjoining her old room, Susan turned on the shower, stripped off her shorts, and stood beneath the shower's stimulating spray of warm water. Her head ached and her eyes burned. Her nose was raw and red. The tips of her fingertips were tender from chewing on her nails. More than anything, her mental state was shifting moment by moment. She knew she needed to keep her wits about her. If she caved in, she would be no good to her daughter. What she longed for, what she *needed*, was something to give her a spark of hope, something to cling to. Since Ashley's disappearance, which according to the police, hadn't been all that long, there'd been nothing to offer even a faint glimmer of hope. Everyone knew the first forty-eight hours were the most crucial in an abduction or kidnapping. Perhaps today would be the magic day. Ashley Rose was her life. And that was it, pure and simple.

Susan poured liquid soap into a mesh sponge and scrubbed herself until her skin protested. She felt grubby and grimy. She found a bottle of Prell shampoo, her mother's favorite, and liberally poured some into the palm of her hand. Her hair was oily, hanging in limp strands. Not only would the Prell strip the oil from her hair, it'd leave a nice, clean smell. She remembered how her mother washed her hair daily with it as a child. Back then she hated to have her hair washed. Not Ashley. Ashley loved bath time. Susan loved wrapping her in a big fuzzy towel and nuzzling her all over. She always smelled clean, fresh, and pure.

The thought hit Susan so fast it felt like a physical blow.

Pure. Had someone taken Ashley to molest her? A pedophile? My God, she hadn't let herself go there, but now that she had, she was enraged! She bolted out of the shower, wrapped a towel around herself, and ran downstairs.

"Mother! Listen to me. Has anyone checked with the police on . . . oh, God I hate to think this, but we have to if we're to get Ashley back. Has anyone mentioned pedophiles?" Susan dropped down onto a wooden chair in the kitchen, a look of horror on her face.

Iris and Jemma were filling a basket with fruit, homemade croissants, and sandwiches for Ashton and the detectives. Both women stopped what they were doing at the same time to stare at Susan.

"Don't look at me like that, Mom. Have they?" Susan's voice escalated, edging toward hysteria.

Iris sealed the loaf of bread before answering her daughter. She wiped the crumbs from the cutting board, then brushed them into the sink. "Of course the police have thought about it, Susan. The police are professionals and they know what they're doing. You need to get hold of yourself. It's all part of kidnapping by sick people with sick minds. As hard as it is to do, try not to think along those lines. Leave all that up to the police. Ashley will come back. I know it, I can feel it here," Iris said, placing her hand over her heart. "You know I'm never wrong when I get one of those feelings. Lily has them, too, from time to time, but her feelings aren't as strong as mine. I remember my father telling Lily and me that our mother had the same kind of feelings. Way back then they said women were fey, or they'd say when we were born we had a veil over our eyes, when they even spoke of such things. You can refer to it as woman's intuition or maybe even a smidgen of psychic ability. Whatever you want to call it, I always pay attention when I get one of those feelings."

"Yes, I know you get those feelings. It used to drive Dad nuts. Thanks, Mom. I needed to hear that. I'm trying to be as positive as I can under the circumstances."

"Your father told me last night the police feel very positive about Doctor Stockard's involvement in this case. They wouldn't have arrested him otherwise. That doesn't mean they're going to ignore other possibilities. The Internet . . . Doctor Stockard's attorney is going to raise all manner of issues. He won't let them off the hook if he believes his client is innocent. There are . . . files, lists, registries where that type of person can be found. This is just my opinion, dear, but why would a man who is a doctor, and who has his whole life and career ahead of him, steal a friend's child? Ask yourself that because the authorities are asking the same thing. He could have been set up somehow, he could just be an unlucky person who was at the wrong place at the wrong time. Why would he throw all of that away, risk prison, when he and his wife were in the process of adopting a child? I know you don't want to hear this, but I'm not buying it."

Susan stared at her mother. "When did you become such an authority on the subject? What do you mean you aren't buying it?"

"Jemma agrees with me, don't you, Jemma?"

"Yes, I agree with your mother, Susan."

"I'm not an authority, dear. However, I do watch the

news and read the papers these days. Every single day there is something in the paper or on the news about sick people doing sick things. It's everywhere you look these days. All I want is for you to keep an open mind and think about Doctor Stockard. Think about what's going to happen to his life. I want you to be honest and fair the way I taught you to be.

"I want you to go back upstairs and get dressed. By the time you get back down here, this will all be ready." Iris motioned to the food basket. Her voice rang with motherly authority. Susan blinked but did what she was told.

Susan hurried upstairs, her mother's words ringing in her ears. Everything she said made sense. Yesterday she had been full of pure, blind panic. In that panic, she had reacted. If Dylan didn't take Ashley, who did?

She found a pair of khaki pants, a black tee shirt in the drawer, along with her favorite black slides. Her mother knew what she liked to wear. She'd chosen her clothes with comfort in mind. Leave it to her mother to think of things like that when it was the furthest thing from her own mind.

Iris stood at the bottom of the steps waiting for her daughter. There were so many things she wanted to say to Susan, but she knew it wasn't the time. Her thoughts drifted to a conversation she'd had late last night with her husband.

"Oh, Ashton, surely you know who he is?" Iris plucked the earrings from her ears and threw them on her vanity.

"What are you talking about?"

Was it her imagination or did Ashton's face turn three shades lighter. "The man they arrested. He's Cameron's best friend. The one Susan was engaged to."

"Oh, him. I think Susan may have said something to me." He undressed and crawled between the cool sheets.

Something made her turn to look at her husband then, really look at him. She stood next to the bed, the lamp shining down on Ashton's face. He looked gray.

"Ashton, whom did you think I was referring to just now?" *One of her alien feelings came over her. Intuition, whatever you wanted to call it, kicked in full force.*

"I don't know what you're talking about, Iris. I want to try and rest. I'm going back to the station at first light. Why don't you try and get some sleep yourself?"

"I think you're lying to me again, Ashton. I'm not tired, so don't tell me to go to sleep. I think I know exactly whom you were thinking about. It's him, isn't it?" Iris persisted. *"I don't think Doctor Stockard took our granddaughter."*

"The police arrested him. That means it's out of our hands. Everything points to him and his wife. Good night, Iris."

"Mom, are you okay?" Susan asked her mother.

"Yes, just woolgathering. I'm ready to go if you are. Do you want to take the Volvo, dear, or stick with your father's Navigator? I want to make sure he eats something today besides peanuts. He didn't look well last night when he came home."

"Dad should be here with you. I can stay at the station. It's my place." Nipper raced for the door, thinking he was going for his morning walk. "It's okay, boy. I'll be back. Jemma can let you run around in the backyard later. I promise." She scratched the shepherd behind the ears and opened the front door. "Stay," she commanded.

"Poor dog, he's suffering, too," Iris said absently as she

climbed in the passenger seat of the Lincoln.

Susan turned the key in the ignition. The Navigator purred to life. "Mom, when you said you knew in your heart that Ashley was okay, were you just saying that to make me feel better or were you serious? And do you *really* believe Dylan didn't take Ashley? I need to know, Mom."

"Susan! I would never say anything just to make you feel good! This is a very serious matter. Ashley is my granddaughter. I know you and your father have always laughed at my . . . *feelings,* but I'm rarely wrong. Of course I meant what I said. It was a feeling I had. Sometimes they just come over me for no reason. I don't know how I know this, I just do. Doctor Stockard did not abduct Ashley Rose. I'm telling you, Susan, the man did not do it."

"I've never laughed at you or your feelings, Mom. I don't think Dad ever laughed either. You spook us both sometimes, that's all. You've been right too many times. What you're saying gives me something to cling to. But if it wasn't Dylan who took Ashley Rose, *who* has my daughter?"

"I think that lunatic husband of yours took Ashley Rose is what I think, Susan. And the reason I know in my heart the child is all right is because I know Richard won't hurt his own flesh and blood."

Susan started to shake behind the wheel. Was her mother right? Would Richard do something so evil and pretend otherwise? Of course he would. Did he have an alibi? She had to admit she didn't know. Well, by God, that was the first question she was going to ask when she met with Detective Simmons.

Iris gazed out the window, her thoughts returning to Ashton. He'd been acting strange lately. Not just because of Richard and the trouble he thrived on stirring up. It was more than that, but she couldn't exactly put her finger on what it was. She had the feeling he was holding back things. Just like he did before they were married. Even before Susan was born. So many years ago . . .

"Iris, she's the hired help, for God's sake! What do you think your daddy will say?" Ashton asked.

"Frankly, Ashton, I don't give a hoot what my daddy says. Maureen is my oldest and dearest friend. If I can't choose my own maid of honor, then we'll just have to elope. Daddy won't like that one little bit, I can tell you that much." She reached for her ice tea and sipped at it, her eyes on Ashton.

"She doesn't fit in, Iris, I'm sorry. She's ten years your senior, and she has that boy. Her husband is a drunkard. How is that going to look? People will talk. I just think it would be best if Lily were your maid of honor."

"Lily doesn't want the job. Ashton, could you just shut up for once? You worry too much. Daddy's still gonna give Burke and Burke that loan. With or without us gettin' married."

"Iris, that's not what I'm worried about. I want a nice wedding, that's all. I don't want to do anything that's going to cause us any embarrassment in years to come. It wouldn't surprise me if that husband of hers doesn't do something . . . wild!"

"Maybe he will, Ashton. Maybe that's what this town needs. Some excitement. I'm sure bored with it. Now, if you'll excuse me, I have things to do." Iris walked inside, slamming the screen door behind her. Ashton Parker Burke, III, could just kiss her rosy red rear end!

She hated it when Ashton started acting like he was better than her dear Maureen. Ashton Parker Burke was a snob. She'd show him, maybe make him sweat a little.

"Iris, is that you?" a voice called from upstairs.

"Yes, it is. Stay there, I'm coming up," Iris shouted back.

Prosperity Place had been in the Weatherby family for more than a hundred years. Located on Peachtree Street, Prosperity Place was within walking distance of Rhodes Hall, one of the last castles in Atlanta. Iris liked to tell her friends she lived near the castle. Their eyes would widen, this bit of information always impressed people since one of the richest families in Atlanta lived there. It hadn't hurt her reputation one little bit.

Though Prosperity Place wasn't nearly as grand, it stood on its own. Upon entering, one would be greeted with a double mahogany staircase, with stained-glass windows trailing up the entire flight of stairs. Each window was a different flower. Of course there was an Iris and a Lily. Her father always teased her and Lily, telling them they were named after the windows, then he'd wink. The windows had been installed after they were born. Maureen told her it was her mother's dream to have a dozen girls and to name each one after her favorite flowers. Her mother had only made it to window number two. Two months after Lily was born, she died quietly in her sleep.

Iris hurried down the long hall in search of the sweet sing-song voice she knew belonged to Maureen.

"Take a rest now, Maureen. You work way too hard. Do you want me to fetch some tea? Or would you like to sneak outside so we can smoke some of Daddy's cigarettes?" she asked, hoping to bring a smile to her friend's face.

Maureen brushed the feather duster across the marble mantel, then sat down on the dainty chintz-covered ottoman. "No, I have to get the upstairs finished. I won't be coming by next Tuesday. I'm taking R.J. to the doctor. You sure your daddy won't mind?"

Iris rolled her eyes and fanned herself with an imaginary

fan. "My Daddy doesn't know what dust is, Maureen. I'm telling you, you could take a year off and Daddy wouldn't be the wiser. But I would. I would dearly miss you. Why are you taking R.J. to the doctor?"

Maureen stood up and went to the window that overlooked Peachtree Street. Magnolias lined both sides of the street, lush green lawns meeting carefully tended flower beds. "It's just his five-year checkup. Nothin' for you to worry about." Maureen smiled at Iris. At thirty, Maureen looked twenty, and Iris, who was twenty, could pass for a girl of fifteen. They made quite a pair.

"Well good, I'd hate to think of R.J. having problems again." They both laughed, then Iris became serious. "You sure that's all? You and R.J. aren't havin' any more trouble out of Hank, are you? I wish you'd leave him for good and come live here. Daddy said you and R.J. were welcome. Daddy and Lily would love having you live here with us. We could take turns lookin' after R.J. He's a good little boy; doesn't get in the way."

"Oh, Iris, it's not that. Hank is all right when he's sober. He's good to R.J. and me. I can't leave him. What would he do without us?"

This was the only subject where Iris disagreed with Maureen. Hank was a bully and a drunkard. Maureen had come to work more than once with a swollen eye or a bruised arm. Iris wasn't stupid. She knew what Hank did to her friend when they argued. She wished Maureen would leave him.

"I think he'd have to find someone else to punch on, that's what I think. He'd have to find someone else to earn the money so he can drink it away. I think that's exactly what he would do, Maureen."

"Well, I'm glad you hold me in such high esteem. I would

hate to think Hank married me for any reason other than my weekly wages."

"You stop that right now, Maureen! That's isn't what I meant and you know it." Iris got up from the chair she was sitting on and stood behind her friend. She placed her hands on Maureen's shoulders.

"I know. It's my life, Iris, let me take care of Hank the best way I know how. Now, let's talk about somethin' else. Let's talk about Ashton. Are you excited about the wedding?"

Iris laughed. "Not really. Ashton is Ashton. A dear, wonderful man, but I've known him so long, Maureen. I don't think marriage to him is gonna change things much."

"You better think again, Iris. Your entire life is going to change. You'll be a wife with certain duties to attend to. That is . . . unless you already . . . Iris?" Maureen turned around and looked at her.

"Before you ask, no, I did not have sex yet. I'm saving myself for my wedding night. Not that I wouldn't have if Ashton wanted to. He's afraid Daddy would find out." Iris giggled like a schoolgirl. "I asked him once, I said, 'Ashton, what do you think? When the deed is done that I'd run and tell him? Or that he'd just know somehow?' His face turned twenty different shades red, do you believe that? I almost couldn't believe it myself."

"Iris Weatherby, you're an ornery one for sure. Ashton is gonna have his hands full with you."

"Let's hope so! I love excitement."

"Well, I'd best get back to work. You get on out of here now."

"I'm making dinner tonight. You'll stay won't you? And R.J., too?"

"I don't see why not. Now, get out of here before I

have to sic Lily on you!"

Maureen's threat had the desired effect. Iris beelined out of the room. Lord, but Lily did make her want to scream!

"I'm sorry, Maureen. I wish there was something I could do. If there is, just tell me and I'll do it. Do you want me to tell Iris or don't you want her to know?"

Maureen choked back a sob and nodded. "Iris is my best friend. How could I keep something like this a secret?"

"Tell me what?" Iris said. "We've only been married for six years and you two are already keeping secrets from me," she teased. "Come on, now, one or the other of you best 'fess up now."

Ashton and Maureen looked at one another, then back at Iris.

"What is it? You two look like you're up to something. Ashton, what is going on?"

Ashton walked over to his wife and reached for her hand. "Maureen has something she needs to tell you."

"So, get on with it?"

Seated at the kitchen table, her husband and best friend looked like they'd both lost their best friends. Iris sat across from them. "What? You're scarin' me now. I don't like what I'm seein' on your faces."

"Oh, Iris, this is so terrible. I don't know . . ." Maureen appealed to Ashton.

"What she means is . . . she's sick, Iris. Very sick. Too sick to work."

Iris let out the breath she'd been holding in. "Well, that's not the end of the world. Lord, Ashton, we can clean this old place. Lily dusts every day. I'm capable of putting a meal on the table." The silence was so thick she could have sliced it with a butter knife. She stopped talking. "There's more, isn't there?"

"Yes, it's a blood disease. The doctor calls it leukemia. The doctor says it won't get any better, Iris."

Iris could feel her eyes start to fill with tears. "Better than what, Maureen?" she whispered in a hushed voice.

"Than anything, Iris. The doctor said it won't get any better. Just worse." Maureen broke down. Iris stood rooted to the floor, tears streaming down her cheeks. Ashton held Maureen stiffly in his arms.

"What do you mean? It has to get better. If it gets worse, then . . . then it means you'll . . ."

"Yes, go ahead and say it. Die, Iris. I'm going to die." Maureen took a great gulp of air. "But that's not what has me so worried."

"I don't understand. Damnation, what?" Iris looked to Ashton, but his face remained as blank as freshly erased slate.

"The Lord has a plan for us from the moment we're conceived. Heck, I've known that forever. We're all going to die at one time or another. I just didn't think it would be so soon." Her eyes flooded, and she reached across the table for Iris's hand. "You know how Hank is. I haven't told him yet. I don't know if I will. He wouldn't understand anyway. He'd just think it was a trick or something, so I'd have an excuse to quit giving him money."

"Maureen, I . . . Ashton, isn't there something we can do? What about another doctor?"

Ashton shook his head. "No, nothing, I thought of that myself. She already had three different blood tests. Maureen?"

"There aren't any treatments. They can make me comfortable and that's all I can hope for. I'm slowly coming to

terms with it. Except for R. J."

"Mom, have you heard a word I've said?" Susan tapped her mother on the shoulder for the third time.

"I'm sorry. I guess I was woolgathering. Lord have mercy!" Iris pointed to the gaggle of people outside the police station.

"I told you it was going to be a madhouse. We can go inside through the back entrance and avoid all this if you like."

Iris reached for the basket of food she and Jemma had made up. "Whatever you want, dear. Don't you think we should talk to them?" Iris stepped out of the car. She handed the basket to her daughter.

"Perhaps later. Right now I want to talk with Detective Simmons to see what he has to say." She reached for her mother's hand. Together they walked to the back of the police station and entered through the rear entrance.

"Susan, we are going to find Ashley. I want you to trust me and I want you to believe what I'm saying."

"I do, Mom. Thanks. Don't worry, I won't give up. I just pray that whoever has her is taking good care of her . . . God, I can't imagine what she must be thinking or if she's even thinking at all. Do babies think? She doesn't have her Pooh blanket, the one that's all soft and worn. It's hard to get her to go to sleep without it. Whoever has her can't know these things!" Susan sagged against her mother. "I don't know what I'll do if she's not found . . ."

Iris's hold on her daughter was fiercely protective. "You're not going to find out because they *will* find her." Her mother's voice was so forceful, Susan believed her. "I told you I can feel it here." She placed her palm over her chest.

Susan wiped her eyes with the hem of her shirt. "I don't know what I'd do without you and Dad right now. Okay, okay, I'm all right now."

"Come along, dear, let's find your father and Detective Simmons."

The women walked through a maze of hallways, following the posted signs that would lead them to the front of the station.

Susan spotted the familiar entrance to the detective's office. Inside, a group of people she didn't recognize were gathered around her father and Detective Simmons. They were talking when she entered the room. They stopped when they saw her.

Her heart lurched. "Did you find my daughter? Did something happen?" She looked left to right, her gaze coming to rest on the last person she had expected to see.

Richard!

Susan pointed a shaking finger at Richard. "What's he doing here?" Her voice was so shrill she could hardly believe it was her own.

Ashton reached for his daughter's arm and led her out to the hall. "Susan, calm down. Richard wants to help. As much as you and I might not like it, he has every right to be here. As much right as you do. He's Ashley Rose's father. He has rights and they can't be denied. Detective Simmons thinks it would be best if we put forth a united front, just until Ashley is returned."

"Who are all those people?" She jerked her head in the direction of the room they had just left.

"Those people are what we need to talk about. But first, I want you to calm down. Forget about Richard right now. He's not important. What is important is getting Ashley back. The police know about these things. They know what to do. I think we should listen to them, Susan."

"I'm listening." Susan clenched her teeth and her fists.

"Detectives Nicholls, Davis, and Simmons all seem to think we need to get the Center for Missing and Exploited Children involved. With their network, if—God forbid—Ashley has been taken out of the state, they have the manpower and the technology to get her picture out to law enforcement agencies all across the country."

"Exploited children, Dad? What's that supposed to mean!"

"It's what they call themselves. The group was founded by a father whose son was kidnapped and murdered . . . we need to hear what they can do for us. For Ashley."

She nodded. "Of course, I understand." She leaned into her father so no one could hear their conversation. "What I don't understand is what *he's* doing here? He accused me of planning this whole thing yesterday. What changed his mind? What changed *your* mind?"

"In cases like this, according to the detectives, when word gets out that you and Richard are going through divorce proceedings, it brings the nasty side out in some people. The media in particular. They'll go after you tooth and nail. Ashley Rose's disappearance will be secondary to the dirt they'll pile on both you and Richard. Then the tabloids start paying people and making up stories. Trust me, you don't want that and neither do I."

"I don't get it," Susan said.

"Ransom. Crazies. If the media learns you two are united in the search to find Ashley, it will just be much easier. Detective Simmons says the nuts come out of the cracks when something like this happens. All sorts of kooks looking for money, publicity, or a cheap thrill call the police. They have Ashley. They saw her. They have information that can only be revealed to the parents for a price. That sort of thing. Simmons thinks your chances of getting one crank too many will decrease if the public doesn't know about your personal troubles. And I agree. When this is all over, you can go ahead with the proceedings, but if I were you, I'd listen to the detective. He's got a hell of a lot more experience in this type of thing than we do."

"What about Richard? Have you discussed this with him?"

"No, I didn't think it was my place. I've had too many words with him lately, and I didn't want to compromise any of this. Plus, I have that contract dispute going on with him. I don't want to talk to him unless I absolutely have to, but I will if you want me to."

Susan placed her hand on her dad's shoulder. "You're right, it is my place to talk to him, and I will. I want to make sure we do everything right. It is my place. He is Ashley's father. I guess in his own warped way he does love her. How is it he's here now? Did Detective Simmons call him?"

"Apparently Richard came in on his own early this morning. He said he wanted to do anything he could to help find his daughter. I think we should take him up on his offer. Every bit of help we can get will only bring Ashley home that much faster."

At some point during the discussion, Iris had come out to the hall and listened to both her husband and daughter. She hadn't said a word. She watched her husband carefully. A good night's sleep had left him looking like the man she knew, not the weary, pale man who had climbed into their bed, refusing to answer her pointed questions.

"Susan, are you sure you're up to this? Richard's a bully, and you're vulnerable right now. Ashton, I don't want that man left alone with her. I'm not so sure it's a good idea no matter what the detectives say."

"Iris, the man wouldn't dare lay a hand on her. They are both going to be under a microscope. The man is not an idiot. Simmons is aware of their . . . current situation."

"Yes, I can handle it. If it will help get Ashley back, then I'll do whatever I have to. If it means putting up a front for the media and all the weirdos of the world with Richard standing next to me, I'll do it."

"Are you sure about this, Susan? I hate the thought of you having to pretend to like that man! I hate the very sight of him! Look at him. The man is actually holding court. I think he's pretending he's a movie star. This is his fifteen minutes of fame."

Ashton and his daughter flinched at the venom in Iris's voice.

A moment later they were back inside Simmons's office, where a group of reporters from the *Orlando Sentinel* and other Florida newspapers had managed to get inside the building. Richard gravitated to them immediately.

"Let Richard do the media thing," Ashton whispered. "He's good at it, and it's one of the reasons I hired him in the first place. Public relations. God, if I'd only known then what I know now, we wouldn't be in this mess."

Ashton watched Richard as he gestured, spoke animatedly but never once raised his voice. He was a master of public relations. He was good, he'd give him that. Hell, he'd have those reporters wrapped around his little finger in five more minutes. When he was finished with them, they'd be out on the streets doing a door-to-door search for Ashley Rose themselves.

Detective Simmons strode over to them. "You folks ready to speak with the people I brought in?" He indicated the group of five or six people from the National Center for Missing and Exploited Children.

"Yes, I'll talk to them myself. Promise me you'll come and get me if there's any news?" Susan pleaded.

"Of course. I've arranged a room where you can talk in private. Follow me."

Susan followed the detective to what she guessed was an interrogation room of sorts.

"Take all the time you need. Open up. Don't be afraid to talk."

The room was approximately ten-by-twelve. The walls were painted an ugly shade of gray. There were no windows. There was, however, a one-way mirror directly across from the entryway. A large, wooden table scarred with cigarette burns and six metal chairs were the only furniture in the room. Susan looked above her expecting to see a single light bulb dangling from the ceiling. A plain fluorescent light did nothing to brighten the bleakness of the room. There was nothing in the room to distract one, she thought as she sat down.

Prayers. She needed to pray. In her head she recited a prayer she used to say every night as a child.

> *Now I lay me down to sleep,*
> *Now I lay me down to sleep,*
> *If I should die . . .*
> *No!*

She stopped. She wasn't going to die because she had to find Ashley. Her daughter was probably taking her afternoon nap about now. She would sleep for at least two hours, then she would wake up wanting to play. Susan always cherished that quiet time with her daughter.

Her entire world had shattered in a matter of a few minutes.

How was it possible that she'd been no more than two feet away from her daughter and this ugly thing happened? She struggled to remember anything out of the ordinary and couldn't. She'd gone over the incident a thousand times in her mind. Surely, she had missed something that would've pointed to Dylan and his evil plan. She replayed the events of the previous day like a broken record. But then her mother said Dylan wasn't the one who had taken Ashley Rose.

Over and over, around and around. Nothing. But, wait, she did remember something! The stroller had moved. A noise, like a thud, as though someone had bumped into the stroller!

She remembered that was when the auditorium had gone completely black. If Dylan had taken Ashley he would have slipped back in at that precise moment to make his move. She thought again about her mother's words.

Was it possible that Renée knew of his plan, and she'd laughed and enjoyed a magic show while her husband kidnapped my daughter? Mother said . . .

What other explanation could there be? One other explanation. Her mother's theory.

Chapter Fifteen

The hand gripping the phone receiver was bone-knuckle white. A murderous expression rode his face, while his foot tapped angrily. "I don't care if the FBI, the CIA, Scotland Yard and the Mossad comes knocking on your door. You don't know me. You never met me, and my name doesn't ring any bells. Is that clear? And, if it isn't clear, I'm the one person who *can* make it clear."

Maximus González rued the day he had met Richard Johnson. He hated what he had been coerced into doing years ago. Greed, his greed in particular, was the reason he was even having this conversation. He didn't need or want Ashton Burke's money. He liked the man. They'd been golfing partners and personal friends for too many years for him to switch his loyalties so late in the game.

"I understand that you are threatening me, Mr. Johnson. I am not asking you any questions, because I do not care to hear any more of your lies. I do not have many regrets in my life, but you are at the top of my short list. Don't ever call me and threaten me again. I will not seek out the authorities, but if they should come to me, I will tell the truth. Let me make myself even more clear. I have written a letter that is in my attorney's possession. It is, of course, sealed and only to be opened in the event of my . . . shall we say, untimely death. Is that clear, *Mister Johnson?*"

"Oh, it's clear all right, González. Remember, all it takes to have your license revoked is a phone call."

Perspiration beaded on the doctor's forehead. If he allowed this evil person to threaten and frighten him again, he might as well hide in a corner and suck his thumb. "Losing one's license is not so bad compared to spending a lifetime in prison. I will be retiring in the coming year, so your threat is rather idle, no?" He was glad Richard Johnson couldn't see the way he was trembling.

Richard Johnson's response was met with the drone of the dial tone.

¡Puedo matar ese bastardo! I can kill that bastard!

Twenty years ago, he might have acted on that thought. Then he'd been a desperate man. The oldest of nine, he would have done almost anything to put food in the mouths of his five sisters and three brothers left behind in Mexico. Now, they were all scattered about the United States, thanks to him and his hard work. He no longer needed to pull a con for money. His practice was legitimate and had been legitimate for many years. Astute investment strategies provided for his well-being far into the future. Gone were the days of writing a prescription for uppers and downers to anyone willing to pay a price.

Maximus González sighed. This phone call definitely was not good news. He had fulfilled the promise he made all those years ago. He owed Richard Johnson nothing.

Though it had taken years to relocate and insinuate himself into the same social circle as the Burkes, he had done so. When Ashton Burke asked him to take over the care of his wife, he had readily agreed. As per Richard Johnson's instructions, he saw to it that Iris Burke was virtually incapacitated. The drugs he had prescribed were powerful as well as mind-altering. He'd done exactly what Richard

Johnson paid him to do. "Make her life miserable like she made mine," he told him that first day at the seedy clinic in Los Angeles. In order to clinch the deal, Johnson had opened his briefcase and dumped stacks and stacks of money on his desk. His greed had kicked in just as Johnson knew it would.

González had treated young Richard for gonorrhea. They struck up an unlikely alliance, his out of greed, Johnson's out of hatred. The first step of Richard's plot to destroy the woman was outlined. If he'd had any misgivings, he couldn't remember what they were. All he could see and think about was the money. In his wildest dreams he never thought he would be anything but a back-alley doctor practicing on the edge of the law. Richard Johnson had made it possible for him to move in the circles the Burkes moved in.

He had been so pleased when the young Ms. Johnson asked that he be replaced. He'd canceled all his appointments that day, gone home, turned on his stereo, and proceeded to get drunk. He'd slept like a newborn that night. His guilt would no longer ride on his shoulders, not that it would ever totally disappear. One day he would have to pay for the years he'd robbed from Mrs. Burke's life.

He looked at his appointment book. Nothing for the rest of the afternoon. He'd really cut back on his practice the last few years. Now he had more time for friendships and golf, his passion in life. Some days he won more money on the golf course than he took in from his practice.

He stepped into the elevator that would take him to his fourth-floor private office. Ashton Burke had designed and built the office building for him. More than pleased with his work, he later asked him to build other buildings for him. Rent poured in faster than he could spend the money.

Maximus González considered himself a wealthy man,

his retirement beckoning. Retirement was something he'd looked forward to since the day he started to treat Iris Burke.

Whatever Richard Johnson was up to now, he was on his own. He hoped he had the courage to follow through if things went awry.

He would not become indebted to a man like Richard Johnson a second time.

Susan waited impatiently, her thoughts ricocheting wildly. She looked up, startled, when a short, slender woman in her fifties blew into the room like a wild gust of wind. She had long, dark hair streaked with gray, which was pulled in a haphazard ponytail with a tortoiseshell clip holding the flyaway hair in place. She had friendly eyes and a generous smile. Susan felt at ease immediately.

"I'm Marlene Smith. I'm with the Center." She held out her hand for Susan to shake, then pulled up one of the metal chairs. "I'm sorry you're here and that we have to meet under such circumstances." She took a pad and paper from her shoulder bag.

"You can't imagine what it's like. It's been more than twenty-four hours and there's no news, no reports. It's like my daughter dropped off the face of the earth. I watch the news and read the newspapers, so I know the chances of finding my baby decrease with each passing minute. We're now counting down on those forty-eight hours that are so crucial when a child goes missing. What can I do to . . . help? I feel so useless right now. My daughter is out there somewhere, and all the police are doing is prying into my personal life. Is that what you're going to do, too?" She wasn't going to waste any more time explaining what she felt was unnecessary, useless information.

The woman looked at her, her green eyes filled with sympathy. "Yes, it is. I lost my only son fifteen years ago, so I do know what you're going through."

"I'm sorry . . . I don't mean to be . . ."

"It's all right. You couldn't know. Now, let me tell you a bit about myself."

Marlene briefed Susan on her background with the Center. She had a doctorate in psychology and had been with the organization for twelve years. Added to her own personal experience, she was a dynamo. Fifteen years ago, her husband had shot her seven-year-old son to death before turning the gun on himself. Grief-stricken beyond help, she'd gone to the Center two years after their deaths looking for answers. It was during her third year that she became actively involved as a counselor and advisor.

"I'm sure Detective Simmons explained to you how we get involved. We're linked with law enforcement agencies across the country. Pictures of—" she looked at the papers she held in her hands "—Ashley Rose, will be distributed to as many of those agencies as humanly possible. We've been very successful in locating thousands of missing children. All we need is your permission. We will keep you and your husband and, of course, the police, updated constantly. All we need from you is a recent picture, then we can get started."

Marlene knew the frazzled woman sitting across from her was sizing her up. It came with the territory. She was in agony with her loss, possibly questioning why a virtual stranger would want to involve herself in her personal tragedy.

Susan shifted in her metal chair. "Yes, do whatever you need to do. My father has a snapshot my mother took of

Ashley about two weeks ago. He gave it to Detective Simmons."

Marlene heard the sorrow in the young woman's voice. Her heart went out to her. She knew what she was going through. "This will mean nothing to you, but from what I've seen and heard, that doctor they have in the lockup, he's not the one. That's just my gut talking here, but I've seen too many of these cases not to know a thing or two.

"We'll get started right away. Now, if there's anything you need, here is my pager number. Call me anytime, day or night." Marlene gave Susan one of her business cards, then bounded out of her chair like a jack-in-the-box.

Susan liked the energetic little woman already. "Thank you, Marlene. I guess I should just sit here and wait for the others?" *She didn't think Dylan was responsible for taking Ashley.* Susan could add her to the list of people who believed Dylan was innocent. She wished she could feel the same way.

"No, you can leave now. The others are waiting for me to give them the go-ahead, which is what I'm about to do. We all have specific functions that enable us to move fast. They report to me, I report to you and the police. We all know this is the worst time of your life. The last thing you need to do is explain yourself to another person."

"I'm up and down, this is so . . . horrible, but I'll tell them anything they need to know. Marlene, thanks."

Marlene picked up her bag and headed to the door. "You're welcome, but this is what I do. It's what I'll do till the day I die. I guess you could say I'm dedicated, but then so are all the others. I'm no exception. Now, I'm wasting precious time. I'll be in touch." A rush of wind swirled into the room when the little woman left. Talk about your human dynamo.

Something nagged at Susan when she thought about her mother's *feelings*. Something she'd heard recently on television while she was scrolling through to find a movie she wanted to see. The man on television said something. What? She thought it was a program her mother liked to watch. She bolted from the room to find her mother. She might know about the program.

"Susan, I was just coming to get you. Detective Simmons just this minute told me they received a call from a young woman who thinks she might've seen Ashley Rose with an elderly couple yesterday. He thinks it's serious, so he's going to interview the caller himself," Iris said.

"Did she say where? When?" Susan asked, excitement ringing in her voice.

"The detective didn't say. He left and your father went with him. They'll call as soon as they can, dear. Don't get your hopes too high. These calls come in all the time."

"Oh God, Mom. I hope this leads to something. I don't know how much more of this . . . this not knowing I can stand! I want my baby back!" Susan embraced her mother, then pulled away. "Mom, you watch a lot of television. Recently I heard this man. I think he's one of those psychics. I thought you might . . . well, know about him since you have those feelings. I can't remember his name, though."

Her mother's eyes sparked with recognition. "Yes, it's a show called *Crossing Over*. The man is a medium. John Edward. I watch him all the time. Your father thinks I'm crazy, but I believe him, Susan."

Susan wasn't sure where she was headed with this. "What does he do? I've heard of psychics who locate missing children. Does he do that?"

"I don't think he does, dear. He reads for people. He connects them with their loved ones who have passed away.

279

He's excellent at what he does."

Susan suddenly understood her father's skepticism. "And you really believe him?"

"Absolutely. We can call him, you know. He does readings over the phone."

Susan pulled her mother back inside the interrogation room. "Call him. Tell him I would like a reading. Maybe he can give me a clue or something. I can't believe I'm even thinking like this! What do you think, Mother? Am I going crazy?"

Susan found the metal chair and pulled it next to the scarred table. Overwhelmed with worry, she sat down, cupping her chin in her hands. Her mother sat in the chair Marlene had used. She wondered if she should tell her mother Marlene's assessment of Dylan's role in Ashley's kidnapping. Maybe she would tell her later. Then again, maybe not. After all, Marlene said it was an opinion, not a feeling. A feeling, especially her mother's feeling, was different.

"Of course not! I want you to stop thinking that way. We *will* get Ashley back. I'm sorry, but I feel in my heart that your husband is responsible for what we're all going through. Maybe John Edward can tell us if Richard is involved. If you want me to call him, I will."

"I think I'm grasping at straws, but go ahead. Make the call, but, Mom, let's keep it between us. I don't want to explain anything to Dad. Or Richard. God, he would have a field day with this."

"My dear, your father will never hear it from me. There's a public phone right down the hall; I can call information and get the number. By the way, I just saw Richard talking on that very phone. You would think with his daughter gone, business would be the last thing on his mind."

"That's Richard for you. Business comes first. I wonder why he was using a pay phone when he has his cell phone attached to his belt. He's never without it. I wish he'd just leave. Just seeing him here, pretending he cares, makes my skin crawl."

"I'm not going to say I told you so because it's too late for that. But watch him, Susan. Watch him closely. He's the missing link. I know it, I feel it, right here!" Iris placed her hand over her heart the way she always did when she had one of her feelings.

"I'll watch him as closely as I can. Let's get out of here. This room is making me claustrophobic."

"I'll make that call."

Susan had agreed with her mother just to give her something to do. She really didn't think some TV medium could help her locate her daughter, but it was something to hold on to. It was more than she'd had before. Any little thing, any spark, made her feel more positive. She prayed Detective Simmons's visit to the woman who had called into the station was a success.

Briefly, she wondered how Renée was holding up. She hadn't known her for very long, but she'd liked her. She had been open, honest, and kind. Or maybe that's what she *wanted* her to think. If Dylan told her of his plans, then she would have done anything in her power to help him achieve their mutual goal. Now she had to think about Marlene's opinion.

Then there was Richard. Could he commit an act so vile and evil? Her mother seemed to think so. As much as she wanted to believe her mother, she simply couldn't. Richard was many things, but a kidnapper—she didn't think so. He wouldn't do something this insane. She knew him. Or did she?

They'd married in haste; at least she had. And for all the wrong reasons. In all honesty, she'd married Richard hoping to forget Cam. She knew now she could never forget Cam. Somewhere along the way, she reserved a special place in her heart for him. Nothing could ever take that away. Richard had given her Ashley, and for that she would be forever grateful. He'd fooled her once, but he wasn't going to fool her a second time.

Detective Simmons adjusted his shoulder holster, which held the .357 Magnum he wore beneath his jacket. In all of his years on the force, he'd never had to use it, but that didn't make him any less aware of the need to carry it.

He checked the address on the mailbox against the slip of paper in his hand. It matched.

"You'll have to wait in the car, Burke."

"Like hell! I didn't ride all the way out here to sit in the car. I'm going inside with you. If this woman knows anything about my granddaughter, I want to hear it with my own ears."

"Only if you agree to keep quiet and let me do the talking, got it? You got it?"

"I got it, Detective," Ashton said promptly.

The caller lived in one of Orlando's older neighborhoods. Though small, the house looked well cared for. It was an older-style Florida home with a flat roof and jalousie windows. Simmons wondered about the caller as he rang the doorbell. Was it another crank or had this woman really seen the missing infant?

The door opened. A young woman in her early twenties stood behind the screen. "Detective Simmons?"

"Yes. This is Mr. Burke. It's his granddaughter you might have seen."

"I'm Ellen Grant. I made the call. Please, come in."

They followed the woman inside. She ushered them into the living room.

A floral sofa and two matching chairs were grouped around a large coffee table. A curio cabinet positioned behind the sofa held a collection of miniature dolls. Beyond that, the room was empty. There were no family photos, no thumbed-through magazines, not a book in sight. Simmons stretched his neck to see beyond the living room. A kitchen with an ice-cream style table for two, stove, refrigerator, and a plain white microwave. Nothing spectacular. It was just a neat, tidy house with no clutter.

"Ms. Grant, I'll make this easy. Tell me exactly what you saw. If I have any questions, I'll wait till you're finished to ask them."

She nodded. "It was yesterday, around one. I'd been to my mother's in Leesburg, they have a condo there. We always have lunch at the Farmer's Market Restaurant. There's a place there where you can get propane gas refills. Now, normally I don't even look in that direction. The place where customers fill their tanks is directly across from the restaurant. You can sit in any of the booths along the wall and see out the window. I was sitting in one of those booths with my mom. Something made me look up; I don't know what it was, but I did. I saw a man and woman with a baby. They were older, like maybe in their sixties. I thought surely they weren't the parents, maybe the grandparents. But something about the way they handled the baby just didn't seem quite right. You know, how you can tell with some people? They either have it or they don't. Well, this couple didn't have it. They weren't comfortable with the child. I mentioned it to Mom. The couple kept passing her back and forth. Maybe she was crying or something. I couldn't hear that, of course, since I was inside. The man, he was short, not much hair from what I could see, looked angry when the woman gave him the baby to hold. He must have said something that scared the woman because she snatched the baby back. She just acted . . . odd. It's hard to say, but it didn't look right and it didn't feel right. My mother felt the same way. A few minutes later, the couple took their tank and left. That's all I can tell you.

"I didn't think anything more of it until this morning when I saw the news. It was the pink shirt and blond hair that made me remember. The news said the baby had been wearing a pink outfit and that she had blond hair. The baby matched the description, and the people just didn't seem like real grandparents. I called my mother, we discussed it, and she said I should call the police."

Simmons flipped to a second sheet on his notepad. "Did you see the vehicle they were driving?"

"No, it was out of my view. Like I said, I didn't think anything more about it. Just a set of grandparents with a baby. If I hadn't seen those reporters, I would have forgotten the incident, but I'm sure it was the missing baby. She was wearing a red shirt."

"What about the woman? Was there anything about her that stands out, other than her awkwardness with the baby?"

The young woman shook her head. "Nothing I can think of. She was average size, I guess, because nothing stands out in my memory. If she'd been really fat or tall or had some distinguishing marks, I'm sure I would remember. She was wearing a dress, though. The man had on jeans and boots. And a baseball cap."

"Can you describe their clothing, color, texture? Did they have bags or anything with them?"

Ellen thought for a moment. "Now keep in mind I was more than a hundred feet away. I think the woman was wearing a plaid dress. The kind my mom calls a housedress. They button down the front, have pockets and a collar. My mother said she didn't think they made housedresses any longer because they're old-fashioned. I think her hair was brown. I'm really not sure about that, though."

"Could you make out the colors?"

"They were dark colors, that much I do remember. Drab. But, if they were green, blue, or black, I haven't a clue. The man was wearing jeans and a denim shirt. His baseball cap was black or maybe navy blue. I couldn't see his hair. Everyone in the restaurant was wearing the same kind of cap, even the young guys. He was wearing sunglasses. So was the woman."

"Burke, does that sound like anyone you know? Family? Friends, neighbors?"

"No. Susan or my wife might know someone who fits that description. Hell, Richard might know someone who fits that description. What about that doctor they have locked up? He might know. Maybe you can put the squeeze on him and let him know we have a lead. He might break down and confess."

"I plan on it, trust me. I'll do it the minute his lawyer allows us to question him." Simmons stood up, tucked his notepad into his shirt pocket. He withdrew a card from his wallet and handed it to the young woman. "Ms. Grant, I'd like to speak with your mother, too. Could you have her call me?"

"Yes, of course. I can call her now if you like."

"No, that's all right. Have her call me at the station later. If I'm not in, tell her to leave her number and I'll call her back."

"Okay. I hope this helps you find your granddaughter, Mr. Burke. I saw her picture. She's a beautiful little girl. I'll say a prayer that she's returned safely to you."

Simmons stopped. "Did you happen to see the baby's face?"

"No. The woman was holding her up to her shoulder. I could just see the back of her head and the pink shirt."

"You've been a big help. If you think of anything else, call me. Any time of the day or night."

Burke followed the detective outside, then turned around. "Ms. Grant, you didn't happen to see a pickup truck with a camper parked anywhere near the restaurant, did you?"

"No, like I said, I didn't have a clear view of the parking lot from where I was seated. Just the area where you wait while they fill the tanks."

Burke nodded and thanked the woman for her information.

"I hope it helps."

Back in the squad car, Simmons quizzed Burke. "Want to fill me in on the camper story?"

"Grasping at straws, I'm afraid. Richard's adoptive parents have a camper. The way Ms. Grant described the couple brought them to mind. But they're from Lakeland, nowhere near Leesburg. I only saw them once, at Susan's wedding reception. If you asked me what they look like, I can't tell you other than to say they're ordinary-looking. My wife said they were nice but shy."

"First, I'm going to ask you some conclusive questions to record your response. Then we'll begin questioning. Please answer my questions with a yes or a no." The polygrapher stood beside the machine, made a few adjustments, then sat down across the table from Dylan.

"Is your name Dylan Stockard?"

"Yes."

"Are you thirty-five years of age?"

"Yes."

"Are you married?"

"Yes."

"Are you a doctor?"

"Yes."

"Do you have children?"

"No."

"Is your wife named Renée?"

"Yes."

"All right, Doctor Stockard, we've established our base-line questions. Are you ready to begin?"

Dylan looked at Seamus seated in the corner, who nodded. "Yes, I'm ready."

"On Saturday did you make a visit to the Magic Kingdom amusement park?"

"Yes."

"Are you adopting a child?"

Dylan caught Seamus's eye before answering. "Well, we're planning on it. We've only recently talked with an agency."

"Doctor Stockard, just answer with a yes or a no. Are you adopting a child?"

"No." Dylan started to perspire. The room was small, and there wasn't a window for ventilation. He lifted his hand to wipe at his forehead.

"I want you to sit still. Please don't move, Doctor Stockard."

"Uh, sure." He thought this would be a breeze, but it wasn't. His heart began to pound. He inhaled, closed his eyes, and visualized a cool stream. Renée swore by visualization. His heart pounded harder. It wasn't working for him.

"Are you friends with Susan Johnson?"

Again, he searched Seamus's face before answering. "Not, really. No. We're acquaintances."

"Just say yes or no, Doctor Stockard." The polygrapher's voice rose just enough to let Dylan know he'd hit a nerve. This was a by-the-book-no-other-way-man. "Are you friends with Susan Johnson?"

"No." He sounded harsh.

"Did you ever remove Ashley Rose Johnson from her stroller?"

Dylan panicked. If he told the truth, he'd incriminate himself. If he lied, it would show on the test. He was willing to take a chance. Either way he was screwed. "Yes."

"I think my client has had enough. Unhook him."

"I still have more questions."

"Tough. We're done," Seamus told the polygrapher.

"Seamus! This isn't going to look good. I'll answer his questions. Look, I don't care what he asks me. I didn't do anything, so there's nothing to worry about."

"I agree, Doctor Stockard, but before we go any further, we're going to get someone else to do this test."

"Sir, I'll have you know I've been giving polygraphs for thirty years."

"Yep, I know. I just remembered. Thanks for your time. Now, unhook him."

The man did as instructed. Dylan was shocked speechless.

Ten minutes later he was back in his cell. "Want to tell me what that was all about? Damn, Seamus, this makes me look guilty as hell."

"His sister is married to the state's attorney."

"So?"

"I don't like it, that's all. I kept thinking I knew the man from somewhere, then it clicked. The state uses his services a little too often to suit me. Don't worry. I'll have another examiner in here ASAP. We need the results for the bail hearing tomorrow."

"You're the lawyer. I just want to get out of this place. It's noisy, dirty, and the guards watch me piss. Damn it, Seamus, I didn't take that kid."

"I'll have you out of here tomorrow, hang in there."

"Is Cameron allowed to visit? I'll need to go over some things with him."

"Yes, he's allowed, but you'll be out of here, so his services might not be needed after all."

"I hope so, because another night in here and I'll go out of my mind."

"I won't let that happen, Dylan." Seamus scribbled something on his ever-present legal pad.

"That's nice to know." Dylan grimaced. He liked Seamus and hoped they could be friends when this was behind them.

"Tell me about Doctor Cameron Collins. How'd you come to be such good friends?"

"Cam and I grew up together. We went to the same schools until we graduated. Why?"

"A little birdie tells me this story about Doctor Collins. And I ask myself why I had to hear it from a birdie."

"Play it straight, Seamus. What are you talking about?"

"Were you aware that your good friend Doctor Cameron Collins was once engaged to the mother of the missing child?"

"You're serious? You didn't know? I thought everyone

knew. I just assumed you knew. Okay, okay, you didn't know. I should have told you. What's the big deal?"

Seamus thumped his legal pad with the tip of his pen. "Maybe it's not a big deal to you, but I'm your attorney, Dylan. I need to know things like that. Before we get inside the courtroom. If we get that far. I hate to be blindsided. Do you have any idea what the prosecution could do with this information?"

Dylan raised his eyebrows. "No, but I feel sure you're about to tell me."

"In the wrong hands, right hands, whichever way you look at it, it doesn't look good. Now, I'm not saying there's anything there, but . . . but in the hands of a good prosecutor we could get royally flushed right down the toilet."

"Okay, so what do you want me to do?"

"Nothing. I want your promise you'll be up-front with me from here on in. I can't defend you if I don't know these little secrets."

"There is no secret, Seamus. You can ask me anything and I'll give you a straight answer. Like I said, I have nothing to hide. Furthermore, Seamus, Cam's name and his relationship with Susan has never come up since I landed here."

"Okay, that's good. Now, I'm outta here. I'll be back with that examiner, so prepare yourself."

"I'll be waiting."

"I made the call and got through." Iris's voice rang with excitement. "Mr. Edward is going to do a telephone reading for you."

"Mom, really. I don't think he can help," Susan said. "I'd be wasting his and my time." Weariness and defeat rang in her voice.

"You can do what you want, Susan. I'm not going to force you, but do me one favor. Watch Mr. Edward's program before you make up your mind. You're the one who said you were willing to do anything. I think this comes under the heading of anything. I saw a television set in the employee lounge when we came in through the back. I'm sure Detective Simmons can arrange for us to use that room for a bit."

"All right, Mom, I'll watch the program, but I still don't know about the reading. What if Richard finds out?"

"What if he does? You'll be glad you agreed when Mr. Edwards helps you find Ashley."

"I want her back so bad. I feel empty. She's part of me and I've lost her. She's still alive, isn't she, Mom?" Susan pleaded.

"Yes, your daughter is alive, and yes, we will get her back. I told you what I thought about Richard. If you're smart, you'll insist that Detective Simmons check him out. If you don't tell him, then I will. Susan, think about it. Richard is about to lose everything. His job that he deceived his way into, his family, his new status in the community. And we all know how important his status is to him. The rug is about to be pulled out from under him. What better way to put a stop to . . . well, everything. Ashley turns up missing, and the focus is suddenly on her and not him. He is still in control of Burke and Burke, the divorce proceedings stopped on a dime. It fits, Susan. Just think about it."

"What kind of man would do this to his daughter? Richard knows how much Ashley depends on me. She's never been cared for by anyone but me, you, and Dad. That has to mean something to him."

"I don't think so, dear. I really believe the man is wicked

and evil. Look in his eyes sometime. The eyes are supposed to be the window on the soul. There is nothing to see in Richard's eyes. The first time I met him was the night your father invited him to our house for dinner. I knew in an instant there was something wrong. I knew, Susan. He knew I didn't like him, knew I suspected something. He smirked at me as much as to say, go ahead, try and figure it out. He damn well *smirked,* Susan. Your father, of course, was oblivious to all this."

Susan considered her mother's remarks. Richard *was* full of rage and he was heartless. He was also arrogant, obnoxious, and hateful. But would he kidnap his own child? Her mother thought so. Why was she having so much trouble believing it? Because it would make her look bad? Because she was stupid for marrying a man like him? Her own guilt for her stupidity.

"I think something happened to Richard in his childhood. I don't know what it is because he never really talked to me about it. But whatever it is, it affected him in his adult life. I couldn't wait to tell him about my childhood. It was like he was born an adult. I think it has something to do with the people who adopted him. Look at the way he treated his adoptive parents at the reception. That pretty much bears out what I just said. I don't think Richard has called them more than twice, if that, since we got married. Maybe I should call them myself and tell them about Ashley before they hear about it on the news. I've been sending them pictures of Ashley. I didn't tell Richard, though. Vilma always sent me a little thank-you note."

"Did you mention any of this to Detective Simmons? I think it bears telling."

Susan drew in a shaky breath. Just talking about Richard made her nervous. "I didn't see the point. Ashley is my main concern right now, Mom. I know you mean well, but until I hold my daughter in my arms again, nothing will be ever be right. I don't care about Richard, his parents, or anything that has to do with him. I want my daughter back, and if it takes an army to find her, then I'll find an army. I can't concentrate on anything else. I keep seeing her face and wondering if she's hungry. Has her diaper been changed? Is she warm? Is she hurt?"

"I'll talk to the detective myself, as soon as he gets back here with your father. Maybe by the grace of God, the woman they talked to will have the information we need to locate the people who have your daughter. Then that poor Doctor Stockard can go home to his wife. I feel terrible about him, Susan, because I know he's innocent. Right here. I feel it right here." Iris placed a hand over her heart for the umpteenth time.

Susan knew her mother thought she was right and there would be no convincing her otherwise.

Chapter Sixteen

Saturday, December 14, 2002

Ashton Burke clinked the ice cubes in his glass. He couldn't remember ever drinking scotch at eleven o'clock in the morning. It was obvious Iris couldn't remember either. His wife scowled at him. She was drinking black rum tea. The flavored kind.

"Don't look at me like that, Iris. I need to drink today to prepare myself for that ridiculous Christmas party Richard is hosting this evening. Do not even think of telling me you aren't going. We're going and that's final. We need to be there for moral support for our daughter.

"Tell me again, Iris, why our beautiful, intelligent daughter allowed that . . . that . . . person to move back into her condo."

Iris's voice was weary. "Ashton, I've already told you a dozen times, Susan did it partly because of the media and because she feels guilty somehow for marrying Richard in the first place. She absolutely refuses, just as you refuse, to believe that man had anything to do with our granddaughter's disappearance. Well, you're both wrong and I am going to prove it to you."

Ashton replenished the scotch in his glass. He glared at his wife as he gulped at the fiery liquid. "Just how in the hell are you going to do that?"

Iris sipped at her tea that was now cold. She didn't care.

"I had a dream the night before last, and . . ."

"Stop right there, Iris. I can't handle any more of your dreams and your cockamamie feelings."

"Do you want to know something, Ashton? Do you know what I think? I think you are a . . . what you are is . . . a *horse's ass*. So there! I said I could prove it, and by God, I will. I've had enough of this pussyfooting around. The police, all those agencies, none of them have found a thing. Not even one clue. Now, I want you to listen to me and listen good."

Ashton shrugged, his thoughts far away. He continued to guzzle the amber liquid in his glass.

"Yesterday, I went Christmas shopping, Ashton. I bought lovely gifts for Vilma and Buddy Johnson. I'm going to Lakeland today, unannounced, to deliver them. I am going to appeal to the Christian side of Richard's adoptive parents. You can either go with me or you can stay here with your snoot in that glass. What's it going to be?"

"What? Why would you want to do a stupid thing like that?"

"Ashton, I am getting mighty sick and tired of the way you talk to me. I will not tolerate it. Let me remind you one more time, the situation we are in is all because of you. We are in this position because of your greed, poor judgment and your ego. Susan is in her own little black world because of that man. I am the only one left who can make this right because I am . . . I . . ." She struggled for just the right phrase. "I am because both my oars are in the water." She was so pleased with her words, she smiled triumphantly.

"Iris, I didn't mean . . ."

"Yes, Ashton, you did mean everything you said. I am this close," she said, pinching her thumb and forefinger together, "to leaving you. I get extreme pleasure out of visualizing you as a homeless vagrant."

Ashton blanched at his wife's words. He could visualize it, too. He poured more scotch into his glass. "Do you hate me that much, Iris?"

"Sometimes. Other times I love you so much it hurts. I can get over the latter real quick. Most times it is easier to hate than it is to love. If Ashley Rose is never found, that man will be in our lives forever. I will not tolerate that, Ashton. I absolutely will not tolerate that. If we leave now, we can be back in plenty of time for the party. I'm driving the Volvo. Are you coming or not?"

"Iris, you haven't driven on the highway for thirty years."

"There's a first time for everything. Now, get your ass in that car and let's go. I'm doing this for Susan. Right now I hate you, Ashton. Don't make me regret extending the invitation to come along."

"When did you get so goddamn peppery?"

"While you were screwing up our lives, that's when. Now, move!"

Ashton moved.

The trailer was a rusty affair, old and ugly. The yard was littered with tires, a junk car, rusty tools and a garden hose coiled like a snake. A strip of plywood that said, JESUS LOVES YOU in red paint, was nailed to a wooden spike in the ground.

"I'm going to drive by the house and park farther down this . . . road."

"Road my ass. It's a cow path," Ashton grumbled. "People don't live like this."

"Yes, Ashton, people do live like this. Suck it up because you might be moving out here and becoming their new neighbor. You didn't have two cents to your name when I married you. This could well be you if it wasn't for me and my family. Chew on that. Now get out of this damn car and help me with the presents. Try not to breathe around them. They don't approve of drinking. To them, we're sinners. Are you listening to me, Ashton?"

"Shut up, Iris. Let's just do this and get it over with." He waited patiently for his wife to load up his arms. Both packages were so elegantly wrapped, he knew that the wrapping alone must have cost a fortune. "You never gave me anything wrapped like this," he complained.

"That's because you didn't deserve it. Remember what I said about breathing around them. I will do the talking, Ashton. Pretend you're mute."

Ashton rolled his eyes. He felt so light-headed he thought he was going to pass out. He sucked in the humid air and followed his wife, trying not to step in dog poop as he went along. He wondered where the dog was.

Iris knocked on the dirty-looking metal door. When there was no response, she kicked it, then hammered it with her closed fist. "Yoo-hoo, Vilma," she trilled, "it's Iris and Ashton Burke. We brought you some Christmas presents," she trilled again.

"They aren't home, Iris."

"Or else they aren't answering the door. They're afraid." Iris continued to bang and kick at the door. She winced when she saw dog poop on the edge of her shoe. She tried to scrape it off on the wooden step but was unsuccessful. She banged again.

The door opened. Vilma Johnson's face turned white. "Mrs. Burke! Mr. Burke! Lord have mercy, what are you all doing way out here?"

"We came to wish you a Merry Christmas and to give

you these presents. You are family now. This is what families do," Iris said cheerfully. "May we come in?"

"Well . . . my husband isn't here. I don't . . . yes, of course. Can you wait just a second? I have to . . . to . . . pick up a little. I wish you had called and told me you were coming. I could have baked something."

"Good heavens, that's not necessary. Ashton and I are both on diets. We'll only stay a minute."

The woman's face took on a desperate expression. "Just give me a minute." She closed the door in their faces. A minute turned into seven or eight. When she finally opened the door, Iris blasted through, Ashton in her wake.

The interior of the trailer was worn and shabby, but it was clean. The walls were decorated with religious pictures. Votive candles were everywhere. A stack of prayer cards sat on a table by the door.

"Where would you like my husband to put your gifts? Are you going to have a Christmas tree, Vilma?"

"No. No, we don't do much celebrating. Christmas is too commercial. People lose sight of the real meaning of Christmas in their greed to make money."

"My husband feels like that, but I don't," Iris chirped, her eyes searching, for what she didn't know. Suddenly she sat down on an old rocker and burst into tears. "This was supposed to be such a wonderful Christmas. It would have been Ashley Rose's first Christmas. We're just devastated. My daughter is being treated for a nervous breakdown. I hate seeing her on all that medication. Most of the time she doesn't even know what day it is. It's just heartbreaking. What kind of evil person would steal a child and not care what the child's mother feels? No good Christian person like yourself, that's for sure.

"I told Ashton and my daughter that God works in

mysterious ways. The person or persons who took Ashley Rose will burn in hell for what they did to us. God will bring down his wrath on the evildoers. Don't you agree, Vilma?"

"Why, I . . . yes, yes, I agree with you."

"Now, I've ruined our little visit. I'm sorry, Vilma. I was trying to do something nice to get my mind off our missing grandchild. I'm just so worried about our daughter. She has to be watched constantly." Iris dabbed at her eyes again. "If something goes awry and she takes her own life, it will be . . . *murder*."

Iris didn't think it was possible for Vilma Johnson's face to get any whiter, but it did somehow.

"Ashton, we have to leave now. I'm too overwrought. Please tell Buddy we missed seeing him, and tell him we wish him a Merry Christmas, and you, too, Vilma." She stepped forward and threw her arms around the woman, at the same time slipping a roll of bills into the pocket of the woman's housedress. She drew in a deep breath and hugged her. Ashton held the door open. He nodded goodbye, his lips clamped shut.

Neither Iris nor Ashton spoke until they were in the car. "Well, I hope to hell you're happy, Iris. This was a wasted trip."

"Sometimes, Ashton Burke, you are so stupid you make me wonder why I ever married you. For your information, Ashton, Vilma Johnson smelled like *baby powder*. I sat next to her at the wedding and there was no scent to the woman at all. It's a woman thing. What do you think she was doing for those eight or nine minutes when she closed the door? I'll tell you what she was doing. She was hiding things. Now, what do you think? Do you still think I don't know what I'm talking about?"

Ashton reared back as he watched his regal-looking wife descend the steps. She looked ravishing in her silver lamé gown. Her hair was upswept with jeweled combs. She looked every bit as good as she had when she was nineteen. He said so. She smiled.

"I can't believe Richard had the nerve to say this party was black tie. Considering the circumstances, the whole idea of a party is in bad taste. I can't imagine how Susan is going to handle it. I feel so much better, Ashton, don't you? At least we know Ashley Rose is safe, and I'm sure Vilma is taking very good care of her."

"You don't know that for sure, Iris. Smelling like baby powder doesn't mean she has our grandchild. If you were so certain, why didn't you let me call the police?"

"Because I feel she's safe. Listen to me, Ashton. If I'm right and the Johnsons do have Ashley Rose, we have to give them time to bring her back on their own. That will be in their favor. The authorities will go very hard on them. Richard ruined their lives, too. I'm sure he threatened them with God knows what. The morning will be time enough if the Johnsons don't bring her back."

"What if they take Ashley Rose and leave? What if they call Richard? If you're so certain, you're gambling with our granddaughter's safety. You're depriving Susan of knowing where her child is. You can't play God, Iris."

Iris sat down on the steps. She eyed her sparkly shoes. "Is that what I'm doing, Ashton?"

Ashton sat down next to his wife. "I think so. I'm stone-cold sober now. Let's stop at the police station on our way to the party. I understand what you're saying, Iris, and I know you mean well, but we can't take a chance. We've already allowed four hours to go by. Four hours is a long time. You can drive two hundred and fifty miles in four hours. And I don't mean to rain on your parade, but I put baby powder in my shoes all the time so my feet won't sweat."

"They aren't evil people, Ashton. I know as sure as I'm sitting here that Vilma Johnson will bring back our granddaughter. If she has her, she will bring her back."

Ashton reached for Iris's chin and tilted it toward him. "Think about this little scenario, my dear. The police come to the party and arrest Richard in front of everyone. Then Detective Simmons arrives with Ashley Rose in his arms."

"Oh, Ashton, can that happen? Can it truly happen?"

"It's the season of miracles, isn't it? If you're right, yes, it could happen. Come on, let's not waste another minute."

Bing Crosby's "White Christmas" flowed from a hidden speaker, reminding Susan of the upcoming holiday. Not that she cared. Since Ashley's disappearance, Christmas would be just another day. It had been two months since Ashley had been taken from her stroller at the Magic Kingdom. Two months since she'd held her in her arms. Gone but not forgotten. Never forgotten.

Sight unseen.

For weeks, Detectives Simmons, Nicholls, and Davis had pursued every phone call, every lead possible in their search to locate Ashley Rose, to no avail.

Doctor Dylan Stockard had been charged with kidnapping and murder. Her worst fears were confirmed when her father gave her the news. Her daughter was gone. Nothing would bring her back.

Richard had showed up at the door three weeks after Ashley's abduction, saying he was moving back in so they could present a united front to the media. He'd gotten what he wanted in the end after all, Burke and Burke.

Days would go by when she wouldn't even see him. It was almost like having a roommate who traveled and was never home. He told her a Christmas party would cheer her up. That's when she knew he really was crazy. But what did she care? A Christmas party wasn't going to cheer her up. The only thing that could make her world right again was seeing her daughter. She knew that wasn't going to happen. Nothing would ever be the same without her daughter, so it didn't matter what he did or didn't do.

Richard could have the condo, the cars, and the bank accounts. Her father might as well sign Burke and Burke over to him because it was all but his anyway.

She had finally accepted the fact that her daughter was dead. Not that anyone said the word aloud. Did they think she was a fool? This year would have been Ashley Rose's first Christmas. And Richard was having a Christmas party.

Thanks to Doctor Dylan Stockard, her daughter would never have *any* firsts.

Susan Johnson stood in the middle of the bathroom staring at her reflection in the mirror. She refused to acknowledge the glass of water and the bottle filled with Valium. Who was this ugly caricature staring back at her? She glared at the person returning her glassy-eyed stare. Not only did she look ugly, she looked pathetic as well.

Dove-gray eyes shadowed with purple half-moons stared vacantly at the image, as though controlled by a remote. Her shoulder-length hair was a dull coffee brown and hung limply around her face. She looked like an anorexic, ugly, pathetic witch.

Mother of God, how did it come to this?

She fingered the lustrous pearls circling her neck. They

looked as dull and washed-out as she did. To still the ever-present tremor in her hand, she balled it into a fist. She winced because her nails were raw and ragged from biting.

She turned around and studied the black, knee-length sleeveless dress she was wearing for the evening's festivities. The off-the-rack Ralph Lauren would do little to disguise her gaunt figure. She could have gotten the same style dress at the Gap for a quarter of the cost and saved some money. Richard considered off-the-rack Ralph Lauren and Gap slumming.

God how she hated the son of a bitch.

She deliberately moved away from the vanity and the pill bottle to stare into the massive walk-in closet. Versace, Yohji Yamamoto, Armani, and Escada decorated the long racks and were a healthy tribute to the fashion industry. She'd always been a Levi's and tee shirt kind of gal. Back in the days when Cameron was in her life, but that was all B.A.—Before Ashley.

Today was the day she was taking matters into her own hands. She was too tired and she couldn't fight anymore. *Couldn't or wouldn't?* What did it matter? It was all a game anyway, a game with no rules. She couldn't win, so why bother to play? She wondered vaguely if this was the way her mother felt when things closed in on her. *God, where did that come from?*

All she had to do was get through the evening. Just one more evening.

Susan reached for a pair of black sling-backs. Slut shoes. Then she remembered that, at five-foot-seven, in heels, she would stand taller than Richard, who at five-foot-eight was self-conscious about his height, or lack of it. Her hand reached out for a pair of black flats. She jerked it back and chose the slut shoes. "Fuck you, you son of a bitch!" she mumbled.

"Susan?"

"What is it, Richard?" Susan asked, stepping out of the closet, the slut shoes dangling in her hands.

"What the hell is taking you so long? That goddamn idiot of a caterer your mother hired doesn't understand a word I'm saying; and the fucking bartender hasn't arrived. He should have been here an hour ago." He looked at the Rolex on his wrist.

She'd given it to him as an engagement present. It was the last gift he'd ever get from her. She felt smug at the thought.

"Move your ass. Christ, can't you do anything right?"

Susan stared at her husband with clinical interest. Richard was forty-five, fifteen years her senior, and didn't look his age thanks to his daily workouts.

Richard still wore his hair close cropped, military style, and it had just the right blend of gray at the temples. He thought it made him look distinguished. Deep webbed lines etched the corners of his pale blue eyes. Richard referred to them as laugh lines. She knew better. Full lips, professionally whitened teeth, and skin tanned without any help from Florida's burnishing sun proved he could pass for an often-out-of-work George Hamilton. And to think at one time she'd thought him handsome.

That night Richard wore an Armani suit, pristine white shirt, and a festive red tie, in apparent deference to the holiday. He looked every inch the consummate professional.

Architect extraordinaire.

Susan took a deep breath. *Screw you, you bastard.* "I just need another minute."

Richard scrutinized her. She knew she was coming up

short. She felt the urge to laugh in his face. *Just let me get through the night,* she thought.

"Christ Almighty, you look like you just came off Forty-second Street. Fix your goddamn hair. If I didn't need you to help with the bar, I'd lock you in this room."

Lock her in her room. Isn't that what my father used to do to my mother? He gave her one last disgusted look before he stomped out of the room.

Susan watched her husband's retreating back until she was sure he'd left the room. Her heart pounded with each step. Actually, it roared in her ears. She laughed, a weird sound. It was like putting a seashell to her ear the way she'd done when she was a child. Sweat dampened her palms. Not caring, she wiped them on her dress.

She tottered over to the toilet tank and looked down at a large, white magnolia candle whose scent was overpowering. Next to the candle stood a statue of a naked woman, Richard's sick contribution to the bathroom decor. With one sweep of her arm, the statue shattered, and the candle broke into three jagged pieces. The sound of the breaking statue sounded loud to her. She paused and listened for Richard's footsteps.

Silence.

She was safe.

Lifting the porcelain top from the back of the tank, Susan found her stash, courtesy of Doctor Emily Watts, safe and sound.

The Ziploc bag dripped on her dress. Like she gave a good rat's ass if it dripped. She removed a second brownish gold bottle of Valium and placed it next to the bottle on the vanity. She uncapped the bottle and shook out several of the blue pills.

She looked up then to stare into the mirror. She blinked

when she saw, not the haggard woman she'd become but a smaller face with blond curls and clear, blue, puppy-dog eyes. The vision was wearing a little pink tee shirt with matching shorts. The last outfit she had dressed her daughter in.

Susan leaned into the vanity, her knuckles white with the effort. *Dear God, help me. Please, help me.* She managed to open her eyes, but everything was out of focus. Was she having one of those out-of-body experiences she'd read about? Probably not since she didn't see any golden light at the end of the tunnel. Damn, there wasn't even a tunnel. *What is wrong with me?*

Her gaze dropped to the marble vanity and the two bottles of "relief" she'd come to rely on since losing Ashley two months earlier.

She dumped the contents of both bottles onto the vanity. They glowed like a beacon to the lost. She was lost, wasn't she?

Since her daughter's disappearance, her life had been nothing more than a performance for the characters who, like her, merely pretended to care. Their act was so well rehearsed, Susan often believed it herself. Richard. Her father. Her mother. No, she wouldn't think about her daughter. If she did . . . she might not be able to go on.

Her fingers traced the pills on the counter until they formed an A and an R. It took forty pills to make the two initials.

Forty pills should be enough to do the job. She picked them up, one by one, hating to disturb her daughter's initials.

She ran water from the tap to fill the glass in her left hand. From somewhere far back in her mind she could hear a stern voice say, *Oh, no, Sue, that's the coward's way out.*

No, no, I won't let you do this.

Susan whirled around. "Cam? Is that you?" She shook her head to clear it. Cameron Collins, her true love. "You dumped me, remember? What do you care what I do?"

She was about to swallow the pills when she heard loud footsteps. Shit! Panic zipped through her as she pulled the stopper to let the pills slide down the drain.

"Goddamn it, Susan, hurry up. Your father is asking for you. I want you downstairs now, or I'm going to do something you aren't going to like."

She didn't have to be on the other side of the door to see the controlled rage that contorted her husband's features. Didn't actually have to stand next to him to hear the venom in his words.

God, how she hated him. She looked around for another means of escape. Other than the skylight twelve feet above her, her only other means of exiting the bathroom was to walk out the same way she had walked in.

Susan took a deep breath. The pills she'd taken earlier had finally kicked in. Familiar fogginess descended, easing her tension. She smiled at herself in the mirror. She looked crazy, dazed.

She thought about the pills sliding down the drain. Oh, well, she'd just have to go to see Doctor Watts again; and if she balked, she'd simply remind her of what she'd been through. Or, if she was desperate enough, she'd look up that quack González. Just the thought made her stomach roil.

It was time to make her command performance. She splashed water on her face, combed her hair. She didn't look one bit better. She looked just as crazy and dazed as she had before. Stumbling from the room minus her slut shoes, she whizzed downstairs so fast she had to stop at the landing to catch her breath.

Susan viewed the throng of guests as though she was in a fun house, the images distorted. Tall, short, fat, and skinny. Smiling, frowning, talking. She didn't know half of them, and she knew they couldn't have cared less whether or not she made an appearance. This party was all about Richard. Not her. Never her.

Peter Breckenridge, Richard's friend and client, and his wife Marilyn. Tall and gangly, Peter reminded her of the scarecrow in *The Wizard of Oz*. Blond hair in constant need of combing, shirttail out, always in need of a tuck here or there. Peter was the complete opposite of Richard, who never had a hair out of place. Marilyn, on the other hand, was the direct opposite of her husband. Flawless skin, cat green eyes that couldn't possibly be her real color, and skin so tight, it looked like a mask. Fake. Rumor had it she'd recently undergone a face-lift. Auburn hair cut in the latest short style stuck out from her head like feathers. She'd always reminded Susan of a bird. One of those drinking birds filled with red water she'd seen at Stuckey's as a child. Marilyn's head bobbed up and down, her mouth in a constant state of movement. Chirp. Chirp. Chirp.

She continued to watch the couple chat with Rose and Reuben Goldberg, old friends of her father's and once practicing attorneys. Susan had enjoyed many lively debates over the years with the retired couple. Reuben, short and rotund, with a snow-white beard and like hair, could have passed for a jolly Santa. At four-foot-ten, Rose fit the image of a petite Mrs. Claus. Always animated, Susan watched her gnarled, jeweled hands wave through the air while she spoke. Take away Rose's hands and she would become a deaf mute.

She sensed Richard glaring at her from across the room.

She held his gaze, and, under her breath, muttered, "Fuck you, Richard. I hate your guts. Do you understand what I'm saying?" She smiled when she realized he understood *exactly* what she was saying. She took a step forward and stumbled. She grabbed for the newel to support herself.

She watched him weave his way through the den, pausing to stop and talk with people who idolized him. *They should only know,* Susan thought grimly.

He was on his way to the bottom step, where she remained a spectator. Scorching anger brightened his eyes. Ashley's eyes.

"Okay, how many did you take this time?" He yanked her by the arm, his fingers digging into the underside of her tender flesh before he half dragged her to the kitchen and slammed her down on one of the kitchen chairs.

Maria, her new housekeeper, looked at her, then quickly averted her eyes. A man dressed in a crisp white shirt and dark, tailored pants, obviously a member of the catering staff, stood at the center island in her stainless-steel kitchen. He was filling a platter with stuffed cherry tomatoes. He looked at Richard, then back at her, his dark brow raised in question. She knew what he was thinking. Was she going to take this abuse or do something about it? She shook her head slightly.

Richard loomed over her like a giant. His voice was little more than a harsh hiss when he said, "What in the hell am I supposed to tell our guests, Susan?" His fingers tightened on her arm.

"I have an idea," she singsonged. "Let's tell them the truth for a change. Let's tell them what a conniving son of a bitch you are. Let's tell them about your temper, how you hit women. Let's tell them *everything*. If you don't want to tell them, I'll do it for you."

Susan eyeballed him, knowing she'd finally struck a nerve. The last thing Richard Johnson wanted was for her father and business associates to discover the *real* Richard Johnson.

He released his grip. So predictable.

She was angry now. She wanted to, no, she *needed* to provoke Richard.

"Well?" she prompted.

He leaned over her and met her glassy-eyed stare. He wanted to beat her senseless, but he didn't dare. She laughed in his face.

"You find this funny? I certainly don't, and I doubt your father will either. We have a house full of guests. This is supposed to be a goddamn Christmas party, not some . . ."

She laughed again. "Some what, Richard?"

Richard looked around before he grabbed her arm again. "You don't belong here, you belong in an institution, Susan. I've warned you that I won't tolerate this behavior. Make no mistake, I will have you committed, and Daddy dearest isn't going to be able to prevent it."

"Tsk, tsk, and just how are you going to do that? Are you going to say *poof*, and make me disappear? I don't think so. My father and mother care about me. And you're wrong about one thing, it's you who doesn't belong here. This is all mine. Not yours. Never yours, you son of a bitch."

Susan turned around when she heard the kitchen door open, heard her name called. She stared, unable to comprehend what she was seeing in her Valium haze.

Chapter Seventeen

The sun suddenly dimmed as thick, gray clouds scudded across the sky. Simmons focused on the cloud but only momentarily. It wasn't an omen. He wouldn't allow it.

"Davis, I want you and Nicholls to ride with Lakeland P.D. in their unmarked cars. I'll follow in one of ours. We don't want to look like a goddamn parade. The Burkes tell me the Johnsons' trailer is at the edge of a trailer park on a dirt road out in the middle of nowhere. The last thing we want to do is spook them." Simmons was excited at the thought of possibly making an arrest, and if their luck held, they just might find the little baby girl alive.

"We'll do whatever it takes, Simmons. What about him, though?" He nodded in the direction of the jail. "Think we can safely release him?" Davis asked.

"Not yet. Before this is all over, Doctor Dylan Stockard will own us. Call Seamus and tell him what we've learned, but don't tell him we're on our way to the Johnsons'. I want to make damn sure that baby is there before we release Stockard. For whatever it's worth, I never thought the doc did it."

"You got it," Davis said.

"This is going to make one hell of a story if we find that kid. I feel like I know her. Her mother's going to have the best Christmas of her lifetime if we find her."

311

"I'd like to be around to see the look on her face," Nicholls chimed in. "I'm a sucker for that mother love stuff. Makes what we do worthwhile."

"I know what you mean. Now, let's get this show on the road. Lakeland P.D. is expecting us."

Two hours later, Simmons drove his dark green, unmarked, Ford Grand Marquis into a pine-tree-covered lot at the beginning of the dirt road leading to the Johnsons' trailer park. After a fifteen minute debate, Lakeland P.D. had agreed to allow him, Nicholls, and Davis to do the actual stakeout. Three LPD patrol cars were hidden farther down the road, just in case.

The three men were spread out, each with a clear shot of the trailer's exits. Simmons watched the front door from the far edge of the trailer park. Davis positioned himself behind a junky Volkswagen van, where he had a clear shot of the sliding glass door leading to the backyard. Nicholls hid in a small orchard where he could observe anyone coming or going out of the bedroom window.

They'd been there for three hours with no sign of activity.

Simmons used his two-way radio to call Davis and Nicholls. "I think it's time to knock on the door. What about you two?"

Static came across the radio before he heard two clear "ten-fours."

Simmons removed the .357 from his holster, gripped the handle, and aimed it at the rusted front door thirty feet ahead. He took slow, cautious steps as he walked toward the door. Twenty feet. Ten feet. Homemade rickety wooden steps led to a stoop that was just as rickety. He held the gun in his right hand and rapped loudly on the door.

Silence.

He knocked again. Then, again. The silence thundered in his ears. He peered inside a small window at the top of the door. A flimsy white curtain blurred his view. Another series of knocks. He waited. One minute, two, then three.

"Buddy and Vilma Johnson, this is the police! If you're inside, come out with your hands up!"

One . . . two . . . three . . .

Silence.

Simmons holstered his weapon and reached for his radio. "You guys copy?"

"We got ya," Davis said.

"What's happening?" Nicholls asked.

Simmons sighed before answering. "Absolutely nothing. It looks like the Johnsons have skipped out on us."

"I can't believe you'd be so danged stupid! Them people ain't as dumb as you, Vilma. Now if you got an idea, let's hear it, cause when R.J. finds out they was here, we are gonna have some surefire trouble," Buddy said. He'd just been to the Pick Quick to buy diapers and was having a hard time with what his wife was telling him.

"I need to think, Buddy. I just need a minute." Five minutes later, she said, "I think we should just light out. We need to get as far away from this trailer as we can get. We can make a plan while we're driving. We have enough money to tide us over. Mrs. Burke slipped five hundred dollars in my pocket. She's a good person, Buddy."

Ashley Rose, or Mary Jane as they'd been instructed to call her, had run low on diapers after a three-day bout with diarrhea. Vilma had sent Buddy to the store. By an act of God, she'd made him take the baby with him.

Vilma packed up what little they had in the way of personal belongings and was waiting on the porch while Buddy pulled the camper around front. "Thank goodness you got the propane tanks filled for the camper, we're gonna be needin' 'em."

"Propane is gonna be the least of our worries. When R.J. finds out we're gone, he'll come lookin' for us. Lord knows with all that money he's got now, he might hire a private detective to come after us. This ain't gonna work, Vilma. We can run all we want, but he'll find us. We got somethin' that belongs to him."

Vilma thought about what her husband said. He was right like always.

"You got any more bright ideas?" he asked as he hefted a battered suitcase into the camper.

"I'm thinkin'!"

They loaded the back of the camper, put the baby's car carrier in the front seat of the pickup. Vilma took Mary Jane and gently placed her in the seat. Her little bottom was sore. "Poor darlin'," she said to the baby. The baby smiled, showing her bottom teeth.

They both climbed in the truck, checked for a map in the glove compartment, then tore off down the dirt road at seventy miles an hour.

"So, what's our next move?" Buddy asked as he headed north on I-75.

Vilma had been thinking about Iris Burke's visit that morning. She was a good woman, Vilma could tell. She'd been nice to them at the reception, tried to make them feel a part of things, even though R.J., *Richard,* had ignored them. The Christian thing to do was to give the baby back to her momma. Lord only knew what R.J. would do, but hopefully they wouldn't be around to find out.

"We need to give her back, Buddy. She don't belong to us. Her poor momma is about to die, at least that's what

Mrs. Burke says. She's on some kinda medicine or somethin'. We got to return this baby, Buddy. It's the Christian thing to do."

"I never wanted to do it in the first place, you know that."

Vilma glanced at Buddy. "Well, you shoulda spoken up. I hope you ain't thinkin' I wanted to do it. I sure didn't. I suppose that threat on our lives didn't scare you enough to do anythin' about it then, huh?"

"Aw crap, Vilma, you know as well as I do we didn't have no choice. That boy ain't been right since we adopted him. I thought he'd make a fine son. He was polite and all. Did what he was told. After a while, I knew there was somethin' not right about him. I'm tellin' ya, it's why he was placed for adoption in the first place. There's somethin' wrong inside his head. I always said that."

"You're probably right, Buddy. But that ain't gonna solve our problem now. We need to stop and think about how we're gonna get her back to her momma. If we take her to her momma, we'll have to face R.J. and the police. We'll spend the rest of our lives in jail if R.J. has any say-so in the matter. He's gonna say we was the ones who took her. Look—" she pointed to a billboard "—there's a Waffle House three miles from here. Let's stop, get a bite, and think on this."

"All right, but we better do somethin' and be quick about it. If the Burkes are as smart as you claim, they'll be hauling the police up this way right about now, if they ain't already."

Buddy steered the camper onto the exit ramp, then into the parking lot of the Waffle House. Just to make sure no one spotted his camper from the road, he pulled in behind the restaurant.

Vilma gave him a sappy grin. "Good thinkin'."

"We're on the lam, Vilma, it's what needs to be done."

Vilma took Ashley Rose out of her car seat, grabbed the paper sack she used for a diaper bag, then headed inside the restaurant. Faith Hill crooned over the jukebox singing something about soaring above the sky. Coffee, grease, and burned bacon scented the air.

"Good thing we stopped. I was gettin' hungry without any lunch."

"Me too. Now let's order and plan, Buddy. We got to think real hard about what's right for this little girl here." She took a plastic baby bottle in the shape of a hound dog out of her paper sack and poured powdered formula inside. "We'll be needin' a glass of water," she called to the waitress behind the counter.

They ordered waffles with sides of ham and coffee.

"I think we could take her to a church. You know that law they have here in Florida that says leaving babies at churches, firehouses, and police stations is the thing to do if ya got a baby you ain't gonna keep. I think it's supposed to be for unwed mothers to keep 'em from abandoning the little ones in a garbage can or something. What do you think of that?" The waitress came with their meals and refilled their coffee cups.

Buddy waited till she was gone before he answered. "I don't think the police station or the firehouse is a good idea, but I don't see no harm in taking her to a church so long as they take care of her." Buddy's eyes glistened. He'd become attached to the little girl in the past two months.

"I think that's what we should do. Now, all we have to do is pick the right church. I saw a pay phone outside when we came in. There's probably a phone book we could look in. We'll find a church and take her there. We'll tell them who her momma is."

"And you think *they* won't call the police?"

"I think we should leave Ashley, then go make the call."

Buddy pondered this. He shook his head up and down. "Okay, I think it'll work. But you better make sure this little one ain't gonna get hurt."

"Buddy, I'd think after forty years of marriage you ought to know me. Why, if I thought this precious baby stood a chance of bein' hurt, I'd take her to her momma and turn myself in. Churches do these things all the time. They don't tell on you. They keep things like this confidential."

"I know that, Vilma. I just want her taken care of." He sopped up the syrup on his plate with his last bite of ham. "This ain't easy."

Ashley Rose cooed, then let out a loud giggle. Vilma looked at the happy baby. "No, it ain't, Buddy, it ain't easy at all."

Their meal paid for along with a hefty dollar tip, they found the phone book on the shelf beneath the pay phone. Taking it with them to the truck, Vilma searched the yellow pages for churches in the area. "Look at this! Our Lady of Redeemer Church. Don't you love that name? We need to be redeemed, Buddy. This is the place. It's the good Lord's way of tellin' us we're doing the right thing." Vilma tapped a cracked, yellow nail over the name. "And it's just right up the road accordin' to this little map they have here next to the number."

Vilma returned the phone book, minus the page with Our Lady of Redeemer's telephone advertisement.

Thirty minutes later, Buddy parked the camper two blocks away from the church. Vilma's idea. She sure was smart these days. They carried the baby in her car seat, and

Vilma brought the bag with the clothes that still fit. R.J. had brought plenty of things for her, but most of them were too small now. So far, the baby had plumped up real good, Buddy thought. Vilma did a good job feeding and caring for little Ashley.

Brick with a white steeple, Our Lady of Redeemer was small but appeared to be well maintained. In the front of the church two stained-glass windows displayed the Virgin Mary and baby Jesus. A garden in the back must help feed the Sisters, Buddy thought, as they traipsed through the gardens to the back entrance.

It was quiet this time of day. They must be between services. Vilma looked about, hoping no one from that Circle K across the street noticed them. She was sure they would look out of place.

Not wanting to wait any longer, she checked Ashley Rose's diaper. Dry as a bone. Her round little tummy poked out because she was full from the bottle Vilma had given her back at the Waffle House. She wrote the baby's real name and her mother's name on a scrap of paper. She didn't know the Burkes' phone number off the top of her head, but she figured with the baby's picture being on the news for the past two months, when the church called the police they would know how to find the child's momma.

Before she lost her nerve, she gave the little girl a kiss on her soft cheek. "You better tell her goodbye now, Buddy."

With tears streaming down his weathered face, Buddy took Ashley from her seat, gave her a quick hug, then placed her beneath the pink blanket Vilma had spread out. "Bye, little one."

Vilma took the seat, the paper bag, and a heart full of sorrow inside the church. It was dim and quiet, the way a church is supposed to be quiet. She placed the carrier at the altar, stopped, turned around to give the baby one last hug, then darted out the door.

"Let's get out of here!" she called to Buddy through her tears. "Let's get out of this place before I change my mind."

They ran the two blocks to the camper, both of them huffing and puffing when they crawled inside. "Get me to a phone and do it quick. I don't want her left alone for a minute longer than she has to be!"

Buddy shifted the old pickup into drive and left dust in his wake as he raced down the street to a pay phone. Vilma hurried out, made the call, and jumped back in the car.

"Let's get out of here!"

The deed was done. Ashley Rose could now be reunited with her mother.

Iris rushed to her daughter. "Please, everyone, give us some room." She dropped to her knees, aware that the caterer was shooing guests back into the living room. "Susan, Susan, dear, are you all right? Someone find Doctor Watts. I just saw her in the den. Move, Richard!" She shivered at the rage she was seeing in her son-in-law's face. He didn't move immediately, his hate-filled eyes going to the stranger who had just entered the kitchen.

"What . . . what happened?" Susan asked groggily.

"You fainted. You probably haven't eaten, and if I had to take a rough guess, I'd say you took a few too many tranquilizers. Just lie still."

"I thought I saw . . . oh, Mom, I just . . . this party, it's so . . . obscene. For one minute there, I thought I saw Cam. I'm all right. I just need to eat something. I'm okay, Mom." She was muttering, her brain struggling to relay the words. The familiar fogginess she'd been living with the past months was like a cocoon, isolating her from the rest of the world. She tried to get up but her legs felt like wet noodles.

She recognized Doctor Watts's calm voice. She felt better immediately. Doctor Watts wouldn't let Richard do anything to her. "What happened, Susan?" She heard the words, felt her probing hands. She was in good hands and she knew it.

"Can you sit up, Susan?" Susan struggled to a sitting position. Strong hands from behind her helped her onto the chair. They felt familiar, comfortable, just the way Doctor Watts's hands felt.

"I'm sorry. I guess I forgot to eat today. Could I have some water?"

Doctor Watts reached for the damp cloth Iris held out to blot Susan's forehead. "You fainted, Susan. And I suspect you've taken more of the Valium than I prescribed. How many did you take? I need to know if we have to pump your stomach."

"Susan, how many pills did you take?" Iris's voice was so anguished, Susan wanted to cry.

How many pills had she taken? Five since midmorning. Maybe it was seven. It must have been seven if she thought she saw Cam. Usually when she took seven, she could see her daughter's face. Seven pills allowed her to pretend Richard didn't exist.

Seven must be her magic number. "Maybe seven," she mumbled.

"Let's get her upstairs to bed," Doctor Watts said. "What I would really like to do is send her to The Willows. What do you think, Iris?"

"No! I don't want to go there! Mom, no!"

"Shhh, dear. We're going to take you upstairs for now." She nodded to the tall man standing behind Susan's chair. The tall man who had remained quiet throughout the doctor's brief examination. The tall man whose eyes were full of sadness.

Before Susan could even think about responding to the doctor, two well-muscled arms scooped her off the kitchen chair. Maybe she did need to go to The Willows because she was seeing Cam again. Maybe she *had* died and was in heaven. Cam was heaven. If she was dead and in heaven, where was Ashley? She looked up through her Valium haze. "Cam?" she whispered.

"The one and only," he whispered in return.

"Follow me," Iris said, leading Cam to a spiral staircase located behind a wall of floor-to-ceiling cabinets that led to the upper floor of the condo.

"In here," Iris said, leading the way to Susan's bedroom. She saw Cam look at the three heavy-duty deadbolts on the door. Her own hand went to her heart in a gesture of disbelief. Her daughter felt the need for three deadbolts in her own house. She wanted to cry.

"Cam. I can't believe it's you. I can't see you clearly. I took some . . . what I did was . . . I almost . . . oh, God . . ." Tears rolled down her cheeks.

"It's me, Susan. If you need me, I'll be downstairs."

"You won't leave, will you?"

"Not this time. Remember the words in that song, *'Just call my name and I'll be there.'* "

"I remember. You used to say that to me all the time."

Cam looked at her, then turned away. "Mrs. Burke, I'll let you and the doctor take over now. I'll be downstairs."

Susan tried to push herself into an upright position. She couldn't. Weakened by the drugs, she instantly felt horrified at what she had done. She wanted to be with Ashley Rose so badly that she'd planned to end her life. She remembered the words she thought she heard as the pills slid down her throat. *Oh, no, Susan that's the coward's way out. No, no, I won't let you do this.* Were they imagined? Had Cam come back to save her from herself?

The hard reality of her situation overcame her. It didn't matter that Cam had found her. She was married to Richard. She had to stay with him. Because . . . because . . . she owed it to . . . to *whom?* Herself? Her daughter? Cam could never be a part of her life again. It was all her fault. She had no one to blame but herself.

"Susan, are you sure you only took six or seven pills?"

Susan didn't want to admit in front of her mother that she'd tried to end it all. Life was just so hard without Ashley Rose. Living with Richard was pure hell. Surely they understood that.

"I did take the Valium, but I didn't take more than seven. I already told you that. I was going to take more, but Richard came to the door. He . . . stopped me." *Does this mean he saved* my *life? Just something else to bind us together. It's all my fault. I never should have married him. Never.*

"If you're sure that's all you took, then I think the best thing for you to do is sleep it off. I would really like it if you would agree to go to The Willows, Susan. We can look after you there."

Susan knew what she really meant was, they'd keep a suicide watch on her so she wouldn't have an opportunity to try a second time. She shook her head. "No, I don't want to go there, I'll be okay. It's just so hard to get through the days. Nighttime rolls around. I think I hear Ashley crying and go to her nursery, and she's not there. I don't really know why I took all those pills. I'm just lost without her." Susan broke down and sobbed. She sobbed for Cam and what they'd shared, then lost. She sobbed for her horrid judgment when she'd agreed to marry Richard. But most of all she sobbed for her baby daughter and the life she would never have.

"I'll stay here with my daughter, Emily. I won't leave her side. I'm going to send Ashton to fetch Jemma. I appreciate all you've done for us. Please, go downstairs and have a drink and something to eat. My husband told me there are a lot of eligible bachelors floating about, so you might want to circulate. That catering service I hired made everything under the sun. Crepes, little green beans stuffed with cream cheese, rumaki. There's cold shrimp, lobster, filet mignon, fruit, anything and everything," Iris jabbered.

Susan half listened to her mother. She knew her too well. She was up to something. She was trying to get rid of Doctor Watts.

"I'll pass on the drink, but I did miss dinner, so I'll check out the food table. Susan, no more pills. I want to see you in my office first thing Monday morning. We need to talk. *Really* talk. Iris, I'll call you later. Now, if you need me, you know where to find me." Doctor Watts gave Susan's shoulder a quick squeeze, whispered something in her mother's ear, and headed downstairs for the buffet.

"I'm utterly amazed that your husband isn't up here. Utterly amazed. You think he would at least *act* like a concerned husband. Instead, he holds court like he's some famous person."

"It's all about Richard, Mom. You know that. It's always been about Richard. Cam is here. Now, that's something really hard to believe."

"Susan, I want you to listen. Please, dear, pay attention. Don't say a word. I'm the one who called Cam to come to the party. He's been here covering for Doctor Stockard since his arrest. I didn't want to tell you before because that's the last thing you needed to hear."

Susan leaned back into the nest of pillows. She wanted to sleep, needed to sleep. Maybe she'd dream about Ashley Rose and Cam. "Did something change, Mom?" she asked, trying her best to keep up her end of the conversation for her mother's benefit.

"Other than you taking those silly old pills? I'm going to make sure you never do a thing like that again. I want you to pay strict attention and listen to me, Susan. Really listen. I know you don't think that . . . that weasel who is downstairs right now acting like he's hosting a movie star roast or something is responsible for Ashley's kidnapping, but I know he is."

"Oh, Mom, please. We've gone over this a hundred times. I know you don't like Richard, but he didn't have anything to do with Ashley's . . . death." She hated that word. Death and her daughter.

"What if I told you I had proof? What if I told you I know our little Ashley Rose is alive and well? She's not dead, Susan. I swear on my life, Susan, Ashley Rose is not dead. I don't care what those people from the Center told you."

Susan bolted up in the bed, dizziness washing over her like a wave. "Mom! What I think is this. I am going through the worst time of my life. I know you want to help, and I truly can't thank you and Dad enough for all you've done these past two months. But Mom, the police have investigated every lead, every call. They've checked into Richard's alibi. While it's flimsy, he was home lifting weights, then he went for drinks at the country club. Don't you remember Detective Simmons checked it out more than once? If he couldn't find anything, how could you find something?"

"Thank you for the vote of confidence, dear. The answer is, because I'm a mother."

"Mom, please. I didn't mean it like that and you know it." Susan fell back on the pillows.

"Shhh, I want you to listen to me." Iris crossed the room to close the door. She snapped all three deadbolts into place. "This morning your father and I took a drive to Lakeland. It's just a bit over an hour. I thought it would be the Christian thing to do if we took the Johnsons a Christmas gift. You know how I feel about Christmas. Vilma and Buddy live in a dreadful little trailer no bigger than this room. I don't understand how Richard can live in the very lap of luxury and not provide for his parents. It's unconscionable."

"Mother! What *are* you talking about?" Susan raked a hand through her hair. How long since she'd had a decent cut? How long since she'd even thought about her appearance?

"Listen to me, dear, because what I'm about to tell you is going to change your life. As a matter of fact, it's going to be the merriest Christmas you'll ever have."

"The only thing that would make this a merry Christmas is Ashley. And we both know that's not going to happen, so I hate to say this, Mom, but whatever your surprise is, thanks, but no thanks."

"That *is* it! Ashley is alive and well. The Johnsons have her! As we were about to leave, something made me hug Vilma. I felt sorry for her, I guess. I don't know what, maybe because the poor thing didn't even have a Christmas tree. She's a kind soul. I know this in my heart." Iris blotted her bright eyes with the edge of the comforter.

Susan adjusted the covers, her heart accelerating slightly. She could tell the Valium was wearing off. Soon she'd be nervous and paranoid and wanting to jump out of her own skin. After they peeled her off the ceiling. "Don't do this to me, Mom! Please. I can't take any more."

"Susan Burke Johnson, get hold of yourself. Listen to me! I'm telling you, the Johnsons have Ashley Rose. I know it. I smelled baby powder on Vilma when I hugged her. I was seated next to her at the wedding reception if you recall. She had no scent. None at all. Not even hair spray. Everyone has their own scent, either manufactured or simply their own body scent. I know these things. Even your father believes that the Johnsons have Ashley Rose."

Susan's heart almost soared out of her chest. Could it be possible? She shoved the covers aside and struggled to get out of the bed. "Then take me there. If they have my daughter, I want to go there and bring her home. Are you saying they had my daughter all this time? This has to be a mistake, Mother! The police and the Center have spent the last two months trying to locate Ashley. They told me, as hard as it was, that I had to accept the fact that she was probably dead! Mom, are you still taking that medicine Doctor Watts prescribed for you?"

"No, I am not taking any medication, thank you very much. I haven't needed it for quite some time now, but you wouldn't know that since you've been caught up in your own misery. I can see you don't believe me, so I think I'll let your father try to convince you." Iris was preparing to leave the room, when Susan called out to her.

She could barely hope. "Mom, you really are serious, aren't you?"

"I've never been more serious in my life, dear."

"My God! I can't believe it! My baby, alive! Let's go now, I want to bring her home. Have you called Detective Simmons? And what about Dylan? Oh my God!" Susan stopped, as though a bolt of lightning struck her full force. "Does this have anything to do with Cam?"

"I called that young man when your husband decided to throw a Christmas party, which, by the way, is in incredibly poor taste. I thought seeing your old friend would cheer you up. I haven't told him about the Johnsons if that's what you mean. I hope you're not angry with me, dear."

Susan shook her head. It was too much to absorb. Cam and now Ashley Rose!

"No, no. How could I be angry?" How could she be angry when the two most important people in her life were back . . . *almost* back, in her life? Ashley could be alive and Cam was downstairs!

"I want you to listen to your father. We have a plan to get Ashley back. This is going to be very hard for you, dear, so you have to trust us. I've said all along I think that devil you married had something to do with the baby's kidnapping. No matter how you look at it, it fits."

Light-headed again, Susan sat back down on the bed. "Dear Lord, if he did, he'll pay the price. I'll see that he does. How could he do that to me? Ashley is his own flesh and blood. You're right, Mom, he's a devil."

A knock sounded on the door. Iris undid the three deadbolts. Ashton entered the room, his gaze going to his daughter. "I take it you told her." He held a plate of food and a soft drink. "Doctor Watts said you need to eat some carbohydrates. It will help the pills to wear off."

Susan reached for the plate and gobbled the food like a starving animal. Her world was looking brighter by the moment. That bright world nose-dived a second later. What if she had taken those forty pills, the forty pills that spelled out her daughter's initials? She shuddered. "I'm sorry I put you through this. I really am. I was so desperate. Then Richard kept harping on this stupid party. He was getting verbally abusive. I don't know, maybe I snapped. Maybe I was planning it all along. My head isn't too clear right now."

"It's all right. Things will clear up soon. You know then what your mother and I suspect? The wheels are in motion, as they say," Ashton assured her. He patted her shoulder like the indulgent father he was.

Susan bit into a chunk of cheese. "Yes, and we can't get there soon enough as far as I'm concerned."

"I'm afraid we're going to have to hold off on that for just a little while longer, honey. Your mother and I spoke with Detective Simmons after we left Lakeland. He wants to do this the legal way, and your mother and I agree with him. Our visit might have scared the Johnsons into fleeing the state. They might have called Richard, but if they did that, he certainly isn't acting like anything happened. He's downstairs having the time of his life. Detective Simmons and the Lakeland police are going to watch the Johnsons' trailer."

"The waiting, the uncertainty, not daring to hope and believe is frightening. If they had called Richard, he wouldn't be downstairs hosting a party. I feel like I'm going to implode," Susan wailed.

"I know, I know, it's terrible, but we have to do everything just right or it could backfire on us, and then Ashley Rose truly will be lost to us. Just be patient, dear," Ashton said.

"Your father is right, dear. I agree with him one hundred percent." She shot Ashton a warning look, daring him to utter another word.

"What about Ashley? She needs me!"

"As awful as this may sound to you, dear, you are the one who needs Ashley, not the other way around. Now stop being so selfish, and that's an order. I know the Johnsons have taken good care of your daughter. They are not Richard, so don't judge them by your husband. They're just his pawns."

"Your mother is right, Susan."

Thanks to the plate of food, her light-headedness was almost gone. Susan got up and started to pace the room. "Why in the world would the Johnsons steal my daughter? To what end? They didn't ask for a ransom. So it wasn't for money. They barely make ends meet according to Richard! How on earth could they feed and clothe an infant? Diapers, wipes, medicine, and formula cost a small fortune."

Iris sniffed. "Obviously, you have not been listening to us, and me in particular." She sniffed again. "The Johnsons *did not* steal your daughter, your husband stole your daughter. Then he took her to the trailer, and my guess is, he threatened Vilma and Buddy somehow. He probably told them you were an unfit mother or some other rubbish." She looked at her husband, daring him to contradict what she'd just said. He didn't.

Susan found her voice. Her head bobbed up and down. "I certainly can't see them as being the brains behind this . . . this scheme. I only met them that once, but Vilma and Buddy seemed like decent, honest people. They haven't had an easy life, but still they managed to adopt and care for Richard. That's got to say something about their character."

"Yes, it does. But when you're frightened out of your wits, you do things you wouldn't do under normal circumstances. I know all about that, don't I, Ashton? Now, we need a plan, something concrete, so we're together on this. Susan, do you think you can keep this to yourself until Detective Simmons confirms the Johnsons really do have Ashley?"

"If it will get my daughter back, I can turn deaf, dumb, and blind. I'll do anything. I'm not sure I can face Richard without killing him with my bare hands, but I will certainly try. If he orchestrated this entire thing just to . . . to keep his position at Burke and Burke, or to stop the divorce from going through, I don't know how I'll be *able* to keep quiet."

"Why don't we tell Richard you're going to take Doctor Watts's advice and spend a few days at The Willows? Instead, you'll be home with us, where you will be safe and sound. You'll be out of this tacky condo, and you won't have to see Richard until this is over and done with. I've never told you how tacky I thought your decorating was because I didn't want to hurt your feelings. I know you decorated with Richard in mind, but it's cold and sterile," Iris babbled.

Susan smiled, her first real smile in weeks. "Again, Mom, it was all about Richard. Yes, it *is* tacky, all this glass and chrome. Richard likes modern and new. I wonder how he'll like living in a jail cell? Do you think he's insane?"

"Yes, I do, Susan. I've thought so since the first time I laid eyes on him. We can thank your father and his greed for that, too."

"Mother!"

"It's the truth, and you know it, don't you Ashton?" Iris flashed her husband an evil-eyed glare.

"I suppose it is, Iris. And I suppose you'll never stop reminding me. It's all right. I'm resigned to being under your thumb for the rest of my life."

Susan felt sorry for her father, but her mother was right. He'd been too concerned with Burke and Burke to give her and her mother the attention they'd needed. Perhaps he could make it up to them with Ashley Rose. She suspected her father had many secrets throughout the years. Secrets she and her mother would probably never know.

"Stop whining, Ashton. It isn't manly. Your days of telling me what to do, when to do it, and how to do it are over. From now on you will dance to my tune. Or, I will simply leave you and go with Lily. Don't say a word, Ashton. Not one word. Before I leave this party, I plan on having a few words with your friend Maximus. I'll want you in attendance, Ashton."

Ashton groaned. It was a pitiful sound. Iris sniffed into her lace hankie.

"Will the two of you please stop your squabbling? Mom, you know you aren't going to leave Dad. Dad, you know you're going to do just what Mom says from here on out, so let's lay the past to rest."

Her parents smiled at her.

Ashton patted his wife's hand. "I'm going back downstairs to try and act as though I like that son of a bitch. Maybe I'll start sizing up that young doctor your mother invited." He winked at Susan, then left the room, not giving her a chance to tell him that it could never happen.

She was married to Richard at the moment. Now, though, if what her parents said came to pass, she could go ahead with her divorce. She thought about Cam then. The way she always did. Maybe . . .

"I'll never doubt you again, Mom. Never. If I had only listened to you two years ago, this might not have happened, but then I wouldn't have Ashley, so at least something good came out of this nightmare."

"This is such a wonderful time of the year for miracles, Susan. And I think that today we've had the most special one of all. That little one will be home before you know it. Now, I'd better go back downstairs. Richard has scared the catering staff half out of their minds. One more night as his mother-in-law is about all I can take. I'm officially disowning that miserable cretin as soon as I leave this atrocious place. Now, dear, if you could just stay in here and snap all those locks, I'll tell Richard you're not well so he won't disturb you. And I think Cameron and I need to have a nice long talk." Iris smiled, pleased with the turn of events. No, pleased didn't quite cover it. Ecstatic was more like it. "I'll be back to check on you later." Iris gave her daughter a kiss and hug before she left the room. She waited, shivering, until she heard all three locks snap into place.

Downstairs the party was in full swing. The bar was the busiest area in the condo. Upbeat music rocked through the rooms. More than a hundred guests were packed into the three-bedroom condo. Cam hated parties like this, where you had to scream to be heard. He wondered if these people knew about the drinking and driving laws in the state. Everyone seemed to be trying to outdo the other. When Iris Burke had invited him to a Christmas party, he'd been under the impression she and her husband were giving the party. He accepted the invitation because he couldn't wait to talk to Susan. He'd seen her on the news pleading for the return of her daughter and it broke his heart. He'd accepted the invitation for that reason alone.

He introduced himself to a few of the guests but was content to remain on the periphery so that he could observe Susan's husband. As hard as he tried, he couldn't picture Susan married to the man. He watched as Richard poured a drink for a young woman. He placed his arm around her waist, then leaned over and kissed her on the neck. Cam felt the urge to beat the hell out of him on general principle. He didn't like the man, and they hadn't even been introduced.

"Cameron, I'm so sorry I had to leave you on your own, but Susan was so distraught I had to do what I could for her," Iris said briskly. "I'm so glad you found the time to join us."

"Not to worry, Mrs. Burke, I've been amusing myself." His gaze settled on Richard and the woman whose neck he continued to nuzzle.

Iris followed his gaze. "There are no words to tell you how my husband and I detest that man. He has made Susan's life miserable. Susan had already filed for divorce when her daughter was kidnapped. My husband was about to terminate his position at the firm. Everything had to be put on hold so the media wouldn't go after them. Divorces tend to get messy, if you know what I mean. Oh, dear, that's probably more than you wanted to know. I'm sorry, Cameron. That man simply brings out the worst in me."

Divorced. "I take it you're not too fond of your son-in-law?"

"I hate him, if you want to know the truth. In the whole of my life, and I'm no youngster, I have never hated anyone. Well, sometimes I get cranky with my husband, but I don't hate him. Richard has ruined Susan's and Ashley's lives. Dear God, my daughter has *three* locks on her bedroom door. That should tell us all something."

"How is Susan? Dylan has kept me informed, but he really doesn't know much, being in jail. His wife told me how much they both liked Susan. What little I know I saw in the papers or on TV."

"At this precise moment, Cameron, Susan is wonderful." She leaned close to him so as not to be overheard. "Between you and me, your friend Dylan is going to be released in a matter of days, maybe as early as tonight. I knew from the beginning that he had nothing to do with this. Unfortunately, he was at the wrong place at the wrong time. We have every reason to believe Ashley Rose is alive and soon to be on her way back to her mother where she belongs! Promise me you will keep this to yourself."

Taken aback, Cam could only stare at Iris Burke, his jaw dropping. "What are you talking about, Mrs. Burke? I saw Dylan at the jail earlier before coming to the party. He didn't say anything. His lawyer, Seamus, was there, too. Both of them were depressed. Oh, I get it, no one knows but you and Susan, is that it?"

Cam grinned then, and Iris thought his eyes sparkled like diamonds. She knew in that one instant that the man standing next to her was the man Susan would end up spending the rest of her life with. This man was her daughter's destiny.

"No, they don't know." She explained to him what they had discovered earlier in the day. She swore later that his eyes *glowed*.

"That's fantastic! Suzie must be beyond elated. I'm happy for her. And Dylan, too. When are they going to . . . you know, bring her back?"

"We're waiting for Detective Simmons to confirm that Ashley is with the Johnsons. He knows we're here tonight if anything goes awry. As soon as he gives the word, Susan will go after her daughter. From there, I'm not sure what will happen except my daughter will be the happiest woman alive."

Cameron grinned. He liked Iris Burke. A lot. She would make a wonderful mother-in-law. "Then I'd say we should celebrate, Mrs. Burke. Would you like something to drink?"

"A ginger ale. I want to make sure I'm not three sheets to the wind tonight. Did I say that right? Inebriated. I have too much to do."

"I'll be right back." Cam went to the den, where they had the bar set up. He walked past Richard Johnson and the young girl in her sparkly spandex dress. She was giggling. He'd never heard Susan giggle. She laughed; her eyes laughed, too.

Iris smiled as the party guests swirled past her. Iris waited patiently for Cameron to return. She really liked the young doctor. Susan had been reluctant to talk about Cameron when she returned home. Whatever it was that had gone wrong must have been either a misunderstanding or something silly. It was clear to her the man still had feelings for Susan. She looked across the room to see Richard staring at her, an ugly smirk on his face. The urge to walk across the room and smack his smug face was so strong, she had to clench her fists and dig her heels into the carpet to prevent herself from doing it. She unclenched the fist on her right hand. She slowly raised her middle finger.

She smiled at her son-in-law's stunned expression.

"I saw that." Cameron chuckled. "Here you are, Mrs. Burke. Let's make a toast to the success of . . . well, just success." Cam lifted his glass and Iris did the same.

"To Susan and Ashley." They clinked their glasses together.

"Hear, hear!" Iris exclaimed.

"What's all this cheering about?" Ashton asked.

"Ashton, I take it you and Cameron have met?"

Cameron reached out to shake Ashton's hand.

"Yes, we have." Ashton released his grip and gave the man a pat on the back. He liked him and could see Iris did, too.

"So, what were you toasting?" Ashton asked. He sipped at his drink.

"I shared the latest turn of events with Cameron. He

promised not to say anything." She turned to Cam, who was still grinning from ear to ear over this gentle lady's finger movement.

"My lips are sealed. I wouldn't dare say anything that would jeopardize the return of Susan's daughter. I hope something happens soon. It's been rough seeing my best friend behind bars."

"Cameron, I told Susan and Ashton from the very beginning that Dylan was an innocent man. Marlene, the woman from the Center, agreed with me. She told Susan right way Dylan wasn't their man. I even tried to get Susan to speak with John Edward, you know the medium from *Crossing Over*."

Ashton's jaw dropped as he stared at his wife. "Iris Burke, tell me you're not serious! Tell me you didn't do that!"

"Yes, I'm serious, Ashton Burke. I'll have you know when this is all over and done with, I'm going to go to New York and have a reading with him myself. I'm going to ask him *all sorts of things,* and you better have your answers ready when I get back."

The two men smiled sheepishly at one another.

"Whatever makes you happy Iris, by all means. I'll even take you there myself."

"I'd like that in writing, Ashton," Iris responded smartly.

Iris focused on the door when she heard the bell ring. Her heart raced. Maybe this was the beginning of the end for her son-in-law. Ashton's face was totally blank. Cameron stared at them both before his eyes, too, went to the front door.

Iris's gaze searched the room for Richard, to see what he would do. He motioned for one of the caterers to answer the door.

Ashton caught her eye and nodded. They both headed for the den because it would afford them a better view of the front door.

The bell chimed again.

Iris turned around to see if Cameron was following them. Cameron stopped to help himself to a drink from the tray in the caterer's hands. The same man Richard wanted to open the door.

Iris watched Richard watching Cameron talking to the caterer. He said something to the group milling around him, dropped his glass on a tray, and headed for the server. She moved then, quickly, to get as close as she could to Cameron. She wanted to hear what they were saying.

"Didn't I ask you to get the door?" Richard snarled.

The man nodded, his eyes apologizing to Cameron.

"You're a real peach, aren't you?" Cameron said quietly.

"Who in the hell do you think you're talking to? And who the hell *are* you? I don't recall inviting you to this party."

Cam laughed. "No, you didn't invite me. If you had, I wouldn't have come. Mr. and Mrs. Burke invited me. Do you have a problem with that?"

Chapter Eighteen

Richard eyeballed the good-looking man standing in front of him. The good-looking, *tall* man standing in front of him. There was something about him that triggered a sense of uneasiness. It was as though he knew a secret no one else knew. The fine hairs on the back of Richard's neck moved as he tried to figure it out. He'd entered through the kitchen. At first he'd thought he was part of the catering crew. He knew that wasn't the case now. He found himself bristling defensively.

"Apparently you don't realize just whom you're speaking to. I'm Richard Johnson, the Burkes' son-in-law. I'm hosting this party."

Cam took a long pull from his glass of ginger ale. "Yes, I know," Cam said quietly. "Susan and I are friends. If you'll excuse me, the Burkes are waiting for me. Nice party, a little too crowded, but still nice. Excellent food." Cam stared into Richard's eyes before he directed his gaze to Iris and Ashton Burke standing by the front door.

"What . . . this is *my place* and *my* party, not the Burkes'!" Richard hissed.

"Excuse me. I was under the impression this was Susan's place. I guess Mr. and Mrs. Burke and Susan were wrong. My apologies. Now, if you'll excuse me."

Richard stared around the crowded room, which was

getting quieter by the moment. Why were his guests gravitating to the front door where the Burkes were standing? His heart started to pound in his chest when Ashton Burke fixed his steely-gray eyes on him, a smile of satisfaction on his face. Perspiration broke out on his face and above his lip. He fought the urge to wipe it away.

Still balancing the tray in one hand, at shoulder level, the server from the catering company still managed to open the door, then deftly stood aside.

Three detectives, badges in hand, stepped inside. Audible gasps from the startled guests ricocheted across the crowded room.

"Simmons! I thought you'd never get here. Did you find her? Have you taken the Johnsons into custody yet?" Ashton asked, his wife's hand clutched tightly in his own.

"Not yet, Mr. Burke. Seems as though they hightailed it out of Lakeland. We'll find them. We have a neighbor lady who saw them. She said they'd had a baby with them for the past couple of months. People out there don't mix with the law. They mind their own business. We're sure it's Ashley Rose. She matches the description." Simmons jammed his hands in his pants pocket. "Where is your son-in-law? We'd like to talk to him."

"Here comes the son of a bitch right now. He doesn't look too happy either."

"Good. I'm about to make the son of a bitch completely miserable." Simmons motioned for Nicholls and Davis to follow him. He walked up to Richard, knowing full well he'd better follow procedure right to the letter. "Are you Richard Johnson?"

Richard rolled his eyes and flashed his Hollywood smile. "Come on now, Detective, I know you haven't forgotten me. Tell me, did the Burkes invite you to *my* party? If so,

I'm glad you could make it."

Nicholls and Davis took up their stance behind Simmons.

"I see you brought your sidekicks along. Welcome to the party. Help yourselves."

"Is there somewhere private where we can talk? Or, would you rather do it here? Makes no difference to me, Mr. Johnson," Simmons said.

Richard threw his arms open as if to embrace the room. "Detective, this is my home. It *is* private. Anything you need to say, you can say it right here."

Simmons looked around. In the background he could hear music. Someone crooning about being home for Christmas. Oh, yeah. There had to be at least a hundred people clustered into tight little groups in what appeared to be the living room. If Richard Johnson thought this was private, it was fine with him.

"All right, if you're sure that's what you want."

"It is. Now, if you could get on with it, Detective. As you can see, I have guests. I really don't appreciate this invasion. Just so you know, your superiors will hear about this the first thing in the morning."

Simmons couldn't have picked a better scenario for what he was about to do. "Mr. Johnson, you will need to come with me to police headquarters. We have reason to believe you were involved in the kidnapping of Ashley Rose Johnson, your daughter. We can do this the easy way, or we can do it the ugly way. Right now, this moment, it's a request. It's your call."

Richard's face turned gray, then white. His blue eyes sparked with rage. Simmons watched as the man standing in front of him clenched his hands in tight-knuckled rage. He took a breath, then another. He watched as he gritted his teeth before he finally spoke. "What the fuck are you talking about?"

"That's what you're going to come downtown and explain to me. As I said, it's a request."

The silence in the room was unearthly. The music that could be heard minutes ago was over. One by one, the guests started to whisper among themselves as they focused their attention on the small crowd of people clustered in the front entry hall.

"I'll do no such thing. I'm not stupid, Simmons. I can't believe you would stoop this low just to make a name for yourself." His defensive sneer didn't go unnoticed by those in the room.

"Now, as I said, Mr. Johnson, you can come willingly, or I can get a warrant for your arrest. If I were you, I'd go with the former rather than the latter. Again, it's your call."

"You're not me, Detective. I want to call my lawyer! Get my wife down here. I want her to listen to this bullshit. Susan, come down here! Now!" he bellowed at the top of his lungs.

Simmons shook his head. "Somehow, I knew that's what you were going to say. All right, everyone, the party's over! Please gather your belongings and leave in an orderly fashion."

Iris pushed her way through the remaining guests, stopping when she stood directly in front of Richard. "You, you . . . *scoundrel!* I just want you to know there are no words to describe how much I detest you. After what you have put Susan through, you'll never live long enough to beg for her forgiveness! Inmates in prison are not kind to child molesters or men who kidnap babies. I want you to think about that when you talk to your lawyer." Then Iris Burke did something so out of character she surprised herself. She drew her hand back and slapped him. Out of the corner of her eye, she saw Maximus González about to leave. She switched her attention to him. "Yoo-hoo, Maximus. I want to talk to you, *too.*"

Ashton shriveled inside his custom-made tux. He groaned.

Richard lifted his hand to return Iris's slap when Cam caught him by the arm, twisting it behind his back so that he couldn't move.

"Get him off me!" No one paid any attention. "I said, get him off me!"

Ashton broke through the small group of people. "Cam, back off, son. I want a turn at him. You think you're so damn smart, weaseling your way into this family. I know who you are and I know what you did. You're a goddamn murderer, that's what you are. If you so much as lay a hand on my wife or my daughter, I will personally kill you, you got that, you son of a bitch!"

As Cam released Richard, Iris had her own powwow going down just a few feet away. Her voice dripping syrup, Iris said, "Maximus, I've wanted to do this since the day I met you. Now stand still, sweetie, and don't move." Iris drew her arm back just the way a star pitcher does before throwing his first pitch. Her balled-up fist connected perfectly. Doctor Maximus González dropped to the floor. Iris dusted her hands dramatically.

"We'll be dropping you from our social circle, Maximus."

Cam gaped at the woman he hoped would one day be his mother-in-law. "Way to go, Mrs. Burke."

Richard lunged at Ashton, but was pulled away, then pushed down on his knees by Detective Simmons. "You . . . you old bastard! How would you like me to tell your wife all about you? Well, how would you? Wonder what she'd think after all these years?" Richard blustered, as Simmons yanked him up from the floor, keeping a tight hold on him by pinning his arms behind him.

"Tell me what?" Iris asked.

"Mrs. Burke, Mr. Burke, please calm down. Let me handle this," Simmons said.

"Tell her, Ashton, go on, tell her," Richard sneered. "Tell her about her dear friend, *Maureen!*" Richard threw his head back and laughed, a crazed, maniacal laugh.

Simmons jerked his arm harder. "I think you need to be a little more quiet, Mr. Johnson. I'm going to release you. If you so much as make a move toward the Burkes, I'll arrest you so fast your head will spin. You got that, pretty boy?"

Iris walked over to her husband. "What is he talking about, Ashton? How does he know Maureen?"

"It's a long story, Iris. One I should have told you a long, long time ago. Now isn't the time. I promise when this is all over, I'll tell you about Maureen."

Iris shook her head. "No, Ashton Burke, you will tell me right now! You've kept too many things from me far too long. I'm waiting, Ashton."

Detective Simmons released Richard, allowing him to get a grip on himself. He had to defuse whatever was brewing between the Burkes. "You can discuss your personal business later, Mrs. Burke. Right now we need a phone so Mr. Johnson can lawyer up."

"You don't think I can find the phone in my own house," Richard snarled, sending the few remaining guests scurrying to the front door. "Go on, get the hell out of here!" he thundered. "Who needs you!"

Ashton turned to his wife. "Later, Iris, I promise."

"You best keep that promise, Ashton. Keep Lily in the

back of your mind. I mean it, Ashton." Iris brushed imaginary lint from her dress as she watched the men moving toward the kitchen.

Not once during the entire scenario that had just played out had Richard even bothered to ask about Ashley Rose. Iris assumed it was because he knew where she was and that she was safe with Buddy and Vilma. How frightened they must've been to do what they did. She made a promise to do something nice for them . . . everything that Richard thought was his would be given to the Johnsons. If they didn't want any of his possessions, then she would personally see to it that they were sold and the money given to the Johnsons. They were too old to be working in the orange groves. One's golden years were meant to be enjoyed.

Nicholls and Davis were watching her. They probably thought she was as nutty as her son-in-law, or at the very least a terrible hostess. "Would you men like something to eat? Drink? We have ice-cold soda, tea, and a variety of fruit juices. I know you're not supposed to drink while you're on duty. I would be honored if you would allow me to fix you a plate of food. I want to thank you. I know those are just words, but until I come up with something better, it's all I can offer. Now, how about a little of everything? You sit right down over there and I'll be right back."

Davis spoke for them. "Yes ma'am, we are still on duty. Some food would be real nice. We missed supper."

Iris whirled through the swinging door leading to the kitchen. Richard, Cam, Ashton, and the detective huddled together around the telephone. She strained to hear what they were saying as she heaped two plates full of food. She carried them into the living room to the grateful detectives. "Now, you eat everything. There's plenty more in the kitchen."

A moment later she was back in the kitchen. "I'm going right upstairs to tell Susan that the Johnsons definitely have Ashley Rose. I'll be back."

"Wait, Iris. Not so fast," said Ashton. "The police still don't have a clue as to where the Johnsons are at this point. Simmons is questioning Richard on their possible whereabouts as we speak."

"Surely you don't think he's going to confess anything now? He's kept secrets for months, why would he do or say anything now? I hate that man, Ashton. I swear, I wish I had it in me to kill, because if I did, he would be my first victim."

"I think Detective Simmons will convince him to 'fess up. He really doesn't have a choice. Cooperation makes for leniency. Sometimes. Once his lawyer gets here, he won't say a word. Don't expect any miracles where Richard Johnson is concerned, Iris."

Iris nodded. "I'm going upstairs to check on Susan."

Ashton nodded and watched her as she flew out of the kitchen. She was something else. He had so much to be grateful for. He owed Iris more than she would ever know. Maybe that was his problem. He had to say the words out loud. All the words, not ones he chose so carefully. Shame and guilt were terrible enemies.

Simmons and Ashton listened as Richard spoke to his attorney, a Burke and Burke lawyer.

"They're going to arrest me. They actually believe I had something to do with my daughter's kidnapping. Yes, I mean murder. You what? Fuck you, too!" Richard slammed the phone down. "I hope you're satisfied, Ashton. That ancient fool of an attorney you've kept on the payroll all these years said he couldn't represent me! Was that your doing or your wife's doing?"

"More power to him! I guess this means you'll have to settle for a public defender. For what it's worth, Richard, there is a clause in that *ironclad* contract that reads if you're ever arrested for anything other than a misdemeanor, the contract becomes null and void. You are going to arrest him, aren't you, Detective?"

Simmons looked at the pager buzzing on his hip. He took the phone from the cradle, all the while keeping his firm grip on Richard's arm. He punched in the numbers. "This is Detective Joshua Simmons. You just paged me."

Ashton watched the series of expressions crossing the detective's face. "Yes. When was that? This afternoon? And where is she now? I see." He listened to the voice on the phone, nodding from time to time. "I think that would be a grand idea. Yes, sir, we thank you very much, sir.

"To answer your question, Ashton, you're damned straight I'm going to arrest this man! Davis, Nicholls, get in here!" He called to the two men still waiting his instructions.

They both bolted through the door. "What is it?" Davis asked.

"Read this man his rights. Nicholls, cuff him and take him downtown."

"Wait just a goddamn minute! You can't arrest me! I haven't been charged with anything. You don't have proof I even committed a crime. I'll have all of your jobs! Susan!" Richard bellowed at the top of his lungs.

Cam whirled around and all but walked right into Susan, who was being led in the kitchen by her mother.

They both stopped. Their eyes locked on one another. Cam took a step forward, his arms outstretched, as Susan fell into his arms. The room was suddenly silent.

"It's really you, isn't it?" Susan asked, smiling. "I thought I was hallucinating."

"As I said, the one and only. I'm sorry, Susan. For so many things. I can't . . ."

"Then don't. Thank God you came back." She refused to even look at her husband, who was glaring at her, his eyes spewing hatred.

She turned to Simmons. "Detective, have they found the Johnsons? Mother just told me what happened. I feel terrible for them, but I want my daughter back!"

Ashton, Iris and Susan clung together. They were a family now, united by loss and bound together by love. Cam stepped closer. Their arms reached out to bring him closer.

"I have something even better!" Simmons looked at Davis and Nicholls. "Remember you two wanted to be there when . . ."

"When what?" Susan asked, suddenly anxious.

Simmons looked at his watch, then back at the Burkes. What was about to happen made his job worthwhile.

"About now—" he paused for effect, a huge smile on his face as he walked to the kitchen door "—several officers from the Lakeland Police Department should be . . ."

A loud knock sounded at the kitchen door.

"What?" Susan darted a questioning glance at the three detectives.

They all looked at one another with grins as wide as the Grand Canyon.

"Why don't you answer the door, Susan?" her father said.

Susan nodded as she moved toward the door. She put a shaky hand on the knob, turned it swinging the door wide. "Yes?"

"Are you Susan Burke Johnson?" two plainclothes detectives asked her.

She nodded, her heart in her throat. "Who . . . who are you?"

Simmons spoke. "You could call them Santa Claus. Or angels."

"I don't understand."

The detectives smiled at her before the taller of the two men stepped aside to reveal a car seat that he had placed on the ground behind him.

Susan looked from one man to the other. "Is this . . . *OHMYGOD!*"

She shoved the door aside and scooped the baby from the seat. "Ashley Rose? Oh my God, it's my baby! She's alive! Mom, Dad, look!" Susan held her daughter tight against her chest, then she held her away so that she could look at the light of her life. Ashley Rose cooed, then smiled a smile so big, Susan thought her plump little face would crack. Tears streamed down Susan's face as she brought her daughter even tighter against her chest. Her prayers had truly been answered!

There wasn't a dry eye in the room. Cam smiled and didn't care who saw him cry. Ashton sniffed and knuckled his eyes. The three detectives wore smiles that could light up a room the size of a football field. Even the catering staff had stopped to view the Christmas miracle.

Iris glowed like a treetop angel. "I told you."

Suddenly, all eyes focused on Richard. He stood back away from the family.

"Mom, take your granddaughter, I know you're dying to hold her."

"Absolutely." Iris cradled the smiling baby in her arms.

Susan crossed the room. "You!" She thought of all the

things she wanted to say, mean, ugly words. Instead she wiped at her eyes and said, "You just aren't worth me wasting my breath."

He stared right through her. "Are these handcuffs necessary?" Richard snarled as he was being led out of the room.

"Well, Richard, you finally got what you wanted. You're now the center of attention. Your name is sure to go down in the . . . criminal books somewhere. I just want to say one last thing, Detective, then you can take him. It's really *not* all about you, Richard."

Epilogue

It was a day of celebration. The weatherman had smiled with the beautiful sunrise. Clear skies, warm and sunny with a light breeze. No dreaded humidity. A perfect day to visit the Magic Kingdom.

"Ashton, for heaven's sake, put on some long pants! Those shorts have a hole in the seat. I swear, since you sold Burke and Burke, you look like a vagrant. I don't think Cameron and Susan will like the father of the bride looking like a . . ."

"Like a retired person who doesn't give a hoot about anything but his family and his comfort? Lord, Iris, they're not getting married yet. This is an engagement party." Ashton rolled his eyes, then grabbed his lovely wife around the waist. "I love you, you know that, old gal? I know I have a lot of making up to do, but meet me halfway, Iris, and we can really enjoy these golden years."

"Old gal, my foot! I bet Lily's friends wouldn't even think of calling me an old gal. More likely they'd call me a slick chick." Iris giggled as she pinched her husband's rear end.

"Are you flirting with me, Iris?" Ashton leered. He sobered almost instantly as he removed a pair of khaki slacks from the closet. "Just don't throw it in my face every day, Iris. I know what I did and I have to live with

350

it. Like I said, meet me halfway."

"I'm more than willing to meet you halfway, Ashton. The other half of me will always remember. I lost so many years, years I can't reclaim. It's the same way with Susan. A mother is the first one who is supposed to see her baby's first tooth, take her first step. Vilma Johnson was the person who saw that. Do you understand what I'm saying? I am going to try very hard. I'm certain I'll slip from time to time.

"The truth is, Ashton, there are a lot of things you and I should never forget. Like my dearest friend, Maureen. Dear God, when I think of Richard, or R.J., and the grief he went through as a child, I want to cry my eyes out. His mother dies by his hand; his father lights out never to be seen or heard from again. Did the boy have a heart back then? Some people are born without a conscience. They call them sociopaths. I think Richard is a sociopath."

"Let's not ruin the day talking about Richard. He's out of our lives for good. When his trial is over, he'll be spending the rest of his life in prison. We said we were going to put the past behind us and look forward to a very bright future."

"Yes, but to think that an eleven-year-old boy could put a pillow over his mother's face is beyond anything I can contemplate! Poor Maureen, I wonder if she knew what a bad seed her son was."

"No, I don't think she ever knew. I suppose that's a blessing. He must have heard us talking that day and decided his mother wasn't dying fast enough to suit him. I will never forget the day I saw him put that pillow over his mother's face. It was so horrible, I convinced myself I didn't see what I saw. I made up every excuse I could think of. I was just so afraid after what I saw him do that I couldn't allow you to take him in and raise him. I just couldn't. To this day, I don't really know whether he suffocated his mother out of hatred or love. I was rooted to the floor, Iris, I literally could not move for minutes. I ran in there as soon as I could move, and he just looked up at me, and said, 'Mama said goodbye, then she asked me to put the pillow over her face and hold it down until she was dead.' But even then there was a look in his eyes that made me shudder; and I simply did not know if he was telling the truth. I still don't."

"I never thought I would say this, but you did the right thing, Ashton. Richard spent his entire life plotting our downfall in his search for revenge. Can you imagine what he might have done to Susan had we kept him? I shudder to think. Doctor González fell prey to him. The Johnsons, poor souls, were coerced into his plot to destroy us. I hope they never find them. I pray they're somewhere safe. Where does it stop?" Iris asked tearfully.

"It stops today. At the Magic Kingdom, where the beginning of the end started. Personally, I think it's very brave of Susan and Cameron to host their engagement party at the park. I think she needs to do this in order to go forward."

"I'm glad her divorce is final. Susan called last week and said Ashley Rose was starting to walk, holding on to things, of course. She's wobbly, but before you know it, she'll be *running* around."

"The girl is smart. Takes after her grandmother." Ashton's voice was so sincere, Iris grabbed him and kissed him soundly.

"You're the best thing that has ever happened to me, Susan Elizabeth Burke."

"I know it." She smiled as she finished dressing Ashley Rose. "I'll just need another minute and I'll be ready. Tristan is bringing the kids and most of the people from her parenting class. I asked Dylan and Renée to come, but I'm not sure if they will. I certainly can't blame them after all I put them through."

Cam wrapped his arms around her waist. "You didn't do anything. If they don't attend, it will be because they need a little healing time. They also know whom to blame for everything, and it isn't you. You've got to stop blaming yourself, Susan. You made a mistake, you corrected that mistake, and you're about to make the smartest move of your life."

"Oh, yeah, what's that?"

"You're going to marry me. I don't know why I let you go, Susan. I thought living in a third-world country wasn't what you'd bargained for. You had a career ahead of you and it wasn't in the wilds of Borneo. It was the biggest mistake of my life."

"Yep," Susan said as she tied the laces on Ashley's tiny Reeboks.

Cam turned her around, taking both Ashley and Susan in his arms. "You girls are my life, you know that? Always and forever."

Susan almost swooned at the words. She kissed him just as soundly as her mother was kissing her father all the way across town.

Always and forever.

About the Author

Suzanne Barr lives in southwest Florida. She is an active member of Mystery Writers of America. When not writing, she loves to travel with her husband Jay in their private plane. She also enjoys reading, snow skiing and spending time with family. She loves to hear from readers. They can contact her by email at *SuzyBarr@aol.com*.